Loonies

By
Gregory Bastianelli

JournalStone
San Francisco

JOURNALSTONE
YOUR LINK TO ARTISTIC TALENT

JournalStone books may be ordered through booksellers or by contacting:

JournalStone

www.journalstone.com

ISBN: 978-1-942712-17-6   (sc)
ISBN: 978-1-942712-18-3   (ebook)

JournalStone rev. date: March 20, 2015

Library of Congress Control Number: 2015932365

Printed in the United States of America

Cover Art & Design: Wayne Miller

Edited by: Dr. Michael R. Collings

To my parents,
for their faith in me

Chapter I

THE TRUNK IN THE ATTIC

Smokey Hollow had the appearance of a quiet and quaint New England town, until the day the trunk in the attic was opened.

Brian Keays left his downtown newspaper office at the end of the day to stroll over to the police station when he got the call from his wife. Darcie had been poking around in the attic of the house they had just settled into when she discovered an old steamer trunk. He didn't like the idea of her going up the drop-down ladder that led to the attic space. She was four months pregnant, and the thought of her missing a step and falling backwards onto the floor unnerved him.

She was curious, she told him, and excited about exploring their new home. When he asked what was in the trunk, she informed him it was locked. There was a small keyhole, and she had been thinking about jamming a screwdriver in it to try to open the trunk. He told her not to, to wait until he got home. Those old steamer trunks were valuable to antique dealers if they were in good shape. He didn't want her damaging it trying to open it. She wasn't happy about waiting, but she ended up being glad she did. If she had opened it by herself, she might have gone insane.

Brian liked the location of his newspaper office, on the corner of Main Street and Hemlock Avenue, not only because it looked out on the business district of Smokey Hollow, but also because it was across the street from Cully's Pub, where he liked to imbibe a cold draught beer after his day was done, and diagonally across from the police station where he was headed now.

Not that the police station was a hotbed of activity. Not in Smokey Hollow. *At least not before the trunk was opened.*

The New Hampshire town lay in a valley. Often on early summer mornings, mist would settle there, bathing the town in a smoky haze, giving the community of about seven thousand the origin of its name. The town's forefathers misspelled the word *smoky*, but it was never corrected.

Smokey Hollow had a minimal staff at its police station. The chief, Noah Treece, was new and young, late twenties, about the same age as Brian. There were only two other full-time officers, both named Alvin by some odd coincidence. One worked day shift and one worked night shift. Chief Treece floated between the two shifts but always said he was never really off duty. There were several part-time officers, a couple of part-time administrative people, and a dispatcher, though most of the emergency calls went through the county office.

Brian walked through the front door of the station, no metal detector or security buzzer to worry about. This was Smokey Hollow, not the precinct stations in Boston, where just a few short months ago Brian Keays was working the crime beat for one of the city papers. Now *that* was a time when walking into a police station was like opening Pandora's box, with any type of depraved crime of passion, greed, or lust just waiting for him at the sergeant's desk. He still remembered the flutter in his chest every time he approached a grizzled police veteran for the nightly report. It was the same flutter in his chest he had when he fell in love with Darcie.

Walking into the Smokey Hollow police station spawned no flutter in Brian Keays' heart. Nothing happened in this town. This wasn't Boston or any of its bustling burbs. This was a town whose highlight was the annual Dump Festival. The only major crime in the past several decades was the unsolved disappearance of four-year-old Timmy Birtch twenty-four years ago, a case that the outgoing police chief had pledged to solve before retirement. That never happened.

Chief Noah Treece had a glass office and always seemed happy to see Brian whenever he walked into the station, which Brian could never figure out because neither of them had any information to share to help their stagnant careers. Brian sometimes thought Noah was just glad to see a friendly face to talk to that would help break up the mundane pace of his job.

Brian greeted Wanda, the dispatcher/receptionist/secretary/not-sure-what-other-functions-she-had, and she half-heartedly nodded as if disturbed he was interrupting her boredom. Noah flung open his door and waved him in. Brian settled in one of the hard wooden chairs across from the chief's desk. He looked at Noah's smile—such a handsome, even pretty face on a man young enough to only be a patrolman in Boston, but here he was at the top spot in this town's Police Department, a job that didn't apparently require a lot of experience.

Brian liked Noah, and he wasn't quite sure what it was about the young chief that drew him. Maybe it was the fact they both had jobs that could be exciting in a different setting than Smokey Hollow, but their career paths had unceremoniously dumped them into their current positions and they were stuck with their lot in life. The only major difference Brian saw was that Noah seemed content, happy overseeing a community where the major scofflaws were people breaking pooper-scooper laws or the occasional peeping tom.

Give me something! Brian wanted to shout. Tell me something happened that will make my heart flutter. Make me be in love with my job again. Would that be so hard?

"How are you, Brian," the smiling face said. "How's your day going?"

"About the same as most days."

"How is Darcie?"

"Good. Thanks."

Not long after Brian had met him, Noah had stopped by their house to welcome them to the town. Darcie had thought the chief charming.

"Finally settling in to her new home?"

"A little too much," Brian said. "She keeps digging through the place. Now she's discovered some trunk in the attic and got all excited about it."

"Oh, nice. What did she find in it?"

Brian sighed. "That's the problem. She can't open it. It's locked. So her curiosity is raging, and she can't wait to see what's inside."

"Locked?" Noah's smile weakened slightly. "No key?"

"I don't know if she's tried looking around for one. She only called me a few minutes ago."

Noah leaned back in his chair, his smile fading as he dropped into a deep contemplative state. Brian studied him, wondering what the chief was thinking.

Noah held up a finger before reaching down and opening one of the bottom drawers of his desk. He dug through it, trying to get to something at the bottom, his smile returning when he pulled an old coffee mug out of the drawer and set it on the desk.

"Let me tell you an interesting story."

Noah began to tell him about former Police Chief Pfefferkorn, now retired and living in Florida. He had run the quiet town for many years but felt his career was tarnished by his inability to solve the Timmy Birtch disappearance. Sure, the State Police took charge of the case, as they did with major crimes in small towns, but it happened on his watch, and he was the one who had to look the townspeople in the eyes every day and feel like he failed them.

Timmy Birtch had been four years old when he went missing. One summer night, he was snatched from his bedroom while he slept. His mother, asleep in the next room, didn't hear a sound. There were no clues as to what happened to him, no evidence. Not a trace.

About sixteen years after the disappearance, and a few years before retiring, Chief Pfefferkorn had made a seemingly innocuous discovery. He had left the station around midnight and was walking along Main Street and some of the side streets around downtown when he happened upon something: a key.

Pfefferkorn had kept it in his front shirt pocket and for most of his last few years on the job had wondered about it, had become obsessed with finding the lock the key opened. He had told Noah how he tried every lock he came upon, usually late at night while walking the streets, hoping he'd get lucky and find the lock the key fit. But it was like looking for a needle in a haystack.

Noah said the chief told him that he needed to find the lock it fit. Somehow, he had gotten it into his head that the key opened something important, that he had been destined to find it, that he couldn't retire until he found the lock. It had become a compulsion.

The chief had told him he never stopped trying until the day he retired. Noah said he could see the sadness in the chief's eyes on the day of his retirement. Not sadness that he was leaving his position, but that he never found the lock that key went to.

"I think," Noah said to Brian, "that his inability to solve the Birtch case sent him over the edge with frustration, and that the key became some tangible object that he could resolve if only he found the lock it went to."

Noah picked up the coffee mug.

"And when he retired," Noah said, "he left this with me."

Noah turned the coffee mug over and a key clattered onto the desktop.

Brian looked at the small black key. It didn't look like the kind of key that would fit a door lock. It was old and looked more like it would open the lock of an antique roll-top desk, suitcase, maybe ...

"And you think this key might go to the steamer trunk in my attic?"

"I have no idea, but why not try it?" Noah said, smiling. "And the interesting thing was, Pfefferkorn told me where the key was found. It was near your house."

Brian and Darcie Keays lived on Ash Street, a U-shaped residential street off the main drag, with both ends connecting to Main Street. It was dotted with Victorian and Colonial houses, some of the oldest in town. They bought the house because of its convenience to downtown. Darcie wanted to be able to walk to the shops on Main Street. She especially liked going to the flower shop and the public library. The elementary school was at the end of Main Street, and Darcie was hoping to do some substitute teaching in the fall, just until the baby came. Eventually she hoped to get back into teaching full time, and having the school close would be convenient.

Noah followed Brian home and Darcie showed them where she had found the trunk. The three of them stood in the attic of the Keays' house. It was hot and stuffy, the air stagnant. Brian's sweat-drenched shirt clung to his back. The floorboards were covered in a layer of dust, stirred up a bit by three sets of footprints.

Darcie had pulled the trunk to the middle of the floor, beneath one of the dim light bulbs. Brian wasn't happy she had done that, but she assured him it wasn't heavy.

"It didn't even feel like there is anything in there."

"Still," Brian said, frustrated she wasn't seeing his point, "you need to be more careful."

"I will," was her curt answer.

Noah stood by quietly till the couple finished, rubbing the key in his right hand. Brian looked at the smile on his face and thought the chief looked excited. It was the most animated he had ever seen the young chief. It made him actually look like a policeman. But what were the odds the key actually went to this trunk?

"Here goes nothing," Noah said, getting on his knees before the trunk. Brian and Darcie leaned over his shoulders.

Noah slipped the key in with a little bit of a struggle. He was trying to force it, Brian thought, to make it fit. But then there was a click, and Brian felt a well of amazement swell up in him as the lock popped open.

"Oh, my, would you look at that," Noah said, looking back at them with a wide grin. He raised the lid of the trunk, standing in the process.

The top of the lid shielded some of the light from the bulb overhead, shadowing the contents somewhat, so all Brian could see were yellowed newspapers wrapped around some objects.

Noah reached in and grabbed one bundle, lifting it out with care.

"Very light, whatever it is," he said in a whisper, as if afraid to let anyone else hear.

He set the parcel on the floor.

"I wonder what it could be," Darcie said, leaning closer.

Brian said nothing, curious but not excited. What could they expect, old pottery maybe?

The chief lifted some of the newspaper, which cracked and tore in his fingers. It was like peeling the layers of an onion. He tried to be gentle in case there was something breakable underneath.

The three sets of eyes gazed down as page after page of old newspapers revealed shoe-store ads, high-school baseball game results, obituaries, and comic strips. Brian peered closer as Noah folded back the last layer.

At first it looked like a bundle of dusty gray sticks. But shapes emerged in the dim lighting: thin bony arms, frail femur and tibia drawn up in a fetal position, cracked ribs, and a small skull, tatters of decomposed skin clinging to it, empty eye sockets staring at them.

It was a human baby skeleton.

The three of them were silent, too shocked to talk, eyes taking in the tiny bones.

Then Darcie uttered a sound, a sort of cry that came halfway up her throat but then caught, which was a good thing, because if it had escaped her mouth it would have come out as a scream.

"Jesus," said Noah, no longer smiling. "What the hell have we found?"

Brian stared, a dozen thoughts running through his head: What had they uncovered? What else was in this trunk? Where did this come from? What did this mean? And most of all, who was this baby?

"That's certainly not the remains of Timmy Birtch," Brian said.

"No," Noah agreed. "I don't know what we've stumbled upon here. This is bizarre."

Brian didn't realize his wife was about to faint. In fact, he had forgotten she was standing right beside him. She staggered sideways and put a hand out on his shoulder to steady herself. He looked up and, even in the dimness, saw the look on her pale face.

"Honey," he said, grabbing onto her arm.

She was turning her head away from the thing on the floor. She tried to say something but could not.

"Let me get you downstairs," he said, not needing to say anything to Noah, who was still mesmerized by their discovery.

Brian guided his wife toward the trap door. He descended the ladder first, not trusting her to go ahead of him, and then helped her down. He led her to their bedroom, helping her lay on the bed covers, and then, even though it was summer, he drew a throw blanket over her. She pulled it tight and clung to it, shivering.

"Just rest," he said, turning to go.

"Don't leave."

He looked at her, torn by the urge to sit beside her to comfort her and his eagerness to get back up to the attic. He didn't want to wait, he needed to see more.

"I'll be close by."

Her eyes stared at him, glassy and dazed, but also with a hint of—what?—anger, or maybe disappointment.

"Just call out if you need anything," he said, trying to break away from that gaze. His heart was thumping, like it used to in Boston. He wanted to get out of this room and back up those steps into that dusty, dark attic with the curious trunk filled with unimaginable mystery.

She closed her eyes, and a puff of air passed through her lips.

He stroked her left shoulder reassuringly and then left the room, looking back only once. When he was in the hall, he moved rapidly to the attic ladder, almost stumbling as he climbed into the darkness. Once through the opening at the top, he saw that Noah had more newspaper bundles spread out on the floor around him.

As Brian approached, the chief turned to face him, his smile wiped off, the color washed out of his face, his eyes round.

"There are five of them," the chief whispered, almost as if afraid to wake the babies laid out on the floor before him like a naptime nightmare at some daycare from hell.

Brian looked at the skeletons, all about the same size, all intact. What he thought might be the remnants of clothing on some he realized were gray flakes of withered skin. He wondered if they had died straight out of the womb. He glanced at another set of bones and saw that it had a small fist up to its mouth, as if it had been sucking its thumb in its last moments. God, he thought, had they been alive?

"This is unbelievable," was all he could think to say.

"Look at the newspapers," Noah said, his voice excited.

Brian knelt and grabbed one of the pages from the floor, holding it up to the light. He looked at the date, and then glanced at Noah.

"This is almost thirty years old."

"Yes," Noah said. "The newspapers are all from around the same time." He gestured to the bundles. "They span a period of about eight years. The newest I found is a little over twenty years ago."

They both sat on their heels in silence. Brian didn't know where to start. He felt like he had stumbled upon a great treasure. This would be something worth writing about. Not like all the superfluous fluff he wrote about to fill in around the town Board of Selectmen meetings and Planning Board agendas. It took a whole week's worth of nothing to fill the pages of one weekly newspaper, and he still was always scrambling at deadline.

Deadline.

He looked at Noah.

"Oh shit."

"What?"

"The paper's going to the printer tonight. I've got to get something in or I'll have to wait a whole week."

Noah studied him for a moment. "Well, I've got to take some action. I need to call the county medical examiner's office to report this, and the State Police."

"You're going to turn this over to the State Police?"

"Of course, my department's not equipped to deal with something like this."

Brian was disappointed. "Once they get involved, I'll get nothing from them. Can't you just hold off on calling them?"

"Once I talk to the medical examiner, he'll expect them to be in charge. That's the way it goes around here."

"Fine." Brian looked at the skeletons. "Let me get my camera and take some pictures. But then I've got to get over to the office and redo my front page and get hold of the printers."

"Yeah, I should probably get the department's camera and take some pics as well."

Brian felt a time crunch. "Go now, and hurry back. I've got to get out of here and get going."

"What about Darcie?"

Brian had almost forgotten about her. Hopefully she was sleeping. "She's resting. She'll be okay. Though she won't be once we have a house full of state officials."

After the chief left, Brian checked on Darcie, who was not asleep but curled up on the bed. Her eyes looked red. Had she been crying?

Brian told Darcie about the baby skeletons in the trunk and that Noah was going to report it. Brian warned her that a lot of officials would be in the house to investigate. She was concerned she'd have to talk to them.

"You were the one who found the trunk. They will have to ask you some questions."

She reached a hand out from under her covers and grasped his arm. "Please, I don't want to talk to anybody."

"It will probably be very brief," he said. "But now I've got to get to the office."

"No, don't leave me alone." Her grip tightened. Her eyes grew wide.

"I'll wait till Noah gets back."

"No," she said, and he thought she was going to cry.

"Just rest, I'll be back before you know it. And Noah will be here."

Brian grabbed his camera and returned to the attic. The air was thick, and he felt like he had swallowed some of the dust. His throat tightened and he forced a cough to clear his scratchy throat. Sweat trickled down the center of his back, giving him a chill.

He heard a soft tapping.

His eyes locked onto the trunk. His stomach clenched.

Brian couldn't move, his legs stiff, feet locked to the floor.

He counted the little skeletons on the floor to make sure they were all still accounted for. Five. Yes, there were still five. What did he expect, one of them to crawl back in the trunk?

Brian approached the trunk.

Don't let your imagination run wild, he told himself.

But the tapping continued. Very soft.

He looked to the window at the far end of the attic.

A fat fly was bouncing off the glass of the window, looking for a way out. Brian couldn't blame the insect. He wanted out of here, too, but he had a job to do.

He walked to the window, wanting to let the fly out and let some air in, even though it was hot outside as well. Maybe it would at least let some of the stagnant heat in the attic out. He set his camera down and unlocked the window, pushing up on the sill. It wouldn't budge. It probably hadn't been opened in years and had swollen shut. He pushed up again, straining, more sweat forming on his brow and under his arms.

Air, he thought. I need air.

He heard a sound and turned to look behind him. The open trap door was at the other end of the attic. It looked far away. He thought maybe Noah had come back, or maybe Darcie was up, but no one was there.

There was no further sound.

He turned back to the window, gritting his teeth and pushing hard. There was a screech of wood as the window released its grip and rose. The fly disappeared out the window. He felt no air coming in, hot or otherwise. Not a slight shift in air at all.

He wiped his sweaty palms on his pants, grabbed his camera, and walked back to the center of the attic. As he approached the trunk and its contents, spilled on the floor in front of it, it occurred to him that this was the first time he had been here alone. The darkness of the attic, with its wooden beams leaning in, and the cobwebs, dust, and shadows heightened the eerie remains on the floor. He felt like he had stepped into a haunted house. He had the urge to just take the picture and get out before one of those skeletons started moving.

Silly, he thought. They were dead, had been for a very long time. But where had they come from and how did they get here? So many questions.

He raised the camera to his eye, looking at the bizarre scene through the lens.

Click. Click. Click.

He snapped the pictures quickly, moving to get a couple different angles. He inched a little closer to get some close-ups, not even sure if he would put something this gruesome on the front page of the paper. No, of course he couldn't. The owners of the paper would have his head. This was a small community weekly, not some supermarket tabloid. But still, he needed to take the shot. He peered at one of the skeletons, its tiny, dark, empty eye sockets looking up at him through the camera lens. Could it see him? The teeth in the jawbone gave the impression it was grinning at him.

He snapped and backed away.

A floorboard creaked behind him. He froze. His hands started to shake, and he thought he'd drop the camera. He tried to swallowed, but his throat tightened. He turned to look behind him.

Noah was climbing through the trap door.

Brian sighed. His nerves tingled.

"Christ, you scared me."

Noah grinned. "Sorry. I guess it is kind of spooky up here." The chief held his own camera.

"Yeah. Now that you're here, I'm going to run over to the paper. Darcie's still in bed."

"Okay. I've made my calls. In about an hour, this place will be crawling with people. I've got officer Alvin stationed outside."

"Which one?"

"Day Shift Alvin."

"Well, things will probably go on long enough for Night Shift Alvin to join us."

They looked back toward the trunk.

"Got everything you need?" Noah asked.

Brian looked down at his camera. "I guess. I don't have a lot to write about yet, so it will be brief and won't take me too long. Give me a couple of quotes for the article."

Afterward, Brian literally ran to the newspaper. He greeted Day Shift Alvin outside the front door and noted that the officer's cruiser was parked behind his car, so he bolted the couple blocks to the office on foot. The whole way he was working out the lead in his head. As he turned up the sidewalk to the building that housed his office, he dug into his pocket for his keys. He looked up just in time to avoid bumping into someone on the sidewalk.

"Excuse me," Brian said, looking at the man, whose eyes seemed to look right past him. He was tall and thin, with thick hair piled on top but short on the sides. He looked to be in his mid-to-late forties. He didn't seem to notice Brian, even though the two had nearly collided on the sidewalk. The man didn't return Brian's comment and brushed past him, continuing along the sidewalk.

Brian shrugged it off and unlocked the front door. Once in the office he started his computer and called the printers, telling them he would transmit a new front page. He downloaded his pictures, selecting the best. It didn't take him long to write, because he really didn't have much information. He tried mostly to paint a picture of the scene in the attic. He hated putting himself and Darcie in the article, but they were witnesses and the owners of the home, so it couldn't be helped. They were immersed in the story, like it or not.

He reviewed what he had written and formatted it on the page, along with the picture. He replaced a preview of the Women's Garden Club tour. It would anger the old ladies in town, but it was the most expendable item on the page and in the best location. He was sure he'd hear about it from Mrs. Picklesmeir, the head of the Garden Club.

He looked at his headline:
Trunk of baby bones found in town
He had room to add a subhead:
Discovery of decades old skeletons in attic a mystery

He proofed it quickly, reading his headlines aloud to make sure there were no typos, and hit the send button. He called the printers to let them know they had the new front page, making sure to thank them for being understanding.

When he got off the phone he took a deep breath, wanting to relax for a moment before racing to the house and awaiting the authorities who would be showing up. And once the word got out, the big papers and TV stations would be on the story. But for now he had the jump on everybody. He broke it. He had the inside track. The whole event had been exhilarating. When he took this job, he never expected it to provide a moment like this. And it was only the beginning.

Shortly after Brian got back home, his house became a flurry of activity involving the county medical examiner, the county attorney, and two officers from the State Police—Capt. Steem, an older, stocky, bald man, and his cohort, Sgt. Wickwire, much younger, tall and athletic, his dark hair cropped close to his scalp. The attic became crowded and Wickwire had to keep his head down so he wouldn't bump it on the slanting beams.

Brian stood in the background, near the trapdoor, so he wouldn't be in the way. Darcie had gotten up and was making coffee, though it was a hot June night and the attic was sweltering, the air thick and humid. He didn't think anyone would really want coffee. Lemonade might have been a better choice. Steem removed his hat and wiped his bald crown several times with a bandana.

Brian had his notebook and was scribbling observations, listening intently as the medical examiner looked over the skeletons. Chief Treece stood by the county attorney, who had unbuttoned his vest and loosened his tie but was still sweating profusely. Brian was jotting something down when Steem turned and noticed him.

"Excuse me," the captain said. "Are you taking notes?" Irritation showed on his face.

Brian stopped, mid-scribble, but did not reply.

"I neglected to tell you," Noah said, gesturing toward Brian. "Mr. Keays is the editor of our weekly newspaper."

"Oh, great," Steem said, glaring at Noah. "Would have been nice to know." He looked at Brian. "I'm going to have to ask you to step downstairs and wait for us."

Crap, Brian thought. "This is my house."

"It's a crime scene," Steem said.

Brian looked to Noah for some help.

"And I'm in charge," Steem said, voice rising. "Not Chief Treece."

Noah grinned and shrugged.

Sgt. Wickwire walked toward Brian, ducking beneath another beam. "Clear the scene, sir," he said with no expression, his hands folded across his chest.

Brian muttered a mild obscenity, slapped his notebook closed, and descended the drop-down ladder. He joined Darcie in the kitchen.

"How are you doing," he said, rubbing her back.

She looked at him, pouting. "This feels like a nightmare. I woke up when I was napping and heard everybody's footsteps above me. I thought it was the babies' ghosts walking around." She shivered. "It's just so creepy knowing those poor babies have been up there all this time."

"They've been dead a long time, honey. And who knows if they were even alive to begin with."

She grimaced, touching her belly, and he realized it probably wasn't a reassuring thing to say.

"What do you mean by that?"

"I don't know what I mean." He turned and walked toward the living room. "I don't have any idea where they came from or what happened. It's all just mysterious."

He sat on the couch, and she joined him.

"You're enjoying this, though, aren't you?"

He looked at her, carefully formulating his response. "What do you want me to say? I'm a journalist. You have to admit, this has some excitement to it."

She frowned. "But they were babies. Little babies." Her eyes got moist.

"It's tragic, I admit." He patted her knee. "But it happened. We can't change that. Now we've got to try and figure it all out and what it means."

She looked at him, and he saw disappointment in her eyes. She would have been happy with him covering the garden tour and the upcoming Dump Festival and crap like that. That's why she didn't mind dragging him here, because she didn't care about his career. She wanted a quiet family life, a nice place to raise their child, and a job where he could come home at a reasonable time and be with her.

She didn't want him out all hours of the night at police stations, crash sites, and late-night fires. This dull weekly newspaper seemed perfect for them—no, for her.

And he went along with it. But he had other reasons for taking her away from the city, reasons that had nothing to do with his job, but more to do with her job. He wanted her away from her job at the school as much as she wanted him away from his, maybe even more.

Brian was itching to know what was going on in the attic. A couple more men showed up at the house, who turned out to be from the state pathology lab. They headed upstairs and into the attic. Brian followed and stood in the hallway by the drop-down ladder, trying to eavesdrop on what was being said, but the words didn't carry well. He had his notebook out and pen ready in case he picked up something. The voices were mostly Steem's and the medical examiner's.

At one point, Brian thought he heard a word and scribbled it into his notebook: *snuffing?*

After a few moments he heard feet shuffling toward the trap door, and he stepped away from the ladder. Capt. Steem came down first, glaring at Brian as he descended the steps, but not saying a word. The pathology men came next, carrying five black plastic bags. They proceeded downstairs and through the front door.

The medical examiner and county attorney came next and stood aside as Chief Treece and Sgt. Wickwire carried the steamer trunk down the steps. Noah smiled at Brian as they went by. Everyone else followed, like a funeral procession behind a casket, though Brian was sure this box was now empty and its contents in those black plastic bags.

In his living room, Brian looked out the window and watched Treece and Wickwire load the steamer trunk into the back of the State Police vehicle. The pathology men had already left with their cargos, and the medical examiner soon followed. As Brian stood there, he saw on the sidewalk across the street the same tall, thin man he had nearly bumped into outside the newspaper office.

The man walked slowly, arms hanging limply by his sides. He stopped at one point and looked at his feet. He reached down to the sidewalk, picked something up, put it in his pocket, and continued down the street. Brian made a mental note to ask Noah if he knew anything about the man.

Brian left the window and joined Darcie on the couch, patting her hand and giving her a reassuring smile. She didn't smile back. She looked tired even though she had been resting earlier.

After refusing Darcie's offer of coffee, Steem sat opposite them. He took out a notebook of his own and asked them about the discovery of the trunk. Brian and Darcie told him they had only moved into the house and the town a few months ago and had discovered the trunk today.

"You hadn't been in the attic at all before today?" Steem asked.

Brian and Darcie exchanged glances.

"Just to kind of peek," Brian said, "but not really to look around."

"And you never noticed the trunk?"

"No," Darcie answered. "It was tucked into a corner, and I dragged it out under the light."

Brian started to tell Steem about the key Noah had gotten from Pfefferkorn, but the captain cut him off with a wave of his hand.

"Chief Treece informed me all about the key." He glanced up from his notepad at Brian. "Very strange coincidence."

"Yes," Brian agreed.

Steem was jotting something in his notebook. Brian took his own notebook out and pretended to write something. Steem looked at him, eyes narrowing.

Noah and Wickwire came into the house and stood off to the side in the living room.

"Now tell me, who did you buy this house from?"

"The previous owner's name was Ruth Snethen."

Steem wrote it down. "Do you know anything about her?" he asked without looking up.

"We never met her," Darcie said. "It was all done through our real estate agent. Ms. Snethen didn't even attend the closing."

Steem looked at them, and turned toward Noah.

"She's a retired nurse," Noah said without waiting for a question. "Lived alone. Don't believe she'd ever been married."

"Hmm," Steem said. "Where did she work as a nurse?"

"Up at the Mustard House." Noah smiled.

Steem's brow furrowed. "What the hell is the Mustard House?"

Noah's smile left his face.

"It's an insane asylum."

Chapter 2

THE MUSTARD HOUSE

It sat on the top of the ridge, overlooking the town like a sentinel.

It was a sprawling nineteenth-century mansion with multiple narrow gables that punctured the sky. It had been originally built by a logging tycoon and had passed through many hands. Townsfolk had nicknamed the building the Mustard House because of its yellowish-brown paint. Its actual name was The Wymbs Institute. Dr. Milton Wymbs had opened the private sanitarium forty years ago.

Dr. Wymbs lived at the institute and rarely appeared in town. He had a small staff of nurses and a housekeeper who cooked and cleaned for him. No one knew exactly how many patients resided at the asylum, but the mansion had enough rooms to house at least a couple of dozen. Noah had told Brian he had never laid eyes on the reclusive doctor in the two years he had been police chief. The doctor kept to himself and his patients, and there were never any concerns.

At least not until the trunk was opened.

Brian sat in his office downtown looking at a copy of the weekly that had come out that morning, pleased he had been able to break the story. He had fielded several calls already that morning from the news syndicates and other media sources. The story had sparked plenty of interest, as he knew it would. Of course he also had to field a call from Mrs. Picklesmeir, the angry head of the Women's Garden Club, and he failed in all attempts to appease her. He assured her that he would do a big photo spread on the tour for the next week's issue, but that did little to satisfy her concern that townspeople wouldn't know the details of the tour since they weren't in the paper.

The Hollow News came out every Thursday, and most people read it to find out about the upcoming weekend's church suppers, club meetings, school fund-raisers, and auctions. From what Brian had gathered when he took the job as editor, news seemed secondary. There was a small staff—basically Brian. He had a secretary, Beverly Crump, who really kept the paper running. She inputted all the press releases from the various social organizations and clubs, and that filled more than half the paper's pages. Brian had to cover the local board meetings and do a feature story or two. The only other staff member was Isaac Monck, in his early sixties, who covered the local sports and recreation as well as writing a fishing column.

Brian remembered how difficult it had been to leave his job and Boston to take over as the editor of *The Hollow News*. He knew what he'd be giving up with his police beat, but he had no idea what he was actually taking on in Smokey Hollow. But Darcie had pleaded with him.

"What kind of life do you want for us?" she had quizzed him six months before.

There wasn't an easy answer. He had the life he wanted, the job he wanted, and he didn't see the need for a change. But all that changed when Darcie got pregnant. His initial reaction to her pregnancy was not good and had almost led to a fight. She was supposed to be the one counting days. He had left that control up to her.

"I told you it might not be a good night," she had said afterward, almost in tears.

It made him feel like a jerk, and he apologized. Then he said something even stupider. He wondered whether they should have the baby. The look of horror she gave him sent chills down his spine, and he tried to backpedal. What the hell was he thinking? She was a school teacher for Christ's sake. She adored children, and for him to suggest something like that....

It was one of those moments he wished he could take back, because he knew it was something that would mark him for the rest of his life.

It took a while for him to smooth that one over. By then she was suggesting they move to the suburbs where maybe he could find work at a small-town newspaper. So he scoured around for job opportunities, and that's when he stumbled upon the job at *The Hollow News*. The longtime editor was retiring.

They drove north to check out Smokey Hollow. Darcie fell in love with its small-town charm, of course. He knew she would. Brian felt nothing but a bad taste in his mouth, like he was choking on the mist the town derived its name from. What he saw were his dreams and hopes of a journalism career going up in flames.

"But just think," Darcie said. "You'd be the editor of your own newspaper."

True. He'd be the editor, reporter, photographer, and copy editor. It was basically a one-man band, and he'd be playing all the instruments, but nobody would be listening except people like Mrs. Picklesmeir and her Women's Garden Club members. That was his audience.

He remembered looking at Darcie as she slept in the car on the drive back to Boston. He watched her sleep, usually something he did with great affection, but this time it was with contempt and…what?…speculation? It wasn't the first time the thought crept into his mind. Did she get pregnant on purpose?

It didn't matter. He took the job, and they moved to Smokey Hollow.

Brian thought back to one of his first feature assignments when he settled in at the paper. Beverly had told him about a visit to the school by the assistant fire chief to talk about fire safety and prevention. He had rolled his eyes and wanted to stick a pencil through his forehead. Damn Darcie for this.

"Really?" was the only response he could give Beverly.

If she was insulted by his comment, she didn't show it. Maybe she already sensed his frustration and understood. Maybe she was just being cordial, like most of the people he had met in Smokey Hollow so far. Certainly not arrogant like a lot of the people he encountered during his city beat.

"It can be quite entertaining," she said. "The kids love it. He brings along Marshall."

"The fire marshal?" he said, perking up a bit. He had loved talking arson forensics with some of the fire marshals in Boston.

"No, *Marshall*," she replied, as if expecting him to know better. "His puppet. I figured you'd seen him at the fire station. The assistant fire chief is a ventriloquist."

Brian sat for a moment, soaking in the information. He grabbed his notepad and camera.

"This I got to see," he muttered before leaving the building.

Simon Runck was the assistant fire chief. He was in his mid-forties, with a square-ish head and sharp jaw, a touch of gray in his hair, and a bit of a paunch. He sat on a stool on the stage in front of the students at the elementary school, his puppet in his lap.

"Say hello to Marshall, girls and boys," he said to the audience, which yelled back a greeting in unison.

Brian stood off to the side of the gym-café-torium. The dummy was dressed in a little fireman's uniform, complete with a cap perched on the shaggy black hair on its oversized head.

"Howdy, boys and girls," the dummy said in a high voice.

Brian watched Simon and could see his throat moving up and down, as if he were swallowing something, but his mouth, open a small crack, barely moved. Not bad, Brian thought, but knew the kids were fixed on Marshall, so the assistant chief didn't need to be too convincing.

Brian began snapping pictures.

"We all know how important it is not to play with matches," Simon said.

"Yes," Marshall piped in. "Especially since I am mostly made of wood."

The students burst into laughter.

Brian jotted some notes.

At the end of the show, Brian took more pictures of the students as they approached the dummy. Some of them shook Marshall's wooden hand. When the kids dispersed and filed back to their classrooms, Brian introduced himself to Simon.

"Nice to meet you," the fireman said. "I heard you had taken over at the paper."

"Yeah, me too," Marshall said. "About time they kicked that old loser out of there and brought in some new talent. Maybe that fish wrap will get a bit more interesting."

Brian chuckled. "Nice. But I think Beverly Crump really runs the place. She's the one who told me to come here today."

"You should put me on the front page," the dummy said. "Class up the rag a bit."

"I will see what I can do." He turned to Simon. "How long have you been doing this act?"

"Act?" Marshall said. "Who's acting?"

Simon laughed at his own crack and looked at his puppet. "That's enough, Marshall. The man's trying to conduct an interview." He turned to Brian. "I came to Smokey Hollow about eight years ago. Guess I started with Marshall a few years before that."

"What made you come up with this idea?"

Simon looked deep in thought, and then brought his eyes to meet Brian's. "I started practicing ventriloquism back in high school. Kind of my way of dealing with teen angst I guess. I was a bit shy and nervous, and Marshall gave me a voice, even though it should be the other way around."

Brian jotted his comments down, before looking up from his notepad. "And I guess a career in ventriloquism didn't look promising, so you decided to be a firefighter?"

Simon chuckled. "Ventriloquism was more a hobby than anything."

"Maybe for you," Marshall butted in. "This is a way of life for me."

"And what brought your act to this exciting town?"

Brian saw Simon's eyes drift away in thought, but they came back and he smiled.

"I had actually become afraid of fire. Not very good for a firefighter. It was somewhat depressing. A town like this, I'll be honest, does not have a lot of action."

"Yeah, I gathered that," Brian said. Which is why I'm here doing this silly interview, he thought.

"It seemed perfect for me. Ends up being a lot of sitting around the fire station. That's how this happens," he patted his belly.

Brian laughed. At least Simon was honest. He thanked him and Marshall and turned to go.

"I'm sure we'll be seeing you," Marshall said.

As Brian tucked his notebook in his pocket and gathered up his camera, he looked back at the pair.

"Are you still afraid of fires?"

Simon grinned. "Around here, there's not too much to worry about." He looked at the dummy by his side. "And Marshall helped me a lot with that."

Brian smiled and waved. Before he left, Marshall had to get the last word in.

"In case you were wondering, I'm not afraid."

On his walk back to the office that day, Brian felt a little depressed. What had he gotten himself into? No, what had Darcie gotten him into? Is this what the rest of his life was going to be like, covering stories like this? Good career move, Keays, he said to himself. They will be polishing up that Pulitzer soon. Who was the real dummy here?

But now Brian had latched on to the kind of story he never imagined he'd find in Smokey Hollow. The whole town was buzzing about the discovery of the skeletons. The only problem was that he now had a whole week before he could put out more details on the story. The other news media would have daily updates. A weekly was not a good way to dispense real news.

Of course, Steem was going to be pretty tight-lipped on any information on the investigation. That was obvious from the captain's demeanor. He wished Noah was taking a more active role in the case instead of just being the local lackey for the State Police. He'd probably be able to goad him into leaking whatever information he could get out of Steem and Wickwire. That was if they'd give the chief any information.

He already knew they were having trouble locating Ruth Snethen. Tax records had shown she owned the house at the time the newspapers in the trunk were published. So the real question was, did the trunk belong to her? If not, what was it doing in her house?

Brian stared out his office window toward the Mustard House atop the ridge, with its gables and four great brick chimneys. Nurse Snethen worked there. But did the trunk have any connection with the Mustard House?

Brian thought maybe he should pay a visit to Dr. Wymbs.

He drove out of town and up the rise. He kept the windows down in his car to let air in. He despised air conditioning, and the day was turning into a hot one. He could feel sweat trickle down his chest. At the top of the rise, he turned left onto Ridge Road and drove along it, the Mustard House looming larger as he got closer. Brian slowed and eased into the gravel driveway that snaked its way toward a small parking area in front of the institute.

There were only two cars in the driveway, a large Cadillac and a small economy coupe. Of course the patients wouldn't have any vehicles, but he wondered where the staff members' cars were parked. Maybe there was an employee parking area in the back.

As he stepped out of his car, Brian looked down toward the town. It was a great view of the small village, and its Main Street looked picturesque. He spotted his newspaper office and Cully's Pub across the street from it. Down the street from that was the police station, where no doubt Chief Treece was summing up his uneventful day of reviewing parking fines and illegal brush burns. He'd had the case of a lifetime fall in his lap, yet he'd rather sit back and let the bozos from the State Police have all the fun. Brian couldn't understand that.

As he studied Main Street, it dawned on him that the town wasn't quite suited for a post card. He scanned the shops and buildings along the downtown drag. On one bookend was the Town Hall and fire station. On the other end were the library and the elementary school. Between the municipal buildings were a hardware store, a taxidermist shop, Wigland, Wibbels Fruit Market and Real Estate, and Mrs. Picklesmeir's Flower Shop. But Brian had never realized how many empty storefronts dotted the Main Street business section, with their soaped up windows and for-rent signs. There were almost as many empty spaces as there were occupied shops.

He remembered Darcie and him taking their first stroll along the downtown sidewalk one Saturday afternoon and her telling him how charming she thought the town was. He hadn't noticed it up close then, but maybe it took a view from a distance to really see the town's condition. It was like seeing someone's smile without noticing the cavities.

Across the way he could see the town's water tower cresting the rise on the opposite side of the hollow. The name of the town was painted on its tank, but *Smoky* was spelled without the 'e'. Brian remembered Beverly Crump telling him it had been that way for a long time and many citizens were embarrassed by the mistake, but the town selectmen never bothered to have it corrected. The letters were faded and chipped from winter winds. Maybe the selectmen were waiting for the mistake to be erased by Mother Nature so they wouldn't have to expend the effort themselves.

As Brian's eyes dropped from the letters, he noticed a figure standing on the catwalk that surrounded the water tank. It looked like a man, and Brian figured it must be a city worker since no one else would have reason to be up there. That would be trespassing, and Chief Treece would have to go up and bring the man down. Now that would be an exciting end to his shift.

The man appeared to be staring down, maybe surveying the town like Brian himself was. But then he thought that perhaps the man was going to jump. There was no reason for Brian to think this, but the idea popped into his head. He recalled several times on the beat in Boston when he'd be sent to the scene of a jumper threatening to leap off a high-rise. Not once did one jump. They never did. All talk, no action.

The man made no effort to climb over the rail. So...he wasn't a jumper. At least it didn't look to Brian like the man was doing anything except standing there, arms resting on the railing. Maybe he enjoyed the view. Brian was about to turn away when he realized the man now seemed to be looking across the valley...at him. Was the man watching him, or did he just happen to notice Brian on the opposite ridge? Brian had the urge to wave, to see if the man would wave back.

It's nothing, he thought, and turned away.

The Mustard House was Tudor style, reminding him of a Swiss chalet except that the building was long with two wings off the main central section. It was two stories, but the many gables lining its front gave it the appearance of being much taller. The narrow windows along the second story were enclosed with bars. Brian wondered if the inmates of the asylum stared out those windows at the town below. How frustrating it must have been for them to be so close to civilization, yet trapped behind bars, locked in their rooms.

He also wondered what the inmates were like. How crazy were they? It was a private sanitarium, so he assumed they weren't dangerous criminal lunatics. Those kinds of inmates would be housed at the state mental facility in Concord. Surely the occupants here wouldn't be like that.

But this was where Nurse Ruth Snethen worked, and she had kept a locked trunk full of baby skeletons in her attic.

Brian approached the large wooden door. The yellowish-brown paint on the building was faded, overdue for refurbishment. He looked for a doorbell but could not find one. There was a large brass door knocker on the middle of the door, and he grabbed it, lifting it up and banging it down three times. He stepped back. His notepad was in his back pocket. He didn't want it in view. That sometimes made people nervous and scared potential interviewees away.

He waited with anticipation, but no one opened the door. After a moment, he grabbed the doorknocker again and rapped it a few more times, this time a little harder. He waited, finally hearing the soft patter of footsteps. There was a sound of a bolt being withdrawn, and the heavy door swung open slowly.

A short, middle-aged woman with graying hair stood on the threshold, apparently startled to see Brian. She had a purse in her hand and a small tote bag.

"My goodness," she said, trying to compose herself. "Where'd you come from?"

Brian smiled. "I just knocked at the door. My name is Brian Keays."

"I didn't hear you."

"But I knocked," Brian said, confused. "And you answered the door."

"Oh no," she said, almost defending herself. "I didn't hear you knock at all. I was just leaving."

"And you are?" he asked.

"I'm the housekeeper."

"Oh. Well, I came to see Dr. Wymbs." He continued smiling.

"For?" She eyed him with suspicion.

"A private matter." Hold off on telling them you're a reporter as long as you can.

"Do you have an appointment?" She stood her ground in the doorway, as if afraid he might barge in.

"Not quite," he said, wondering if the doctor was that busy. Then he thought of something. "Police Chief Treece sent me." Not quite a lie—Noah had told him about the doctor, so surely the chief expected him to come up here.

She looked puzzled. "The police have already been here."

Steem and Wickwire, he thought. Of course.

"This is separate from that." He still smiled.

She stared at him for a few seconds. He could read the uncertainty on her wrinkled brow.

"Just a moment," she said. "I will check with the doctor."

She set her pocketbook and bag down on a table just inside the foyer. She closed the door, and he heard the bolt thrown.

Hmmm, he thought. Maybe she was afraid he'd follow her in. As he waited, he turned and looked back across the valley. The man was no longer standing on the water tower. If he had jumped, Brian might have missed witnessing next week's front page story. But no, there was only one story going on the front page for a while, Mrs. Picklesmeir be damned. Of course, that was if the police and he could uncover any more developments in the trunk case.

He stopped smiling, knowing that the longer this took, the less likely the good doctor would be to grant his request for an interview. Maybe he was just wasting his time. It was hot outside, and he wanted to go inside or go home.

The door opened and the suspicious housekeeper stood there again. She was not smiling either.

"The doctor said no visitors."

Brian's mouth dropped open, but he couldn't release any words. They were stuck inside his dry throat.

She had her bags in her hands and was leaving, looking at him to step out of the way. "Excuse me please," she said, and was polite about it, though he could tell she wished he would leave.

"But you don't understand," he said. "I've come a long way." That was a lie, but it was all the way from the bottom of the hill.

She looked at him but said nothing.

"Please," he said. "I can't tell you how important this is." That was true.

She released a sigh of exasperation and then placed her bags back down on the table.

"Wait right here," she said, and the door closed again and the bolt thrown.

Thankfully this wait was shorter, and when she returned, she motioned for him to come inside.

His smile returned, and he thanked her. Upon entering, he was surrounded by cool air. The discomfort of the heat outside was now replaced by an equally discomforting chill along his bare arms.

The housekeeper closed the door behind him and threw the bolt. Brian had the impression that he was now locked in the asylum with the inhabitants.

His first thought was how quiet it was. He wasn't sure what he had expected (screams, rants, and mad laughter?), but silence was not it. He was in a spacious foyer. Before him a grand staircase curled up toward the second floor. Up there, he thought. That's where the patients' rooms must be. If the inmates were being quiet, then so were the staff members, because there appeared to be no one about except for the housekeeper.

"This way," she said, gesturing down a hallway.

He followed her toward a door at the end of the hall. She rapped twice on it, and he heard a muffled response from the other side. She opened the door, but he couldn't see inside the room because her body blocked his view.

"The visitor is here," she said.

"Yes, send him in." The voice was deep.

"I'll be leaving now."

"Of course."

She stepped aside, and Brian entered what looked to be an office. The door closed behind him, and the housekeeper was gone.

Dr. Milton Wymbs rose from behind a large mahogany desk and walked around it, hand outstretched. The doctor was short and had a bald dome surrounded by wiry tufts of brown hair. Brian guessed the man to be in his sixties, but there was not a speck of gray in his hair. He wore a brown tweed sport coat with leather patches on the elbows. He also had on a bowtie.

Brian met him halfway and grasped his small hand, shaking it firmly. The doctor returned to his padded leather chair behind the desk, leaning back in it. He motioned to one of a pair of smaller chairs before the desk, and Brian sat. He resisted pulling out his notebook just yet.

"Thank you for seeing me," he said. "Let me introduce myself...."

"Oh, I know who you are, Mr. Keays," the doctor interrupted. "I may not get out into town very often. Hardly at all, in fact. But I manage to keep aware of the events of the town, such as the new editor of that esteemed rag that comes out every Thursday. What I don't know is what you expect to accomplish by coming here."

"Well, I was thinking...."

"I've already spoken to the State Police," he said, interrupting again. "As my housekeeper made you aware. That is why you are here, is it not?" His eyes locked on Brian's.

"Yes, it is. I...."

"I really didn't think you were interested in doing a feature expose on the wonderful work the Wymbs Institute has been doing in treating people who suffer from various mental deficiencies, phobias, and disorders. You know I've been running this place for forty years and treated hundreds of patients successfully."

"I wasn't aware of that. I...."

"Of course not." The doctor stood up and strolled to the front window overlooking the parking area.

Brian took this opportunity to discreetly remove his note pad from his back pocket and a pen from his front.

"You were hoping," the doctor continued, still staring out the window, "to find some connection between the discovery in your attic and this institute of mental disorders." The doctor turned to face him. "That would be a scoop wouldn't it?"

Brian didn't get a chance to answer.

"That is what you call it, correct? A scoop? An exclusive none of the other media has?" He stepped forward. "But there is no scoop here. I am a psychiatrist and this is a medical facility. I don't treat lunatics here. These are normal people. Just as normal as anyone in that town down there." He pointed toward the window. "Just as normal as you and I." The doctor was smiling.

"I wasn't suggesting...."

"No, of course you weren't." He returned to his seat and plopped into it. "As I told the State Police, Nurse Snethen retired a couple years ago. I have no idea why she had that trunk and the...contents, but it has nothing to do with the Wymbs Institute. I can assure you of that. And you can even put that in your little notepad you've been trying to hide."

Brian swallowed, but did scribble down the comment from Dr. Wymbs. "Have you heard from Ruth Snethen lately?"

The doctor shook his head. "Not since the day she retired. We had cake and coffee and bid her farewell."

"We?"

"The staff."

"And how many staff do you have here?"

The doctor glared back at him. "Why is that any of your business?"

"I just thought maybe one of Ms. Snethen's co-workers might still be in touch with her. Though I haven't seen too many staff members about here. Do you have a lot of patients? It's such a big facility."

The doctor leaned forward and placed his elbows on the desk. "The number of patients at this facility is only of importance to me and nobody else. As are the members of my staff." He leaned back in the chair again. "As you would hopefully comprehend, the privacy of everyone in this institute is highly regarded. People wouldn't come here if they couldn't expect privacy."

"So people come here voluntarily?"

"Yes, of course. They come here seeking treatment, and I provide it. People are not brought here under restraint. Like I stated earlier, they are normal people seeking treatment. Just like anyone would do for any kind of ailment. Their ailments just happen to be of the mental variety."

"And you cure them?" Brian asked, almost wishing he hadn't, judging from the flushness in the doctor's face upon hearing it.

"Cure?" The doctor loosened his bow tie but left it draped around his neck. "These people don't have gonorrhea or athlete's foot. They need to learn a way to cope with the mental functions that trouble them. There is no cure. There is adjustment."

"So you adjust them?" Brian knew he was trying the doctor's patience, but he also knew he would get nothing helpful from this interview.

"You mean like a chiropractor?" The doctor rose from his seat. "I think that is all." He came around to the front of the desk. "I will show you out."

Brian snapped his note pad shut and stood. The doctor led the way out of his office and down the hallway to the front door. Brian turned to the doctor.

"I didn't catch your housekeeper's name," he said.

"That's because I didn't throw it." Dr. Wymbs opened the door, and Brian felt the blast from the heat outside. "Good day, Mr. Keays. I look forward to the next issue of *The Hollow News*. I can't wait to see how the garden tour went."

"Thank you," Brian said and left. When the door closed behind him with a loud thud, he heard the bolt thrown in place.

On the drive down the ridge, cool air blew in the open car windows, lifting the sweat from his face and arms. But inside he boiled. Dr. Wymbs had made him feel like some cub reporter. Had those few months away from his city beat in Boston softened him already? Damn. He had let the doctor intimidate him and sidetrack him. He had accomplished nothing by going up there. He wondered if Steem and Wickwire had the same problem with the good doctor. No, probably not as bad as he had. And, of course, he would get no information from the two State Police detectives.

If only Noah would take a more active involvement in the case. Brian thought maybe he should push the police chief a little bit in that direction. It was the only way he'd likely get any helpful information.

Back in town he pulled into his driveway, getting out of his car and calling Noah on his cell phone. While the phone was ringing, he glanced across the street, drawn by the sound of whistling. It came from a chimney sweep perched on the roof of the house opposite his. The man was dressed in a top hat and black coat with tails and was pushing a brush down the chimney. His face was obscured by soot and a thick black mustache. Brian remembered during his home inspection that it was recommended he get his chimney cleaned. He saw the sweep's van in the driveway, a silhouette of a chimney and sweep painted in black on the side. Brian made a mental note to jot down the phone number on the side of the van for future reference.

"Hello."

"Noah," Brian said. "Not much luck with Dr. Wymbs."

"That's a shame," the chief said. "Not surprised, though. I don't think Steem and Wickwire got much out of their visit either."

That made Brian feel better for a second, until he realized that the two State Police detectives probably weren't too forthcoming with information for the chief.

"He has a housekeeper," Brian said. "Do you know her name?"

"No, but I'll do some checking. Why?"

"I don't know. Maybe I can get the names of some of the other staff members and talk to some of them. But the housekeeper seemed pretty protective of the doctor."

"I'll let you know if I find anything out."

"Thanks. I appreciate it."

"I can let you know tonight if I find out."

"Tonight?"

"Yes. The Boston Post Cane presentation? At the Odd Fellows Hall. Have you forgotten?"

"Oh shit." Brian had. "No, of course not. I'll see you there." He was so caught up in the trunk case that he forgot all about the trivial events he had to cover for the newspaper. The kind of things the Picklesmeirs of the town expected to read about. Tonight, the Boston Post Cane was being passed on to the current oldest resident of the town. That was something he had to attend.

As he walked to his front door, he looked across the street again. The chimney sweep waved. Brian waved back and entered his house, forgetting to jot down the sweep's phone number.

Darcie greeted him with a tight hug. Her eyes looked red. She seemed tired.

"I'm so glad you're home." Her grip tightened.

"What's the matter?" he said, stroking the back of her hair.

"People have been calling all day."

"People?"

"Well, first it was friends and family, hearing the news about our discovery. That wasn't too bad. But then news people were calling. How'd they get our number?"

"News people?" Damn, he thought. "If you're resourceful enough, a number is not hard to get. Did you tell them anything?"

"No, not really."

"Well, which is it. No or not really?"

She pulled away from his grip. "No. Of course."

"Good," he said. He didn't want to hand out information to the competition. Pesky reporters. Now he kind of understood how Dr. Wymbs felt. Ironic.

"A TV news van even stopped out front. They filmed the house."

"Wow," Brian said, though he shouldn't be surprised that the story had attracted that much attention. There was only one local TV news station in the state, and they were bound to jump on something this unusual. "Don't worry," he told Darcie. "They'll move on to something else pretty quick." Especially if nothing more developed with the case, he thought. And it looked like that's what would happen.

The Odd Fellows Hall was on Main Street across from Picklesmeir's Flower Shop. Like most private social clubs, until recently it had been exempt from the no-smoking ban for public buildings. The scent of stale smoke had seeped into the woodwork of the dark paneled walls. The slow-turning ceiling fans in the second-floor function room pushed the hot air around but never came close to cooling anything. The windows facing Main Street were open, as were the ones in the back.

Brian Keays sat in one of the hard folding chairs in the front row of the hall, with Chief Noah Treece beside him. Brian had his notebook out and his camera ready. The Board of Selectmen Chairman Eldon Winch stood at the podium. Winch had thinning gray hair and a thick white mustache. He started by talking about the previous recipient of the Boston Post Cane. She had passed away recently at the age of 102.

Brian was lazily jotting notes and had missed the woman's name. He'd have to make sure to ask for it later. It was hard to concentrate. All he could think of was his talk with Dr. Wymbs at the Mustard House. He glanced around the room, which was only half full. He spied Mrs. Picklesmeir, a large, top-heavy older woman with heavy rouged cheeks, and she glared back at him. She was probably mad he had time for this event, even though he had scrapped her garden tour preview. He would have to make sure to stop by that damn event this weekend to at least snap a stupid photo. Brian winked at her and she looked away in a huff.

Next to her was Leo Wibbels, who owned Wibbels Real Estate and Fruit Market. He was the broker through whom Brian had bought his house from Ruth Snethen. Maybe he would have some idea where the retired nurse had moved. He jotted a note to remind himself to ask the man later.

The guest of honor was seated in a high-back, throne-like chair to the left of the podium. Though he was the oldest resident in town, he still had a full head of puffy white hair. His name was Rolfe Krimmer, and Brian made sure to jot it down. Chairman Winch pointed out that Rolfe had been an upstanding citizen of Smokey Hollow for the past thirty years. After Chairman Winch's speech,

Krimmer rose out of his throne on sturdy but thin legs, a grin showing few teeth.

When the cane was presented, Brian snapped the picture of the two grinning men while everyone applauded. The crowd began to mingle, a few people filing downstairs to the bar, and Brian went up to the old man to get some quotes. Rolfe was ninety-six, and it shouldn't have surprised Brian that he was younger than the recent recipient. Didn't women live a lot longer than men?

The old man worked his gums before answering any of Brian's questions, as if he were chewing over his thoughts before spitting them out.

"Where did you live before settling in Smokey Hollow?" Brian asked, always curious what brought people to this off-the-road spot.

"I was all over the east coast," Rolfe said. "Worked as a ticket conductor on the passenger trains back in the day, in a time when a lot of people traveled by rails."

"What brought you to Smokey Hollow?"

"Seemed like a nice fit," he said. "At all the stations the trains would stop at, I'd look out the windows at the towns. Some of them looked nice and peaceful. I remember stopping at Smokey Hollow, seeing that big beautiful mansion on the ridge overlooking the town. Just looked like a nice place to retire."

"What keeps you busy in retirement? Any hobbies?"

"I still wanted to work when I retired, too restless to just laze around, so I got a job at the movie theater downtown. Started out as a ticket taker and worked my way up to projectionist. But then the theater closed down. Business was slow. That was sad."

"So what's your secret to longevity?"

"Hmm," the old man said, thinking. "I don't drink, don't smoke, haven't got laid in a long time." He burst into laughter, his gums flapping. "Oh, and I try to stay fit. Exercise. Keep my strength up."

Brian couldn't imagine what the man's workout regimen was at his age.

"And I try to keep my mind sharp. That's important. I do crossword puzzles, play dominoes, checkers, anything to keep thinking. I have a pretty good memory. I can recall things from way back."

As Brian scribbled in his notepad, trying to keep up with the old man's gibbering, sirens sounded outside on Main Street. His portable scanner was clipped to his belt, but he had it turned off so as not to interrupt the evening's proceedings. Back in Boston he would have been glued to every twitch of static from his scanner, never knowing what excitement might be sparked on its waves. Here he wasn't too concerned. There was the occasional late night car accident or maybe a drunk-and-disorderly call, but never anything to keep him awake at night.

Someone at the back of the room exclaimed "Oh God!" and he realized how wrong he was.

A flickering glow filtered through the windows at the rear of the room. Brian was still in mid-scribble—Rolfe Krimmer's comment about how disappointing it was when the movie theater had closed—when he turned to look at the back of the room, not noticing Chief Treece sidle up beside him. A row of people had gathered at the windows at the back of the room, and over their silhouetted shapes Brian could see the source of the glow beyond the glass. It was flames.

"The Mustard House," Noah said softly into his ear. "It's on fire."

In a flash, barely hearing Noah's words because he could see for himself, Brian pushed his way to a space at one of the windows and stared at the mansion on the ridge, great orange flames shooting up into the dark night sky. Now it was his turn to exclaim "Oh God," and he turned to run to the stairs, not even noticing that Noah was already gone.

Brian raced down the stairs, feet barely touching the wooden steps, and out onto Main Street to his car. Across the street he spotted the tall thin man with the high hair again, ambling down the sidewalk, hands hanging by his side. The man stopped and picked something up off the ground, putting it in his pocket before continuing down the street.

Other people filed out of the Odd Fellows Hall and into their vehicles. Brian hopped into his car and was soon part of a convoy heading up Hemlock Street toward Ridge Road. Through his windshield he had a view of the blazing building and the huge plumes of thick black smoke billowing above the pointed gables.

His heart raced as he pressed on the accelerator, climbing the steep grade. This is what his heart used to feel like, racing as fast as the thoughts in his head. Why was the asylum burning so fast? How long had it been burning before the call came in to the Fire Department? He did some calculating. Smokey Hollow had no ambulance service and relied on paramedics from the county. How many ambulances were in the surrounding area? He thought about the size of the structure and the number of rooms it must have. He wished Dr. Wymbs had told him how many patients were in the asylum. There could be dozens. Would they have been able to get out in time? The place seemed to have erupted in an instant. Were the patients' rooms locked? How many staff members were there at night? God, why hadn't he gotten these answers earlier? Damn Dr. Wymbs and his stubbornness. Would there be enough ambulances?

Sirens screamed in the night as Brian reached the top of the ridge and got as close as he dared, not wanting to interfere with the emergency vehicles. Blue and red lights flashed in a spasm, and fire engines streamed in from neighboring towns. Brian was able to find a spot at the front of a crowd of onlookers who had gathered and were being kept back by Night Shift Alvin and a few others of Smokey Hollow's finest. He spotted Noah and moved to his side.

"Holy shit," Noah said, not looking at Brian, staring at the conflagration before him.

"This is unbelievable," was all Brian could think to say, trying to hide his excitement. What was it about a fire that turned grown men into little boys?

A ring of fire engines surrounded the blazing structure, pouring water from their hoses in what Brian had often heard of as a "surround and drown" technique, usually a last resort for a fire so out of control that there was no way to save the building.

Brian looked up at the second floor windows, expecting to see hands and arms thrusting through the barred windows in frantic pleas for help, but there were none. God, had they all succumbed or had they gotten out before it was too late? He looked around, searching for people wearing—what? What did the patients wear, some kind of gowns? He saw nobody dressed like that.

"Where are they?" he shouted into Noah Treece's ear.

"Who?" the chief asked, giving him a puzzled look.

"The patients, the staff. Did they get out?"

The chief shook his head. "Nobody's gotten out."

Brian looked back at the building, glass shattering from a burst of flames in the gabled windows on the second floor.

"Oh, shit."

Huge plumes of thick black smoke billowed into the dark night sky, blotting out the stars. The yellow-brown clapboards blistered and blackened, peeling away from the walls. Brian's face seared in the heat from the blazing structure, forcing him to step back, sweat dripping from his scalp down his neck.

No screams, he thought. Had they all been overcome by smoke inhalation already? No one screaming, no one trying to get out. Had it happened that fast? This was a hellish nightmare. He almost felt guilty for thinking it would still be another five days before the weekly went to press. But still, there would be nothing then to top this story.

Brian was so mesmerized by the inferno that he almost forgot to take pictures. He took out his camera and moved a little to his left to get a good angle on the firefighters helplessly pouring jets of water on flames that refused to give up. He began clicking away, circling the face of the asylum to get different shots. He kept sidestepping and snapping before almost bumping into somebody.

It was Capt. Steem, along with Sgt. Wickwire. The captain glared at him, the glow from the blaze lighting up his bald crown and the deep furrows in his forehead. Brian smiled and began retracing his steps back toward where Noah stood. Steem looked at him with disgust. Wickwire held no expression, just stared. They weren't in authority up here, Brian told himself, so he needn't worry about them trying to remove him from the scene. It did make him wonder if they had gotten more out of Dr. Wymbs than he had. After all, it couldn't be just a coincidence that the institute was going up in flames like this, could it? Of course not. That was obviously why they were here.

With a loud crash, part of the roof on the west wing caved in, and a shower of sparks rose up into the air. The pointed tips of the gables on the front of the façade looked like teeth, as if the head of a giant dragon had tipped back and opened its mouth, belching fire and brimstone into the night sky.

The crowd gasped, and Brian turned to look at them. Most of the people from the Odd Fellows Hall had gathered to watch. There was Leo Wibbels, Eldon Winch, Mrs. Picklesmeir, and even Rolfe Krimmer, holding his brand new cane. Brian felt bad for the old man. Sorry, Mr. Krimmer, it looks like you just got bumped from the front page. You picked the wrong time to be the town's oldest resident.

He spotted the local priest from St. John's Church standing in the front of the crowd, beside a nun. The priest was overweight. The nun was homely with a rugged face and bent nose. They both made the sign of the cross as they stared up at the devastation. The nun grasped her rosary in her large hands. No amount of praying was going to help here, he thought.

Brian glanced to the left and saw a slim, tall, gray-haired woman, clutching the front of her housecoat as if she were cold, but she looked more frightened than anything. He didn't remember seeing her at the Boston Post Cane ceremony. She must have just come to the scene, like so many of the other townspeople, curiosity drawing them to the big fire. The whole town could look up and see the scene on the ridge.

"Damn!" Brian yelled, shoving his camera in his pocket and pulling out his phone. He dialed home, wondering what time it was.

"Finally," was all Darcie said when she answered.

"Honey, I'm sorry I didn't call. Things got real crazy."

"I know," she said. "I'm watching out our bedroom window. Of course I knew that's where you'd be."

"Yeah, it happened so fast, everyone just rushed up here."

"It looks pretty bad."

Brian took a few steps along the perimeter as he talked. "Worse than bad."

"Anyone hurt?" Her voice cracked with genuine concern.

He didn't know what to tell her. He didn't even know himself, but it sure had all the markings of a real tragedy. She was still nervous because of the skeletons in the trunk, so he didn't want to pile much more on her, especially when he couldn't be with her right now.

"Don't know yet," was the only response he could think of. "What time is it?"

"After midnight."

He didn't think it was that late already. "I'll probably be up here most of the night."

"Of course." Was that disappointment in her voice, or resignation?

"Don't wait up."

"I never do."

"Goodnight. I'll try to be quiet when I come in."

"Love you."

"Me too," he said, shutting off his phone and shoving it into his pocket.

He scribbled some notes in his notepad, jotting down the communities that had sent fire apparatus. Eight towns had sent trucks. He spotted the Smokey Hollow fire chief's truck and the department's engine. Simon Runck was standing beside the fire chief, Warren Shives. The chief was speaking into his radio, no doubt coordinating the operation with the other units.

Brian sidled up beside Simon Runck, thankful the assistant chief didn't have his ventriloquist dummy with him. That would have made for too bizarre a scene. He had spotted Simon in the bay of the fire station a few times with Marshall, entertaining some of the firefighters with the puppet during their down time. He hoped the assistant chief had better jokes than he used for the kids at the school performance he had witnessed.

Brian stood quietly, listening to Chief Shives bark orders into his radio. The rest of the crew from the town's engine poured water from their hose through the window on the first floor where Brian remembered Dr. Wymbs' office was located. Simon's eyes beneath his fire helmet looked jittery.

"Hello, Simon," Brian yelled, trying to be heard over the barking chief and the roar from the flames and the snapping and cracking of timbers. Simon almost jumped, not aware Brian had been standing beside him.

"Oh," he said. "Hi."

"Quite a scene," Brian said.

The assistant chief nodded, looking back at the fire. "Went up very fast. Too fast."

"Nobody got out?"

Simon turned to him. He didn't answer and didn't need to. He looked away again.

"Not the quiet place to work you thought it would be, huh?"

Simon cracked a smile and nodded. "Not at all." He looked at Brian. "This shit scares me." Brian could see that in Simon's eyes. "That fire is out of control and eating everything like a hungry beast and we can't do anything about it."

Brian jotted that down. Great quote.

"Several towns had to bring tanker trucks," Simon continued, "because we wouldn't have had enough water to fight this one." The assistant chief shook his head. "Doesn't matter. Not enough water in the state to drown this sucker."

Another crack, and another section of roof caved in. Part of the façade above the front door pitched forward and crashed onto the ground with a roar of splinters and glass. Brian took his camera out and shot more pictures. He turned and took some shots of the onlookers. Crowd reactions often made some good pictures and this group was displaying expressions of startle and amazement at all the right moments.

Brian took in as much as he could, scribbling in his notepad. His heart was racing as fast as he was writing. As the night wore on, his heart slowed at the same pace as his scribbling, and before long he put the notepad and pen away. The crowd began to dissipate in the same ratio of the flames, people getting into their cars one by one and taking the road down into town. Soon there were only wisps of white smoke curling upwards from the heap of timbers as firefighters milled through the ruins of the Mustard House, dousing embers.

The sun rose over the tall pines beyond the ridge. The last spectator was gone, and Brian sat in his car and waited as the fire crews started digging through the rubble. He knew what he was anticipating: the removal of the bodies. Multiple ambulances remained on standby, the EMTs huddled together.

Brian sat up in his seat as he saw a quartet of firefighters carrying something out of what remained of the mansion's front entryway. He got out of his car and approached the group that was beginning to gather near the front steps. The county medical examiner who had been at Brian's house just last night was there, as well as Steem, Wickwire, Fire Chief Shives, and Assistant Fire Chief Runck, and of course Noah Treece. The firefighters set something down that was covered by a blanket.

Brian inched closer, trying to get a look past the bodies blocking his view. The medical examiner crouched and pulled the blanket away. The head revealed resembled a charcoal briquette after a day of grilling on the barbecue, but the singed wiry hair surrounding the faceless lump gave no doubt to the identity of the corpse: the late Dr. Milton Wymbs.

Faceless?

The body didn't appear to have a face.

The medical examiner withdrew a pair of tweezers from his front pocket and reached toward the top of the head. He plucked the edge of what looked like a flake of skin and pulled back some kind of cloth that had been covering the face. Once it had been removed, even from his distance Brian could see the doctor's open eyes. Whatever had been covering his face was placed in a plastic bag.

The group of men began discussing something, and now Steem appeared to be giving orders, gesturing with his right hand, his voice raised but not enough for Brian to make out any words. Steem began talking to the firefighters. Brian was growing impatient. It had been a long night. Too long, but he couldn't leave now. He walked toward the group of men, but Steem must have spotted him out of the corner of his eye and immediately turned and put his hand out, palm up.

"Stay back," he barked, and the curled lip and narrowed eyes stopped Brian cold.

Helpless, he could only watch as the state policemen and the fire chiefs entered the rubble. There were shouts and hollering from the various firefighters and law enforcement personnel, and then everyone filed out of the debris. Steem barked more orders, and Wickwire went to the State Police vehicle and got on its radio.

Brian wanted to get Noah's attention, but Steem had corralled him and there was nothing to do but wait. Steem did all the talking and Noah nodded appropriately. Several of the out-of-town firefighters headed to their trucks and started their engines. It looked like most of them would be heading home, no longer needed now that the fire was out and the mansion just a smoky hull.

It looked like Steem was done with Treece, since the young chief turned and walked away. Brian intercepted him.

"What's up?" Brian asked.

It had been a long night for Noah, too, but his grave, ashen face was new. The chief met Brian's gaze, his lips not spreading in his usual smile, and shook his head.

"Man," he said, looking back at the Mustard House. "It's weird."

"What?" Brian asked, heartbeat picking up again. "Are they going to bring out the rest of the bodies?"

Noah looked at him. "That's what's weird. There are no bodies."

"What do you mean?"

"They found Dr. Wymbs, but nobody else. No staff, no patients. There are no bodies. There was nobody else in the place." He gazed at the smoky remains, shook his head again, and walked to his patrol car.

Brian stood dumbfounded, not sure what to think. He got his camera out and took one last picture of what was left of the Mustard House and walked back toward his own car. Before getting in he stopped and looked down the ridge at the town of Smoky Hollow, a light mist settling around storefronts getting ready to open for business as usual.

But this was anything but usual, he thought. It was crazy. And that was followed by another thought.

Where had all the crazies gone?

Chapter 3

A MYSTERIOUS MESSAGE

Brian sat at his desk in his office holding a strange envelope.

It hadn't come in the mail. There was neither stamp nor address on it. It must have been slipped through the mail slot in the building's front door sometime before Beverly Crump arrived to open. Scrawled in black ink on the front were two words: "Mr. Editor." Black marks stained the envelope where the ink had smudged.

Brian flipped the envelope over and back before deciding to work his thumb under the flap and rip it open. A sheet of simple white note paper was inside, with two lines written in the middle of the paper in the same handwriting:

Do you know the secret of Smokey Hollow?
The Silhouette

Brian stared at the question, wondering what it meant but more importantly who or what The Silhouette was. He figured it had something to do with the trunk. It had to. And maybe even the fire at the Mustard House. He thought about calling Chief Treece, but if this was someone who could be a valuable newspaper source, he needed to protect the identity in case the person came forward.

But the letter wasn't much help, posing a question Brian had no way of answering. Did the letter writer know the answer? Brian's gut said yes. So why the tease? Why not just come right out and tell him. Someone liked a mystery, it appeared.

He tossed the letter into his top center drawer. There was really not much else he could do with it. Brian began downloading pictures of the fire from his camera onto his computer.

After he had gotten home from the Mustard House, he had collapsed onto the couch, not wanting to go upstairs to bed and disturb Darcie. Even though he had been jittery from the night's event, he had managed to drop off to sleep for a bit until his wife came down in the morning. He had felt obliged to talk with her briefly, telling her all about the excitement of the night and the mystery it held.

But he knew it wouldn't be long before he'd be back at the office, even though it was almost a week before the next edition was scheduled. He wanted to jot down descriptions of the scene while they were fresh in his mind, and he wanted to look at the pictures. He was surprised by how few photographs he took. He remembered being so mesmerized by the blaze that he had found himself just observing it, forgetting that he wasn't a spectator.

A call to Fire Chief Shives confirmed what he had already suspected. The state fire marshal had determined the blaze to be arson. Evidence of an accelerant had been found—a couple empty gasoline cans. No real attempt to hide them. They had been outside the back of the mansion.

Brian brought up the crowd scene and stared at it, scanning the faces of the spectators. He remembered how often fire marshals told him that arsonists liked to watch the fires they set. Was the culprit in this crowd shot? Many of the people had been at Rolfe Krimmer's Boston Post Cane ceremony, so none of them could have been involved. But there were plenty of others in the picture, such as the priest and the nun.

He remembered the gray-haired woman standing by herself. He zoomed in on her, though the picture's clarity weakened as the picture got closer. Her eyes looked wide and round, her lips clamped tight. It wasn't quite the look of amazement that the other onlookers had, it was more…what? Shock? Fright?

His attention returned to the crowd as something caught his eye—a woman near the back. He hadn't noticed her before because she was mostly obscured by other bystanders. But he noticed her now and recognized her: Wymbs' housekeeper. He hadn't seen her at the scene, but there she was, watching with the others. Brian remembered her getting off duty earlier that night. He also remembered how he wished he had gotten her name. If only he had noticed her at the fire.

Brian looked through the glass window of his office at Beverly, at her desk in the reception area, typing press releases.

"Bev," he called, looking back at the picture on the computer screen. "Come here."

The diminutive round woman pushed herself out of her chair and strolled to the open door.

"Yes," she said, removing her cat's-eye glasses and letting them hang from the chain around her neck.

"You know everyone in town," he said, looking at her—she was so short it really was like looking at eye level. "Look at this picture."

She waddled around his desk to peer over his shoulder, raising her glasses and setting them on the end of her nose. Brian pointed at the screen at the housekeeper.

"Do you know this woman?"

Beverly bent forward and then immediately straightened. "Don't recognize her."

"Damn," he said. "It's Dr. Wymbs' housekeeper, but I didn't get her name when I went up there earlier in the day. I'd love to be able to talk to her." He leaned back in his chair, dejected.

"Oh, my gosh!" Bev squealed.

Brian bolted upright in his seat. "What?"

"That's her!" She pointed to the edge of the picture, to the gray-haired woman off to the side.

"Who?" He was confused.

"The woman you were looking for. Ruth Snethen. The one who owned your house."

Brian looked at her in amazement. "Really?" He couldn't believe it, and excitement rose in his chest again. "That's Ruth Snethen?"

"I'd recognize her anywhere."

He looked back at the screen. "Wow." She was there, at the scene of her former place of employment where her former employer met his death. What was she doing there? Concern? Or something more?

"The State Police haven't found her yet?" Beverly asked.

"No," Brian said, laughing at the thought she was right there under their noses and Steem and Wickwire hadn't even known it. They must not know what she looks like, or they were so preoccupied with the blaze that they didn't pay attention. He wanted to call Noah and was reaching for his phone as Beverly was heading out of his office. She stopped at the doorway and turned to face him.

"How long are you going to be here?"

"Why?"

"Aren't you supposed to be somewhere?" Her expression told him she knew something he didn't. She often did.

He put the phone down and racked his brain. Nothing came to mind. He looked at her and shrugged.

"Today's the Women's Garden Club tour. Remember." It was as if she were scolding him.

"Oh shit," he said, banging his fist on the table. He looked at the clock on his desk, and then at the picture on his computer.

"You're not going to blow this off again are you?"

He thought about it for a second, then rose from his chair, looking through the papers on his desk for the tour schedule. "No," he said. "Dammit." He ruffled more of the papers but couldn't come up with anything.

"Would you like this?" Beverly asked, fanning herself with a small flier that she seemed to pull out of thin air like a magician, which he was learning pretty quickly she practically was.

Brian grabbed his camera and notepad and plucked the schedule out of her hand as he whisked by. He would call Noah from the road to tell him about Ruth Snethen. But first he had to get in the good graces of Mrs. Picklesmeir.

He stepped out of the news office into the warm afternoon sun, the Garden Club flier in his hand. He wore khaki pants and a jersey on an early summer day that could call for shorts, but Brian felt those were less than professional. No one takes a reporter seriously who's wearing shorts. He was about to head to his car when he glanced across Main Street. Wibbels Real Estate and Fruit Market caught his eye and a thought popped into his head. He glanced at the flier in his hand and thought, in a few minutes, one stop first.

He shoved the flier into his back pocket with his notepad and secured his cameral strap over his shoulder before darting across Main Street. Not much traffic on a Saturday afternoon, of course. Once on the other side he looked up at the marquee for the abandoned cinema. The movie theater was closed when he and Darcie moved to Smokey Hollow, and he wasn't sure how long it had been since it last operated. He remembered Rolfe Krimmer telling him his last job was as a projectionist for the cinema, and he told him he was in his eighties when he worked there. There were still two letters up on the marquee, a "Y" and a "C," the remains of the last movie the theater had shown. The "Y" was loose and dangled at an odd angle. It wouldn't be long before it would break free of the marquee, like some autumn leaf clinging to the branch of a tree, and drift down to the sidewalk.

Past the cinema Brian walked by the taxidermist shop, whose front window boasted a menagerie of stuffed wildlife: a fox, beaver, raccoon, several deer heads, and even a bear up on its hind legs, arms raised in a menacing gesture. In the center of the window display, a wooden tiered rack contained several rows of glass eyes in a variety of sizes and colors.

Brian glanced back as he passed the shop and the eyes seemed to be watching him walk by. He looked away with a shiver.

After passing an empty storefront, its windows soaped over, Brian went by Wigland. Its window display contained multiple mannequin heads adorned with long flowing locks of women's tresses: blondes, brunettes, redheads. If the plastic heads had the eyes from the taxidermist shop, it really would have freaked him out.

The bell over the door tinkled as Brian pushed his way into Wibbels. A citrus odor engulfed him, and goose bumps erupted on his bare arms in the cool interior of the shop. Bins of fruits formed two rows in the center of the market. A big wooden pickle barrel was planted near the front, exuding a vinegary odor through its round cover. The priest and the nun from the local church were picking through bins of fruit. Behind the counter on the right, an older man in an apron smiled at him. He was short, with a thinning dome and thick black glasses. There was something familiar about him.

"Mr. Wibbels around?" Brian asked.

"Out back," the clerk said.

Through a doorway at the back of the market was Leo Wibbels' real estate office. Brian and Darcie had sat in there not long ago, pouring through listings of homes. He thought about how deciding on Ruth Snethen's home on Ash Street had set in motion the odd series of events that followed. What if they had picked some other house? Would the steamer trunk be still locked in the attic, keeping its grisly secret?

"Good afternoon," Leo Wibbels said, rising from the chair behind his desk and extending his hand. Leo had a pinched, bulldog face topped with silver peach-fuzz hair and squinting eyes.

Brian shook his hand.

"What can I do for you?" the real estate agent/fruit seller asked.

Brian dropped into the chair in front of the desk as Wibbels sat.

"I was wondering if you knew where Ruth Snethen lives now."

Wibbels shook his head. "Those State Police guys asked me that too, but I wasn't able to help them either."

"She didn't buy another property after selling her house?"

The man shrugged. "If she did, she didn't use me as her agent." He leaned back in his chair and scratched his head. "I thought she made some comment about moving into a retirement home, over near Keene somewhere."

Brian didn't really hope for much here but figured it was worth a shot.

"That's pretty crazy about that trunk in your house," Wibbels said.

"Yeah," Brian said. "And it's not surprising that she didn't take it with her."

"I don't know why she didn't throw the damn thing in the dump." Wibbels leaned forward and lowered his voice. "I mean, why hold on to something like that? Especially knowing what was in it. How could she even sleep at night, with that box of horrors right above her in the attic?"

"I know," Brian said, thinking how he and Darcie had spent several months with it above their bedroom. Of course, they didn't know it was up there and what was in it.

He thought about something Wibbels had said. "Did Ruth know what was in it?"

"Huh?" Wibbels grunted.

Brian hadn't realized he had spoken out loud.

"Nothing," he said, rising from his seat. "Thanks, anyway." He extended his hand and Wibbels slapped an apple in it.

"Here, on the house," he said with a grin.

"Thanks," Brian said and left the office, waving to the clerk on his way out the door and still thinking he had seen the man somewhere.

On the sidewalk he bit into the fruit. It was soft. He fumbled the Garden Club flier out of his back pocket. A map on the interior showed the locations of the homes in the tour. The closest was just around the corner, on the street behind the library. He could walk to it. He headed up Main Street, tossing the disappointing fruit in a garbage can chained to a lamppost.

A paved walkway between the library and the elementary school on Main Street led to the homes on Cricket Lane. When Brian got there, a few women were milling about in the front yard gardens of a small Cape-style home. A white picket fence enclosed the front yard. Several rose bushes grew along the fence, sporting red flowers.

Once inside the front yard, he removed the camera from his bag and started taking pictures of the spectators admiring the bushes lining the picket fence and the front of the house. He approached a couple of the women, introducing himself, and asked what they thought of the tour. He scribbled their comments and then asked if they minded him taking their photograph looking at the flowers. They were thrilled, of course, and he snapped a couple of pictures.

He thanked them, turned to look for other shots, and came face to face with Mrs. Picklesmeir.

The large woman startled him.

"Hello," he said, with a big smile.

"Mr. Keays," she said. "I wouldn't have believed it if I weren't seeing it with my own eyes."

Brian faked a laugh. "I told you I would be here."

"And how many homes have you visited?"

He hesitated, almost afraid to answer. Boy, he thought, Steem and Wickwire should enlist her for their side.

"This is the first."

"Humph." Her eyes bore into him, and sweat seeped down the back of his neck. He could not hold her gaze and looked away.

"Very beautiful," was the only thing he could think of saying while looking as some unknown flower. "What is that?"

"Delphinium." She offered no more.

"I like it." He turned to face her but she had already walked off and was now chatting with the two elderly women he had just photographed.

A wooden bench stood beside a stone bird bath, and Brian sat to jot some notes in his pad. He was wondering how to describe some of the plants when he heard whistling and looked up, spotting someone on the roof of the house across the street. It was the chimney sweep he had spied across from his house the other day. The man, grimy and black, was pushing a wire brush attached to a long handle into the mouth of the chimney. The man wore the same outfit—black coat with tails, dark shirt, and top hat. Brian wondered how comfortable it could be wearing a costume like that on a roof on a hot summer day. It might have made for a good publicity gimmick, but didn't seem very practical.

"Brian?"

He looked up, drawn out of his daze, to see his wife.

"What are you doing here?" he asked.

She looked disappointed in him. "I told you before you left this morning that I was going to take in the garden tour. Remember?"

"Oh, sure." He didn't. "Having a good time?"

She sat down on the bench beside him. "Yes, very much so." She was smiling. "It's given me so many wonderful ideas for our own yard. I can't wait to get started."

"Great," he said, and he really meant it. It would give her something to do and take her mind off the awful thing she had found in their home and the ongoing story that was unfolding because of it.

"I hope you'll be able to help me with it."

He feigned enthusiasm but really didn't offer any kind of answer, just nodded politely.

"I was also thinking," she said, "that I'd like us to go to church Sunday."

"Church?" And he knew from her expression that he had used an inappropriate tone. They had not been in a church since their wedding day.

"Yes."

"What's brought that on?"

"I heard that there's going to be a Mass in special remembrance for the children."

He was confused. "Whose children?"

Her face flushed red, and he immediately regretted asking the question.

"The children found in our home." He felt her distaste in the enunciation of her words.

"Oh." How stupid could he be?

"You do realize they were human beings, don't you. They weren't just bones in a box."

"Of course," he said, patting her knee. "I didn't mean it to sound that way. I've just got so much stuff rumbling around in my head from these past couple days."

She stood. "You know, you're not the only one."

He looked up at her and felt like a child.

"I'm sorry, dear. Of course, we can go to the Mass."

"Thank you," she said. "Now I think I will go take a look at some of these beautiful flowers. I'll see you back at home later."

"Yes," he said, and then added, "I'm not sure when."

"Of course," she said, and walked away.

Brian left the garden tour knowing that he wasn't going to stop at any of the other houses. Mrs. Picklesmeir be damned. There were more important things to spend his time on. He walked back to Main Street, stopping at the convenience store for a small purchase that he shoved in his camera bag. His next stop was the police, and Wanda greeted him when he walked in.

"Noah in?" he asked, though he could see the chief through the glass window of his office. Noah looked up and waved him in.

Brian dropped into the chair in front of the chief's desk, noticing the ashen appearance of Noah's face and assuming that something was wrong.

"I know it was arson," Brian said, taking a guess. "I already talked to Fire Chief Shives."

Noah looked up, with an expression that said he wasn't paying attention to Brian. Then he nodded. "Yeah, well, there wasn't much doubt about that. They found a couple gas cans at the scene."

"Then what's the look for?"

Noah met his gaze. "Just got off the phone with Capt. Steem. He heard from the county medical examiner."

"And?" Brian leaned forward.

"Dr. Wymbs didn't die in the fire." The chief paused for reaction. Brian had none. "The doctor was already dead. It's been ruled a homicide. Steem's in charge of the investigation, of course." Noah ran his hand through his sandy hair and blew out a deep breath.

"Murdered," was all Brian could come up with. "Did he say how?"

"Strangled," Noah said. "With his own bow tie."

"Wow," Brian said. "The fire must have been set to cover it up."

Noah stood and paced behind his desk, pausing to look out his window to the street beyond. "There hasn't been a murder in Smokey Hollow since…." He didn't finish, just shook his head.

Brian finished it for him. "Since someone stuffed five little babies into a steamer trunk?"

Noah's head turned sharply toward him. "We don't know what that was yet."

Brian stood as well. "How else did they end up there?" He took his camera out of his case. "Let me show you something." He scrolled through his pictures, past the shots of people admiring the flowers on the house on Cricket Lane, till he got to the one of the crowd of onlookers at the fire scene. He showed it to the chief. "See that woman there?" he said, pointing to the woman standing off to the side. "Do you know her?"

Noah examined it for a moment, and then shook his head. "Doesn't look familiar."

"That's Ruth Snethen."

Noah's eyes widened. "She was at the fire?"

"Yes, watching the place burn to the ground. And none of us knew she was there."

The chief sat down. "Steem has had no luck trying to find her."

"All he had to do was turn around."

"Why was she there?"

"Very good question," Brian said. "Watching her former place of employment burn to the ground and her former boss with it?"

"What are you suggesting?"

Brian didn't want to sit. He was too excited. "I'm not suggesting anything. Just look at what's happened. I find a steamer trunk of baby skeletons in the house that I bought from Ruth Snethen, who just happens to be a retired nurse who used to work at the Wymbs Institute, which burns to the ground the very next night, and the only thing inside is the strangled body of the doctor who ran the place."

"Coincidence?" The chief's brow furrowed.

Brian looked down at him in frustration. "That's not the feeling I get in my gut."

"Steem's going to want to look at that picture of yours."

"Yeah," Brian said. "But I'm going to want some mutual cooperation."

He thought about telling the chief about the mysterious note he had received but decided to keep it to himself. It might be important, but it came from someone who wanted to keep quiet.

Brian thought of something. "Almost forgot, Wymbs' housekeeper was in that crowd shot, too."

"Really. I was talking about her with Steem earlier. No one seems to know who she is or where she is. She's the only other person we know who was working at the institute. She could clue us in on the other staff members and patients."

"And where the hell they all went."

"It just doesn't make any sense," the chief said. "They had to have some staff on duty overnight, even if it was just a skeleton crew."

"Ooh, bad choice of words," Brian said, chuckling.

The chief grinned and Brian was glad. That was the look he was used to seeing on the young man's face, not this grim mask.

"Any records in the place went up in flames. Who knows how many were confined there."

"Maybe it was a mass break out." Brian was only half-serious.

"The lunatics leaving the asylum?" His grin looked mad.

"You said it."

"Or maybe there was just nobody there." His gaze met Brian's, only he wasn't smiling.

Brian's house was empty when he got home, and he called Darcie to see if she was still on the garden tour.

"I'm just heading to the supermarket," she said. "I should be home shortly."

"Okay," he said, grateful to have a few minutes home alone.

He walked outside the back door to the small yard behind their house. He had his camera bag with him.

An old maple at the back of the yard rose taller than the roof of his house, its limbs extending almost to the boundary of his lawn. Many of the branches were dead, devoid of bark, skeletal, creaking in the slight breeze that cooled the ending of the hot summer day. A hole in the trunk, about eye level, looked like a gaping mouth. Above it were two eyelike knots that gave the whole trunk the impression of a face, its mouth open in a scream.

Brian approached the tree. He removed his purchase out of the camera bag—a pack of cigarettes and a book of matches. He tore open the package, glancing over his shoulder at the back of the house, making sure no one was there. He plugged a cigarette into his mouth and lit it. He took a deep drag with his eyes closed.

It was the first one he'd had since they moved to Smokey Hollow, and it felt good. He could already feel his nerves relaxing. Darcie would be furious if she found out. When they decided to get married, she said he would have to quit smoking. It was time to be responsible, she told him, and think about the importance of being a family and having children and setting good examples for them.

She let him do it gradually, and it hadn't been too hard. Once he got to Smokey Hollow, he didn't miss it at all. The pace of the city crime beat in Boston stimulated the urge to smoke. But this town had changed all that...until the events of the past few days. Now the craving had come clawing back, and he caved in to it. But he'd need to keep it hidden.

He sucked one last drag on the butt and stamped it out on the side of the tree. He tossed the butt into the hole in the tree and tucked the matches under the cellophane wrapper of the pack and put it into the hole as well. There was no chance his wife would go poking around there.

He looked at the tree, thinking how unhealthy it looked. It should probably come down before it crashed onto their house. Their bedroom window was in line with it. Those dead limbs would smash through the window like hands trying to rip them from their bed.

He opened another pocket to his camera bag and took out a bottle of antacid tablets, another staple from his days on the Boston beat. He popped a couple of the fruit-flavored tablets into his mouth, crunching down on them. As he walked to the rear door of the house, he turned and looked back to make sure the cigarette package couldn't be seen. The gaping hole in the trunk beneath those dark knot-eyes no longer looked like it was screaming. It looked more like it was laughing at him.

In the house, he made a pot of coffee. While waiting for it to brew, he heard a noise on the front steps. He figured it was Darcie back from the supermarket and went to open the door for her and help her with the bags. But before getting to the front hallway, he heard a second sound — the slight clink of metal.

When he entered the hallway, he saw a small envelope on the floor below the mail slot. He bent down to pick it up and saw the familiar writing: "Mr. Editor."

Not taking the time to open it, he flung open the front door and stepped outside. There were no cars on the street. A squirrel scampered across the road and raced up a maple tree on the other side. A couple houses down, three girls played jump rope. The two swinging the rope were chanting, while the third girl skipped over the swinging rope.

"Don't try and hitch a ride with your thumb," the girls chanted, "'cause the Knackerman will get you and turn you into bubble gum."

He looked the other way. Nothing. Nobody. How could someone get away that quickly?

He looked at the envelope and opened it in a rush, his hands shaking. He looked at the lines printed on it:

What was the Somnambulist doing up on the ridge?
The Silhouette

Chapter 4

CONTENTS OF A SOMNAMBULIST'S POCKETS

Brian made two quick phone calls. The first to the police station. Wanda said the chief had left for the day but that he was going to stop at Cully's Pub before going home. The next call was to Darcie's cell phone. He told her he had to run out.

"But I'm on my way home with dinner," she said, exasperation in her voice.

"Something important came up," he said, glancing at the message in his hand, wondering what the hell it meant.

"There's always something important lately."

"And you thought this was going to be a nice quiet town." He waited to hear laughter in response to his wisecrack, but there was only silence on the phone. "I'll try not to be too late."

"Okay," she muttered, and clicked off without saying goodbye.

He got in his car and drove the short block to Main Street and then around the corner to the pub across from the news office. The chief's car was parked out front. Once inside, he saw the place was about half full, a good crowd for a Saturday night. The place did its best business after work during the week. Brian looked around for Noah.

The pub was dim, with dark, barn-board walls, the wooden floor scuffed and worn. Dim lights from ceiling fans cast faint glows over the round tables. The long bar was at the back of room, before the kitchen. The walls were covered with old framed photos of Smokey Hollow from fifty or sixty years ago, revealing a thriving downtown with shops and restaurants when the town was in its heyday.

Eldon Winch, the selectmen chairman, sat at one table with Leo Wibbels. They were engaged in conversation when Brian walked in, but now both men eyed him. Laughter distracted him and his gaze shifted to a table where Fire Chief Shives, Assistant Chief Runck, and a couple other firefighters sat, still in uniforms, off-duty for the night. Simon Runck had his puppet, Marshall, at the table. At another table toward the end of the bar was a slim woman with luscious long, blonde hair. She sat alone, sipping a glass of white wine. It surprised him that such a young woman would be by herself.

Brian glanced around the rest of the people at the other tables—some he recognized, others he didn't—before he looked over at the bar. He saw his sports editor, Isaac Monck, at the bar sitting next to a dirty-faced man who looked familiar. It took only a second for Brian to recognize him as the chimney sweep. Noah Treece sat by himself at the bar, and Brian headed in that direction.

He brushed past the firefighters' table, nodding but not wanting to stop.

"What's the rush?" Marshall said. "Where's the fire?" The men at the table burst into laughter.

Brian stopped and turned to face the puppet and couldn't help but grin.

"Just trying to catch Noah," he said, without realizing he was addressing the puppet. He quickly shifted his eyes to Simon.

"Any break on the case?" Simon asked. "We haven't gotten anything more from the state fire marshal's office."

"Nothing I've heard."

The puppet's head turned toward him, and its mouth dropped open. "That was quite a scene at the House of Dijon," Marshall said.

"What? Where?"

"Dijon mustard," the puppet said. "The Mustard House." The puppet's mouth jittered as laughter emanated from it, or at least it appeared to Brian that it was coming from there, though he knew it really wasn't. Shives and the two young firefighters chuckled.

"Oh, yeah," Brian said, still trying to remember to look at Simon when he responded, but it was difficult. "It certainly was a show."

"And I had to miss it," Marshall exclaimed, "because these jerkos left me behind." He gestured to the others at the table.

"Marshall," Simon said. "You know you can't get too close to fire. You're made of wood."

Marshall turned to look at his master. "But you know how much I like fires. You're the one who's afraid of them." He looked back at Brian. "Why he ever became a firefighter I'll never understand."

"We've discussed that," Simon said.

"I would have gone by myself," Marshall said, "but my feet can't reach the pedals in the fire truck."

The young firefighters forced laughter, as if trying to appease their bosses. Or maybe they had enough beer for it not to matter.

"Maybe you can make the next one," Brian said to Marshall and turned to go.

"Hey, Clark Kent," Marshall said, and Brian stopped and turned to face the puppet.

"Next time you go to a fire," Marshall said. "Stop by and pick me up, cause these schmucks won't take me."

"Sure," Brian said.

As he made his way to the bar, he passed by the blonde woman's table, noticing now he was closer that he was wrong about her age. She was not a young woman. The thick, shiny blonde hair that tumbled in waves down nearly to her waist had fooled him. Up close he could see the creases on her face and lines around her eyes and realized she was probably in her sixties. He was sure the hair was a wig.

He greeted Noah as he sat down beside him at the bar, the laughter of the firemen continuing behind him. The bar owner and namesake, Hale Cullumber, a fat, greasy haired man who also tended bar, came over, and Brian ordered a beer. He knew the chief didn't drink and noticed a glass of lemonade in front of him.

"Tough day at the office?" Brian asked.

The chief smirked. "Enough for me to warrant needing one of these." He lifted his lemonade.

"Talk to Steem?"

"Called him after you left, told him about your photo. He's going to be paying you a visit."

"Can't wait." Brian took a swig from his beer. It was borderline warm. "Cully," he said to the bartender. "Turn the cooler down a couple notches. Jesus."

Cullumber waved his bar rag at him in a gesture of disgust, but it could have easily been the white flag of surrender. Brian had harped on the bar owner before that his beer wasn't cold enough, but it had no effect. He guessed that since Cullumber had the only drinking establishment in town, it didn't really matter to him.

"So what brings you down here?" Noah asked.

Brian pulled the envelope out of his pocket and waved it in front of the chief before setting it on the bar between them.

Noah glanced at the writing on the envelope and looked up at Brian. "And?"

Brian told the chief about the first letter he had received, apologizing for not bringing it up when he stopped in the police station.

"I wasn't sure if it meant anything. And when I got this one, I still debated telling you, because if some anonymous source wanted to communicate with me, I should keep it between the two of us."

"But?"

Brian looked at Noah. "With this note, I think I might need some help."

"What does it say?"

"I'm not quite sure," Brian said, taking the note out of the envelope and handing it to the chief. He studied Noah's face as his eyes rolled across the short message. When he was done, Noah's eyes met his.

"Do you know this Somnambulist?" Brian asked.

"Yes," the chief answered. "His name is Sherman Thurk. He works for the city Sanitation Department, rides on the back of the garbage truck, picks up the trash barrels. Has a little problem with sleepwalking."

"Little problem?"

"Yeah." Noah nodded. "Kind of wanders around town at night asleep. Never causes too much of a problem. Usually wakes up at some point and just walks home."

Brian thought for a moment, remembering the man who almost bumped into him the night they opened the trunk. "Is he a tall, lanky kind of fellow? Big hair?"

"Yeah," the chief said, smiling. "That's him."

"I think I've seen him a couple times."

"He's pretty harmless."

"But what would he have been doing up by the Mustard House?"

"When he's sleepwalking you never know where he might end up. I'm sure it's just a coincidence." The chief took a sip of his lemonade.

"Does he remember anything when he's in that state?"

"You mean, if he saw something up there?"

Brian nodded.

Noah shrugged. "I don't know. It's usually a pretty deep sleep. Sometimes my boys have had to pick him up and give him a ride home. He rarely remembers anything. I'd be more concerned about who it was who saw him up there."

Brian waved the note in his hand. "This person thinks it's worth mentioning."

"I can let Captain Steem know about it."

Brian dropped his head. That was the last thing he wanted. How could he get Noah to be more excited about investigating this case on his own? Where was his drive?

"I don't think you should," Brian said.

"It's his investigation."

"It's still your town. There's no reason you can't check this out."

"Don't you mean 'we'?"

Now it was Brian's turn to grin. "Of course I'd like to go, too. And if anything comes of it, we can let Steem know after." Brian finished his beer. "Do you know where this Thurk guy lives?"

"Yeah, at a rooming house over on Cheshire Road. We can take a ride out there now, before he goes to sleep." The chief grinned.

A hand clasped Brian on the shoulder, startling him as he was getting off his bar stool. He turned to see Selectman Winch.

"Good evening, Mr. Keays," Eldon said, smiling. "Nice to see you."

"Same here, but I'm just leaving."

"No problem. I just wanted to let you know how I'm looking forward to your coverage of the garden tour. I hope a lot of this other nasty stuff happening doesn't distract too much from the kind of things people want to see in the paper."

Brian had to keep from chuckling. "I will certainly try to give everything its fair play," he said, without really giving the chairman a direct answer. He bid Eldon farewell, and he and Noah headed toward the exit.

"It's our chief and Jimmy Olson on the case," Marshall yelled out as they went by the firemen's table.

Brian glanced back as the puppet laughed along with the others. The only one not laughing was Simon Runck. Except that since he was really the voice of Marshall, he kind of was laughing.

The two of them didn't have far to go. Just a block after the newspaper office was Willow Street. Brian followed the chief in his car as he turned onto Willow, which led to Cheshire, a curved lane that looped around. Noah pulled up in front of a two-story house with a front porch topped by a second-floor porch. It was set back from the road and fronted by a long lawn. Brian stopped his car behind the chief's, and the two men walked up a stone walkway that cut through the middle of the lawn.

"Eldon Winch owns this place," Noah said, as they strolled side by side up the walkway.

Brian noticed a familiar face up ahead. It was Rolfe Krimmer, and what he was holding wasn't his newly acquired Boston Post Cane. The old man stood on the lawn wearing a white tank top and work pants. He held the long handle of a sledge hammer in his hands, dangling it in front of him, his legs spread. Rolfe swung the hammer back and forth, like a pendulum, its arc getting higher with each stroke. The old man's arms were surprisingly muscled. Sweat beaded up on the tip of his nose till drops fell one by one.

"Good evening, Rolfe," Noah said as they approached.

The old man set the sledge hammer down and nodded, too out of breath to actually speak.

"What's this?" Brian said, curious about the strange scene.

"Just my," Rolfe started to say between puffs of breath, "daily exercise…routine. Way to…keep my…strength up." The old man smiled.

Brian wondered why Rolfe hadn't told him about this when he interviewed him about his secret to longevity. He supposed he could still add it to the article, though with all the news that had happened since, there might not be too much interest in the old man's story.

"Keep up the good work," Noah said as he and Brian ascended the front steps to the boarding house. The chief pressed the button next to a nameplate that read: S. Thurk. Brian glanced back to watch Rolfe Krimmer and his exercise regimen.

A wheelchair was parked on the front porch. Its occupant was a short man wearing a white Panama hat, his long, stringy gray hair flowing over his collar. His right leg ended at his knee, the left leg missing its foot. His left arm was missing everything below his elbow. He waved at the two of them with the three fingers he had left on his right hand.

"What's up, Doc?" Noah said, returning the gesture.

The wheelchair man grinned but did not speak. He was missing a couple teeth.

"Hello?" came a sleepy voice from the intercom.

"Chief Treece," Noah said. "Just wanted a minute with you."

There was no response at first, and then a buzzer sounded.

Brian followed Noah in and up a narrow flight of stairs. Down a hallway at the top of the stairs, a door opened before they even got to it. A tall, lanky man stood in the doorway, bent a little so the nest of hair on his head didn't brush against the lintel.

Noah introduced Brian, and the three entered the one-room apartment. A bed stood against one wall, a couch against the opposite, with a coffee table before it. A small television sat on a wheeled wooden stand. A bureau was on the front wall between two windows that looked onto the porch. That's all there was for furnishings in the tiny room. Brian thought that a tall man might feel claustrophobic in such cramped quarters.

Sherman Thurk sat on the end of his bed, and Noah and Brian took their places on the couch opposite him.

"What can I do for you?" Sherman asked. He sounded tired. He had bags under his eyes.

"You were out wandering last night," the chief said, sounding matter of fact, not accusatory.

Sherman grunted. "What else is new?" Though it really wasn't a question.

"Do you know where you were?"

Sherman shrugged. "Not really. Think I was downtown when I woke up."

Brian remembered seeing him on Main Street when he came out of the Odd Fellows Hall to go to the fire scene.

"Someone said you were up on the ridge." The chief locked his eyes on Sherman's.

There was a blank look on Sherman's face, though he held the chief's gaze. Then he shrugged again. "Could be. Don't know."

"No recollection?"

Sherman shook his head.

Noah nodded, looking around the room, from one corner to the next. Then his gaze fell back on the man opposite him. "Your clothes from last night still around?"

Sherman didn't look surprised by the question. "In the hamper."

"Can I look at them?"

"Sure," Sherman said, rising and going into the bathroom.

Brian looked at Noah once Thurk was out of the room. "Clothes? What gives?"

"Sherman has a habit of collecting things when he's sleepwalking," the chief said.

"Collecting?"

"Yeah. Picks things up off the ground." The chief kept his voice down. "Totally unaware of it. Must be related to being a sanitation worker. Always picking up trash."

Sherman returned with a pair of pants and a jersey, handing them to the chief.

Noah looked up at the man who now towered over him. "Do you remember emptying the pockets when you got undressed?"

"No." He sat on the end of his bed.

The dark blue shirt had one chest pocket. The chief reached in, but came out with nothing. He set the shirt on the couch. He picked up the pants and dug his hands into the front left pocket. He pulled out a comb and a hole punch, setting them on the coffee table. He reached in again and extracted a cigarette lighter.

Brian's eyes widened. "Do you smoke?" He asked.

"No. Not mine."

The chief flicked the lighter and a small flame popped out. He put it out and put the lighter in his front pocket. The whole time the chief never took his eyes off Sherman, who remained expressionless. Brian watched the chief reach into the front right pocket and could tell as his eyebrows arched that Noah had found something. The chief withdrew his hand, turning it over and uncurling his fingers. The three men looked at the object sitting in Noah's palm.

It was a glass eye.

Chapter 5

A SERMON FOR LOST SOULS

St. John's Church was at the beginning of Main Street, just before the business district, a brick building with tall, arched stained-glass windows depicting the Stations of the Cross. A white steeple pointed toward a bright blue sky. A brick house connected to the side of the church served as the living quarters for Father Lehman Scrimsher and Sister Bernice.

As Brian and Darcie exited their car in the parking lot, he noted another building, set back from the road. It was a two-story, flat-roofed structure, also made of brick. It had been abandoned for quite some time. The windows on the first floor were boarded up with plywood. The second floor windows were mostly broken. Cracked slate letters above the wooden front door said "St. John's Home for the Aged."

Darcie had insisted they come early because she wasn't sure how crowded the Mass would be. It had been quite some time since Brian had gone to church, and he wondered if they still drew a lot of people. Once inside, they took their seats in a pew about halfway down the aisle. Brian wanted to watch the people who turned out for the Mass and scanned the faces as they all took their seats.

Like Noah's Ark, almost everyone showed up in pairs. There was Leo Wibbels and his wife. He was dressed in a suit and tie. His wife, silver haired, wore a flower-print dress and pink hat. Beverly Crump was there with her husband. Selectman Eldon Winch and his wife, an old, crabby looking woman. In fact, all three selectmen were at the church with their wives. Must look good to the voters, Brian thought.

Also in attendance were the Shives, the Moncks, the Cullumbers, and, of course, Mrs. Picklesmeir, who glared at Brian, as if doubting his right to be in the church.

Several people arrived solo. Rolfe Krimmer came down the aisle, his Boston Post Cane tapping in rhythm with his steps. He took a spot in a pew by himself. Brian recognized people whose names he didn't know: the chimney sweep he'd seen around town, and the man who worked at Wibbels Fruit and Real Estate. He saw the woman from the bar, only this time instead of being a blonde, she had long, red hair. Also alone was Wanda, the police receptionist.

For all the people Brian knew who were in attendance, there was an equal number he didn't know. He wondered, but doubted, if Ruth Snethen would show up. He suspected she was in hiding.

A buzzing drew Brian's attention to the church entrance, where a motorized wheelchair cruised down the aisle, bearing the man he had seen in the rooming house on Cheshire Street. He was still wearing his Panama hat. He operated the wheelchair by a controller on the right armrest, his hand pushing the knob forward with his three remaining fingers. He motored to the front and took up a spot to the right of the pews. Brian had asked Noah about what happened to the man, but the chief didn't know. Nor did he know what kind of doctor the man had been, just that everyone in town called him Doc, so Noah did as well.

As Brian scanned the people in the crowd, the one thing on his mind was if any of them had a glass eye. He studied the faces around him, trying to determine if someone had that odd look, where one eye didn't seem to look in the same direction as the other. The glass eye Noah had found was blue, so Brian immediately dismissed anyone with dark eyes.

He was surprised the chief wasn't in attendance. He thought Noah would be the church-going type.

Brian didn't pay much attention to the service. Church had always bored him as a kid. He saw a lot of couples with young children in the pews, and it reminded him of being dragged to church by his parents. He was grateful as an adult that he could choose not to attend. He hoped today's Mass wasn't the start of a new trend for Darcie. It was hot in the church for so early in the morning, portending the kind of day it was going to be. The summer had already been too hot way too early. Brian tugged at his collar, which was sticking to the sweat on his neck. Why was it always so stuffy and hot in a church? It was as if they wanted to give the parishioners a small taste of hell to keep them on the straight and narrow.

When Father Scrimsher got to his sermon halfway through the Mass, Brian paid a little more attention.

The reverend was tall and pear-shaped with a long face that melted into his thick, fat neck. His hair was gray and thinning, his eyes narrow, his mouth wide. Brian guessed he was in his early sixties. Probably riding out the twilight years of his priesthood before he was sent out to whatever pastures men of the clergy retire. Brian was glad to get a chance to sit as the sermon began.

"I look out at all the lovely parishioners," Father Scrimsher began, his voice deep and thick, "and I see such a devoted group of followers. Nice families and couples, old and young." His hands made a sweeping gesture. "And the children, of course." He paused. "Children accompanying their parents to such a great holy event before the eyes of our Lord. It brings such sweetness to my heart." He placed his right hand over his chest. "For it is the children, the innocent young children, who are indeed our most valuable blessings from God. We bring children into the world, to perpetuate our race, to pass on our knowledge, our love, and our belief in the Almighty." He looked around. "So fortunate for our children to have so much love and faith bestowed upon them. To have parents to cherish them." He paused again.

"But not all children are loved!" His voice suddenly boomed, waking up a few of the dozing older folks. "No, not all." Softer. "Right here in the midst of our town, you all know, it was discovered, five young children, children of God, who were not loved. No. They were cast aside."

Brian glanced at Darcie and saw that her eyes were moist.

"But the good Lord has not forgotten about those children," the priest continued. "Because God loves those children. Even though they were hidden from the rest of the world. God still loves them. And it was God who made sure that those children were found, that they weren't lost forever. He let them be discovered, so they can at last be at peace. And now the good people of Smokey Hollow mourn those dear children."

Brian took out his notebook and began to scribble down quotes from Father Scrimsher's sermon. But then he felt watched and glanced up from the page to see Darcie's eyes upon him. They were still moist, even a teardrop clinging to an eyelash in the corner. But her eyes held another look, abhorrence. She mouthed the word 'no' and shook her head. He closed the notebook and shoved it back into his pocket.

As Father Scrimsher continued his sermon, Brian heard sobbing behind him. He glanced over his left shoulder. A middle-aged woman sat alone in a pew, eyes red from crying. She had long hair with streaks of gray. She sniffled throughout the rest of the Mass.

When the service had ended, the priest and Sister Bernice, along with a couple of altar boys, walked down the aisle to the front doors. Immediately following them was the man in the wheelchair, as the rest of the parishioners waited for him to pass before filing out of the pews. As his wheelchair passed, the man's head turned Brian's way. At least, to Brian it seemed like the man was looking at him, but it was hard to tell. His left eye looked at him, but the right eye looked off in another direction. The man had a glass eye.

On Monday afternoon, Brian found himself staring at the rows of glass eyes in the window of the taxidermist shop. It was another stifling hot day, and he wiped sweat from the back of his neck with the palm of his hand and then rubbed it off on his pant leg. This week's edition of *The Hollow News* was mostly done, ahead of schedule. The front page was going to be entirely devoted to the asylum fire, Dr. Wymbs' murder, and the latest update on the skeletons in the trunk. He never imagined he'd be putting out this kind of front-page news when he took this job.

The bit on the garden tour and Rolfe Krimmer's Boston Post Cane award were getting shoved inside, Mrs. Picklesmeir be damned. He did feel bad for Rolfe, though. The poor old guy deserved his time in the spotlight. He picked the wrong moment to be crowned the oldest resident.

As he scanned the eyeballs on the tiered rack, Brian saw another set of eyes on him. Not the ones in the window, but reflected in the storefront glass. He turned to see Police Chief Treece on the sidewalk and greeted him.

"Just because it was in his pocket, doesn't mean it has any connection," Noah said, smiling.

"True," Brian said, but something was nagging in the back of his mind. "But you knew enough to look in his pockets. Why?"

The chief shoved his hands in his pockets and looked down at his feet. Brian got the feeling he was embarrassed.

"What?"

Noah looked at him. "I wasn't being completely forthcoming about something."

"More secrets in this town?"

"No, nothing like that." He looked up the street, then back at Brian. "When I told you Chief Pfefferkorn found that key that he carried around all these years, the one that ended up unlocking the trunk."

"Yes," Brian leaned forward.

"He actually found it in the Somnambulist's pocket."

Brian was surprised. "That's interesting."

The chief shrugged. "I didn't tell you right off the bat, because I didn't want you to jump to conclusions about Sherman Thurk."

"So you don't think it's possible the key belonged to him?"

"Heck no. He picks things up, that's all. He can't help himself. He's just a harmless sleepwalker."

"Who just happened to be walking on the ridge the night of the asylum fire and had a key that belonged to a trunk full of baby skeletons."

"Sounds ominous when you put it that way."

"It would sound ominous no matter what way I put it. But you don't think so?"

"If I did, I would have told Capt. Steem about the eyeball. But I didn't think it important enough." The chief flashed his toothy smile. "At least not yet."

Brian cracked a smile of his own. Now that was more like it, he thought. The chief holding a few cards to himself. Maybe it wasn't too late to make an investigator out of him.

"Care to join me inside for a talk with the taxidermist?" Brian jerked his thumb toward the store's door.

"I'll have to pass," Noah said. He nodded down the street. "On my way to Leo Wibbels'. Someone's been stealing fruit from his market."

And that dashed his hopes for him, Brian thought, feeling a little dejected for the chief.

"You've got the crime of the century happening right here," Brian said. "A few stolen bananas ain't going to matter."

"Duty calls," Noah said.

As he turned to go, Brian reached out and stopped him, grabbing his arm, gently though. Something had caught Brian's eye. Whenever he saw Noah, the thing that always stood out was his cheery smile. But ever since they found the glass eye, Brian found himself focusing on people's eyes, looking for someone with a glass eye like the wheelchair man. But now, looking at Noah, he noticed something about his eyes and he peered closer, almost causing the chief to lean back with surprise.

"You're not about to kiss me are you?" The chief laughed, but he seemed nervous.

Brian couldn't help but crack up at this unexpected joke from Noah. "No," he replied.

"Good, because, I like you, but in a working kind of relationship. And I like your wife, too."

"I just noticed something I hadn't before." He looked deep into the chief's brown eyes. In the right eye, there was a spot of orangish-yellow mixed with the brown.

"Your eye color," Brian said. "You have a spot."

"Oh, the fleck. Yeah."

"I've never noticed it before."

"Always been there. Born with it. It's called Heterochromia. It's hereditary. Nothing that unusual."

"I just wonder why I didn't see it before." Brian stepped back, out of the chief's space.

"It's because you've become obsessed with eyeballs now." He started to walk away backwards. "You'll go cross-eyed if you don't watch out. Good luck." He turned and headed down the sidewalk.

A bell jingled as Brian pushed open the door and entered the taxidermy shop.

A tall, slim man with combed-back white hair and a white goatee approached.

"Good afternoon," the man said, extending a knobby hand. "Jonas Fitchen."

Brian shook his hand, introducing himself, thinking he had seen the man either at church or the pub, or maybe both.

"Looking for something?"

"Not quite," Brian said. "More of a curiosity." He gestured toward the window display. "I see you carry a lot of glass eyes."

"Why yes." Jonas walked closer to the display and Brian followed. "I have an even larger assortment in the case out back. Every size and color imaginable for whatever your taxidermy needs require. Something to stuff?"

Brian shook his head. "Nothing like that. I was just wondering. Are there people in town who purchase glass eyes from you?"

Jonas Fitchen's eyebrows raised in confusion. "Of course. People buy them all the time. I put them in the animals I stuff for them."

"Oh, no," Brian said, grinning. "You misunderstand. I meant do people in town buy them for themselves?"

Jonas scratched the side of his head, trying to dig out a thought. "I guess there are a couple fellas I've sold eyes to who do their own stuffing. Not as many as there used to be."

He wasn't getting it.

"No," Brian said. "What I mean is, people who buy glass eyes for their own eyes, in their own heads."

Jonas Fitchen's eyes widened in comprehension and then shook his head, almost starting to laugh, but then hesitating. "Of course not. These eyes," he gestured toward the display, "are not fit for human use." His expression grew serious. "They are only for animals. Not people."

When Brian got home from downtown, Darcie was in the kitchen, putting flowers in a vase. He stopped short as he watched her, his heart a little weak in his chest. She didn't know he was standing there and was startled when she turned around.

"Who are those from?" he asked, knowing his tone was accusatory.

"Don't jump to conclusions."

"Are they from him?"

Her eyes narrowed and her face flushed, but not with embarrassment, more with anger.

"Why would you say that?" She appeared on the verge of either rage or tears. He couldn't tell which.

"I'm just asking." He thought she was avoiding the question, but maybe she was only mad about what he was insinuating.

A year before they got married, Darcie started to get doubts about their relationship. The summer that year, she wanted some time apart. He wasn't very understanding. They had been dating two years, and she was suddenly having doubts? She had said she just had been feeling in a rut and wanted to make sure that she really wanted a future with him.

"So you want time away from me?" he had asked, sitting on the couch at her apartment—it came out like a sad plea.

"Just a break, to figure some things out." She had tried being soothing.

"I don't understand." He was pouting and knew she hated that, but he couldn't help himself.

"I just don't feel that you're very passionate about me."

That stunned him.

"Passionate." He was dumfounded. "Of course I'm passionate about you. How can you not see that?"

"I see you're passionate about your job."

"That's what this is all about. My job, isn't it? You don't like my job."

"It's just that you're always running off, all times of the day and night. I never know when you're going to be there for me."

"I'm always there for you," he said angrily. "Even if I'm not right there. It's my job, for Christ's sake."

"You don't have to swear."

He jumped up from the couch, pacing back and forth. "It's my job. I have to do my job."

"I just wish you'd pay me the same attention." Her voice was raised, as her tone adjusted from sympathetic to displeased.

"I pay attention to you." He tried to remain calm but wasn't very successful. "When I'm here."

"That's right," she said, almost spitting it out. "When you're here."

Before he left that night, she gave him a half-hearted hug.

"I just need some time to think things over." It was summer, so she wasn't teaching. Though she did a bit of tutoring on the side, she had a lot of free time. So did the other teacher. Brian didn't know his name at first but soon found out.

Brian didn't see her for most of that summer. One night Brian went to see her to talk about the situation. He saw a bouquet on her kitchen table. When he asked who they were from, she finally told him about her co-worker. They were friends, she said. They had worked together for several years and got along well. She was sure she had mentioned him to Brian, and maybe she had, but it was nothing he would have paid attention to. Her world at the school was foreign to him. She had never invited him to work-related functions or activities, always saying that he'd be bored and feel out of place. Maybe now Brian knew the real reason.

"Are you spending time with him this summer?"

"Yes," she said, not looking directly at him.

He left her apartment angry, thinking the relationship was over, though she pleaded with him to stay and talk. He went to the bar where most of his newspaper cohorts hung out and got really drunk. This is where I belong, he thought, among the lonely journalists whose jobs took precedence over relationships.

It was a couple of weeks before he finally spoke to her. She tried to explain, but he wasn't very receptive. He was more than willing to give her the space she wanted. As long and much as she wanted. She kept in touch, but he didn't make any effort in return.

Before the summer ended, she came back to him, professing her love and desire to have a future with him. And Brian felt relieved, figuring she had found the answers to her doubts, though spawning some in himself.

"Then, who are they from?" he asked about the new flowers.

"I don't know," she answered with a whimper.

"What do you mean, you don't know."

"I found them on the front steps." She paused, trying to gain her composure. "Someone placed them there."

He didn't understand. "Why?"

She looked at him with moist eyes.

"Don't you get it?" she said, and now her lip was trembling. "It must be from the mother of one of those babies found in our house." And now she did begin to cry.

The next day, Brian took a break from getting some of the final inside pages done, including the pieces on the Women's Garden Club tour and the Boston Post Cane award. He walked to Mrs.

Picklesmeir's flower shop on Main Street, which was sandwiched between a couple empty stores. He smoked a quick cigarette during his walk over, thinking there was no chance Darcie would be wandering around downtown and catch him. She would be furious if she did, but the cigs helped calm his nerves, and dealing with Mrs. Picklesmeir put him on edge. He wasn't sure why. He stamped out the cigarette butt and deposited it in a trash can before entering the flower shop.

He was assaulted by fragrances as soon as he pushed through the front door and he had to catch his breath. Thank god he had no allergies. The shop was bright, almost hurting his eyes. Big glass cases bloomed with vases filled with colorful arrangements. One case contained bright red roses.

A slim young woman with long hair stood behind the counter. He saw no one else and smiled, thinking he had caught a break. He approached the counter and greeted the woman, who offered a friendly smile in return. But before he could even get two words out, a large form stepped through an open doorway behind the counter.

"I will handle this customer," spoke the deep voice of Mrs. Picklesmeir. The young woman gracefully excused herself, disappearing into the back room.

"What a surprise to see you, Mr. Keays. What brings you here? Flowers for the Mrs.?"

That actually wouldn't be a bad idea, he thought, but then remembered that she had fresh flowers, which was the reason he was here.

"What I actually was hoping for was some information."

"Let me guess," she said. "You need some background on the Women's Garden Club to go along with that nice feature of the tour you'll be displaying in this week's edition of the paper."

He flashed a smile. "Not exactly."

"I can't tell you how excited the members of the club are to see the article and beautiful color photos of those nice gardens."

An image flashed in his head of the page he had just finished. It was not on a color page and he only used one photograph.

"I'm sure they will enjoy the write-up, but as you may be aware, it's been an unusually busy week of news in town."

"Oh, you mean those terrible events from several days ago? Yes, very dreadful. I saw all about them on the television news already."

Her eyes on her large face narrowed. "I can't imagine there is much more to say on the topic."

Once again he chuckled, trying to stave off his annoyance with the woman. "Well, television doesn't always devote the time to divulge all the details of a particular incident. I'm sure there are many details you will find interesting when the edition comes out. I don't think you will be disappointed."

"I certainly hope I'm not disappointed."

"What I came in here for is some information about a bouquet of flowers left on my doorstep yesterday by an anonymous person." He pulled his notebook from his back pocket where he had written down the names Darcie had given him of the types of flowers in the bouquet. He had pretended to be interested in them, not giving his wife the real reason for wanting to know the names. "There were red snapdragons, some daisies, purple lilacs, and chrysanthemums." He looked at her, hoping the bouquet would register with her.

"And what do you wish to know about the flowers?"

"Well, I was hoping to find out who left them."

"There was no note?"

She knew the answer; he had told her they were anonymous. She was toying with him.

"No," he answered. "They were anonymous. No note or anything."

"Were you expecting flowers from someone?"

"No."

"If they were anonymous, then it appears that whoever delivered them did not want to be identified."

"Yes, I understand that. But I was hoping to thank the person, and would really consider it a favor if I could find out the person's name."

"I see," she said, leaning back and crossing her arms. "But I really can't divulge the confidentiality of a customer, especially if their intent was to remain anonymous. It just wouldn't be ethical."

What does she think she is, he thought, a doctor? "I appreciate your concern, but I was hoping you would make an exception for me."

"I see." She looked deep in thought for a moment and then leaned forward on the counter on her big beefy arms, her face inches from his. "And I would appreciate it, as a favor to me, if the Garden Club tour is prominently displayed on the front page." She smiled.

Blackmail, he thought. That's what she's resorting to. His mind drew up an image of the front page he had laid out, with the fire, the murder, and the latest on the trunk full of skeletons. There was no way he could ruin that layout for some little bit of information.

"Of course," he lied. "I see no reason why that can't be done."

She leaned back and smiled.

"Now if I could just have that name," he said, almost pleading.

"Let's say we wait till the paper comes out Thursday morning. Come back and see me then, and I'll see what I can do for you." Her cheeks grew even larger as her grin reached the ends of her fat face.

As soon as he left the flower shop, he lit another cigarette.

In the middle of the night, Brian was awakened by his emergency scanner. Darcie lay beside him, long accustomed to sleeping through the static, tones, and dispatch calls. Brian awoke to the slightest chatter, an innate reaction from his years as a reporter. It was a fire call, but didn't sound serious. Turned out to be a dumpster fire at the old shoe factory, a vacant four-story brick building at the beginning of Main Street, where the road branched off State Route 113.

The factory had closed down decades ago, and Brian remembered it being the topic at several Board of Selectmen meetings. Most townspeople wanted the structure torn down. It was an eyesore, they complained. It often was the scene of vandalism and teen parties. The selectmen were hesitant, hoping something good would come of the building. Selectmen Chairman Eldon Winch was behind a proposal to renovate the building into housing for the elderly or low income families, maybe even with shops on the ground floor. He had been CEO of the shoe factory before it closed down and probably still had a vested interest in the facility. But with the economy being the way it was, many people in town thought it wasn't a wise investment. Besides, they said, there were enough empty storefronts downtown; it didn't seem practical to open businesses on the edge of town.

With no consensus on what to do with the property, it remained abandoned, windows shattered, bricks crumbling, and the interior wooden beams and floors rotting. The railroad tracks beside it, paralleling Route 113, hadn't seen a train in decades, either freight or passenger. It was the same rail line Rolfe Krimmer had worked for, long before he became the oldest resident in town, back when passengers actually rode the rails.

Across from the shoe factory was the old train station, also falling into disrepair, and town folks thought it, too, should be demolished. But Eldon Winch believed passenger train service might one day be revived and hoped Smokey Hollow would be a stop once again. Why anyone would deliberately come here, Brian could not understand. Maybe Winch figured people would come and shop in the stores at the renovated shoe factory. Brian would never have found his way here, or even heard of it, if he hadn't found the job at *The Hollow News.*

Brian ignored the call, rolled over, and went back to sleep. An hour or so later he heard another call on the scanner—a police call, asking Chief Treece to come to the fire station for an undetermined incident.

Brian sat up, staring at the scanner waiting for more. Incident, he wondered. What the hell did that mean? It seemed unusual enough for him to want more, but nothing else came from the scanner. He glanced at Darcie, still sound asleep, and climbed out of bed. He dressed as quietly but as quickly as possible. Something didn't sound right about the call. He could easily wait till the morning and check with Noah, but he would find it hard to get back to sleep now that his curiosity was tweaked.

He thought about waking Darcie to tell her he was leaving, but she seemed really tired now that she was pregnant, and he didn't want to disturb her. She was used to waking up and finding him gone. She had come to expect it.

He scribbled a quick note and left it on her night stand, just in case. Then he scurried downstairs and out to his car. He lit up a cigarette on the short ride to the fire station.

When he approached the station and eased into a parking spot on Main Street, the fire engine was sitting in the middle of the street, lights on, before the open bay doors of the station. Chief Treece's car was parked near the station, along with another patrol car. Some of the firefighters were standing in the street by the engine, looking into the open bay.

Brian didn't see the State Police car belonging to Steem and Wickwire and was glad that whatever the incident was, they weren't involved. Night Shift Alvin greeted him as he approached the brightly lit bay.

Noah was there, standing between Fire Chief Warren Shives and Assistant Chief Simon Runck. They, and everyone else, were looking up. Brian followed their gaze to a fire hose running up and over one of the rafters in the ceiling.

Dangling from the fire hose wrapped around his neck like a noose was Simon's dummy, Marshall.

Chapter 6

VIEW TO AN EXHUMATION

Brian thought it was some kind of firehouse prank, something firefighters might do to rib each other. But when he looked at Simon Runck and saw his trembling lower lip and ashen face, there didn't seem to be any humor in the incident.

Simon stepped forward, reaching his right hand toward the dangling feet of the puppet, and then turned to the crowd. "Let him down," he yelled, he face flushed. "Dammit! Someone let him down!"

Fire Chief Shives approached, put a hand on Simon's shoulder, and motioned to another firefighter, who ran to where the end of the hose was attached to a wall strut and began untying the knot. Once it was loose, he lowered the dummy till Marshall was within reach, and Simon pulled his friend into his arms, gently resting him on the concrete floor. He untied the hose from around the neck and cast it aside with disgust.

The puppet's eyes were open, and Simon stroked its cheek.

Brian looked at Noah and shrugged his shoulders, begging for some sense to the bizarre scene. Noah smirked and shook his head.

"Who would do such a thing," Simon said, now almost on the verge of tears. He lifted the puppet's right hand and let it go. It fell limply by its side. He reached up a hand and closed the puppet's eyes. "He's dead," Simon said.

Brian scanned the faces in the bay and the others standing outside by the fire truck. All the faces were solemn. He expected a few grimaces or gazes of bewilderment. But everyone was taking the scene seriously.

"Why would someone want to kill him?" Simon said, still on his knees by Marshall's side.

Murder? Brian thought. Was this now a murder scene? It was ridiculous. He didn't even have the urge to take a photo. This wasn't something he'd consider putting in the paper. He almost got the feeling everyone was pulling a big prank for his benefit. He might even have believed that was the case if not for the look on Noah's face.

He wanted to ask the police chief if Simon really believed Marshall was alive.

Simon scooped the puppet up in his arms and took him into a back room.

"Let's get that engine in here," Chief Shives barked before following Simon.

The firefighters broke out of their trances and began to move, unloading their gear and directing the engine into the garage. Brian finally got a chance to approach Noah.

"Noah, what the hell is this?"

"I guess someone got tired of the mouth on the little guy," Noah said. He wasn't cracking his usual smile.

"Is this thing serious?"

"It seems Simon thinks so. Someone silenced Marshall."

"Does he think that thing's real?" Brian couldn't believe he had to ask. "It is just a puppet."

Noah looked at him. "Of course. Don't you think I know that?" The chief seemed insulted.

"Phew," Brian exhaled. "I was getting worried I was the only one who could see that. It's just kind of strange."

"No. The strange thing," Noah said, "is whether someone else believed Marshall was real."

On Wednesday afternoon, Brian put the weekly edition of *The Hollow News* to bed, transmitting the final galleys to the printer. He kept the front page intact, with the dramatic stories and photos of the asylum fire, Dr. Wymbs' murder, the missing inmates, and the latest update on the trunk skeletons—of which there was little. He did not connect the trunk and the asylum, other than through the fact that the mysterious container was found in the home once owned by a retired nurse from the Wymbs Institute.

He had included a short bio on Dr. Wymbs, what little he could find with the help of the newspaper's archives. In that dimly lit cellar were bound books of all the past editions. Brian had scoured those editions for some history on when the institute had opened forty years ago. He had interviewed a few people in town who knew the doctor, including Selectmen Chairman Eldon Winch and real estate agent Leo Wibbels. But no one knew the doctor that well. It seemed in years past he'd visit town infrequently, but in the last decade or so had become more reclusive. Brian's notes from his conversation with the doctor were not very useful, but he added them. He might have been one of the last people to talk to Wymbs.

If only he had gotten the name of the housekeeper. That would have been helpful to paint a picture of what went on in the Mustard House and how many patients and staff were usually there. It surprised Brian and Noah that no staff member had come forward to provide any information to the authorities. That was a piece of this puzzle that just didn't seem to fit.

The story on the Women's Garden Club tour and Rolfe Krimmer's Boston Post Cane award went inside as planned. That meant Brian wouldn't get the name of the mysterious flower sender from Mrs. Picklesmeir. It was a shame. If an anonymous woman was indeed the mother of one of those babies, it would be imperative to find her. Brian would have to tell Noah about it. Maybe under the guise of a police investigation, the crotchety woman would divulge her information.

Brian decided against putting anything in the paper about the lynching of Marshall. The more he thought about it, the more he chalked it up as a firehouse prank, despite the odd reaction Simon Runck had to the strangulation of his dummy. Whatever it was, it didn't seem like something that belonged in a news story.

There was commotion by the front desk, and Brian looked through his office windows to see Capt. Steem and Sgt. Wickwire talking to Beverly Crump. She directed the State Police officers toward his office, and Brian waved them in.

"What a pleasant surprise," Brian said.

"I'm sure," Steem grunted, removing his hat and settling in a seat in front of Brian's desk. Wickwire stood by the door, rigid. He didn't remove his hat.

"What can I do for you? Paper's already gone to press. No chance for any last minute quotes."

"Can't wait to see it," Steem said, wiping beads of sweat from his bald head with his bare hand. "No air conditioning in here?"

"Not one of the luxuries the paper can afford. These are tough economic times for the newspaper industry."

"Well, nothing like a good arson and murder story to pump up circulation."

Brian chuckled at that. "This newspaper sells to the same number of people no matter if the front page features the Fishing Derby results or a UFO abduction. I'm just glad I have something newsworthy to publish."

He smiled. "Now what brings you here?" He wondered if Noah told them about the discovery of the glass eyeball.

"Noah tells me you have a photo from the fire scene with Ruth Snethen in it."

"Yes," Brian said. "I didn't know it was her, but my receptionist identified her to me."

"I'd like a copy of the picture," Steem said, his tone demanding. "In fact, I'd like copies of all your pictures from the fire scene for evidence."

Brian leaned back in his chair, his hands behind his head, thinking how to approach this request. "You still haven't found nurse Snethen?"

"Not a trace." Steem's brow furrowed. "We discovered she was living at a retirement complex out on Twistback Road, but she hasn't been at the place for several days."

"Since the fire?"

"Exactly." Steem seemed hesitant to answer. "But we don't have any pictures of the woman, so we'd like a copy of yours." He leaned forward. "If that isn't a problem."

Brian didn't want to hand over copies of the picture without taking advantage of the opportunity it provided. He placed his hands on his desk, pretending to rummage through some papers. Steem looked impatient. Wickwire was emotionless behind him, a statue.

"I don't see any problem cooperating with the authorities," Brian said. "As long as I know they will co-operate with the media as well."

"I could get a subpoena," Steem said.

"I'm sure you could, though I see no need for that. I'm asking for mutual cooperation. Just keep an open line with me on developments in the case. That's not much to ask."

"I keep Chief Treece informed," Steem shot back. Then he hesitated. "I supposed I can pass information along to you."

Brian spread his hands wide. "That's all I'm asking. I'm not looking for special treatment."

"Of course you are. You want details that I don't give out in statements to the press."

"I guess if you put it that way. Yes. I'd like to think, since I'm the only media representative in this town, that I get some kind of—let's say, home-field advantage." He smiled.

Steem did not smile back. "I guess that's only fair," he said.

"Very good," Brian said, getting into his computer picture folder and bringing up the photo of Ruth Snethen on his screen. He turned it around for Steem to see. "Here's the picture of Snethen." He pointed to the gray-haired woman on the screen. "I can burn a disc of all the pictures for you."

"Great," Steem said.

Brian rummaged through his desk for a blank disc and had trouble finding one.

"Need one of these?" Beverly Crump said, standing at his door, holding up a computer disc.

"Thanks, Bev."

She handed the disc to Wickwire, who in turn handed it to Steem, who passed it along to Brian, who put it into his computer and began downloading the files.

While it was burning, he leaned back and looked at the impatient Capt. Steem, who wiped more sweat off the top of his scalp. "Now there are a couple things I'm interested in."

"Such as?" Steem looked irritated.

"I was wondering if you had located the housekeeper? And what her name is."

"Hettie Gritton," Steem said.

Brian grabbed a pen and jotted the name down. "And have you talked to her?"

"No."

Brian looked up from his notepad. "Because?"

"We can't locate her either."

Brian sat upright. "Hmm. Since when?"

"We only discovered her name yesterday. She lives alone in a house out on Fogg Road. Nobody home when we've gone to the place. No one answers calls to the house."

Brian remembered her leaving the night he went to the Mustard House. "Her car?"

"In the driveway."

"That is strange." The computer file finished copying, and Brian popped the disc out. He held it to Steem. An image popped into Brian's head of a faceless Dr. Wymbs. "One other thing."

"Yes?"

"There was something covering Dr. Wymbs' face when they pulled his body out of the fire. What was it?"

Steem's face grew rigid. He plucked the disc from Brian's fingers and held it over his shoulder; Wickwire stepped forward and took it. "That I'm afraid I can't answer." He got up from the chair. "And I expect you to cooperate with us if you come across anything in your journalistic inquiries."

It was a statement Brian thought would be accompanied by a sarcastic grin, but Steem's face showed no such thing. Brian thought about the notes he had received from the mysterious Silhouette, the anonymous flowers left on his doorstep, and the glass eyeball found in the Somnambulist's pocket. "Of course," he said to Steem, smiling.

The State Police captain turned to go.

"Oh, there is one thing," Brian said.

Steem halted and turned back.

"The assistant fire chief's ventriloquist's dummy was found hanging at the station from a noose made from a fire hose." Brian shrugged his shoulders. "Not sure what that could mean. I didn't know if you were aware of it."

"Of course I'm aware of that. Not much in this town gets by me. But I have no interest in a firehouse prank"

Wickwire actually cracked the only smile during his silent visit.

"Then I guess I have nothing more," Brian said. "But I'll keep cooperating if anything else comes up."

The two men left.

Brian left the office when he received confirmation the printer had all the pages set and was ready to roll. Bev had long since gone, and he locked up and went to where his car was parked out front. There were employee parking spaces behind the office building, but Brian often found it more convenient to park in the two-hour-limit spaces in front. The police never bothered to ticket his car, and he appreciated that. Brian saw the envelope under his windshield wiper as he approached and smiled, knowing what it was. He had hoped he would hear from his pen pal again.

He looked around, wondering if his mysterious ally was nearby, waiting to see him find the note. Maybe he was watching Brian right now. He gazed down Hemlock Street, past the pub and the police station, alert for someone concealed in a doorway or alley. Nobody. Looking over his shoulder, back toward Main Street, he saw a few people on the sidewalk. Rolfe Krimmer was standing near the vacant cinema, Sister Bernice was walking into Wigland's, and a gray-haired woman was picking through baskets of fruit displayed outside of Wibbels Fruit Market and Real Estate. The woman slipped a couple apples into the pocket of her housedress and walked off.

Nobody paid Brian any attention, but he couldn't help the feeling in his gut that eyes were watching him.

He grabbed the envelope, noting the same black ink lettering and dark smudges. His heart beat faster. He wanted to light a cigarette to calm down but didn't want to waste time. He opened it and pulled the note out.

How much do you know about the puppet master? The Silhouette

He stared at the words. Obviously it referred to Assistant Fire Chief Simon Runck, the only person Brian knew of in town who had a puppet. So maybe the hanging of the dummy was more than a prank. He pictured Marshall, hanging from the noose, eyes wide open. Brian thought about Runck, leaning over the body, reaching his hand up, and closing its eyes.

Eyes.

What color were Marshall's eyes?

Brian realized why he thought he was being watched. He turned around toward Main Street and saw what was watching him—the eyes in the window of the taxidermist shop. Racks of eyes of all different colors and sizes.

Of course, he thought.

He sprinted across the street to the police station, glad to find Noah still there. Wanda greeted him, and he went right to the chief's office, pausing in the open door frame to catch his breath. Noah looked at him quizzically.

"What color are Marshall's eyes?" Brian managed between gasps.

Noah looked at him as if he had two heads. "What are you talking about?"

Brian tossed the note onto the chief's desk. "The puppet. It has glass eyes."

Noah picked up the note and read it, lifting his eyes over the paper to look up at Brian. "And you think the eye the Somnambulist found belongs to Marshall?"

"Why not?"

"But he had both his eyes when we saw him the other night."

Brian thought for a minute. "So? Runck might keep spares just in case."

"In case he loses an eye?"

"Maybe. Can we check? Where's Marshall now?"

Noah grinned. "That might be a bit difficult."

"Why?"

"He's been buried."

"Buried? As in a grave?"

"Funeral was earlier today."

"Does anybody realize that thing wasn't a human being?"

Noah shrugged. "It was what Simon Runck wanted. He seemed to feel that Marshall was really gone. Maybe he was just looking for a chance to get separation from his act."

Brian arched his eyebrows. "Or maybe he was just trying to hide evidence."

Noah contemplated this. "I suppose."

"Where is he buried?"

"There's a spot out behind the town cemetery, where people bury their pets and stuff." He looked up at Brian. "I suppose you want me to dig him up?"

"I'll go with you."

The chief opened a desk drawer and pulled out the plastic bag containing the blue glass eye. "I'd rather wait till dark. I don't want anyone seeing us do this. Go home. I'll pick you up in a couple hours. And bring a flashlight."

The town graveyard was on Cemetery Road, which branched off Fogg Lane. Treece drove through the gate, going slowly past rows of tombstones. He stopped before one grave and shone a light on the headstone.

"Timmy Birtch's mother," the chief said.

Brian scanned the dates on the headstone. The woman was only forty. "What happened to her?"

"Chief Pfefferkorn said she never got over Timmy's disappearance. She slipped into depression. Her health faded. Drinking, drugs." Noah shook his head. "A downward spiral from the night she woke up and her little boy was missing from his bed." He turned to Brian. "A couple years after she died, Pfefferkorn retired. I think he felt he let her down."

"A shame," Brian said, still looking at the woman's grave.

"It sometimes seems like the town's forgotten about her and Timmy. That's the real shame. I've come by here a few times and brought flowers for her grave. My way of keeping the two of them relevant."

Noah put the car back in gear and drove forward, parking the police car in a rutted lane before the last row of gravestones. They both got out and, flashlights and spade shovels in hand, walked past the tombstones to a clearing beyond them. The night was warm. A three-quarter yellow moon was embedded in a thick blanket of clouds.

The beams from their lights bobbed along the ground, and Brian could see small, white wooden crosses. A chill crept up his spine, despite the warm night, and he shivered. Both men were silent, and the night was as well, except for the soft crunching of grass beneath their shoes.

Noah led the way. Brian followed close behind but kept glancing around at the markings on either side of him. He bumped into Noah before realizing the chief had stopped.

"Here," Noah finally said, pointing his beam at a wooden cross. The name "Marshall" was printed in black marker.

Brian thought about the dummy's cackling laugh and decided that if he heard it coming from the grave, he was going to drop the shovel and run like hell.

They bent and removed the loose sod from the burial spot. They set their flashlights down, beams pointing at the grave, and began digging. No words were exchanged as they flung shovelfuls of dirt onto a pile beside the grave.

Brian heard someone call out "Who," and he stopped dead in his tracks, a pile of dirt on his spade. He looked behind him at the woods beyond the cemetery. His heart thudded. Was someone watching them? The sound repeated, and he realized it was an owl. *Who?* he thought. Us, that's who. Just a couple of grave robbers.

There was a thunk. Noah had struck wood.

The two of them scraped dirt away in silence until a tiny dark pine coffin was revealed. Brian's first thought was to wonder how much the casket had cost, and if it had been worth it for Simon to get rid of his sidekick.

"Here goes nothing," Noah said, no trace of a grin as he pulled open the casket.

Moonlight cast a glow into it. The dummy looked stiff, dark hair neatly combed, lips shut (thank god), and eyes closed. Brian's skin crawled, the hair on his arms tingling.

Noah pulled the plastic bag out of his pocket, looking at the eyeball inside. He glanced at Brian, who nodded and kept his flashlight trained on the dummy's face. Noah bent and pulled the puppet's right eyelid open.

The blue eyeball stared up at them, and Brian grew cold, feeling as if it could really see the two of them. No, him. It was looking past Noah and directly at him. With just the one eye open, the dummy appeared to be winking. *(I know what you're doing.)* He felt the urge to flick the flashlight off and plunge the coffin into darkness. But that might be even worse. Because in the darkness, he might hear it move, trying to climb out of the casket.

Hurry, Brian thought. And let's get the hell out of here.

Noah held the glass eye in the bag and placed it beside the dummy's eye.

It was a perfect match.

Chapter 7

CONFESSION TO A CRIME

Noah and Brian steeled away from the burial field beyond the cemetery, with Marshall's wooden corpse in hand, cradled in the arms of the police chief as if it were a young child. Brian followed behind, carrying the shovels and flashlights.

"Whooo," called the owl from the woods one last time.

Brian stopped and turned to look at the dark trees bathed in shadows. Us, he thought, that's who.

Back at the police station, Noah decided to contact Capt. Steem, despite Brian's objections. "It's his investigation," Noah said, "and this is a possible development."

Brian was frustrated. "It could be your investigation too." But he knew it fell on deaf ears.

"That's not how it works."

When Steem and Wickwire showed up, they were not too pleased with Chief Treece. Brian sat outside the chief's office, watching through the glass. Steem was loud enough that the closed door had little effect on keeping the conversation private and at one point Brian saw the State Police captain point out the office window toward him but only heard the words "this asshole."

He felt bad for Noah, who looked like a cowering school boy being reprimanded by the principal. It was almost lost on Brian how young Noah was. Christ, he was still in his twenties. He had taken a head position in a small town that was probably beyond his experience level if not for the fact that the size and location of the town made it an easily manageable job. No one could have expected events of this magnitude happening in Smokey Hollow.

When Wickwire came out and motioned for Brian to join them, he hesitated, worried he'd get the same treatment, but then realized he didn't work for them. What could they do to him?

Inside the office, Steem glared at him.

"Mutual cooperation, huh?" he said.

Brian looked at him perplexed.

"You kept those anonymous notes from us?"

Brian cast a sour glance at Noah, who shrugged apologetically.

"Of course he had to tell us," Steem said, reading his thoughts. "What other reason would he have to dig up the stupid puppet?"

"Look," Brian said, stammering a bit. "I was trying to protect a newspaper source."

"But you told the town police chief about it," Steem shot back.

He had him there. Brian just shook his head. "I haven't been working in town that long. I needed some help."

"And you have no idea who these notes came from?"

Brian shook his head. "Of course not."

Steem huffed. He turned to face Noah. "Well, let's go pick up Simon Runck and bring him in for questioning."

The Hollow News came out Thursday morning and for the first time since he moved to this town, Brian was actually proud of the newspaper he had produced. Unfortunately, because so many days had gone by since the incidents he wrote about had happened, it was mostly old news. Now everyone in town was talking about the arrest of Assistant Fire Chief Simon Runck for the fire at the Mustard House.

Brian was mad at Noah for divulging the information about the notes from The Silhouette, but understood the chief's hands were tied on this, as much as he wished the chief would just conduct his own separate investigation.

Before leaving the newspaper office in the afternoon, he grabbed a stack of copies of *The Hollow News* that he knew he'd look back on with great pride. Beverly looked up at him with a curious glance.

"What?" he asked, knowing something was on her mind.

"Don't forget your interview," she said, adjusting her glasses on the edge of her nose.

He stood silent for a minute, knowing he should remember this.

"The Knackerman is retiring."

"Oh, yes," he said, the memory suddenly jarred in his head. That was the dead animal guy, the last of that profession still operating in the state. "Of course," he said, returning to his office to grab some notes he had made about the guy.

"And you have to see Selectman Winch about the Dump Fest preview," she yelled from her reception desk.

"I know," he yelled back, finding the sheet of paper he was looking for amongst the clutter on his desk.

"You can't blow that off like the garden tour."

"I would never," he said, walking by her desk toward the front door.

"It's the town's signature event," she yelled, her voice fading as he stepped outside.

He crossed the street to the police station, to see what information Noah would give him about the assistant fire chief's case. Once inside, he greeted Wanda and she buzzed the chief who waved him in. To his relief, Noah still greeted him with a smile.

Brian couldn't be mad at him.

"I know you're upset," Noah said, brushing a hand through his light brown hair.

Brian plopped down into a seat. "You couldn't help it," he said. "I just wonder if I'll ever hear from The Silhouette again."

"I bet you will."

He stared across the desk at the chief and a thought crept into his head. What if the chief was the one leaving him notes, trying to help him out without shirking his official duties? It was possible. "Why do you say that?"

The chief shrugged. "Just a hunch. Obviously this guy has some interest or information in the things that have been going on around town. Maybe it's someone who worked at the Mustard House. Or maybe it's someone who was a patient there."

Brian hadn't thought of that. "So, what's up with Simon Runck?" He pulled a notepad out of his pocket.

"He's at county lockup, being charged with arson only, for the time being. He claims he never went inside the institute."

Brian looked up from his pad. "So he admitted starting the fire."

Noah cracked a smile at this. "Not exactly."

"What does that mean?"

The chief stood up. "How about if I make it up to you for giving your information to the State Police?"

"I'm listening."

"Would you like to watch the interrogation video?"

They sat in a small room that looked into the interrogation room through a two-way mirror. Noah turned the television monitor on and loaded up the interview clip. On the screen, Simon Runck sat behind a small table opposite Capt. Steem. Sgt. Wickwire could be partially seen standing at the edge of the frame. Noah fast-forwarded the video a bit.

"The beginning is just incidentals," he said, before stopping the film. "This is where it gets interesting."

Simon looked jittery, rubbing his hands together.

"What were you doing up at the ridge that evening," Steem asked, his voice stern, but flat, with no emotion.

"I was trying to stop him," Simon said, his eyes averting the State Police captain.

"Trying to stop who?"

"He said we needed to burn the place down."

"Who are you talking about?"

"Marshall," Simon said. "He wanted to torch the Mustard House."

Brian looked at Noah, not believing what he was hearing. Noah just nodded at the monitor, urging him to pay attention.

"The puppet?" Steem sighed.

"He's not a puppet." Simon cast his eyes down at his hands.

"Marionette? Dummy?"

"Oh, he's no dummy." Simon looked up. "He's very smart."

"Intelligent enough to outsmart you?"

"He could outsmart anyone."

"Why did you bury him?" Steem asked. "To hide any evidence?"

Simon shook his head. "I buried him because he was dead. Someone killed him."

"Did you kill him?" Steem was playing along.

"NO!" Simon banged his fist on the table. Wickwire took a step forward, but Steem raised his hand and he backed off.

"No need to get upset," Steem said, his voice softer. "Who killed Marshall?"

"I don't know." He reached his hand up and wiped something from the corner of his eye. A tear? "I guess the same person who told him to burn down the Mustard House."

"Someone told you to do that?"

"Not me." Simon's voice rose. "Someone told Marshall."

"Someone told Marshall to burn down the Wymbs Institute?"

"That's right."

"Who told him to do that?"

"I don't know." His head slowly moved back and forth. "Marshall wouldn't tell me. He said it was on a need-to-know basis. Maybe he was protecting me."

"Who are you protecting?"

Simon looked at the captain. "I told you I don't know."

Steem leaned back in his chair. "Let me get this straight. Marshall told you someone told him to burn down the institute. So the two of you got some gas and drove up to the ridge?"

Simon nodded. "I went along to try and stop him."

"But you didn't stop him?"

Simon slumped in his chair. It looked like he might be on the verge of tears. "No. I couldn't."

"You replaced one of his eyes," Steem said. "How did he lose an eye up on the ridge?"

Brian leaned forward, in anticipation of this answer.

"We had a fight," Simon said.

"A fight?"

Simon nodded. "I was trying to stop him, and we got in a fist fight."

Steem glanced over to Wickwire, shaking his head. Brian couldn't see the captain's expression on the monitor but imagined it was one of wonderment. Wickwire was expressionless.

Steem looked back at Simon. "So you had a fight, and his eye came out."

Simon could only nod.

"I need to hear an answer," Steem said, his tone up a notch.

"Yes, I punched him and his eye popped out. I tried to find it, but it was dark."

"And you never went inside the building?"

Simon leaned forward on the table. "NO! I swear."

"And you didn't see Dr. Wymbs?"

"No. I didn't even think he'd be there."

"Why is that?"

"Marshall said no one would be there."

"Why did Marshal think no one would be there?"

"He said he was told that."

"By whoever told him to set the fire?"

"That's right." Simon leaned back in his chair. The questioning seemed to drain him. His face was sweaty.

Steem stood up and stepped over to Wickwire, whispering something in his ear. The sergeant nodded and left the room. Steem sat back down. He looked at Simon, but kept silent. Wickwire returned, carrying something, and set it down on the middle of the table between the two men. It was Marshall.

Simon jumped up from his seat and stepped back, up against the wall.

"What is he doing here?" He yelled. "He's dead! I buried him!"

"He's not dead," Steem said, his voice calm. "He was never alive."

"That's not true!"

"Who told you to burn down the Wymbs Institute?"

"Marshall told me."

"And who told Marshall?"

"I told you! I don't know! Marshall wouldn't tell me! Just that it needed to be done!"

Steem rose to his feet. "Why did it need to be done?"

"Marshall said so they don't find out." Simon was pressed up against the back wall, as if he wanted to be far away from his ventriloquist dummy.

"Find out what?"

Simon looked directly into the video camera, knowing where it was, and Brian felt as if he were looking right at him.

"The secrets of the Mustard House!"

Chapter 8

A POT OF BONES

The video interrogation was unnerving. The experience left Brian wondering if Simon Runck was crazy. Noah suggested it could all be an act. They couldn't be sure if the firefighter really believed Marshall was alive and talked with him. It certainly looked like he believed. Either that or he was an incredible actor.

Regardless, the county prosecutor was prepared to charge him with arson. The State Police would continue their investigation into whether he was also responsible for strangling Dr. Wymbs.

There was also no indication of whether the fire and murder had anything to do with the trunk of skeletons. But Brian thought it likely that there was a connection. He could feel it.

In the meantime, Brian had to continue with some of the routine tasks of his job, and he was on his way to visit Hester Pigott, the last of the knackers in New Hampshire.

At the end of Main Street, heading out of town, Brian hesitated. Fogg Lane was to the left, and that was where Hettie Gritton lived, the late Dr. Wymbs' housekeeper. He had the urge to drive by her house, just to check it out, though Steem had said she hasn't been seen.

He looked at the clock on his dashboard and realized it was almost time for his appointment with Pigott, and Beverly Crump had warned him not to be late. The Knackerman was eighty-six years old, followed his own schedule, and would have little patience with a flatlander. Bev had to explain that that meant Brian was a city boy who didn't fit in with the country folk in Smokey Hollow.

To the right was Twistback Road, the direction Brian drove. It was an old curvy cow road. (Bev also explained to him that some of the older country roads were winding because they were formed by the trails cows made meandering from one location to the next.) The road wound its way past hilly meadows, farmlands with wide open pastures, cornfields, and meadows of goldenrod. Noah had told him locals nicknamed it the Rollercoaster Road because of its hairpin curves.

The road continued for a couple miles before Brian spotted Pigott's house. He saw a large black mailbox with the name stenciled on it in white block letters, atop a tilted post at the end of a long dirt driveway that wound its way up a sloping field. He turned in and drove up, eyeing the Colonial farmhouse, its white paint in need of a new coat. To the right was a red barn, its coat bright and shiny in the sunlight. Brian parked between the two structures and got out.

Bev had said Pigott would be in the barn, and that was the direction he headed. He spotted half a dozen ducks, waddling from the path to the barn. The sliding door was half open, and light spilled out. Brian looked for some kind of doorbell, but not finding anything, he stepped through the opening.

The lights were bright inside the barn, and Brian wasn't prepared for what it would reveal. Bev had tried to explain to him what a knacker was, but it was lost on him. All he understood was that it had something to do with dead animals and that Hester Pigott was the last knacker in the state, probably one of only a handful in the whole country.

The old man stood bent over a broad table in the middle of the barn beneath fluorescent lights. A half-skinned cow lay on the table. A vile odor hung in the air. Flies swarmed around the man's head as he bent over the table, a long sharp knife in his hand, cutting the skin of the cow away from the muscle. Brian cleared his throat, almost thinking he might cough up some vomit. Pigott looked up from what he was doing and straightened.

He was tall and thin, wearing bib overalls and a white tank top stained with brown and red spots. His face looked like an owl, long with a thin hooked nose, round eyes, and high arched eyebrows beneath a tall forehead. His jowls hung loose around his chin. Wispy white hair formed a widow's peak beneath a dusty ball cap perched on his head, a tractor logo on its front. He opened his mouth to speak, and Brian could see lips and gums but few teeth.

"You the paper boy?" the old man asked, his voice gravelly.

"Yes," he answered, stepping forward, about to extend his hand, but Mr. Pigott made no move to reciprocate the gesture, and Brian was glad when he saw the blood-stained bony fingers, the right hand still clutching the knife. "Brian Keays."

"Watch yer step," Pigott said, gesturing to a spot on the floor in front of Brian's feet, where a small pile of what he supposed was animal fat lay.

"Thanks," Brian said, glancing around the brightly lit barn. On one wall were pinned animal hides he recognized as bear, raccoon, possum, skunk, and fox. A counter along the opposite wall had bones spread across a portion of it. "Quite a place you have here."

"It's home," the old man replied, and bent back over the table. He flicked the knife, cut off a piece of meat, and flung it over his shoulder. It landed on the floor near an old hound Brian hadn't noticed before. The dog scooped up the meat in its jaws and lay patiently, waiting for more. "So why is the paper interested in what I do?"

"You're retiring," Brian said, wondering himself why he was here.

"So?" Pigott said, looking up at him.

Brian stepped around the animal fat on the floor and approached. "From what I've been told, there's no one left in the state that does what you do."

The old man's eyes narrowed, as if to get a better look at Brian. "And what is it you've been told I do?"

Brian was stumped. He looked at the cow on the table and pointed. "You take care of dead animals. You do your knackering thing." He knew he sounded stupid.

The old man flashed a gummy grin. "You have no idea, do ya?"

Brian shook his head. "Not really."

Pigott laughed. "Then let me tell you, sonny, and you can decide if it's worth a story. I don't quite see the point. It's just a job. Lots of people have jobs. Everyone has to do sumthin'."

"But yours is supposed to be—" he fumbled for the right word, "—unique."

"Oh, that it is." He sliced some more with the knife. "Not many of us do this. I've been at it for seventy years."

Brian scribbled it down in his notepad.

"No one today would choose a profession like this." The old man straightened. "Not really much need for it."

"So let me ask a dumb question."

Pigott looked at him. "I wouldn't expect any other kind."

"What is the point of what you do?"

He pointed at the cow with his knife. "I take old, dead, crippled, useless farm animals, and I make use of them."

Brian looked at the animal. "Use how?"

"Mostly they go to the rendering plant over in Grafton."

"Rendering plant?"

"Yes. They turn the animal material into useful products. The meat, fatty tissue, bones, offal."

"Offal?"

Pigott glared at him. "The internal organs and entrails."

"That sounds awful," Brian said, but Pigott didn't crack a smile. "And what does the rendering plant do with this...stuff?"

The old man scratched the top of his head through his ball cap. "Oh, the fatty tissues get used for lard or tallow, that's used in animal feed. The bones get turned into fertilizer." He glanced at Brian. "Shouldn't you be writin' this down?"

"Oh yes," Brian said, scribbling in his notepad. "And where do these animals come from?"

"I get calls from farmers, veterinarians, and go pick them up. Or sometimes they just get dumped here. In the old days, stray animals would end up at the Town Pound, and if they were crippled or diseased, no farmer would want them back, so I'd go collect them in my truck."

Brian had driven by the Town Pound on Fogg Lane. It was a corral-like structure made up of four stone walls of granite blocks with a metal gate covering an opening in the front. He had asked Beverly about it when he first moved into town. She had explained it was used years ago as a place to corral loose farm animals until the owner could be contacted to come down and retrieve them. Now it was kind of a historic landmark in town.

"I prepare the dead animals for the man from the rendering plant, who comes by once a week."

Pigott continued to slice up the cow on the table, tossing scraps of meat every now and then to the eagerly waiting hound, while Brian asked questions. Pigott talked while he cut, telling Brian of his early days trapping raccoons and foxes and how he used to butcher horses for a pet-food plant that was no longer in business. Pigott looked up at him at one point, bloody knife gripped tight.

"Don't you need to take a picture?"

Brian had not even thought about the camera around his neck. "Oh, of course," he said, snapping pictures he knew he could never put in the paper. He would have to get a profile photo later. For now, he watched the old man work, flicking the knife like some fancy chef in a Japanese restaurant.

"Do you ever work on unusual animals?" Brian was hoping for some kind of angle that might make the story more interesting.

Pigott stopped and straightened. "Unusual animals?" He was confused by the question. He shook his head. "Just cows, horses, pigs, sheep, and goats. Regular critters."

"Nothing that caught you by surprise?"

Pigott rubbed his chin. "There was a time, couple decades ago, when some unfortunate carcasses showed up around town."

"Like what?"

"Dogs. Skinned."

Brian hesitated, pen in hand, fingers unwilling to write this bit down.

"For a stretch, pets went missing. Chief Pfefferkorn found the remains of a few dogs, necks broken, skin removed. He turned the remains over to me. It was the only time I was reluctant to take a dead animal." Pigott wiped something from the corner of his eye. "Not a fitting end for man's best friend."

"Did they ever catch who did it?"

Pigott shook his head. "No. Never."

"What happened?"

"They stopped." The old man cleared his throat and spat onto the floor. "Either the person stopped doing it or found better hiding spots for the carcasses. Peoples' pets still went missing from time to time. Every time I see a poster on a utility pole for a missing cat or dog, I wonder."

"That's horrible. And strange."

The old man set his knife down on the table. "You want strange? I have something I could show you." He motioned for Brian to follow him over to the counter along the side wall. Brian watched his step. Pigott stopped in front of a large, dusty ceramic pot on a shelf above the counter. The old man reached up and lowered the pot to the countertop. He removed the cover.

Brian stepped up to the counter and peered into the pot. It was filled with old, gray bones. He looked at the Knackerman.

"What's this?"

"The remains of a ribcage."

"Huh?"

Pigott told him a story. More than twenty years ago, a fisherman snagged his line on something in Thrasher Pond, three-acres of water by the railroad tracks parallel to Route 113. What he eventually managed to pull up was a ribcage.

Police Chief Pfefferkorn had been alerted by the fisherman and had checked it out. This was about two years after the disappearance of Timmy Birtch, and some residents speculated that maybe the remains of the poor boy had been found. Some wanted the pond drained to see if there were more remains. But Pfefferkorn decided the bones belonged to a pig that might have fallen victim to whoever was killing animals. He turned the bones over to Pigott to be disposed of.

"But you kept them," Brian said, looking at the old man.

"Them ain't no pig bones."

"Couldn't they tell?" Brian would have thought the difference would be obvious.

"I could," Pigott said. "Grant you, the abdomens of a pig and a human being are almost identical, including the internal organs. That's why pigs are often used in scientific testing. But there is a difference."

"There is?"

"The human ribcage has twenty-four ribs, twelve per side. A pig has fourteen per side, twenty-eight ribs." He pointed into the pot. "This ribcage has twenty-four."

"Are you sure?" Brian peered inside to the pile of bones.

"If it's one thing I know, it's bones." He seemed insulted. "Besides, I may have been homeschooled by my ma, but I can count to twenty-four."

Brian didn't doubt the man. "Did you tell Pfefferkorn?"

Pigott nodded. "Sure did."

"And?"

"He wouldn't listen. That puzzled me. I thought that maybe he didn't want to believe it could be that poor kidnapped boy, the Birtch kid. He'd rather the boy remained missing than be found dead, so he dismissed it."

Brian looked into the pot of bones and decided to take a couple pictures. He looked at the Knackerman and asked the main question on his mind.

"Could it be Timmy Birtch?"

The old man paused. "Crossed my mind at first," he finally said, working his gums. "The ribcage was small, which is why the chief thought about a pig. But it was still not small enough for a boy Timmy's age. And the main reason it couldn't have been the boy's is because the bones were kind of narrow."

Brian looked at him. "Which means?"

"They belong to a woman."

Chapter 9

DISCOVERY AT THE TOWN POUND

Darcie was preparing dinner when Brian got home. He was disappointed that there was no new note from his secret correspondent. Maybe The Silhouette had gotten spooked by the authorities. Whatever the case, he missed his mystery messenger.

His wife called out that dinner would be ready soon and told him to wash up. That was something he urgently wanted to do, feeling the odors of the Knackerman's workshop clinging to his sweaty body. He almost felt flies buzzing around him but knew it was just his imagination; still, he waved his hand over his head as if shooing away something.

After a quick shower, he checked his camera, skipping past most of the shots of Hester Pigott at work, stopping only to view the profile shots he took. The old man flashing a gummy grin, his round eyes wide. Brian noticed a spot of blood on the ball cap on the knacker's head. It was visible in every profile shot. Damn, he thought. Maybe nobody would notice, especially if he ran the picture on an inside page in black and white.

When Brian got to the shots of the pot of bones, he skimmed them. He wondered if Noah knew about them. Maybe Pfefferkorn had never told him about the rib cage in Thrasher Pond. More mystery bones, Brian thought, things decaying and rotting in Smokey Hollow and nobody noticing.

Brian went into the kitchen while his wife was tossing a salad. He crept up behind her, wrapping his arms around her, startling her a bit. She giggled, and it sounded good. He felt the bump in her belly and kissed her neck.

"Good day?" she said.

"Every day I have with you is good," he answered, bending his head to brush her cheek with his lips. He hugged her tight but mindful of what she carried inside her.

"The hard-nosed reporter getting all soft?"

He pressed his crotch against her backside. "Does that feel soft?"

She laughed and pushed him away. "What's got you all riled up?"

He released her and shrugged. "I don't know, just feeling good."

"Dinner's almost ready. Go sit down. Eat first, play later."

He went to the table and sat. Darcie brought over a couple bowls of salad, placing one before him.

"I know why you're in such a good mood."

He looked up at her before reaching for the bottle of salad dressing. "Oh yeah? Why?"

"Because your paper looks so good this week."

He grinned. "It did come out fantastic."

She frowned. "You shouldn't show so much glee in such tragic stories."

He shrugged. "I can't help that they happened."

"But you feel fortunate they did."

He smiled. "I just never thought I'd have something like this happen to me here, of all places." He was worried she might ruin the mood he was fostering, but he couldn't help but gloat a little.

"Well, for what it's worth, the paper looks really good."

"Thanks, darling."

She took his empty plate to the kitchen counter. "Though it would have been nice if the one garden tour picture you ran was in color. I'm sure Mrs. Picklesmeir will be extremely disappointed."

He sighed. "I have no doubt about that."

Darcie returned to the table, setting his plate before him. Brian stared at the porterhouse steak sitting in reddish juices next to a small pile of rice. He eyed the bone in the meat. His mind retreated to the images inside the Knackerman's barn. He frowned.

"Something wrong?" Darcie asked, sitting down with her own steak.

Brian looked across the table as she began cutting her meat, not looking up at him.

"I think I might have just salad and rice tonight."

She stopped sawing mid-stroke and looked at him. "What? Are you feeling okay?"

He didn't know what to say. "I'm not that hungry," he lied.

"But I made it medium rare, just the way you like." She pouted. "Nice and juicy."

"And it sure smells delicious," he said, feeling his stomach rumble. "Just not tonight." He pushed the plate to the side and pulled the salad bowl in front of him, avoiding the disappointed look in her eyes.

"Doesn't sound like you," she said, her tone flat.

"I might have some later."

After dinner, he helped her clean up and then went to his office upstairs. Darcie wanted his company, and he told her he'd be down soon. He wanted to write a quick draft of the Knackerman story while the images were fresh. What he really wanted was to sneak outside for a cigarette, but that was out of the question.

He joined her later on the couch while they watched an old black-and-white movie on one of the retro channels. His portable scanner was on a table in the hallway by the front door, where he had left it when he got home. It was plugged in, recharging. He always kept it running, usually with the volume turned low. There was quite a difference in the amount of chatter on the scanner in this town than back in the city. He could not bother with it and probably not miss much, but after the past few days, he liked to keep it close.

Toward the end of the movie, Brian drifted off. Some chatter from the scanner perked him up, something about the Town Pound. He got out from under the arm Darcie had wrapped around him and walked to the hallway, picking up the scanner and bringing it into the living room, placing in on the coffee table and turning the volume up slightly.

Darcie shot him a look but said nothing.

When the credits rolled at the end of the movie, she got up and tugged at his arm.

"Come on," she said. "Let's see if you're still frisky before you doze off."

He smiled and rose from the couch, following her toward the staircase.

The scanner squawked.

He looked back at it, habit telling him to grab it and bring it upstairs.

"Leave it," she pleaded, her eyes dour.

He actually thought about it and started to move toward the stairs, his hand still in hers, when he heard something that stopped him in his tracks. He looked at the scanner, deciphering the words he was positive he heard. He looked at Darcie.

"They're calling for the medical examiner."

The disappointment etched on her face cracked his heart. Her hand released his and dropped to her side.

"Go," she said, matter-of-factly.

It was ten o'clock at night as Brian headed down Main Street, lighting a cigarette on the way. He knew he shouldn't have left, not with that look Darcie had in her eyes, but he also knew he had to go. It was who he was. Sometimes he wondered why they were together; he wasn't the kind of person she should be with.

That's why when the trunk was opened in their attic, they saw the contents with different eyes. He saw the tiny skeletons as a big headline and a set of questions: Who, what, when, where, and why. He saw a story that lead to more mysteries and more headlines. Darcie, on the other hand, saw the flesh wrapping those decaying bones. She saw the living, breathing babies that those tiny remains could have been, should have been, like the tiny body growing inside her own belly. The body he had put there. Not the school teacher she could have ended up with, but him, a news junkie chasing sirens and salivating at the thought of murder. Just what he was chasing tonight. A call for a medical examiner meant a death.

At the stop sign at the end of Main Street, where earlier that day he had turned right onto Twistback Road, he now turned left onto Fogg Lane. He drove past Cricket Lane and a short time later saw the emergency vehicles ahead on the right—a couple police cruisers, a State Police vehicle, an ambulance, and a couple of unmarked vehicles. He pulled over a safe distance away and got out of his car.

The Town Pound stood in a grassy clearing about fifty yards off the road, a rutted dirt drive leading up to it. The entry gate hung crooked, and apparently falling off its hinges.

As Brian approached, he saw that most of the people were gathered in front of the gate. The county attorney was there, along with a couple of the Smokey Hollow police officers, including Chief Treece and Night Shift Alvin. When he spotted Noah, he casually walked up to him. The chief greeted him.

"What's up?" Brian asked, trying to peer through the gate. There were no street lights on this portion of the road. Over the wall of the pound, he could see the heads of Steem and Wickwire, along with someone who might have been one of the paramedics.

Noah's face was solemn and, though it was hard to see in the dark of night, even a bit pale. "We found the body of a woman."

"Ruth Snethen?" Brian asked, craning his neck to try and see better.

Noah shrugged. "No ID yet."

Another car pulled up. The man who stepped out of it was the medical examiner who had been at his house the night the trunk was opened. He spoke briefly to the county attorney and then headed toward the pound. He pulled open the metal gate, which squeaked loudly in the quiet night, and stepped inside.

Brian moved to one side to look through the opening. The two police cruisers had their spotlights shining into the pound, but they couldn't completely penetrate the dark shadows that filled the structure. The medical examiner's feet crunched on old pine needles and dried leaves as he walked toward the back left corner where Steem and Wickwire stood.

Now Brian could see bare legs, pale beneath a skirt that fell just below the knees. The upper portion of the body was still bathed in darkness.

"How'd you find her?" Brian asked, realizing his voice was low, just above a whisper, almost afraid to break the silence of the night.

"He found her," Noah answered, pointing toward one of the cruisers.

Brian saw the dark figure of a man in the back seat. It was too dark to make out a face, but he saw the outline of the man's head and recognized the high wiry hair.

"Is that—?"

"Sherman Thurk," Noah finished.

"How?"

"He says he was sleepwalking, woke up out here, and started to walk home. Needed to take a piss, so he stepped inside the Town

Pound. That's when he saw the body, lying in the corner. He went to one of the nearby houses, and the homeowner called us."

Brian looked at the Somnambulist in the cruiser. "Is he under arrest?"

"Not exactly," Noah said. "More like protective custody. At least until Capt. Steem can check out his story."

"You don't think...?"

The chief shrugged. He was probably thinking the same thing Brian was. Thurk had been spotted up on the ridge the night of the Mustard House fire, when Dr. Wymbs was murdered. And now he happened to find a body. And the glass eye had been found in his pocket. That made Brian wonder.

"Have you checked his pockets?" he asked Noah.

"Of course," the chief said. "Found a garden tour pamphlet, a rubber ball, and a compass."

Wickwire came to the entrance of the pound and gestured Noah and the county attorney inside. Brian wanted to go with them but saw the distasteful look Wickwire shot him and knew that was out of the question. Night Shift Alvin remained behind to guard the gate. Brian walked up to the wall and leaned against the cold granite to peer over the top. Shadows filled the clearing, especially the back left corner where the body lay.

The men gathered around it, blocking Brian's view even further. Noah and Wickwire trained flashlight beams on the corpse while the medical examiner crouched and made his examinations. Steem's body obscured the upper part of the victim's body, and Brian kept moving his head, trying to get a better angle. He kept wondering if it was the missing Ruth Snethen.

Steem bent to point something out, providing an opening for Brian to see the upper torso of the body. It was bathed in the beams of light from the flashlights, but he could not see the woman's face.

The victim's head was covered by a pillowcase.

Chapter 10

DEATH BY STRANGULATION

In the morning, before work, Brian told Darcie about the night's events. He hadn't wanted to wake her when he got home, given her current condition, knowing she needed rest. He hadn't slept well himself, tossing and turning, his mind working over the events at the Town Pound. At one point he had even got up and stepped into the back yard, getting his cigarettes and matches out of the hole in the maple tree and lighting one up. He figured it might calm his nerves and help him sleep. He stayed outside, sucking the smoke deep inside, releasing it with a gentle exhale. Just one, he told himself, and then back to bed, after rinsing with mouthwash first, of course.

He had stayed at the Town Pound until they loaded the body in the ambulance and took it away. He tried to get a glimpse of the face as the stretcher was carried out past the squeaky iron gate, but Wickwire kept him at a distance. He wanted to see if it indeed was Ruth Snethen. If so, then a clue to the mystery of the trunk full of skeletons could be lost.

"Obviously, that's why she was killed," Brian told his wife over a breakfast of toast with cinnamon sugar, scrambled eggs, sausage links, and a glass of pulpy orange juice.

"And you think it was the same person who killed Dr. Wymbs?" Darcie asked, eating a small bowl of maple oatmeal with a glass of milk.

He set his fork down and looked across the table. "Has to be. They have a connection. It can't be a coincidence."

"And of course you think it has something to do with the trunk we found?"

Brian pierced some eggs with the prongs of his fork and stuffed a bite into his mouth. "Makes sense," he said after swallowing. "That seemed to trigger everything that's happened since."

Darcie shivered. "It just gives me the willies. Thinking it all started here in our house, with those poor babies." She played her spoon around the oatmeal and then set it down, as if she didn't want any more. She looked at him. "Are we safe?"

He hesitated. That hadn't occurred to him. "Of course," he said. "We had nothing to do with what happened in that trunk. We only found it. Apparently, someone out there has some vested interest in it and the people involved. The police need to find out who."

"And by police, you don't mean Noah?"

He shook his head. "I wish. He's not experienced enough to deal with this kind of thing, though. Investigations are not his expertise. Steem and Wickwire are running the show. They're having a press conference outside the police station later today."

She stood and took her bowl to the counter. "And there will be more press than just you? Like when we found the trunk?"

"Unfortunately, yes. Two murders in a week, in a small town like Smokey Hollow. That's bound to attract some outside attention. The dailies, the wire services, the state TV station, who knows, maybe even news outlets from Boston." The thought was annoying. This was his town. No one else cared about it. Hell, he barely did. He watched Darcie scrape the remains of her oatmeal into the garbage.

"You need to be eating well," he said.

"I know," she answered, almost an apology. "Just not this morning. I might go down to Wibbels later and get some fresh fruit."

Brian brought his dishes to the sink. He paused and kissed her on the cheek. "Don't worry," he told her. "We're fine."

She closed her eyes and drew a deep breath. "It's just things seem so rotten in this town all of a sudden." She opened her eyes, drawing close to him. "And it feels like it's our fault."

"Why would you think like that?" He took her in his arms.

"If we hadn't opened that stupid trunk, maybe none of this would be happening."

"We can't change that." He reflected for a moment. "Besides, maybe it was a good thing we found it, before someone came looking for it."

She pulled back, her brow furrowing. "And that's supposed to make me feel better?"

He hugged her. "Shush. And you know, bad things happened in Smokey Hollow before this. Remember that Timmy Birtch disappeared more than two decades ago. And that rib cage the fisherman found in the pound. They don't know who that belonged to. And no one is trying to find out."

She burrowed against him. "You're not helping."

"I'm just saying, bad things happen, and it's not because of anything we did." He stroked her hair. "Now, I have to go to the office and get ready for that press conference. Though I'm not sure what the point will be. Steem isn't going to say a lot. Hopefully, they will have identified the body. Not that it matters, since I can't publish anything about it for almost a week. By then, everyone will probably have lost interest."

"I doubt that."

"I wonder how the owners would feel if I suggested turning the paper into a daily."

Darcie laughed, and it felt good to hear that sound coming from her, even if it was at his expense. "There isn't enough news in Smokey Hollow for that," she said.

"I don't know," he replied. "There seems to be an awful lot lately."

At the office, Brian wrote up a base file for the Town Pound murder story. He had hoped to talk to Noah before the press conference and get some inside information, but Noah was off doing chiefly duties, whatever they were. Before the authorities had taken the body away that night, Brian had asked Noah if they had established an identity once the pillowcase had been removed from the woman's head. Noah had told him the body was too bloated to be recognizable and that there was nothing on the remains to identify the person.

He wished he knew some people who were acquainted with Ruth Snethen that he could interview about the woman, in case it was her body, but he didn't know anybody. He thought he might talk to Leo Wibbels again, since he had handled selling her house. There must be something he knew about her.

Looking out his office, Brian could see a van from the state TV station setting up in front of the police station. His stomach roiled and he grabbed a bottle of antacid tablets from his top desk drawer, popping a couple in his mouth and crunching them. He washed the chalky remains down his throat with the last of the black coffee in his mug. It was lukewarm, and he stepped out of his office to the coffee maker near the reception area.

He smiled at Beverly as he poured another cup. In the back, Isaac was pecking away at his keyboard, probably writing about the latest softball-league happenings. A sports reporter Brian could never be. Talk about mundane.

"Don't forget this afternoon you're meeting with Selectman Winch about the Dump Fest," Bev said, almost as if she were reading his mind and reminding him that his job wasn't devoid of monotony.

"Of course," he said, sipping coffee that burned hot in his mouth.

He retreated into his office, thinking about the annual festival scheduled for the following weekend. It wasn't actually held at the dump but on the grounds where the dump had once been, now just an open field on Blackberry Road north of Fogg Lane. It was the town's big summer celebration, with food, crafts, and carnival-type games and activities. He needed to preview it, and that one definitely had to go on the front page. Dealing with Mrs. Picklesmeir was one thing, but this was run by the town selectmen.

He sat at his desk and was preparing to head to the press conference when Beverly buzzed him on his extension.

"What is it, Bev?"

"I have a call for you."

"Who is it? I'm just getting ready to head out."

"A woman, but she won't give her name. She said she needs to talk to you."

Needs? Brian thought. Not wants, but needs.

"Patch her through," Brian said, curiosity getting the better of him.

"Hello," he answered.

There was a pause on the other end, and he wondered if Beverly had screwed up the transfer, but that wouldn't be like her. Finally a voice spoke in a hushed tone. "Is this Mr. Keays?"

"Yes," he said. "Brian Keays, editor of *The Hollow News*."

"I know that," the woman said, irritated. "I know what you do; I just wanted to make sure it was you."

Brian was annoyed, but knew he had to treat the public with respect. "And who am I speaking with?"

Again another pause on the other end. Brian kept an eye on the clock. The press conference would be starting soon.

"Will this conversation be kept private?"

An odd question he thought at first, till he remembered the notes he had been receiving. Could this be The Silhouette, though he had assumed it was a man?

"It will be kept private, but I need to know who I am speaking with." He waited, worried that the woman might hang up.

"Okay," she said. "I will take a chance."

"Good. You can trust me."

"Oh, I don't trust anybody." There was fear in the woman's voice.

"I need to know your name," Brian tried not to sound desperate, but he was afraid of losing the woman. He heard a deep breath from the other end of the line.

"My name is Ruth Snethen."

Brian had been certain the body found at the Town Pound was the missing retired nurse, but now he had her on the phone.

"Is this for real," he managed.

"Of course I know who the hell I am," she spat.

He was worried he'd lose her. "I'm sorry. It's just that I—"

At that he stopped, realizing that he was about to tell her he thought she was dead. But how would she react to that? Not very well, he assumed. "I didn't think—"

"I was alive?"

"N-no," he stammered. "It's not that. I just wasn't expecting –"

"You thought that was me they found at the Town Pound?"

He heard a touch of levity in her tone.

"I don't know what I thought," he admitted, throwing in the towel. "It's been so crazy around here."

"Well, it could have easily been me."

"Where have you been," Brian said. "The police are looking for you."

"Don't you think I know that? I've been hiding."

"Why?" Though he thought he knew the answer.

"I'm afraid." Short and simple.

"What are you afraid of?"

"Can't you see what's going on?"

"Let's get together and talk," he said, trying to sound soothing.

"I don't know," she said, hesitant. "I don't know who to trust."

"Tell me what's going on." He decided to ask the big question. "What do you know about the trunk I found in your house?" He could hear breathing on the other end of the line.

"Not on the phone," she said, her voice hushed. "Someone could be listening."

"Can you meet me somewhere?"

Again, silence. For a second he thought she was gone. Then he heard another breath.

"Meet me tonight." She paused. "Alone."

"Where?" he said, heart racing. "When?"

She paused, and he was again afraid she had hung up.

"Sunset," she finally answered. "At the old train station."

"Okay," he said, trying to keep his tone calm. "I'll be there."

"And don't bring anyone with you." She was emphatic. "I mean it." He knew she did. He heard fear in her voice.

"Don't worry. I'll—"

There was a click and the line was dead.

Brian sank back in his chair, his heart pounding. Wow, he thought. Ruth Snethen was alive and still out there somewhere. He had the urge to tell someone but knew he couldn't. This was a source he definitely had to keep to himself. He couldn't even tell Noah, and certainly not Capt. Steem. They hadn't been able to find her, but he had. Not really. She had found him. But it didn't matter. She was a big part of the puzzle, and maybe now some of the pieces would fall into place.

Brian smiled.

He gathered his camera and notebooks and headed for the door, stopped by his secretary.

"Who was that?"

He just smiled at her and left the building.

On the opposite side of Hemlock Avenue, a small crowd had gathered before a podium set up outside the police station. Half of the crowd was reporters from daily newspapers in the bigger cities. And there were the television crews. The rest of the crowd was curious citizens of Smokey Hollow. Selectmen Chairman Eldon Winch stood next to Leo Wibbels. Rolfe Krimmer was near the back, leaning on his Boston Post Cane. Mrs. Picklesmeir stood beside the old man and glared at Brian. Next to her was Jonas Fitchen, the taxidermist. The older woman with the youthful hair Brian had seen around town was there as well, this time wearing a chestnut wig curled to her shoulders. Hale Cullumber stepped out of his pub and leaned against the doorjamb. Brian wondered if the town's shopkeepers had all closed to hear the press conference.

Brian heard a hum and saw the man in the motorized wheelchair maneuver down the sidewalk and stop near the front of the crowd. He was wearing his white Panama hat, which on a hot sunny day like this was probably a good idea. Brian already felt sweat beading on his scalp.

He glanced toward Main Street, his eyes drawn upwards to the hill beyond. Maybe because it was hot and the coffee he'd been drinking had left his throat warm and dry, his gaze fell upon the water tower overlooking the town. Or it could have been that he sensed what he now saw, a figure up on the tower. He could only guess that it was the same man he'd seen on the tower the day he'd visited the Mustard House. It was hard to tell, since the figure was small and indistinguishable in the distance. Once again, the man stood there looking down at the town, so he didn't give Brian the impression he was a city worker. Maybe he could ask Eldon Winch about the man when he went to interview him about the upcoming Dump Fest.

The doors to the police station opened, quieting the murmuring onlookers as their attention was drawn to the four men approaching the podium. Capt. Steem stood in front of the microphone. To his right was Sgt. Wickwire; to his left Chief Treece. In the background stood the fourth man, the county attorney.

Since Ruth Snethen was alive and still in hiding, Brian could pretty much guess who the murdered woman in the Town Pound was. He doubted any of the other reporters had a clue, and that made him smirk.

Steem's eyes scanned the crowd as he stood before the podium, a folder of papers in his hand. He seemed to be waiting for the television camera crew to give him his cue before starting. That figures, Brian thought, thinking he'd never get that kind of courtesy.

Steem cleared his throat, which reverberated in the microphone.

"Thank you all for coming," he said. "I won't keep you long."

Of course not, Brian said, not really expecting much information. He snapped a couple of pictures of the trio of law enforcement officers and then zoomed in on the captain.

"As you may be aware," he continued, "there has been another murder in Smokey Hollow. The body of a middle-aged woman was found inside the Town Pound on Fogg Road." He paused, looking up from his notes. "The victim's family has been notified, so we are allowed to release the name. The victim has been identified as Hettie Gritton, who worked as a housekeeper at the Wymbs Institute."

There were some gasps and more murmurs from the crowd. It was as Brian had anticipated. The police had been unable to locate her after the night of the fire and now Brian knew why. Besides, he remembered Steem telling him she lived on Fogg Road.

"The medical examiner has ruled the cause of death as asphyxiation from strangulation."

Gasps again, and even an "Oh no," from a woman, maybe Mrs. Picklesmeir.

"At this time we are not linking the crime to the murder of Dr. Milton Wymbs a week ago, as it is too early in the investigations. But law enforcement personnel will be looking into all leads in both murder investigations."

By that, he meant him and Wickwire, Brian told himself.

"We are asking that anyone who may have any information about either of these cases contact the State Police." He recited the phone number and then repeated it. "Any information anyone might have about either of these two victims could be helpful, no matter how insignificant it might seem."

That sounded like desperation, Brian thought. It meant they had zero leads.

"We'll take a few questions," Steem continued. "But there is not much more information we can release." He paused, waiting for a barrage from the reporters.

"Do these murders have any connection to the trunk of skeletons found recently in town?" one of the newspaper reporters asked. Brian felt that question was the main reason most of the media were here. That was the hook that reeled everyone in.

Steem hesitated. "There has been no determination that the discovery of that trunk has any bearing on these murder cases. That is a separate investigation."

Sure, Brian thought.

"Are there any persons of interest?" This came from the television reporter.

"Not at this moment," Steem answered.

"Any idea when the murder took place?" another reporter asked.

"The medical examiner has yet to determine the time of death."

Brian knew Noah had told him the body was bloated, so it had been there at least a few days. For that reason, Brian knew a question to ask that the others didn't.

"Is former Assistant Fire Chief Simon Runck considered a suspect in Hettie Gritton's death?"

Steem's lips tightened.

"Or Dr. Wymbs' slaying?" another reporter yelled.

Steem leaned into the mic. "Simon Runck has only been charged with arson at this moment. There are no identified suspects in the two murders at this point."

"What happened to the patients at the Wymbs Institute?" someone asked.

"We have no confirmation there were any patients at the institute."

A buzz ran through the crowd.

Brian considered the possibility that there was maybe one patient at the asylum, the one who strangled Dr. Wymbs the night of the fire. And no one asked the obvious follow-up question: Where was the institute staff? But maybe he could find out when he met with Snethen. Though she had retired, she should know who else worked there.

There was another question Brian wanted answered, but he didn't dare ask it in front of the crowd. He was sure the police would keep quiet about Hettie's head being covered with a pillowcase, but he had seen it, so that made him the only journalist who knew and he wasn't about to bring it up in a public forum. He would ask Steem about it privately.

"Are we in danger?" someone called from the back. It didn't come from a reporter. It came from Mrs. Picklesmeir. "Should we be worried?"

Steem braced himself before answering. "We don't believe there is any danger to the public. We don't believe these murders were random."

"Why not?" someone yelled.

"We're not at liberty to discuss that information at this time. And that is all the time we have for questions." The captain stepped back from the microphone, examining the crowd with steely eyes.

Brian looked at the people around him. Was the captain wondering if the murderer could be here watching? Brian looked from face to face. Besides the reporters, the crowd was town folk. But it made him wonder. He looked up over the rooftops of the businesses downtown to the water tower and the man who stood there, staring down.

Chapter II

A SECRET RENDEZVOUS

Brian sat patiently inside the police station, waiting to get a word with Capt. Steem, who was conferring with Noah in the chief's office. After a while he was permitted to enter, though Steem seemed less than enthusiastic about his presence.

"We gave all the information outside at the press conference that we intend to give," Steem said, seated in a chair in front of Noah's desk. Wickwire stood silently behind him.

Brian leaned against the glass interior window of the office.

"That was why we held the press conference," Steem continued, "so media could all have the same information."

Brian chuckled. "Well, all the media doesn't have the same information," he said.

Steem's lips tightened. "Meaning what?"

"The pillowcase covering Hettie Gritton's head."

Steem's brow furrowed and he glanced at Noah.

"The chief didn't tell me," Brian said. "I saw it for myself that night."

Steem sucked in a deep breath, and his lips cracked into something that could almost qualify as a smile, but not quite. "Here's where we stand," he said, leaning forward. "There are always details of a crime the police like to keep quiet. It often goes a long way in helping identify the eventual perpetrator, or at the very least, eliminate potential kooks who like to confess to random crimes." He folded his arms across his chest. "The pillowcase is one of those details. The police know, the killer knows—"

"And I know."

"But the public doesn't. We'd like to keep it that way."

"So you're asking me not to write anything about it?"

Steem sighed. "I'd like to tell you not to, but I don't have the authority to."

Brian glanced from Steem to Noah and back. "Listen, I've got quite a few days before I put out another issue of *The Hollow News*. Everyone else will have all kinds of stories to print and broadcast before I get my chance." He waited for reaction from the captain, but there was no impact. "This is the one thing I have."

Steem stared at him. "I understand the situation you're in. But my main concern is this investigation and finding the culprit responsible."

"Culprit? So you think one person committed both murders?"

Steem's eyes narrowed. "I didn't say that."

Brian thought about something that had bothered him since the night of the fire. "When Dr. Wymbs' body was pulled out of the fire, something was removed from his face." He waited for a reaction, but Steem's expression was stone. "It looked like a piece of cloth." Still no movement. "Could there also have been a pillowcase covering his head?" Maybe a tremor in Steem's lower lip, but definitely some color on his face.

"Off the record," Steem said, "that item is being analyzed. But given the circumstances surrounding the condition of Gritton's body, our best guess is, yes, a pillowcase was most likely covering Wymbs' head."

"Was Gritton smothered to death by the pillowcase?"

"No. The medical examiner confirmed that. There were marks on her neck. She appears to have been strangled with bare hands. We don't know what purpose the pillowcase served, but we still don't want anything in the press about it."

"That doesn't really help me," Brian said, "if I can't put anything in the paper about it."

"My job isn't to help you."

"But it does mean you are focused on one culprit for both murders."

Steem shrugged. "You can go as far as to print that. But don't attribute it to me."

"Sure," Brian said, nodding. "Just 'police sources say.'"

"Fair enough," Steem said, rising. "Now we have work to do." He turned to Treece. "Chief, we'll be in touch if we need anything more from you."

"Sure thing," Noah said, standing and looking as if he were going to extend his hand but realizing that the captain wasn't expecting a handshake.

Steem and Wickwire left the office.

Brian looked at Noah, who had sat back down.

"Such a cheerful man," he said to the chief.

Noah laughed. "His job doesn't come with a lot of cheer. Not like mine."

"Yeah," he said. "Not as much stress with your position."

Noah's grin faded. "I can't help the way things are handled around here. I just follow protocol."

Brian looked at Noah, thinking he should be grateful the chief shared as much with him as he did. He didn't have to, and Brian appreciated that. He almost wished he could tell him about his call from Ruth Snethen but knew it wasn't the wise thing to do. This was a secret source that could lead to some valuable information.

He had sensed the concern in the woman's voice and hoped she would not back out of their secret meeting. He wished he could bring Noah with him, but knew that would frighten her away. Hopefully, after he got whatever information she was willing to divulge, he could convince her to see the chief. That way, she might feel safe, and Noah could get credited with finding an elusive piece to this puzzle.

But first, Brian needed to hear what the woman had to say about the trunk with the skeletons and its connection to the Wymbs Institute.

At the Town Hall, in the second-floor office of Selectmen Chairman Eldon Winch, Brian met with him and Leo Wibbels, both on the organizing committee for Dump Festival. Brian and Wibbels sat in large padded chairs in front of a big oak desk, behind which Winch sat in a high-backed leather chair.

On the walls in the large office were photographs of the town, taken when it was a bit more vibrant. It reminded Brian of the pictures gracing the walls of Cully's Pub. There was one of the movie theater, though from where he sat he could not see the title of the movie on the marquee, but there was a line of people at the box office waiting to get their tickets. From the appearance of their clothes, the photo must have been taken about thirty or forty years ago.

Another photo on the wall was of the train station, with people lined up on the platform to board. The wooden siding on the depot was bright red, the shingled roof black. This photo looked even older than the one of the movie theater, once again based on the subjects' dress. Brian thought about going to that place later this evening, and the anticipation made him fidget. He wanted to get the day over with so he could be ready…and he feared that Ruth Snethen would change her mind and not show up. It made him edgy and his stomach twitchy.

Winch twirled the end of his mustache with his right hand before placing both palms on the desk. "I can't tell you," he began, "how important the Dump Fest is to this community. It's something people look forward to in the summer."

"That's what I've heard," Brian said.

"The economy has made it tough for a lot of folks in town. This festival gives them a chance to relax and enjoy a simple day of celebration."

"It's inexpensive, too," Wibbels chimed in.

"Yes," said Winch. "It's an event for the whole family. People bring their kids—it's a fun time for everyone. And with the terrible events lately, people need an escape."

"These things couldn't be happening at a worst time," Wibbels said.

"There never is a good time for murder," Brian said, though he couldn't disagree more. At least for him, this was all happening when he needed something to bring him out of his doldrums.

"I'm glad the State Police said there is no reason for people to be afraid. I think that put a lot of minds at ease," Winch said.

"It did my wife's," Wibbels added.

"It does appear the killer has targeted specific people," Brian said.

"Hopefully they will catch the culprit and be done with this nasty business, maybe before the festival," Winch said.

"That would be a blessing," Wibbels agreed. The real estate agent had a folder in his hands and extracted a paper from it. "Here's a list of the vendors that will be at the festival," he said, handing Brian the sheet. "We want you to make sure you don't leave anyone out."

Brian took it, glancing at it without comment.

"And we will have lots of activities—balloon rides, a petting zoo, a carousel, games, and contests," Winch said.

"Oh, and the cow-pie roulette," Wibbels emphasized.

"Cow-pie roulette?" Brian couldn't even imagine what that was.

"Oh, yes," Wibbels said. "It's one of the most popular events. A field adjacent to the festival grounds is fenced off and lined with numbered squares, and people purchase a ticket that corresponds to a number. Then a cow is released into the field, and if the cow craps on your square, you win."

Brian glances at the two smiling men. "You've got to be kidding?"

"Oh, no," Winch said, leaning back in his chair and letting loose a guffaw. "It's a real hoot."

"Everyone squeals with anticipation, watching the cow wander the field, cheering her on." Wibbels said. "It's a gas."

"And a good fundraiser," Winch added in a more serious tone, pointing his finger at Brian as if to emphasize how seriously he should take this.

Brian shook his head. "And what are the funds for?"

"Well," Winch said. "Most of the money ends up going back into the town coffers for next year's festival."

"I see," Brian said.

"And a portion goes to the church," Wibbels pointed out.

"Yes," Winch said. "Don't forget that. That is important to note. The church is an active participant."

Wibbels handed Brian a couple more sheets of paper.

"Here is a list of all the activities and sponsors of the festival."

"You can't forget to mention the sponsors." Winch emphasized.

"I'll be sure not to," Brian said.

Winch leaned forward. "And I can't stress enough that you must promote this on the front page of next week's edition."

"Well, if you haven't noticed, there has been a lot of pretty important news lately."

"I don't disagree. But people don't want to just read the nasty stuff."

Brian disagreed.

"This is our big town event," Winch said. "It is important to everyone in Smokey Hollow. It must get its proper attention."

Brian waved his hand. "Okay. I get the point. I will make sure it gets on the front page." He had expected that all along, but drew a little pleasure in making the duo uncomfortable.

"Hopefully," Winch said, "people will forget about these unfortunate events."

As the sun set behind the water tower, dusk enveloped Smokey Hollow. Brian sat in his car in the lot at the old shoe factory across from the abandoned train station. He had arrived just before sunset, wanting to get there before Ruth Snethen, but not wanting to park at the depot. He was trying not to attract attention to himself and thought the parking lot at the deserted factory would be better. A low brick wall with iron fencing along its top separated the parking lot from the road. Parked behind the wall, his car wouldn't be immediately visible to passersby. His view over the top of the wall was enough that he should see anyone approach the train station.

He chewed an antacid tablet, washing the gritty remnants down with hot coffee from his thermos. His stomach churned and his palms sweated. He lit up a cigarette and cranked his window down all the way. The setting sun did little to drag away the heat from the summer day. He drew on the cigarette and blew the smoke out the window. It was a good thing Darcie never rode in his car.

He watched the building across the street, wondering when the retired nurse would show up. He had so many questions swirling in his brain, and he was excited to get some answers. But he was afraid she would back out. He wished she would have let him meet with her when she called. She had too much time to change her mind.

He also wished he could have brought Noah, but that would be too much of a risk.

Brian wondered how Ruth would get to the station. Would she come by car? Walk? How was she getting around these days? The police hadn't been able to find her. Where was she hiding? A thought occurred to him. Maybe she was already here.

She could have been hiding in the station all along, and that's why the authorities hadn't been able to locate her. That could be why she picked this spot. But she had called him from somewhere. Surely there was no electricity or phone service at the depot. She could be shacking out in the woods behind the station, near Thrasher Pond. That made him think of the Knackerman's pot of bones. He lit up another cigarette.

If she was there already, she might not wait long for him. Brian grabbed his flashlight from his glove compartment and got out of his car, closing the door gently. He dropped his half-smoked cigarette to the ground and crunched it out under his shoe, wiping his sweaty palms on his shirt.

There was a clunking behind him and he whirled around, his heart leaping.

The dark hulk of the shoe factory loomed over him, four stories high, with rows of tall windows lining each floor. None were boarded up, but only jigsaw pieces of glass remained in most. A tall smokestack at the right rose higher than the building. Some bricks at the top were missing, giving the smokestack a turret-like appearance.

Brian turned on his flashlight and shined it along the dark windows of the upper floor. Maybe this was where Ruth was hiding. There was a flapping sound, probably a bird or bat. He kept expecting the flashlight beam to catch a shadow beyond the empty windows, but he was glad it didn't. But still, before he turned to cross the street, he couldn't help but feel someone watching him from behind those windows.

He kept the flashlight off while crossing the street, not wanting to draw unneeded attention but also not realizing how dark it was out here.

The nearest street light was out, and the next one was at least a hundred yards away. It made Brian remember that one of the resolutions the town selectmen passed to cut the town budget was to turn off every other streetlight. It seemed unfortunate that the one by the train station was the odd pole out.

The fact that the night was cloudy, obscuring what moonlight there would have been, didn't help. A large bank of gray clouds hovered over this end of Main Street. The clouds didn't look dark enough to be thunderheads, which was too bad, because some rain would cool the summer heat.

A few cars drifted by on Route 113, the whooshing of their tires on the night pavement reassuring Brian that he wasn't alone—till he realized that he might not be alone anyway.

He stepped onto the wooden platform in front of the depot, its wooden planks creaking beneath his shoes. Brian stopped. If she were inside, she would now know he had arrived. He turned on his flashlight, pointing the beam along the platform to its edge by the lonely tracks. Even by what little light the flashlight beam cast, he could see the brush growing up between rusty rails. Tracks to nowhere, he thought.

Brian shifted the beam to the front door. One step at a time, each followed by a creak, he approached the door. Should I knock? he wondered. It wasn't like this was her home, or maybe it was. Regardless, she was expecting him. He grabbed the wooden knob and pulled. The door was wedged shut, most likely swollen from the summer heat, and it took him a couple strenuous tugs before it lurched open, almost striking him in the face.

A whoosh of stale air escaped the interior of the dark station like some trapped spirit being released.

"Hello?" he called softly, as if afraid of waking somebody. "Ms. Snethen?" Was she Miss, Ms., or Mrs.? He didn't know. He recalled she lived alone at the house he had bought from her. "Anyone home?" He thought it odd to phrase it that way. This wasn't anyone's home, just a dilapidated old structure from a bygone era, whose usefulness had long passed, no matter what plans the selectmen intended for it.

He stepped inside.

Broken glass crunched beneath his shoe and he stopped, just inside the doorway. The flashlight struggled to penetrate the interior, thick with dust that danced in the path of the beam. He probed the four corners. Nobody—though the floor showed disturbances in the dust that covered it. Someone at least had been here.

Brian's mouth was dry from tasting the dust in the air, and he licked his lips. He wanted to spit but thought it would be rude to do so. His nerves, which had tightened, relaxed a bit...he was alone. But he was also disappointed, thinking maybe Ruth Snethen had changed her mind and retreated back into hiding. He scanned the flashlight beam around.

The light caught something.

He was *not* alone.

A ticket booth protruded from the front wall, its rectangular window partly covered by steel bars open at the bottom. The flashlight beam partially lit up a shadowy figure in the booth.

Brian's breath caught in his throat, and his stomach tightened.

"Uh," he started to say, but could not find words. He raised the beam a little higher and realized that the person could not hear him.

The light caught the top of the figure and the pillowcase covering its head.

"God," Brian said, blowing dust from his lips as he spoke. He took a step toward the booth, pausing before the barred ticket window. The light shined brighter now, and he could tell the person was a woman. The cloth clung to the face, outlining its features, the indentations of the eyes, the protuberance of the nose, and the shape of a mouth open in what could have been an attempt to cry out before its scream was cut off. He knew whose face was beneath that pillowcase, a face he had only seen in that picture he took the night of the Mustard House fire. "Damn."

Don't touch anything, he told himself, now that it dawned on him that he was in the middle of a crime scene. He actually had to glance at his hands to make sure they weren't in contact with any part of the station. The only thing they had touched was the flashlight now gripped so tightly in his hand that he could see the white along his knuckles, even in this darkness.

He looked back at the figure perched on some kind of stool and leaning against the back wall. If the bars of the ticket window weren't separating him from it, he might not have been unable to resist the urge to reach through the window and pull the pillowcase off. He had never been this close to violent death. Sure, he had been at many crime scenes, but he was always separated by crime tape and a uniformed presence.

Here it was just him and a dead body.

And nothing else.

Unless....

He looked over his right shoulder, then his left, not wanting to turn around. How long ago had the killer been in here, maybe standing where he was right now? Brian felt helpless and knew he should get out of this building and call Chief Treece. But his feet felt frozen in place, as if stuck to the dust on the floor.

Move, he told himself, but he couldn't. There was one thing he thought he should do first, before bolting out the door.

Brian's left hand dropped to the camera at his waist. Take a picture, he thought. Not because it was something he'd ever be able to publish in the newspaper, but because he could. There was no one here to shield him from this gruesome scene. No one to stick a hand in front of his lens or block his view. Take a picture.

But to do so he had to put the flashlight down.

Leaving it on, he shoved the flashlight into his right front pocket, the beam now shooting up at the ceiling and leaving the figure in the ticket booth bathed in shadows. Brian raised his camera, making sure the flash was on, and brought the view finder up to his eye, adjusting the focus. The shrouded figure in the booth looked further away, as if he had stepped back from the window. But he knew that was not the case. He knew he was close; if the figure behind the bars had been still alive, it could have reached out through those bars and grabbed him.

He snapped the picture. The camera flashed, exploding a bright light inside the ticket booth.

The head moved.

In that second of light that had temporarily blinded him, the pillowcase had shifted.

The flash went out. He couldn't see. There was only the bright spot in front of him from the intensity of the blinding flash. He felt vulnerable. Those bars wouldn't be able to hold back the figure if it reached for him.

The spot in front of his eyes shrank and disappeared. The figure was still.

Of course it hadn't moved, he assured himself. It was just his imagination. It was dead, and nothing could ever make it move again.

But he could move, and that's what he needed to do. He pulled the flashlight out and made his way to the door, half fearing that it wouldn't open and would trap him here with that thing. He pushed, it swung open, and he escaped onto the dark platform, not daring to look behind him. The door slammed with a thick thud that echoed in the quiet, dark night.

Stay shut, he thought.

The platform creaked even louder as he ran across it. He wanted to get across the street, back to the safety of his car. The shoe factory no longer seemed ominous compared to the train depot. His heels clicked on the asphalt as he crossed the road, every sound he made amplified.

Once on the other side of the street, he fumbled for his keys, unlocked the car, and threw himself into the driver's seat. He needed to call the authorities right away, and felt the urgency of it, but he had been holding his breath and now, as he released it, he knew he would have to wait a few seconds till he'd be able to speak and make the call.

It was just a few seconds, but it seemed endless as he sat in his car staring at the dark, silent station on the other side of the street.

Chapter 12

THE STORY OF THE PILLOWCASE

Yellow police tape encircled the old train station. Brian stood by his car smoking a cigarette. It was where Steem had told him to wait after the authorities had arrived. That was fine by him. He didn't want to go near the depot, knowing what took place inside there. He was satisfied being on this side of the caution tape and this side of the road. Though something about the shoe factory behind him left him unsettled, and he dared not turn his head or look over his shoulder. No, that wouldn't do. He didn't like the fact that he couldn't see through those dark windows, and didn't like the fact that he wondered if someone or something was looking out them at him.

No, it was better to stare across the road at all the flashing lights from the police vehicles and feel the security that so many law enforcement officials provided, even Night Shift Alvin. It made him feel less alone over on this side even though he was by himself. It provided some level of comfort, much like the smoke he just had.

He lit up another cigarette. Was it his third? No, might even be his fifth since he made the call to Noah and waited for the troops to arrive. Darcie would be furious, but maybe she would understand. She was the second call he made, and though he reassured her that he was okay, he knew she sensed something in his voice that wasn't quite right. He had tried to sound calm, but his heart was jittery and that's what smoking helped. It relaxed him, and he needed to relax. Otherwise he thought his heart would explode.

When this was all over, he swore to himself he would quit smoking for good again. But till then, he would need this. And the way things were going, he doubted it would be over very soon.

Something dark was at work in Smokey Hollow, and maybe Mrs. Picklesmeir got the wrong message earlier today. They were not safe.

Brian certainly did not feel safe. This was close. He had come close to death. Not his own, but who knows. What if he had gotten to the train station earlier? What if he had walked in on the commission of the murderous act? And most importantly, what information did he have that the killer might know or even think he knows? He had crossed the line from being a reporter on this story to becoming part of it. He no longer cared that all the authorities were on the other side of the road, processing the crime scene. That's where Brian would normally want to be. But he didn't feel like a reporter just now. He was more than that. He was a witness. He was part of the story.

Police Chief Treece walked across the street toward him, carrying a thermos of coffee. He flashed his typical grin, as if this were no more than a night out catching a hunter jacking deer.

"Thought you might need this," Noah said, holding up the thermos.

Brian tried to crack even the slightest hint of a grin, but his mouth felt like it barely moved, as if his face had grown stiff. "Sure could," he muttered. His own thermos was long empty. Even though the night was still hot and his lungs burned from the cigarette fumes and his mouth was dry and pasty, he felt another cup of hot coffee would do him good.

Noah poured some into the thermos cap and handed it to him. Brian took a sip, noticed it was only a notch above lukewarm, and gulped down a swallow.

"You okay?" Noah asked with genuine concern.

"I'm fine," Brian lied. "Just a bit unnerved."

"Can't say I blame you." Noah turned to look back at the station.

"I've seen plenty of dead people before in my profession," Brian said, as if in protest. "Just that this was a little different. Usually I'm not all by myself in such a dark place."

"I understand. No need to explain."

But Brian needed to. But more importantly, he needed to explain why he didn't tell Noah about the phone call from Ruth Snethen. He wanted—no, expected the chief to ask him about it, but Noah didn't say anything. Brian was sure he felt betrayed, that he wasn't being open with him, and he wasn't. Noah had a job to do, but so did Brian. And contact from a potential source was an issue of confidentiality.

That was how Brian tried to justify it to himself, and he hoped Noah saw it that way. But what Brian couldn't justify to himself was the fact that if he had told Noah or Steem about the phone call, Ruth Snethen might still be alive. Sure, she'd be pissed at him for turning her in. But at least she'd have the ability to feel angry. Now she couldn't feel anything.

"It's definitely her?" Brian asked, almost hoping that maybe this was all a mistake and that someone else lay dead inside the depot and he couldn't be held responsible.

"It's her," Noah said, still looking toward the station. "Medical examiner's looking her over now. There are marks on her neck, so early guess is strangulation." He turned to face Brian. "Of course, that is strictly off the record." He wasn't smiling now. "You didn't get that from me."

Brian had never heard Noah phrase anything like that. He was always forthcoming with information. More forthcoming than he himself had been, and apparently that hadn't gone unnoticed.

"Of course," Brian said, making it sound like an apology. He hoped that was the way it was taken.

"Steem wants to talk some more with you when they wrap up in there."

"No doubt." Brian took another swallow of the coffee. "I'm not going anywhere."

After the body was zipped into a black plastic bag and wheeled out of the station house on a stretcher, Noah fetched Brian from across the street. He sat in the back seat of the State Police vehicle. Steem and Wickwire got in the front, the younger detective in the driver's seat.

It was dark inside the car, and both men appeared as large, shadowy figures. Steem's bald head looked as large as a big black block of granite. The head turned to look at him in the back seat.

"Are you purposely trying to thwart this investigation at every step?" the captain asked.

Brian knew it wasn't a question the man expected him to answer.

"I try to keep our lines of communication open with you, and once again, you withhold information."

"I understand how you see — "

"Someone's life was at stake!" Steem bellowed. "A woman is dead! Someone who most likely had valuable information on this case."

Brian glanced out the window. He didn't want to look into the intimidating face of Capt. Steem. He felt like he was back in school, in the principal's office for pulling some prank that had gone wrong.

"She didn't want to talk to the police," he said, defending his actions. "She wanted to meet privately, and I chose to respect that. She was a source I was willing to protect. I have that right."

"Not if it impedes a criminal investigation!" Steem was still shouting, and it reverberated inside the close confines of the vehicle. "That is more important than anything. I could bring you up on charges."

Brian looked at Steem and, even in the darkness, could tell the man's face was flushed with anger. He doubted Steem's threat but did not want to push the issue. He thought maybe he should divert the conversation away from his actions.

"You know what this death means, don't you? Three murders, all following the same pattern."

A pointed finger jutted out from the front seat. In the dark, he didn't even have to see the expression on Capt. Steem's face. In the rearview mirror, he could not so much see but feel Wickwire's eyes on him. "If you print anything in the paper with the term you're thinking of—"

Steem didn't finish his sentence, nor did he have to. And neither did he have to mention the phrase. He knew what they were all thinking: serial killer.

When Brian got home, sometime after midnight, Darcie put her arms around him and hugged him tighter then she had in a long time. He could feel the baby bump pressed against his abdomen. She had been worried about his mental wellbeing after such a traumatizing event. He worried that she'd detect the cigarette smoke on his breath, even though he had gobbled down several breath mints before coming home.

"I'll be all right," he told her, and he believed that.

"It's just that something like this must be so unsettling," she said.

He rubbed her shoulder. "I'm sorry," he said after a moment's pause.

She pulled away and looked up at him. "What are you sorry for?"

"It's just that I know I haven't been very sympathetic about the effect finding that trunk in the attic had on you, and the emotional toll it's taken. Now, with this happening tonight, I have more of an understanding of how you feel."

She pressed her head against his shoulder. "Events have put both of us through a lot of stress. And I need to be more understanding of the job you have to do, no matter how unpleasant it is sometimes."

Sleep did not come easily that night, and when it did, his dreams were filled with the image of the nurse with the pillowcase over her head. Or was he even sleeping when those images appeared? He might have even been awake. He thought he heard noises in the house, creaks and thumps. Probably just pipes and floorboards of an old house settling, but he couldn't help conjuring an image of Ruth Snethen wandering around the rooms with the pillowcase over her head, bumping into things as she tried to find her way.

Find her way where? Why, up to his bedroom of course, looking for him, angry that he hadn't shown up at the train station earlier so he could have saved her. He imagined her standing beside his bed, looking down at him even though she couldn't see through the fabric of the pillowcase, her hands reaching out to grab him and stir him from his slumber. *Wake up,* she called, her voice muffled from the cloth covering her face. *Wake up and help me.* Help you what? he asked, looking at the hooded figure beside him in the dark bedroom. *Help me save the children.* What children? *The children in the trunk.* What are they doing in the trunk? *Suffocating!* Who put them in the trunk, Ruth? *We don't have time for that; I have a train to catch.* The train doesn't come to Smokey Hollow anymore. *I must find my way out of here. I can't stay.* But Ruth, how can you leave when you can't even see where you're going.

He reached up and pulled the pillowcase off her head. Her eyes bulged in their sockets, her mouth hung open, and finger-sized abrasions marked her scrawny neck. That was when Brian realized he was dreaming and no one was standing by his bed. But he was holding on to something and looked down at his hand. His fingers gripped the pillowcase he had ripped from his own pillow. He threw it onto the floor.

Despite the sleepless night, he felt rested in the morning and his nerves relaxed, with no desire for a cigarette, a cup of coffee, or an antacid. Downstairs, another note had been slipped through the mail slot. He was excited because it had been a few days without hearing from his anonymous friend, and he had worried the attention had driven the mystery messenger into hiding. But what good had hiding done for Ruth Snethen?

He picked up the envelope, seeing the familiar black ink and a dark smudge, thinking his mystery writer needed a better pen. He wondered how long ago the envelope had been shoved through the mail slot, and opened the door, stepping out and not surprised to see Ash Street quiet and deserted. He opened the envelope and pulled the white piece of note paper out. Written on the blank sheet was the latest message, once again a question:

Why has The Pillowcase returned?
The Silhouette

Darcie had no idea he was getting these notes. It was a conscious decision he had made to keep from worrying her too much. She had enough to deal with since the discovery of the trunk. He saw no need to add undue stress to her situation, with a baby in the belly. He tucked the note into his pants pocket and told her he was heading to the office.

"But it's Saturday," she complained. "I thought we could do something together."

"I have a murder story to follow up on," he said, firmly back in reporter mode. "I need to call the medical examiner's office, the State Police, lots to follow up on." He kissed her on the check. "Maybe we can do something later." Then he was out the door.

Sitting behind his desk in his office, he stared at the note. He took particular notice of the capital letters in "The Pillowcase." It wasn't just that all three murder victims had their heads covered with a pillowcase. It was stated as if it were a proper noun, like someone's name. He fired up the computer on his desk and went to a search engine, typing in the words: The Pillowcase.

The list that popped up on his screen started with links to linen companies but was soon followed by another reference: a series of murders committed by an unknown culprit dubbed The Pillowcase.

Brian stared at the screen, his mouth agape. He couldn't believe what he was seeing. He clicked on a link and began reading. A string of murders had taken place throughout New England—seven known victims, male and female. The bodies were mostly found in wooded or deserted areas. One was found in an abandoned barn, one at the bottom of a dried-up well, and one beneath a railroad trestle. The victims had two things in common: they were all strangled, and they were all found with a pillowcase over their head.

There was no pattern to where the bodies were found—some in Rhode Island, Connecticut, Massachusetts, and Vermont, none in Maine or New Hampshire. Most of the locations were fairly remote but not what would be considered very rural, at least at the time. And here was the real kicker: *the murderer was never identified and never caught.* The killings spanned a decade. Then all of a sudden they stopped. No suspect was ever named. No one was ever brought to justice. The killer just faded away.

Being a reporter on a cop beat for many years, Brian was surprised that he wasn't familiar with the story. But he saw the reason why. The last murder attributed to The Pillowcase, before he seemed to disappear forever, was more than fifty years ago.

Brian stepped out of his office. Beverly Crump and Isaac Monck were at their desks, typing away. He glanced from one to the other. Bev was in her late fifties; Isaac a little older. Both of them would have been kids at the time. And that would have been at the end of the killing reign.

"Either of you ever heard of a serial killer known as The Pillowcase?" he asked, eyes darting back and forth between the two. He was met by perplexed glances.

"No," Bev said. "Though it's a cute moniker."

No, Brian thought. Not if you'd seen what I saw in the train station. He looked at Isaac.

The older man scratched his head with the eraser end of a pencil, as if trying to unearth some forgotten memory. "I have a vague recollection," he said. "Something a long time ago, when I was a kid." He closed his eyes for a second, and then reopened them. He shrugged. "Not sure. You need to talk to someone really old."

Brian licked his lips, thinking. "Thanks anyway," he said, grabbing his camera and a notebook and heading out the door. In a minute he was across the street at the police station, greeting Wanda as he entered.

"Chief around?"

She looked up at him with a smile. "He's out."

"Any idea where?"

She gave him a look of reluctance to answer.

"Please," he said, with a smile.

She sighed. "He's checking out a house on Whispering Lane."

"What's going down?"

She cocked her head. "Someone reported seeing lights at night at a vacant house that's up for sale."

Didn't sound like anything important. "Let him know I need to talk to him," he said, turning to head out the door. He stopped. "Make that, I'd like to talk to him."

Wanda smiled. "Sure thing."

Once outside, Brian stood on the sidewalk, hands on his hips, thinking. Something Isaac had said resonated with him. Talk to someone really old. Well, Brian just happened to know the oldest guy in town.

He drove to Cheshire Road, to the rooming house, parking in front. As he approached the two-story structure, he noticed a man leaning on the railing of the second-floor porch. The man had thin hair and glasses and was looking down. When Brian got close enough to the house, he recognized the man as the clerk he had seen at Wibbels' Fruit Market and Real Estate. There was something else familiar about the man, the way he stood against the railing, but he couldn't quite place it.

When Brian walked up the front steps, he saw Rolfe Krimmer sitting on the first floor porch, Boston Post Cane in hand. He was sitting next to the man in the wheelchair, playing dominoes.

"Howdy, Mr. Krimmer," Brian said. His greeting was returned with a warm smile.

"You're the newspaper boy," Rolfe said, less a question than a statement.

"Yes, you remember." Which was good. It meant the man's mind was still sharp despite his age.

"Never forget a face," he said. "Even though I've tried sometimes." He looked at the man beside him and laughed, tapping his cane on the floorboards of the porch. "Where's my manners though, this is Linley Droth." He indicated the man in the wheelchair.

Droth lifted his hat off his head with his remaining hand, tipping it before placing it back on his head. "Greetings," was all he said, with a bit of a lisp. His hair hung in stringy clumps to his shoulders.

"You can call him Doc," Rolfe said. "He's accustomed to that."

"Nice to meet you," Brian said, glad the man hadn't extended his three-fingered hand. It would have felt awkward shaking it. Brian sat on an empty seat beside Rolfe.

"What brings you out our way on a nice sunny day like this?" Rolfe asked.

"I came to see you."

The old man chuckled. "In need of more stories of a life less extraordinary?" He laughed again, as did Linley Droth.

"I thought you might be able to help me with something, using that accumulation of years of knowledge."

"That's a fancy way of saying I'm old," Rolfe said to Linley, both men grinning. "Fire away," he said to Brian.

"I'm trying to learn about an old serial killer, dating more than fifty years back. Killed some people throughout New England. The police dubbed him The Pillowcase."

Rolfe gave him a blank stare, and Brian couldn't tell if he was thinking or just plain stumped. The old man scratched the top of his white head. "Hmmm," he muttered, closing his eyes for a moment. For a second, Brian thought the man had fallen asleep, but then his eyes popped open and he banged his cane on the floorboards. "Dagnabbit. I do recall something. Long time ago it was. I was a young man." He paused, staring at Brian. "Don't recall them using that term serial killer back then."

"No, probably not," Linley added. He was not nearly as old as Rolfe.

"But there were some strange killings, in some remote towns."

"Strangulations?" Brian said, not meaning to pose it as a question.

Rolfe thought this over hard before nodding. "Yes, I suppose that's what they were. I think. I don't quite recall. I was working on the train line back then. Remember passengers gossiping about it from time to time. Had folks kind of shook up. Don't believe they ever caught the fella."

"No," Brian said. "They never did."

The old man nodded. "Not much else I remember. That was a long time ago. Killings happened back then you know. People today think those things didn't happen in the good old days. But folks killed each other then, just like they do now. Just didn't always get so much attention in the news. Your kind changed that." He poked a finger toward Brian. "Killing's big news nowadays."

"Can't argue with you there," Brian said, not even wanting to defend himself.

"Don't know what more I can tell you," Rolfe said, shrugging. "It was a long time ago."

"Very long," Linley Droth reiterated.

Brian stood up. "Well, thank you for your time." He reached out to shake the old man's hand.

"That's all I got is time," Rolfe said, laughing. "Just don't know how much more of it."

"Plenty, I'm sure," Brian said.

He turned to the man in the wheelchair. "Nice to meet you, Mr. Droth." He started to extend a hand, thought better of it, and pulled it back.

Droth tipped his white hat and smiled.

Brian walked to his car. Before he got in, he looked back and saw the small man still leaning on the second-floor railing. He got into his car and drove around the loop to where Whispering Lane connected to Cheshire. He looked down the road and saw the police chief's car and another cruiser in front of a house. He also saw a State Police vehicle. Wanda hadn't mentioned the State Police checking out the house with Chief Treece. Odd, he thought, wondering if she purposely kept that information from him.

He turned onto Whispering Lane. Day Shift Alvin stood sentry outside the front door to the small saltbox-style home. In the front yard was a For Sale sign with a picture of Leo Wibbels, with his smiling face, squinty eyes, and silver peach-fuzz hair.

Brian walked up the brick walkway.

"Hey, Alvin," he said, greeting the patrol officer, who managed a grunt. "What's going on?"

The officer shrugged. "Crime scene. Sort of."

"So you can't let me in?"

"That'd be right."

"Can you let the chief know I'm here? Please."

"Sure," Alvin said, and almost cracked a smile. He disappeared inside for a brief moment and returned to the front stoop. "Said he'd be out in a bit."

"Okay. Thanks."

Brian stood on the front lawn, waiting and trying to have patience. It was hot. The sun burned bright in a cloudless blue sky. He wondered what this house had to do with anything. But the State Police were here, so it had some importance. There was no crime scene tape, nor any other vehicles, so he doubted another murder had taken place. He took a couple pictures of the house just in case, with Day Shift Alvin in the shots, standing guard. The officer seemed to take pleasure in being part of the photo.

Brian looked around. No one was about, which seemed odd for a Saturday afternoon. What were people doing? Over on Cheshire, he could see the chimney sweep up on the roof of one of the houses, whistling while he worked. It reminded him he still hadn't gotten the guy's number to call about cleaning his own chimney.

Finally, Chief Treece stepped outside, greeting Brian with a warm smile.

"What's happening here, Noah?" Brian asked, looking up at the quiet house.

"Broke a big case today," he said, peaking Brian's interest.

"Yeah? What?"

"Found out who's been pilfering fruit from Wibbels' market." The chief grinned.

Brian was confused. "And that brought the State Police out?"

Noah chuckled. "Not exactly." He looked back at the house. "Turns out this is where Ruth Snethen was hiding out."

"Really?" Now Brian was interested.

The chief nodded. "The place has been on the market for a while. Owners had moved out several months ago. The place has been empty, except for some staging furniture. But one of the neighbors reporting seeing lights on some nights. Thought it was strange, decided to give us a call. Looks like she's been squatting here for a while. Found some apple cores and orange peels in the kitchen sink. Figure she's been the one stealing the fruit from Wibbels' bins."

"How'd you figure it was her?"

He shrugged. "We can't be positive just yet. Wickwire's dusting for prints. But we found some of your newspaper clippings about the trunk and the asylum fire." Noah squinted into the bright sun. "And we found a scrap of paper with your name and the phone number to the newspaper office scribbled on it. Steem seems pretty confident she's been here."

Brian looked back at the house and then the For Sale sign. "When was the last time this place had a showing?"

"Don't know. We'll check with Leo on that." He glanced around the street. "Nice neighborhood. Wouldn't be surprised if they've had someone look at the home recently, even though the housing market's a bit down."

"Like everything else," Brian added. He thought about the note and pulled it from his pocket, handing it to Noah. "Got another message this morning."

Noah took it from him and opened it. Brian studied his face as the chief read the note. There was no obvious reaction. If anything, his expression, or lack thereof, showed puzzlement.

He looked up at Brian. "The Pillowcase?"

"Ever heard of him?"

The chief shook his head. "No."

"A serial killer."

Noah's eyes grew wide. "Wow." He looked back at the note, as if he'd missed something. "How come I haven't heard of him?"

"Because he stopped killing over fifty years ago."

"Arrested?"

Brian shook his head. "Never caught. The cases remain unsolved."

Noah fanned the note, looking back at the house before them. "I wonder...."

"If Steem knows about it?"

The chief nodded.

"He seemed pretty emphatic that I not write anything about the victims being found with pillowcases covering their heads."

"But why would the guy return after all this time?"

Brian thought about the trunk in the attic and figured Noah was thinking the same thing. "Unfinished business?"

Noah took the note inside to talk to Captain Steem, and once again Brian waited patiently outside. It was only a few minutes before the chief returned with the State Police captain in tow, an unpleasant look on his face.

"When did this arrive?" Steem demanded, waving the note.

"Just today," Brian answered. "Brought it right to you guys, just to show you how cooperative I'm being." He smiled but got no reaction from the captain.

"I want to keep this as evidence."

Brian nodded. He was reluctant to give it up, but he already knew everything he could from the note. "Sure thing."

"And I'd like you to turn over all the other notes."

"I can do that. It's nice to see you taking an interest in them."

"Of course, they've been contaminated as evidence."

Brian shrugged. "Sorry."

"Let me know directly if any others turn up," he said, looking at Chief Treece as if to usurp whatever authority the local official had.

"I will," Brian said, "but I plan on reading them first."

Steem bit his lower lip and nodded. "I expect you would. Thanks for bringing this by." He turned to go back into the house.

"Captain," Brian called, and Steem stopped in his tracks and turned around. "What's the significance of The Pillowcase? Do you know about him?"

"Of course," he said, matter-of-factly. "Most cops do. But that was an unsolved case from a very long time ago. I can't imagine any bearing it would have today. The murders stopped half a century ago. That most likely means the killer died, or ended up in prison for some other crime. He's either rotting in a cell somewhere or rotting in a grave." He waved the note in his hand. "Whoever's sending these is playing some kind of game with you. Maybe it means something, maybe it means nothing. I'll look into that."

He started to turn again.

"So you don't think this Pillowcase character has come back?"

Steem's body tensed. "No, I don't. Killers don't just stop. Where the hell would he have been all this time?" The captain walked into the house, slamming the door shut behind him.

Noah looked at Brian and shrugged. There was nothing for the chief to say. Brian said goodbye and walked to his car. Before getting in, he stopped. He was thinking about what Captain Steem had said, about where The Pillowcase had been all these years.

Fifty years is a long time for a killer to lay low. Killers don't retire do they? Steem didn't think that was possible. As Brian opened his car door, he looked across town to the ridge and the burned-out hulk of the Mustard House looming over the town. It should be torn down, but it was still the scene of an unsolved crime.

The mystery of where the patients of the asylum were was also unsolved. Maybe there was only one patient in the Wymbs Institute. Maybe that's why the doctor didn't need a large staff. Maybe that one patient was held behind barred windows for decades, looking at the town below. Maybe that one patient was the only survivor of the fire that destroyed the mansion. And maybe that one patient was The Pillowcase, who got his freedom the night the place burned to the ground.

Chapter 13

MEMORIES OF A RETIRED DETECTIVE

Brian was surprised how little information he could find about The Pillowcase. He contacted reporters from the towns in the four states where the murders had taken place. None of the staff librarians at any of the newspapers covering those towns could dig up much information. They were unknown murders committed for unknown reasons and were long forgotten. He even contacted the police departments in those towns. Everyone involved with investigating the cases was long retired, some no longer alive. Not one of the seven departments holding jurisdiction even kept an active file open on the cases. They remained unsolved.

The victims had nothing in common, all seemingly chosen at random. There was a farmer in Vermont, a mailman in Connecticut, a housewife in Massachusetts. Nothing connected the victims.

Brian did finally manage to get a hold of a retired FBI agent who had worked on the case, a man named Gordon Kreck in an assisted-living facility in Virginia. Brian called him from his office at *The Hollow News*. Fortunately the man still seemed to have most of his faculties.

"Of course I remember The Pillowcase murders," Kreck said, wheezing. "Spent several years on that case."

Brian's pulse quickened. "Is there anything you can tell me about it?"

"Not much to say," Kreck answered. "Never saw a case with so few clues in my whole damn career. It was just a dead end. There wasn't any evidence, no witnesses, no motive, nothing. It was like the devil himself snuffed those victims."

"And there were never any suspects?" Brian was disappointed.

"Suspects? Hell no. I think we took a couple plaster casts of some footprints. Size nine and a half. Did you know that is the most common shoe size of the average male? Anybody could have committed those killings."

"And nothing more came of the case?" Brian's was dejected. "Even years later."

"The killings stopped, just like that."

Brian could imagine the old man snapping his fingers.

"And you closed the case on it."

"Pretty much. With nothing to go on, we just packed up the notes and photos and filed them away. Probably sitting in a box on some shelf at the FBI headquarters' warehouse."

"How could a serial killing case just end like that?"

The old man cleared phlegm from his throat. "Listen, there were some who even doubted it was a serial killing. Some started to think it wasn't one person committing the murders."

"But the pillowcases?" That couldn't be just a coincidence, Brian thought.

"Yeah, I know, that was the lynchpin. But a few at the Bureau started to wonder if some of them were just copycat killings. The first ones made big headlines, and sometimes people just get ideas."

"Do you really think so?" It seemed unlikely to Brian.

"There were seven killings spread out over nearly ten years. That's a long time to go between killings, even for a psychopath. And then they just stopped. A thrill killer doesn't just stop."

"Unless something happened to him."

The man cleared his throat again. "True. He could have died, moved to another part of the country, or even overseas. Some people believe Jack the Ripper moved to America. There were killings at the Chicago's World's Fair around the same time that some think were committed by him. Or maybe The Pillowcase ended up in prison for a murder or crime unrelated to the others."

Brian remembered Steem suggesting the same thing. "But what do you really think?"

He heard a sigh over the receiver. "I only saw the bodies of the last four victims by the time I got involved in the case. And one thing always struck me as odd."

"And what's that?" Brian asked.

"Those damn pillowcases were all the same type. Like they all came from the same set of linens."

"Really," Brian perked up. "Were you ever able to trace them?"

"No." Brian could hear disappointment in the old man's voice. "They were a pretty common brand. Nothing unique to them. But seeing those bodies with those damn pillowcases on their heads sure made me think the same person committed the murders."

"And they were all strangulations, right?"

"That's right. Initial investigators thought the victims were smothered in the pillowcases, but that wasn't the case. In every slaying, the death was ruled strangulation."

Brian was curious. "Then what was the point of the pillowcase? It's not like the culprit was worried the victim would be able to identify him."

"We had an FBI psychiatrist we consulted on the case, and we talked about that. He had a theory."

"And what was it?"

"He thought maybe the killer couldn't bear to look into the eyes of his victims. So he covered their faces with a pillowcase."

Brian let this sink in. "Almost like he was ashamed of what he was doing. A killer with a conscience?"

"Never met one of those," Kreck said. "Maybe it was more of a way to dehumanize the victim."

"I guess that's possible," Brian said. "I want to thank you for your time."

The old man laughed. "Time, that's all I got left." Brian remembered Rolfe Krimmer saying the same thing. Probably something most old people related to. "Why the interest in that old case, sonny? Writing a book or something?"

"No," Brian said, though the idea intrigued him. He then told Mr. Kreck about the murders in Smokey Hollow.

"You don't think this guy has started killing again do you?"

"I don't know," Brian said, and he didn't.

"God, that was fifty some odd years ago. Where the hell's he been hiding all these years?"

"That's what I'd like to know." Brian meant to say this to himself, but realized he had spoken it into the phone.

"Well, I hope not," Kreck said. "I still picture to this day seeing the bodies with those pillowcases. Gives me the creeps thinking about it."

"I know what you mean," Brian said, and he did. He still had the image of the pillowcase on Ruth Snethen's head. He couldn't shake it. Especially since it had shown up in that dream the other night.

When Brian sat in his office, putting the stories together for that week's edition, he felt grateful for what he had to work with, even though there were still too many missing pieces. But that was the newspaper business. Every article was incomplete. All you could do was go with what information you had at the moment. He had two murders to write about and the arrest of the town's assistant fire chief for the Mustard House arson.

Of course, he had to make sure he put the Dump Fest preview on the front page. But the whole top of the edition was devoted to the grim news unfolding in town. He felt bad about putting the story on the Knackerman inside, but the photo of Hester Pigott at his work table was better hidden inside the newspaper. There was enough graphic material on the front.

Brian decided not to mention the pillowcases. He partially did this as a favor to Steem, hoping to smooth things over with the State Police captain. Steem was appreciative when Brian called to let him know. He wouldn't use the term *happy*; he doubted Steem knew happy, but he could tell in the captain's voice that he was relieved.

But part of it was out of necessity. Brian didn't have enough information on the old serial killer to really bring that angle into the story of the recent murders. Keeping the information on the pillowcases quiet also gave him a slight advantage over the other reporters. None of the other media knew that detail, and he figured Steem would keep it that way.

Taking a break, Brian walked to Wibbels' Fruit Market and Real Estate to see if Leo was there. When he walked in, the owner was near the back of the shop opening a crate of fruit with a crowbar. As he walked down the rows of fruit and vegetable displays, he saw the sales clerk behind the counter—the man with the glasses he had seen on the second-floor porch at the rooming house.

"Hello, Mr. Keays," Leo said over the screeching sound made when he pried the nails loose from the crate cover. "Need some last minute information about the festival?" The man was smiling.

"No, I'm all set with that. Already have it laid out in tomorrow's edition."

"Front page?"

"Of course."

The man clapped him on the shoulder. "Good to hear. You don't know what this means to the town." He set the crowbar down on a nearby counter.

"I guess I don't," Brian said, though he didn't think Leo was really listening.

The man grabbed the crate and began walking down one of the aisles. Brian followed.

"So, to what do I owe this visit?" He set the crate down and began scooping the cranberries into a bin.

"I'm sure you are aware Ruth Snethen had been living in a house you've been trying to sell."

"Of course. The State Police asked me a few questions about that."

"Yes," Brian said. "I heard. You told them you didn't know she had been staying there."

"That's right. I represent a lot of houses in town, several of them vacant. Real estate's been a bit slow in this economy. Hadn't had a showing at that one in several weeks."

"I gather that."

"That's why you got such a good deal on your house." Wibbels flashed his smile.

"And I certainly appreciate all the help you provided."

"You and Darcie like the house?"

"Very much so," Brian said. "Of course, with the exception of the trunk in the attic."

Wibbels grin evaporated. "Unfortunate. I should have done a more thorough check of the house before listing it."

"Hindsight," Brian said.

Wibbels stopped what he was doing and looked at Brian with his squinting eyes. "So what did you come see me for?"

At that moment, Brian wasn't really sure. Everything Wibbels said corroborated what Steem and Noah had told him. Ruth Snethen broke into the vacant house and had been basically living there. Obviously the woman had feared for her life and didn't want to stay at the retirement complex she had moved to after Brian bought her house. And as it turned out, she had good reason to be afraid.

"I guess I'm just double checking my facts," Brian said. "Want to make sure I have everything accurate."

Stepping outside, Brian looked up and down Main Street. It was quiet. He looked up at the marquee of the cinema. The "Y" and "C" were still there, but the "Y" was crooked and looked like it was barely clinging to the marquee, as if a strong breeze would knock it loose. The problem was, there was no breeze. It was another hot day, too many for this early in the summer. And there hadn't been rain in a while to cool things off.

Brian saw Jonas Fitchen in the window of his taxidermist shop, setting up a stuffed fox. The display of glass eyes stared out the window. *Don't watch me*, Brian thought. It made him think of Marshall lying in that tiny coffin in the graveyard beyond the cemetery. He wondered if Simon Runck was still at the county jail, or if anyone had posted bail for him by now. Since the murder of Ruth Snethen took place while Runck was in county lockup, it paid to reason he was not involved in the murders, at least not directly. But he had burned down the institute.

Time to pay Noah a visit. He walked to the police station. The chief was in his office and welcomed him. Even though Brian had talked to him first thing in the morning, he still asked about any new developments.

"Got something you will be interested in," Noah said with a smile.

"That's what I like to hear." Brian whipped out his notebook.

"Looks like our former assistant fire chief has quite a history."

Brian looked up. "As in?"

"Apparently, the fire department he worked at before he came to Smokey Hollow had a string of unsolved arsons."

"Where was that?"

"Up north in Coos County." Noah named some town Brian had never heard of. "Mostly abandoned houses and small buildings. No injuries. But no one was ever caught. At least a dozen cases of arson. They stopped when Runck left there."

"So he's a regular firebug." Brian thought that odd since the firefighter had told him he was afraid of fire. He had said that he'd moved to Smokey Hollow because he thought it'd be a safe town with little activity. Brian looked at Noah. "Any unsolved arsons in this town since he's been on the department."

"Two," Noah said, "not counting the dumpster blaze at the shoe factory the night Marshall was hung."

"That was obviously a ploy to get Runck and the others out of the station. So what are the two?"

"The Mustard House fire, of course," Noah said.

"And the other?"

The chief grinned. "That's what I thought you'd be interested in."

Brian leaned forward in his chair.

"The other arson was a fire at your house, back when Ruth Snethen lived there."

Chapter 14

VISIT WITH A FIREBUG

Brian wanted to see if Simon Runck would grant him an interview. Noah had some connections at the jail and said he'd make a call and see if it was possible. In the meantime, Brian paid a visit to the fire station to see Chief Warren Shives with the news Noah had given him.

"There was no connection to Simon concerning those arsons up north," Shives told him. "There were no suspicions. Otherwise we never would have hired him. It does explain a few things about the fire at the Wymbs Institute, though."

"Such as?"

"I was out of town the night of the blaze," Shives said. "Simon took the initial call and was in charge when the first crews got to the scene. In a small town like this, with any kind of a serious fire, a mutual aid call goes out to surrounding towns immediately."

"And that didn't happen here?"

Shives shook his head. "Simon delayed the call for mutual aid. And delayed calling me. By the time I got to the scene, Simon had already given the surround-and-drown order, giving up on any real attempt to save the structure."

"Of course," Brian said. "He wanted the place to burn to the ground."

"That's apparent now. Never would have suspected it."

"Tell me about the fire at my house." That's what most concerned Brian.

"A small blaze. Started by the bulkhead in back of the house. We got there right away and quickly had it contained. Minimal damage."

"And it was arson?"

Shives nodded. "That's what the state fire marshal determined. They and the police investigated it. They came up empty."

"And Runck was never suspected?"

Shives seemed offended. "No reason to. He was a great employee."

"Hmm," Brian thought, looking at his notes from what Noah told him. "How long ago was the fire at my house?"

Shives tipped his head back, closing his eyes for a second. "About seven years," he said upon opening them.

Brian scribbled dates down, forming a timeline in his notes. "And how long had Runck been on the force before that."

"Couple years."

"And he came right here from the fire department up north?"

Shives hesitated. "No," he said. "Not quite. It was about four years after he left that department."

Brian looked up. "Where did he work between then?" He wondered if he worked at some other firehouse and committed other arsons.

Shives shrugged. "Not really sure."

Brian lowered his notebook. This sounded odd. "What do you mean not sure?" He looked at his notes, flipping back a page. "There was a four-year gap from when he left his last firefighting job and started here, and you don't know where he spent it?"

"That's right," Shives said, his voice stern.

Brian slumped back in his chair. "Was it on his resume?"

"I didn't see his resume."

Now Brian was dumbfounded. They had hired Runck as an assistant fire chief. That was a pretty important position. "Why not?"

Shives leaned forward over his desk. "Listen, I don't do the hiring around here. All municipal positions are hired through the Board of Selectmen's office."

"The selectmen?"

"Yes," Shives said, sitting back. "So if you want to know any more than what I can provide you, I suggest you talk to Eldon Winch."

Brian certainly intended to. As he got up to leave, he thought of one more question and turned back. "Did Runck have his ventriloquist dummy when he worked for that other fire department?"

"Yes," Shives said, a curious look on his face. "Had it for some time from what I've heard."

Brian wondered if Runck brought Marshall to the interview process, grinning a bit at the thought. He would ask Winch that as well.

When he left the station, he got a call from Noah telling him an interview with Runck was set up at the county jail. It was only a half-hour ride up Route 113, and Brian managed to smoke five cigarettes on the ride and down a cup of coffee.

Now as he sat on the other side of a plexi-glass window waiting for Runck to arrive, his nerves were jittery. He doodled in his notepad. When Runck was led to the seat on the other side of the glass, the man seemed nervous as well.

Brian picked up the phone to connect with the man opposite him. "Hello, Assistant Chief Runck," he said, hoping that extending the aura of authority would encourage the man to cooperate.

"No more, I guess," Runck said, his voice sad. His eyes looked bloodshot. Maybe he wasn't sleeping well.

"Thanks for seeing me," Brian said.

"I've really made a mess of things," he said. "It just got out of control."

"They know about the other fires," Brian said, taking a gamble, not knowing if Steem had already spoken to Simon about the arsons. "The ones in the town you used to work for."

Runck showed little reaction, though his eyes dropped. "That was a long time ago. I was younger then."

"But you don't deny you started them."

He looked up. "Not exactly."

"What does that mean?"

"I was more like an accomplice."

"How's that?"

"Marshall always started them. He liked fires. He was obsessed." He looked up, making eye contact with Brian. "I tried to stop him, but he never listened to me." His eyes pleaded for understanding.

"You couldn't stop him, could you?"

Runck shook his head. "No. Marshall was stronger than me. I never liked fire. That's why I became a firefighter, to stop fires. But I couldn't stop Marshall."

Brian remembered watching the interrogation footage with Steem the night Runck was arrested. He had wondered then if it was all an act. Now he felt certain it wasn't.

"Did you stop setting fires when you came to Smokey Hollow?"

"Yes. I had gotten better."

"*You* had gotten better? I thought Marshall had the problem."

Runck's brows dipped as his eyes narrowed. He looked confused. "I meant we got better. The two of us. We stopped setting fires. I mean he stopped."

"What about the fire at Ruth Snethen's house? Where I live now."

The large man sat back in his chair, his shoulders slumped. He looked like a child caught in a lie and trying to figure a way out of it. He let out a long sigh. "That was Marshall again. I thought we had overcome it, but he had a relapse."

"Why? Did something happen?"

Runck leaned forward, his face almost hitting the glass. "It wasn't his fault! He was tempted." His voice rose, prompting concern on the face of the jail guard standing nearby.

"Tempted by what?" Brian asked, relieved that the guard made no attempt to interrupt their conversation.

"Not what, who."

"Who?"

"Someone convinced Marshall to set the fire. I tried to talk him out of it. You have to believe me. We had made such progress."

"Who wanted him to set the fire?"

"I don't know. He wouldn't tell me. Marshall was very secretive. He said it would be dangerous if I knew."

"Is it the same person who told you to set the fire at the Mustard House?"

"Told Marshall," he corrected. "Yes, Marshall said it was the same person."

"And you don't know who this person is?"

"No. I never spoke to him. He only spoke to Marshall."

"But you know it was a he?"

"That's what Marshall said. A man spoke to him, in private."

Brian was frustrated. If only Runck could see that the man had to have talked to him. But in Simon's world, Marshall was his own identity, with interactions separate from him. "Did this man want the fire set because the trunk was in the house?"

Runck looked at him through the glass. His face was pale. "I swear I knew nothing about that trunk. And I didn't kill Dr. Wymbs either."

Of course he hadn't. It was obvious to Brian and the authorities that all three murders were committed by the same person (*The Pillowcase?*) and Runck was here the night of Ruth Snethen's murder.

"Have you heard about the other murders?" Brian asked.

Runck's hands twitched and he almost dropped the receiver. "Yes. There's a lot of talk about it in here amongst the guards."

"Do you know who might be involved?"

He shook his head. "No."

"The culprit is still on the loose. A lot of people are worried."

"That's why I told them I didn't want to be bailed out."

"Told who?"

"Chief Shives and the others at the department. They wanted to pool money to bail me out, but I didn't want any part of it." He leaned forward again and his voice dropped to just above a whisper. "It's not safe out there."

"Who are you afraid of?"

Runck looked around him, and then faced Brian. "I don't know, but I don't want to find out. That's why Marshall was killed, to keep him from talking.

"Because Marshall knew the person who told him to set the fires?"

"Exactly."

This was no help, Brian thought. "I'm sure you'll be safe in here." He was about to end the conversation when he thought about something. He flipped back a few pages in his notepad. "Simon, you said you and Marshall got better and stopped setting fires till he had a relapse."

"That's right."

"Did you get treatment somewhere?"

His question was met by a stone face. Color flowed back into the man's cheeks.

"It's good if you got help," Brian said, trying to allay the man's concerns. "There's no shame in that."

"We got better," was all the man said.

"Simon, there was a four-year gap between your last firefighting job and the time you got hired at the Smokey Hollow Fire Department."

The man thought for a moment. "Sounds about right."

"Was that when you were getting treatment?"

Runck bit his lower lip. It looked like he was struggling to hold back his response. "Yes," he finally said.

"Where did you get treatment, Simon?"

"I'd rather not say."

Brian felt dejected. He tried to sound more concerned than inquisitive. "It's okay, Simon. You're safe in here. You don't have anything to worry about."

Runck's eyes kept moving around.

"Please tell me where you and Marshall were getting treated during those four years, Simon." He didn't think the man would respond, though Brian figured he knew the answer. He just wanted to hear it from Runck himself.

Finally the former assistant fire chief responded.

"The Wymbs Institute."

Chapter 15

DUCKS IN A ROW

When Thursday's edition came out, Brian thought it was even better than the previous week's. He had two murders and the arrest of former Assistant Fire Chief Simon Runck as a serial arsonist. His story on the murder of Ruth Snethen even contained a first-person sidebar about his discovering the body. That was good enough to win a press award, he believed. He also included his exclusive interview with Runck, taking a peek into the disturbed mind of a firebug.

But to keep good faith with the State Police, he had contacted Steem after his interview at the county jail and shared the information Simon had confessed. There was no need to keep it to himself; it was all going into the newspaper anyway. Steem seemed either impressed or pissed that Brian had gotten Runck to speak so openly. Or maybe it was a combination of both. Either way, the State Police captain appreciated Brian being forthcoming with the information and that he chose not to include the detail of the victims' heads being covered with pillowcases.

It was difficult for Brian to leave that out, but he wanted to try to find out a little more about this Pillowcase character before automatically drawing the line to what was going on in Smokey Hollow. And he didn't want any of the other media learning about that detail just yet.

Two things that Runck had revealed had most fascinated Steem. One was that the former firefighter claimed he didn't know about the trunk being in Ruth Snethen's house when he attempted to burn the place down. The second was the fact Simon Runck had spent four years as a patient in the Wymbs Institute.

That little tidbit fascinated everyone involved in the investigation. Brian discussed it with Noah that day. The most important aspect of it was they finally had someone connected to the Mustard House, even if it was ten years ago. Maybe he could recall some of the people on the staff. Maybe he knew some of the other patients. And most important, what if had heard anything about a patient who had been a serial killer known as The Pillowcase?

It was a proud day for Brian. He had put out another great edition. And even though he already had to start preparing for the following week's release, he felt a sense of ease from the deadline stress and could breathe a little easier. He didn't even feel the urge to smoke a cigarette. It was hard being a one-man show (not that Beverly Crump didn't help out a lot, and Isaac handled all the boring sports-and-recreation crap), but he could relax for at least today before thinking about what he needed to do next.

He told Darcie she didn't need to bother with cooking, because he wanted to take her out to dinner at Cully's Pub. Heck, Brian even thought he could manage to eat a steak tonight. The thought of Hester Pigott's knackering job didn't bother him anymore. He wasn't sure how many people would even read the old man's story in today's paper, given all the other juicy articles.

And of course there was the big Dump Festival this weekend. That was something Brian and Darcie could go to together, even though he'd be covering it for the paper. That was the kind of assignment where they could enjoy the festival like regular patrons while he took some notes and photos for *The Hollow News*.

When he got home from work, Darcie was on the telephone.

"I've got to go now," she said to whoever was on the other end. "It was so nice to hear from you, and we'll talk again soon."

His feeling of elation sank a little, and that craving for a cigarette crept back. His immediate urge was to ask her who she was talking with, but he didn't want to sound intrusive. Not after how awful he felt about the flower incident. But as her husband, he wanted to know who she was talking to. It was normal for him to be curious; that's what made him a reporter. It was in his nature.

So he put his smile on when she came into the living room.

"Your day must have been good."

He held up the paper. "A banner day," he said, flashing the large-type headlines about the two murders.

She hugged him, kissing him on the cheek. "I know how much it means to you. I picked up a copy myself today." Her smile faded slightly. "I almost didn't want to read about those poor women. So tragic." Her eyes looked moist.

Don't, he thought to himself. Don't ruin this for me.

"Then we won't think about it the rest of the night," he said. "Let's just be a man and his wife going out on the town." He thought for a second. "Or at least what amounts for a night on the town in Smokey Hollow."

This meant the only restaurant in town, not counting the pizza joint and the breakfast diner. Cully's Pub was the only place that served alcohol in Smokey Hollow besides the Odd Fellows Hall social club. It had only opened ten years ago, when the selectmen rescinded a longtime ordinance banning the serving of alcohol in the town. Thank god that had changed, Brian thought. He didn't know if he could have lived in a town without at least one beer joint. And the fact that it was directly across the street from the newspaper office made it even more of a bonus. A nice cold beer always balanced off the stress of deadline pressure. Not that owner Hale Cullumber kept his beer very cold. And not that a weekly newspaper deadline was that much pressure compared to what Brian had been used to on a daily. But it's different when you're the one doing most of the work, and even a lukewarm beer made it worthwhile.

At Cully's, the hostess sat the Keays in the center of the dining area. They looked over the menu, Brian going right to the beef section. He had crunched down a couple antacids to make sure his stomach would be ready for whatever he decided to send its way. He eyed the listing of the porterhouse steak and set his menu down.

He looked around the other tables, to see who else he might know in the place. He saw Eldon Winch and Leo Wibbels, along with their wives, at one table. That probably meant that the selectman would stop by their table to either praise him or damn him about the placement of the Dump Festival preview. It was on the front page, even though it was at the bottom. What could he expect? There was big news in town, no matter how much some people wanted to pretend it wasn't happening.

Fire Chief Shives and his wife sat at another table, reminding Brian he wanted to ask the chief why he and his firefighters tried to post bail for Simon Runck, considering how poorly his arrest reflected on the department. Jonas Fitchen, the taxidermist, sat at a table by himself. Also sitting alone was the woman who always wore an obvious wig. This time it was chestnut. It looked like too much hair for her age. Brian had asked Beverly Crump about her earlier today, and she had told him that the woman's name was Ivy Mockler and that she owned Wigland. Taking her wigs out for a test run must be her way of advertising her products, he thought. Though the creased, aged look of her face beneath all that youthful hair did not make for a pretty picture.

Hale Cullumber tended bar as usual, pouring drinks for the waitresses to pick up and for the handful of men sitting at the bar. Brian recognized Isaac Monck, his sports editor, and Sherman Thurk, who was no doubt enjoying a beer or two before his nightly sleepwalking adventure. Hopefully he wouldn't stumble upon any dead bodies tonight. Brian knew what that was like and could sympathize with the man. Maybe the beers would help Thurk sleep deeply enough to remain at the rooming house.

Not a bad crowd for a Thursday night. People in town probably couldn't afford to eat out too often. The waitress came to their table and introduced her name as Gwen, asking if they had a chance to look over the menu. Her long hair, pulled into a ponytail, had streaks of gray. She looked to be in her forties. Brian was surprised, since most women that age colored their grays.

Darcie ordered fish and Brian stuck with his steak, the large cut.

"Aren't you Mr. Keays, the newspaper editor?" the waitress asked.

"Yes," he said smiling. "Brian Keays."

"I recognized your picture in the paper today."

Brian had included a headshot of himself with his first-person piece. He thought it important for the community to recognize their newspaper editor. It was a way to be in touch with the readers.

"Thank you," he remarked, flattered by the recognition.

She dropped her smile. "Such terrible things happening in town these days."

So much for forgetting about it for the night. He looked at Darcie, figuring she was reading his thoughts. She tried to keep an upbeat expression. "Yes," he said to the waitress. "Really terrible."

"Makes you wonder if anyone is going to the Dump Fest," Gwen said. "I know I probably won't feel up to it."

"There's no need to let bad news spoil things," Brian said, wishing she would leave and put in their orders.

"You must understand, considering what you two have gone through these past couple weeks."

Darcie looked down, grabbing her water glass and taking a sip. She looked up at the waitress. "We're being strong," she said.

The waitress frowned. "It's hard to be strong sometimes. Believe me." Her smile reappeared. "I'll go put in your order." She spun around and headed toward the kitchen.

Brian looked at his wife, who managed a half smile. "It's hard being a celebrity in town."

She laughed, the effect he was hoping for. It was nice to see her laugh. The two of them hadn't been doing much of that lately. It was good to hear her voice when she was in a good mood. But then he thought about the tail end of the phone call he had walked in on earlier. She had sounded in a good mood then, too, and it was bugging him. Just ask, he told himself. You know you won't rest until you find out.

He knew there was a chance it would ruin the mood of the evening, but if he kept it in, he'd need either another cigarette or more antacids. Just ask.

"So, the phone call today?"

Her lips flatlined. "Yes."

"Anybody I know?" She was reading his mind, but it didn't matter. It was out.

"It was him," she said, locking her eyes on his. Her lower lip fluttered slightly.

He collected himself, careful with what he wanted to say next. "I guess I didn't realize you've been keeping in touch."

She frowned. He had done it now. "We're still friends. I've explained that to you."

He had to admit she had. "I know," he said. "It's just—"

"It's just nothing. There's no need for you to think anything more of it."

She reached her hand across the table and their fingers interlocked.

"I'm here with you," she said, again reading his mind. "I'm going to have a nice dinner with you, and then we are going to our home and we will lie in our bed next to each other." She squeezed his hand. "And maybe if you're not too disgusted by this bulge in my belly, we can make love before falling to sleep."

He smiled, looking into her sweet, pleading eyes. He couldn't help it. He should feel lucky she had chosen to be with him. Brian wasn't sure he had that much to offer her. Maybe that was why he still felt bitter, because he was sure she had made the wrong choice and he felt guilty for it. Brian wanted to think she came back because she deserved him. Even though he really didn't think he deserved her.

He squeezed her hand back. "I won't think about it anymore."

At home, Brian was admiring Darcie as she got ready for bed in the bathroom. It would be nice to make love tonight, and the thought got him a little excited. Then she made a weird noise and vomited into the toilet.

"Okay, no more fish while I'm pregnant," she said, the skin on her face pale and clammy.

"Are you all right?" he asked from the doorway.

"I'll be fine," she said through a grimace and shut the door in his face, though not in a rude way, just in a 'give me some privacy' gesture that he completely understood.

His phone rang, and he was grateful for the distraction.

It was Noah Treece. "Hope I'm not catching you at a bad time?"

Brian looked at the closed bathroom door. "Not at all. What's up?"

"I'm out at Hester Pigott's place," he said. "Got something I'm sure you're going to want to see."

Brian felt a wave of panic swamp him. Not the old guy. Did something happen to him? He could picture a pillowcase pulled down over the old man's owl-like face. God, no, please. "Is Hester—"

"No, no. Hester's fine. He's right here with me"

Brian's heart relaxed. Was this going to keep on, him worrying every night about who in town might fall victim to the strangler? "Then what is it?"

"You really have to see it for yourself. And I know you're going to want to."

That tweaked his curiosity. He glanced at the bathroom door. "Honey?" he said.

"Go," came a muffled voice.

"Are you sure you're okay?"

"I'm fine. Don't worry. Do your thing."

Driving up the winding dirt driveway to Hester Pigott's farm, Brian could see two town police cars parked near the barn. There was no sign of the State Police, which meant Steem and Wickwire either weren't here yet or this case didn't involve them. That kind of disillusioned Brian, and he felt some of his excitement deflate. If the State Police weren't here, then whatever Noah wanted him to see wasn't part of the strangling investigations.

He parked near the cruisers and got out. A spotlight over the doorway to Pigott's barn illuminated the area in front. He could see the Knackerman standing between Chief Treece and Night Shift Alvin. Hester wore his tractor cap, jeans, and a white tank top. The tank top had splatters of red, and Brian thought maybe the old man had been attacked after all. Leave it to his gusto to have thwarted the culprit.

Noah held a flashlight, though it wasn't turned on.

"So what's going on?" Brian asked Noah, then looked at Hester. "Are you okay, Mr. Pigott?"

"Course I am damnabbit," the old man spat. "Been out all night fetchin' a cow carcass over in Vermont, only to come home to this damn thing." The man's face was flushed with rage.

Brian realized that the blood was probably from his knackering and not any scuffle he had been in, and he was glad about that.

"Alvin," Noah said. "Why don't you take Mr. Pigott inside and finish getting his statement. We'll be right along."

The patrolman led the old man into the brightly lit barn.

"So?" Brian said, once he was alone with Noah. "What gives?"

"You have to see this." The chief turned on his flashlight, took a few steps toward the side of the barn, and pointed the beam of light at the ground.

Brian came up beside the chief and stared, not believing what he saw.

Seven sets of duck feet stuck out of the ground.

"What the hell?" was all Brian could think to say. He bent to get a better look.

"There were eight," Noah said. "Hester dug one of the ducks up when he got home, then decided to call us before touching anything else."

"Why would someone do something like this?"

"The worse thing is," Noah started to say. "Judging from the one Hester dug up, he figured they were buried alive."

Brian put his hands on his knees and bent his head. He closed his eyes for a second, picturing those ducks kicking their little webbed feet as they suffocated. He thought of Darcie vomiting and thought about doing it himself. The steak he had stuffed himself with tonight felt unsettled. He straightened and turned to Noah.

"Who would even think of this, Noah? And why?"

"Did you notice how the ducks are in a straight line?" He scanned the flashlight beam along the trail of feet.

"All in a row," Brian muttered. "Do you think that means something?"

"Maybe someone came looking for Hester, and since he wasn't here, left him that."

"Like a message?"

"Or more like a warning. Telling Hester he better keep his ducks in a row."

Brian looked at the chief. "You think our killer did this?"

Noah shrugged. "Entered my mind."

"But what affairs would Hester need to keep in order? Does he have some connection to all this?"

The chief locked eyes with Brian. "Do you think it's a coincidence that this happened the day your story about the Knackerman appeared in the paper?"

Brian thought about that for a moment. "It was just a harmless story about an old man's unusual occupation. How could that—"

Brian didn't get to finish his comment. Hester's voice rang out from the barn and Brian and Noah ran inside, seeing the old man and Alvin standing near the counter on the side.

"It's gone!" Hester yelled.

"What's gone?" Noah asked as they approached the old man.

"The pot of human rib bones!"

Chapter 16

INCIDENT AT A FESTIVAL

Most of the town turned out for the annual Dump Festival on Saturday at the field on Blackberry Road. The attendance surprised Brian as he and Darcie strolled along the grass past booths offering a variety of crafts and food. Maybe this was what the town needed. People could come and enjoy themselves and their fellow town folk without worrying about what had been happening. It was a release everyone deserved, especially Darcie and himself.

Most of the people Brian knew were there, some running vendor booths. Mrs. Picklesmeir had a booth for her flower shop, selling floral arrangements and bouquets. Leo Wibbels had a stand displaying a selection of fruits and vegetables. Other vendors offered handmade crafts, knitted clothing, or homemade canned jams, jellies, and pies.

Brian and Darcie paused at the booth for St. John's Church where Father Scrimsher and Sister Bernice ran a bingo game. There was a crowd of older folk gathered at that one. Brian saw Isaac Monck and Beverly Crump, bingo cards laid out before them and markers in their hands. Sister Bernice pulled a bingo ball from the cage she had spun, and Father Scrimsher announced the letter/number combo as participants frantically searched their cards. As he and Darcie walked away, he heard Bev cry, "Bingo!"

Another part of the festival grounds was set aside as a children's section, with face painting, pony rides, and a petting zoo with sheep, alpacas, and goats from local farms. Nearby was a hot air balloon, tethered to the ground, where rides were available.

"Would you like to go up in that?" Brian asked Darcie.

"Goodness no," she said, her hand dropping to her belly and caressing it. "I think that would make me too queasy."

In the center of the field was a carousel, calliope music playing, kids and adults alike taking spins on the wooden horses. Brian figured that would be out of the question as well. If going up and down would bother Darcie, going round and round would be even worse.

At the far end of the field was a beer tent where Hale Cullumber dispensed what was most likely lukewarm beer. If he couldn't keep his kegs cold at his pub, what chance did he have here where the hot sun poured down on a field devoid of shade? Still, the beer tent was where Brian and Darcie ended up.

"I need to quench my thirst," he said, as they stepped to the counter. "A nice cold one," he said to Hale, smirking. He turned to Darcie. "How about a glass of wine?"

"No," she said, almost offended he had asked. "I can't have that." Once again her hand found her belly as if to remind her, or him, of what was in there.

"Just a little glass of wine. That can't hurt, can it?"

"No," she said. "I'm taking good care of this baby."

He had no doubt about that. He thanked Hale as he accepted the plastic cup of beer, frothing at the top. He took a sip, surprised that it wasn't as warm as he thought it would be. Maybe the hot weather made the beverage seem cooler than it really was. He noticed Hale was drinking a beer between waiting on customers.

"Hello, Brian," called a voice, and he turned to see Eldon Winch and his wife approach.

The foursome exchanged cordial greetings.

"Quite a turnout, huh?" Eldon surveyed the crowd.

"Yes, certainly is," Brian agreed.

"Hope you get lots of good pictures," Eldon said. "Will be good to see something pleasant on the front page of your paper."

"I haven't taken any shots yet," he replied. "But I certainly will."

"The carousel always makes for nice photos. Lots of smiling faces there."

"I'll keep that in mind." Brian had actually looked at past issues of *The Hollow News* to see the previous coverage of the Dump Festival. Every edition had a shot of people on the carousel. He'd hate to disappoint anyone this year.

"The cow-pie roulette is about to begin," Eldon said. "Hope you've bought a square."

"That I can't miss," he said, and he was serious. It was one of those too-hard-to-believe events he needed to witness. He ushered Darcie over to a roped-off section of the field. People had gathered along the ropes.

Brian bought a ticket for a numbered square and found a spot along one side.

The field inside the roped area had been chalked off in a grid, with numbers assigned to each square. Brian looked at his number, 42, and moved along the crowd until he could get a decent view of his square. He spotted Rolfe Krimmer standing along the rope with his Boston Post Cane in hand, and they stood in an empty space next to him, greeting the old man.

"This is unbelievable," Brian said to Darcie, as a man led a cow by a rope to the center of the field.

"Never would have experienced this back in the city." Darcie laughed.

"No argument there," he said.

The man in the field removed the rope from the cow's neck and walked away. At first the cow didn't move. It bent its head, bit off a clump of grass, and began chewing, still not moving. This went on for about fifteen minutes.

"Not quite as exciting as I thought it'd be," Brian said, looking at Darcie.

She smiled back. She seemed happy, and he liked that. Everything lately had been dragging her down, and he hadn't been much help. Her pregnancy should be a time of bliss, but somehow that had changed when they opened that damned trunk.

"Oh, look," she exclaimed, pointing to the field.

He had been about to kiss her, but now looked where she indicated. The cow was on the move. Well, he guessed one could call it moving. The animal took about three steps in one direction and then stopped, head lowered to grab another bite of grass. Brian looked down at the numbered slip he had paid five dollars for, thinking he had made a bad investment. What the heck, he thought, it was all for a good cause.

People along the rope began calling and shouting at the cow, trying to get the beast to move toward their squares. Some even yelled out the name Bessie, though Brian wasn't sure if that was really the cow's name.

"Is that fair?" Brian asked no one. "Can they do that?" It seemed like cheating to try to coerce the cow to a specific spot.

"Of course it is," Rolfe said, before yelling at the cow. The old man put his fingers in his mouth and let rip a piercing whistle that almost silenced the crowd.

"Go ahead," Darcie said, poking him in the side. "Call it this way."

Brian looked at his wife. Even though she was smiling, he knew she was serious. He looked at the cow. People on all sides of the grid were hollering and whistling, like the cow was a pet they were trying to attract. He was about to call himself and had even partially opened his mouth, but before he could utter a sound, he felt ridiculous. He didn't want to embarrass himself. The whole thing seemed silly.

"I can't believe all these grown adults are cheering for a cow to take a shit," he said.

"Oh, loosen up," Darcie said, laughing. "Don't be such a stick in the mud."

Before he could respond, there was a roar from the crowd and he looked over. The cow was now in a trot, toward the northwest corner of the grid.

"Hey!" Brian yelled. "Not that way." It was moving farther from square number 42. "Back this way." He began waving his arm.

The cow stopped, and Brian believed it heard him. But the animal didn't turn around. It stood still, raised its tail, and out of its ass came three small round brown objects, dropping to the ground.

The crowd roared. It was a combination of cheers and jeers as the man who led the cow out into the field ran to the spot. When he got there, he looked down, examining carefully before calling, "Number seventeen!"

Someone yelled, and, as the crowd parted, a grinning Linley Droth buzzed over in his wheelchair. He came to a stop at the ticket counter and raised his right hand, a ticket stub clutched in his three fingers.

"How nice he won," Darcie said, linking her arm in Brian's.

"Yeah, sure," Brian said, crumpling up his numbered ticket and putting it in his front pocket. "Oh crap!"

"Don't be a sore loser," she said, beaming at him and squeezing his arm.

"No, it's not that. I got so caught up in the event, I didn't even think to take any pictures for the paper. Damn." He was mad at himself. How stupid could he be? He forgot his place. He was here as a reporter, not just a patron. He had a job to do. Plus, how many chances would he get to take pictures of a cow-pie roulette? After thinking about that, he realized that he could do it next year, and the year after, and the year after that. It kind of depressed him, but that was what his career had come to. He should be thankful for the ongoing murder case while it was happening. Before long, it would be over, and this is what he'd be left covering.

"Don't fret," Darcie said. "There's still plenty of stuff left you can shoot."

He looked around as the crowd began drifting away from the roped-off grid. "Yeah, I suppose."

"Tell you what," his wife said. "I'm going to go look at some of the craft booths, and I know you can't stand that kind of stuff, so why don't you go do your thing."

"Okay," he agreed, almost dejected that his wife was shooing him away. It felt good to be spending the day with her. There had been so little of that lately. It was ironic that one of the reasons she wanted him to take this job was that the hours wouldn't be as demanding and they could spend more time together as they prepared to become a real family. But now, he had less time with her, and here she was ditching him. But she was right. He didn't want to look at a bunch of crafts, and she didn't want to watch him take pictures and interview people.

As she started to walk off, it struck him again that they didn't share a lot of interests. As he watched her stop at a booth with hand-carved bird houses, he wondered if her teacher friend would have shared her interest in that as well. But he tried to put that thought out of his mind and decided to head toward the hot air balloon.

Wading through the crowd, he spotted the chimney sweep handing out fliers. The man smiled as he handed his fliers to passersby. Some brushed past the man; others took the papers, only to discard them a few feet further on.

Those were picked up by Sherman Thurk, who strolled around with a burlap garbage bag slung over one shoulder and carrying a stick with a nail at the end. He poked the trash on the ground and deposited it in his bag.

Brian approached the chimney sweep and accepted a flier.

"Thank you," he said, looking at the paper. It had the same darkened image of a chimney sweep in coat and tails and top hat, holding a broom, that Brian had seen on the side of the man's van. The words advertised: "Corwin Dudle, Chimney Sweep." Below that it read "Heating and air conditioning vents and ductwork cleaned as well." A phone number was printed at the bottom.

"I've been meaning to get your number," Brian said, looking from the paper to the man. "I'd like to get my chimney taken care of."

"I'd be happy to. I have lots of openings this time of year. Where is your house?"

"I'm on Ash Street," Brian said. "Number 10. I will be in touch."

"Very well." The two men shook hands.

"Mr. Dudle!" The voice was familiar, and Brian turned to see Eldon Winch approach. "You did not pay a vendor fee for a booth," he said in his official Board of Selectmen chairman voice. "That means you don't get to go around soliciting. I spoke to you about this before."

"I'm just handing out fliers," Dudle said sheepishly. His eyes dropped and Brian felt sorry for the man.

"There's no harm in that, is there?" Brian said to Winch in defense of the chimney sweep.

"It wouldn't be fair to the other vendors," he said, looking at Brian. "They all paid a fee to promote their products and services. How would that look if they see someone handing out advertisements for free?" He turned to the chimney sweep. "Mr. Dudle knows the rules of the festival. Besides, his fliers are littering the grounds." He swept his hand in an arc around the area where, indeed, fliers were scattered.

"Fine," Dudle said. "I'll stop."

"Thank you," Winch said and walked off.

"Sorry," Brian said to Dudle, though he wasn't sure exactly why.

"At least it wasn't a total loss," Dudle said. "I'll look forward to hearing from you."

"Definitely." He folded the flier and tucked it into his back pocket.

Brian sauntered over to the hot air balloon ride. That would make a good photo, especially with its bright red, white, and blue pattern. People were lined up to take the brief ride. The balloon was descending, a young couple in the basket. The balloonist was a thick-bearded man with a riding cap. Brian raised his camera and took some long-range shots before zooming in to get a closer look at the young couple.

The balloon landed, and the giggling couple climbed out of the basket. Brian approached them, introducing himself, and asked to get a few comments for the paper. He jotted down some random quotes about the balloon ride and the festival, and then got their names and ages. He thanked them as they walked off hand in hand.

Brian looked at the balloon as the next passenger got in—the balding man with the dark-rimmed, round glasses who worked at Wibbels' Fruit Market and Real Estate. He was in the basket with the balloonist, who released a jet of flame as the balloon rose. Brian watched, snapping several pictures, though this passenger wasn't as photogenic as the cute young couple. Romance made for a much better image than some lonely, middle-aged guy, but Brian took the shots anyway.

Before the balloon reached half the height of its previous trip, the passenger began yelling.

At first Brian couldn't hear what the man was saying, but as the balloonist began a premature descent, he could make out a few words.

"Let me down," the man yelled in a panic. "Let me down now. Please!" He gripped the edge of the basket, looking toward the ground.

Don't look down, Brian thought, if you're afraid. But the man stared straight down, his eyes wide in terror. Brian half-thought the man was going to jump out of the basket before it had a chance to reach the ground.

When the balloon landed, the man clambered over the edge of the basket, legs shaking as they touched the ground. He turned to the balloonist, apologizing profusely. The balloonist didn't seem sympathetic and more likely glad to be rid of his unruly passenger.

The man in glasses slunk away, his face pale. He bowed his head as he passed the crowd waiting for their turns for rides. Brian approached the man, who almost bumped into him before looking up.

"Excuse me," Brian said, introducing himself. He had already determined he wouldn't use the shots of the man, given the circumstances, but he was curious.

The man introduced himself as Nyle Potash.

"If you don't mind me asking, what happened up there?"

The man looked wary, almost taking a step back. "You're not going to put this in the paper are you?"

"Oh no," Brian said. "I was just curious."

The man looked at the balloon as it ascended with a young family. "I have a fear of heights," he said, turning to Brian.

"Then why on earth did you go up in it?"

"I thought I could handle it," he answered. "Face my fear." He rose up on his toes, throwing his shoulders back in an attempt to seem taller.

"That's pretty brave," Brian said.

"I've made some progress," Potash said. "I got some treatment, but I guess I'm not quite there yet." He smiled.

Brian thanked the man for his time, watching him walk away, thinking something the man said sounded familiar.

The next stop was the carousel, and on his way he spotted Darcie in the distance talking to a woman with long streaks of gray in her hair. He recognized her as their waitress from dinner the other night. Brian waved, but Darcie was too involved in her conversation and didn't notice him.

Nearby, he saw Eldon Winch talking with Leo Wibbels at the fruit booth. The two seemed to be in a heated argument, and Brian was compelled to find out if it was anything that might interest him. Maybe there was some problem at the festival. That was Brian's natural curiosity, but when he saw Winch walk off, he kept his trajectory for the carousel.

The calliope music drowned out all other sounds at the festival. This attraction had the largest crowd, eagerly waiting their turn. A waist-high metal fence surrounded the ride, and Brian approached it and raised his camera. He snapped a series of shots as the ride spun around and around. Young and old alike rode the wooden horses, smiles and laughter on their cheery faces. The breeze generated by the ride blew their hair back and no doubt cooled the sweat off their faces. That in and of itself was probably reason enough for people to take a spin. Brian felt his own shirt sopping with sweat underneath his arms and down the middle of his back.

The music wound down as the ride slowed. Brian took more pictures, figuring the shots would be better now that it was spinning more slowly. He zeroed in on the children, whose gleeful laughter captured his attention. He would be a father soon, and one day he'd take his child here and ride with him, or her, on the carousel. If not next year, definitely the year after. Watching the parents with their children made him look forward to it. It would be a new experience. He hadn't really thought about being a parent. He had been nervous before, wondering how he'd hold up to the task. But seeing these kids on the ride gave him a feeling of comfort and anticipation. He couldn't wait for his chance.

The ride slowed to a stop and the passengers disembarked. Brian sought out a young family and approached them, asking questions about the ride and the festival. He jotted their names and comments in his pad and thanked them. He looked around for someone else to get comments from as other people stepped onto the carousel, each selecting a wooden horse.

Most needed new paint. The brightly colored horses were dotted with white spots where the paint had chipped or peeled away. It probably wouldn't take much to touch them up, but it made the wooden animals look old and worn.

He spied a young mother and daughter who had just gotten off the ride and headed toward them. Before he got to them, he heard a man wailing. He stopped and looked toward the carousel where the sound came from.

Jonas Fitchen, who owned the taxidermist shop, had stepped onto the carousel and stood before a black horse.

"I've missed you so much."

The people climbing onto other horses had stopped and looked at the man, wariness on their faces.

"It's been too long," Fitchen said, draping his arms around the horse's neck. He laid his cheek against the horse's face. "Why have you stayed away so long?"

Brian forgot about the mother and daughter and moved closer to the carousel. The people nearest Fitchen and the black horse dismounted and moved away, selecting horses further from the taxidermist.

Fitchen stroked the black horse's wooden mane. "I'm so happy you've come back to me." He planted a kiss on the horse's cheek.

The carousel operator left his control station and wove through the passengers and horses toward Fitchen and the black horse. He seemed cautious, almost afraid to approach the man. Brian moved a few steps closer.

"I love you so much," Fitchen said to the horse, tightening his hug around the animal's neck.

"Mister," the carousel operator said. "We're not going to go through this again."

"Leave us alone!" Fitchen yelled, not turning to look at the man.

"Enough of this!" the operator yelled, somehow finding his courage. "You gotta leave. You're scaring the children."

"I'm not leaving without her," Fitchen said, his voice forlorn.

Brian wondered if the taxidermist had had a bit too much to drink at the beer tent. He thought about stepping onto the carousel to assist however he could, but instead stood his ground and watched. That was his job as a reporter, to observe, not interact. He had inadvertently become part of one story. He didn't want to become part of this one.

The crowd was murmuring around him when out of nowhere strode Selectman Winch, pushing his way through the onlookers. He stepped onto the carousel and approached Fitchen, putting a gentle hand on the man's shoulder.

"Come, Jonas," he said. "It's time to go."

"But I can't."

"Yes, you can." Winch put both hands on the man's shoulders and, with a much firmer grip, pulled the man away from the black horse.

"No!" Fitchen cried, tears streaming down his cheeks.

"We must go," Winch said, his voice soft and soothing.

Fitchen looked at the carousel operator, who seemed relieved that Winch had taken control.

"You can't keep us apart!" Fitchen yelled at the operator, his voice choked with sobs.

"Easy," Winch said. "No one's trying to do that." He guided the man off the carousel.

Fitchen looked behind him. "I'll be back for you!"

At first Brian thought he was threatening the carousel operator, who looked stunned. But then Brian realized that Fitchen was talking to the horse.

"We're going to be married," Fitchen said to Winch as the selectman guided him through the crowd, his arm around the man's shoulders. "We're in love."

"I know you are," Winch said.

"There's no treatment in the world that's going to prevent that," Fitchen said as Winch led him away.

Chapter 17

CAUGHT IN A PICKLE

On Monday, Brian worked on his story on the Dump Festival and sorted the photographs he had taken. He selected some nice shots of the couple on the balloon ride and some of the families riding the carousel. He selected another shot he had taken during a pie-eating contest, a chubby kid with his face smothered in blueberry.

He looked at his agenda for the week with dismay. There was an interview with Selectman Winch later but not much else. The chairman was going to be honored at the board meeting the next night for forty years of service as a selectman. That seemed a long time for one man to be in office, he thought, but with no term limits, it was up to the townspeople to decide if they didn't want him representing them, and apparently the voters believed he was doing something right.

There was no new information on the murders, and that disappointed Brian. The last couple issues of the paper had been dynamic; he should have known it wouldn't hold out. He had the story about Hester Pigott's ducks being buried alive upside down, and that certainly was bizarre enough, but even missing bones elicited little reaction from Capt. Steem. If he saw a connection with the other events, he wasn't sharing that with the media, whose interest in the happenings in Smokey Hollow had waned.

Chief Treece had shown a bit more interest in Hester Pigott's rib bones. Noah was surprised and a bit perplexed that Chief Pfefferkorn hadn't told him about the discovery at Thrasher Pond. But it had been a long time ago, and if the former chief truly thought the bones were animal remains, he must have felt it was insignificant and not worth mentioning.

Beverly Crump strode into his office with a stack of mail in one hand and waving a single envelope in the other. "More fan mail."

Brian put his head in his hands. He was discouraged by some of the mostly anonymous letters from readers who didn't like how he was putting so much negative news in the paper. They missed the way the paper used to be. Didn't they understand what real news was? They were just used to nothing much happening in town, but he couldn't ignore it. He wouldn't be surprised if it was a letter-writing campaign instigated by Mrs. Picklesmeir. She had never forgiven him for the lack of attention the Women's Garden Club tour received.

When Bev handed him the mail, he plopped it down on the only empty spot on his desk, envelopes fanned out like a hand of playing cards. He spotted the white envelope with the black lettering as Beverly left his office. He grabbed it, excited, tearing open the back flap and retrieving the note inside.

Do you think Dr. Wymbs told you the truth?
The Silhouette

His eyes scanned the words several times. He wished his anonymous ally would just tell him something instead of making everything a guessing game. It was frustrating. Brian felt his stomach churn, and he opened his top drawer, grabbing his antacid tablets and popping a couple in his mouth.

He had only spoken to Wymbs once, and the doctor hadn't really told him anything. Brian went to his files and retrieved the copy with the Wymbs interview. Finding it, he re-read the article. When he finished, he dropped the paper. Nothing. This wasn't much help, he thought. He looked at the mysterious note again, thinking even Steem might not be interested in seeing it. It said nothing. But there must be some meaning to it, otherwise The Silhouette wouldn't have sent it.

Brian shoved the note into his drawer. He would think about it later.

He left the office to pay a visit to Wibbels' Fruit Market and Real Estate. Wibbels was going to give him a list of contest winners and craft awards handed out at the festival. As he crossed Main Street to the market, he noticed a "Closed" sign in the window of the taxidermist shop. When he entered the market, Wibbels was removing several large pickles from the barrel for Sister Bernice. He greeted Brian and rang up the nun's purchase.

"Thank you," the woman said in a gruff, aged voice before exiting the store.

"How are you today, Mr. Keays?" Wibbels didn't have his usual flashy grin.

"Fine, Leo," he answered, looking around the store for the clerk he had spoken to on Saturday.

"I trust you and your lovely wife enjoyed your first Dump Festival?" Now the smile was there, though it seemed forced.

"Yes, better than I expected."

There was no one else in the store.

"I take it you're here for that information you had called about?"

Brian nodded and Wibbels disappeared into his back room office, emerging seconds later. He handed Brian some papers.

"Everything you need should be there. If not, give me or Eldon a call and we can help out."

"I think this should suffice," Brian said, looking the sheets over but not really paying attention to them. He glanced around the store again.

"Something else I can help you with?" Wibbels asked, arching his eyebrows.

"I was just hoping to catch your clerk here, Mr. Potash."

Wibbels' eyebrows lowered. "He's out on an errand. Anything special you needed him for?"

"Oh no. I just wanted to see how he was doing?"

A look of confusion crossed Wibbels' face. "Doing?"

"He just had a little trouble on the balloon ride at the festival. Guess he has a bit of a fear of heights. I wanted to make sure he felt better. It gave him quite a scare."

"Oh, he seemed fine when I saw him earlier," Wibbels said, heading toward a pile of crates near the counter and grabbing a crowbar off the top box.

"That's good," Brian said. "Just tell him I was asking."

Wibbels held the crowbar in one hand and tapped one end into the palm of his other hand. "Asking what?"

"Just if he was feeling better." Brian turned to go, and then paused and looked back. "Has he worked here long?"

Wibbels seemed caught off-guard by the question and at first stuttered. "F-for quite some years," he finally managed.

"Has he always been afraid of heights?"

Wibbels shrugged his shoulders. "I guess. He doesn't really talk about it much. Why?"

"He said he'd been getting help for it. I was just wondering how he was progressing, that's all."

Brian left the market.

In Winch's office on the second floor of Town Hall, Brian scribbled notes as the town official pontificated about his forty-year career of service to the town of Smokey Hollow. The man did a good job of trying to sound humble while bragging about his achievements for the community. He certainly was a man of the people. How else could you explain his continued re-election?

"The people appreciate all I do for this town," he said, standing behind his desk and gesturing out the window toward Main Street. "I didn't ask for this honor they are bestowing on me tomorrow night. Make sure you write that down. I do what I do because I have invested my life in this town and its people." He paused. "Am I speaking too fast?"

"No," Brian said, scribbling. He wished he had thought to bring a recorder, not anticipating how much the elder statesman would spew. "I'm good." He knew he wouldn't put even half of what the blowhard prattled about in the article he was expected to write.

"This town has been through a lot of ups and downs," he continued. "Some good times and bad times. The economy is fickle. And that's the most important thing. People are trying to make a living, and some are just getting by. The businesses in town have struggled."

"I've noticed a lot of empty storefronts," Brian said, and was glad he did when he saw the sudden reaction in Winch's face.

"This town has suffered," he said, pounding his fist on his desk.

Brian wished the man would sit back down.

"When the economy started to go, it was tough," the chairman continued. "The shoe factory closing down was quite a blow. Lot of jobs went with that, including my own. That factory was the lifeblood of this town, the people who worked there, the families who depended on those paychecks, the money it brought into the town in business-tax revenues." He took a deep breath. "God, that was hard. Some families moved away, the breadwinners drawn to work elsewhere. That made it hard on other businesses in town. Shops that couldn't survive closed." He glared at Brian across his large desk. "Nothing kills a town like a crumbling business district. If there's nothing to draw the people who live here to shop downtown, what's going to attract people from surrounding towns?" He looked at Brian as if expecting him to answer.

Brian just shrugged.

"Exactly!" Winch said, pounding his fist on the desktop again. "There is no reason." He turned his back to Brian, looking out the window.

Brian waited for the man to continue. There was one good thing about interviewing a man like Eldon Winch. You didn't have to ask a lot of questions. Once the man got started, he just kept going.

"I've worked hard in this office to try to revive this town. I've brought forth proposals and ideas to generate business in this town."

Brian cleared his throat. "Through your commercial-development firm?"

Winch turned to face him with a look of a school teacher who feels upstaged by a smart-aleck student. The man chuckled, but it didn't put Brian at ease.

"Sure, I've used the firm I started after leaving the shoe factory to help develop business in town. But no one's mentioned any conflict of interest."

Of course not, Brian thought.

"All my dealings have been out in the open, on the table. Nothing shady. I've got nothing to hide. I've worked with the town as a developer and a town official. But my goal has been the same in both, helping the town." Finally he did sit down, and it made Brian feel a little less intimidated. "Have I benefitted from it? Yes. I'm the first to admit it. But I don't think anyone in town will complain about any of the dealings I've made, both as a selectman and as a businessman. I spearheaded rescinding the town ban against drinking establishments and helped set up Hale Cullumber's pub and restaurant. And look how many people in town enjoy a good meal and beverage at that establishment." He pointed a long, bony index finger at him. "Including you and your wife." Big emphasis on this last comment.

"It is a nice place," Brian said, thinking of no other response.

"And there are plenty of other businesses I've had a hand in helping develop. Wigland, the taxidermist shop, the hardware store." He leaned back in his chair, putting his hands behind his head. "Is that enough?" He didn't wait for an answer. "No. Of course not. It's never enough. There's still much more work to do. There are still too many empty storefronts. I won't rest until every one of them is filled and open for business. I still have hopes the old movie theater can be revived, if not as a cinema, then as some kind of arts-and-entertainment centerpiece for the community."

"Is that one of your properties?" Brian asked.

"Yes, I am handling that parcel. And I believe it has great potential for the right person. And believe it or not, I still have hope for that old shoe factory."

"Really?" Brian thought about the decrepit state of the structure.

"I know how it looks, pretty run down." He leaned. "But that's one of our biggest facilities in town, and I think there could be great things for it, with the right ideas and the right money."

"And where would this money come from?" Brian wasn't even sure where his question came from.

"Money can be found," Winch said, leaning back again. "If one looks hard enough."

"Would you call that one of your main goals for the town?" Brian asked. "Reviving the shoe factory building?"

"That would be a major achievement. If this town could make that structure viable again, it would go a long way toward the recovery." Winch must have seen the doubt on Brian's face. "You don't think that's possible?"

Brian shrugged. "Given the state of that building, it would be quite an undertaking."

Winch's eyes narrowed. He twirled one corner of his mustache. "People used to say that about the Mustard House. The first year I became selectman, it was just an old, crumbling, empty mansion most folk said would be better off torn down."

"That so?" Brian's interest peaked.

"But we helped Dr. Wymbs turn it into the fine medical establishment it was until its, and his, unfortunate demise."

"That's very interesting."

"The doctor struggled at first, but the town worked with him. That's what I've always made sure this board strived for, to work with businesses to make them work. Because what's good for business is good for the town. The whole community benefits. It's the lifeblood of the town."

"Did you know the doctor well?" Brian was curious about this.

"Just in business dealings. The man pretty much kept to himself." The selectman had suddenly grown sparse of words.

"You are involved in hiring for town positions, correct?"

Winch glared, tempering his thoughts before answering. He seemed thrown off by the sudden direction of the interview. "Yes."

"And that would include hiring Assistant Fire Chief Simon Runck?" Brian watched the man's eyes for reaction. There was little. The man had great control.

"I believe so. It was quite some time ago."

"But you did review his records?"

"Yes, and I recall he was never implicated in any arsons at the previous fire department that employed him." Winch shifted in his leather chair.

"What about the time after he left that department?"

Confusion reigned on the selectman's face. "I'm not sure what you mean."

"Did Simon Runck's resume account for the four years after he left his previous employment?"

Winch hesitated, locking eyes with Brian. His face flushed. "I don't recall."

"No?" Brian asked, giving the man a chance to rethink. There was no response. "Because apparently, he spent those years as a patient at the Wymbs Institute." Brian sat back, watching.

Winch worked his tongue inside his mouth, as if looking for the right words. "Where did you get that from?"

Brian grinned. "I'm sorry. I can't reveal my sources."

When Brian got home after work, Darcie had a visitor—the waitress from the night at the pub. He remembered her name was Gwen.

"She's a teacher's aide at the elementary school," Darcie said after they were re-introduced.

"Yes," Gwen said. "Waitressing is my moonlighting gig." She jerked her thumb at herself. "Single mom."

"That must be difficult," Brian said, trying to remember if he left a good tip the other night.

"I manage," Gwen said with a smile.

Brian thought maybe she couldn't afford to color her hair.

"Gwen was giving me the lowdown on local babysitters and daycares," Darcie said, "in case I can get a job at the school."

"And there's lots of opportunities as a substitute if you can't," Gwen said. "And speaking of kids, I've got to run."

Brian said his goodbyes, and Darcie walked the woman to the door.

"What brought her over?" he said after Darcie closed the door.

"I ran into her at the festival and we chatted for a bit. Started talking about kids, of course."

Brian gave his wife a kiss. "That's nice."

"It was nice to have company while you're at work. I can't live by shopping and chores alone, you know." She smiled. "And speaking of that, I'm in the middle of finishing laundry." She headed to the room off the kitchen where the washer and dryer were kept. He followed her.

"Is it hard?" he asked.

She looked up at him while pulling clothes out of the dryer. "Is what hard?"

"Being home alone?"

She started to fold a pair of pants and then stopped. "Sometimes," she said. "I keep wondering about what happened here." She didn't say what, but pointed her finger at the ceiling. He knew what she meant.

"Whatever happened," he said, "didn't necessarily happen here." He tried to sound reassuring.

"But it ended here," was her response as she continued folding.

He only wished that were true, but it wasn't.

"Oh, and how many times have I told you to empty your pockets before putting your clothes in the hamper?" She handed him a folded piece of paper that was on top of the dryer. "I didn't know if this was important."

He unfolded it and saw it was the flier from the chimney sweep. "Kind of," he said. Then he noticed something at the bottom of the paper that he hadn't before. He repeated himself. "Kind of."

The call on the scanner came before 11 p.m., just as Brian was getting ready for bed. Darcie was half asleep already. There was a request for the medical examiner and the State Police. Here we go again, Brian thought. It had been quiet for too long. He had almost felt relaxed. He should have known something was lurking just around the corner. The thing with Hester Pigott's ducks indicated that. Whoever was doing this was not finished.

Brian kissed Darcie on the check. "Go to sleep," he whispered. "I'll be right back." He hoped she would be able to sleep. He hated leaving her alone at night. He knew she felt uncomfortable, maybe even scared. But he had to go.

Whatever had happened had taken place at Wibbels' Fruit Market and Real Estate. There was the usual assortment of emergency and law enforcement vehicles out front. Brian patiently waited outside for someone to let him know what was going on. It was a long and boring wait, with nothing to do except take some shots of the exterior of the store and the police vehicles in front of it.

He looked up and down Main Street and marveled at how quiet the rest of the downtown block was. The storefronts were all dark. The only other light came from two businesses, the Odd Fellows Hall and Cully's

Pub. The rest of the town was asleep. The letter "Y" still clung to the movie marquee along with the "C". Brian spent the time waiting trying to make up movie titles that those letters could belong to. It helped pass the time.

A three-quarter moon in the clear star-filled sky helped illuminate the ruins of the Mustard House on the ridge. Brian thought how much had happened since that fire.

Finally, Police Chief Treece exited the store, talked to Night Shift Alvin for a bit, and spotted Brian. There was no smile to accompany the greeting when he came over. Brian was leaning against his car, smoking a cigarette when Noah leaned up beside him, head lowered, looking at the curb.

"What is it this time?" Brian asked. "Or rather, who is it?"

Chief Treece told him the story.

Noah had been making one last round downtown before retiring for the night, just as Chief Pfefferkorn had done years before him. He walked down the sidewalk checking doors. When he got to Wibbels' Fruit Market and Real Estate, the door was ajar. Not much, just a few inches. It wasn't like Leo to forget to close and lock his door. In fact, in the years Noah had been performing this nightly ritual, he had never come across an unlocked door.

Never mind an open one.

He took out his flashlight, clicked it on, pointed the beam at the crack, and pushed the door further open. The light darted inside the store, grazing the bins of fruits and vegetables lining the aisles.

"Hello," Noah called. "Anybody in here?" There was no answer, only the hum from the refrigeration system cooling the bins of fruit. Noah thought about drawing his gun, a thought that had never occurred to him before. But then, murders hadn't happened in Smokey Hollow before. At least, not for a very long time.

He switched the flashlight from right hand to left, just in case he needed to reach for his holster, and stepped inside. His right foot landed on something soft and squishy, and he pulled away, shining his light down at his feet. He had stepped on a pickle. The floor was covered in a pool of pickle juice, with several gherkins scattered throughout.

He shifted his light to the wooden pickle barrel a few feet away. Its lid was on but the outside of the barrel was wet. He walked across the sticky floor, careful not to slip, and stopped before the barrel. Noah gripped the flashlight tight, reached out with a trembling left hand, lifted the lid, and shone the light inside.

He saw the top of a man's head, submerged in the pickle juice.

Noah knew he shouldn't touch anything. He was a law-enforcement officer, the chief of police in fact. But he was also human and couldn't resist what he did next.

Holding the now shaky flashlight, he grabbed the hair on the top of the head and pulled up, the body rising out of the container of pickles till the face broke the surface.

Noah stared into the eyes of Leo Wibbels. The eyes no longer squinted; they were wide open, as was his mouth. He let go of the clump of hair and the body sank back down into the barrel, pickle juice flowing into the open mouth of the dead man.

Chapter 18

STEPPING OUT OF THE SHADOWS

There was no pillowcase on his head.

That's what was troubling Brian the next morning as he went to the scene of the crime where the State Police had returned to further examine the site. Day Shift Alvin stood outside the entrance of Wibbels' Fruit Market and Real Estate. The front was marked off with police caution tape. At this rate, Brian figured the department would have to put in a budget request for extra rolls.

The town was shocked by the death of Leo Wibbels. While standing on the sidewalk waiting to talk to Capt. Steem or Chief Treece, curious onlookers had come by, some even laying flowers near the store. The other murders had been people with a fringe connection to the town, but Leo Wibbels was one of Smokey Hollow's prominent citizens. Not only had people in town bought their fruit from the smiling, talkative businessman, but as a real-estate agent he had probably sold many of them their homes.

Even Mrs. Picklesmeir came out of her shop with a bouquet of orchids, laying them on the sidewalk with the others and glancing reluctantly at Brian. He could only imagine what those eyes were hinting at. He was the one who started this, she probably thought. He and his wife opened that damned trunk and released madness and mayhem on the town. They were outsiders and look what they had wrought. She turned and walked away, not saying a word.

People who had stopped to glimpse the goings-on inside the market gradually dispersed, leaving Brian alone on the sidewalk, except for Alvin. But it wasn't long before he was joined by someone else—Father Scrimsher.

"Hello," the priest said. "Such a sad day for our community."

"Yes, tragic," Brian responded, but was also thinking that he now had his lead story for this week's edition. Just when he thought he would have to make do with the festival and the dead ducks.

"I just came from visiting his widow."

Brian thought he too should pay Mrs. Wibbels a visit to give her a chance to comment on her husband. It was a thankless, yet necessary task of his job. The one he hated the most.

"Hopefully, faith will help her stay strong," Father Scrimsher said. "He was a pillar of the community and a devoted servant of God. Never missed a Sunday Mass."

"And sold some really nice fruit," Brian added.

"It's the devil's work in Smokey Hollow. Only the Lord can put a stop to it."

Not if Capt. Steem has his way, Brian thought, but he kept that to himself. Scrimsher left, and Brian was once again alone except for the silent officer. Downtown Smokey Hollow resumed its daily routine.

Noah came out of the store, ducking under the police tape, and joined Brian on the sidewalk.

"You holding up okay?" Brian asked, thinking of how traumatic the man's experience must have been. Even though Noah was in law enforcement, Brian was sure the man had never experienced anything like this.

"I'm doing all right," Noah said. "Now I know how you felt the other night."

Brian nodded. Finally, Capt. Steem and Sgt. Wickwire came out of the market, and Brian got to ask the question that had been bugging him.

"There was no pillowcase on his head, correct?"

"Keep your voice down," Steem said, his stern tone matching the look in his eyes. He looked up and down the street.

Brian didn't think it mattered. Everyone else had gone about their business. "Why change his M.O.?"

Steem shook his head. "Hard to say. Maybe this one wasn't as planned out as the others. Maybe, for whatever reason, it was more impulsive."

Brian wondered if Steem really believed that. "Why do you think the body was put in the pickle barrel?" Brian asked. "Some lame attempt to hide it?"

"Doubtful," Steem said. "More likely it was some form of staging."

"Kind of like Snethen propped up in the train-station ticket window," Noah added.

"Exactly. This killer seems to have a flair for the dramatic."

"Has a cause of death been determined?" Brian asked. "Was it strangulation, at least?"

"That's also different from the others. It appears he was struck in the back of the head with a blunt object."

"Do you have a weapon?"

"There was a crowbar on a shelf with a blood stain and hair specimens on it."

"So, killed by a blow to the head." Brian jotted this down in his notepad.

"Not quite," Steem said.

Brian looked up. "What do you mean?"

"The blow to the head most likely just knocked him unconscious. His lungs were filled with pickle juice. He drowned in that barrel."

Brian looked up from his pad. "But his eyes were open?"

"The poor guy must have come to in the barrel right at the end," Steem said. "Or when the killer held his head under."

The Board of Selectmen's meeting went on as scheduled that night, despite the previous evening's events. The plan was still to honor Chairman Eldon Winch's forty years of service to the town. Brian felt the honor would be diminished with the sudden death of Winch's close friend. It would tarnish the ceremony.

Brian took his usual front row seat. At most selectmen meetings, there would be dozen or so in attendance, unless there was a major topic on the agenda, and that had rarely happened in the few months Brian had been living in Smokey Hollow. Tonight, though, it was standing room only. That could attest to the popularity of Chairman Winch, but Brian thought it was more likely that Leo Wibbels' disturbing death had brought the crowd for comfort and support. It was as if people didn't want to be home alone; they wanted to be amongst their fellow citizens and sought stability from the town leaders.

Brian wasn't sure they'd get it here.

Brian looked around the crowd. He spotted Beverly Crump, Rolfe Krimmer, Father Scrimsher, Mrs. Picklesmeir, and Nyle Potash. There was also the woman who owned Wigland, wearing long, auburn locks. To begin the meeting, Eldon Winch spoke a few words about Leo Wibbels, then called on Father Scrimsher, who led a brief prayer and moment of silence for the fallen citizen.

The rest of the meeting was eventless, per usual selectmen meetings. Brian rarely got more than a dozen inches in the paper out of one of these affairs. It was hardly worth his effort, but he had to attend every one, along with each school- and planning-board meeting. Brian jotted down the brief notes as the three selectmen went through the agenda, starting with how much money the Dump Festival had made and ending with a reading of the proposal to request Historic Building status for the old train station.

Since Ruth Snethen's murder, there was probably less enthusiasm for that project than before. Brian actually shivered as the image of her hooded face rose up before him. No, most people in town now thought it best to tear that eyesore down. The sooner it was forgotten, the better. Only Rolfe Krimmer stood and spoke out in favor of saving the depot. He cited his many years riding the rails and the importance of trains linking communities, and argued that the town shouldn't lose such a cherished landmark.

Once Krimmer finished, the floor was open for general comments. Everyone was silent. Brian looked at the crowd seated behind him. No one offered to come forward. It was like a flock willing to sit quietly and let their leader speak. They might be too stunned to say anything.

After a moment, the panel moved to the final item of the night. Selectman Burton Slane stood and began to talk about Eldon Winch. It was mostly what Brian had heard from Winch the day before, about how he had run for selectman as a young man with a desire to serve the community. Slane talked about the many achievements Winch had made, all for the betterment of Smokey Hollow. When he was finished, he presented Winch with a plaque.

Brian stood and moved forward to take a photograph. He focused as a smiling Eldon Winch accepted the honor from Selectman

Slane. Brian viewed the two men through the camera view finder, snapping a couple of pictures. He had zoomed in for a close-up of Winch when he heard a commotion behind him—the chamber door opening and footsteps approaching. A murmur swept through the crowd.

Brian never moved his eye from the view finder and thus saw the smile fade from Winch's face, to be replaced by a frown. A lone bead of sweat dropped from his forehead and trailed down the left side of his face. Brian turned to look behind him.

Capt. Steem, Sgt. Wickwire, Police Chief Treece, and a couple of uniformed State Police officers were approaching the council podium.

"What is the meaning of this?" Winch said.

Steem held up a piece of paper in the air. "Sorry for the interruption," the captain said, though he didn't really sound sorry. In fact, Brian thought he detected a hint of delight in Steem's voice. "I have an arrest warrant."

"For whom?" Burton Slane asked as the noise in the crowd increased with the captain's announcement.

"It's an arrest warrant for Eldon Winch," Steem said, and the crowd gasped. "On a charge of homicide."

"This whole town's gone nuts," Brian said to himself in his office the next day. He had spent most of the night after the meeting in Chief Treece's office. Chairman Winch's arrest had sent shockwaves through everybody, and Brian could tell it even stunned Noah. Steem wasn't able (or willing, more likely) to release any information on the arrest, so Brian went to see Chief Treece to find out what he could glean from him.

Brian could hear Winch in the holding cells, hollering about speaking to his lawyer and how outrageously he was being treated. He kept yelling, "But I'm the chairman!" Brian didn't think that would get him far. The State Police eventually escorted him from the station to the county jail. Only when that was taken care of did Brian get some answers from the chief.

"Unbelievable," he had said to an obviously exhausted Noah Treece, who was slumped in his chair behind his desk.

"Just when I think things can't get any weirder," Noah said.

"What do they have, Noah? You have to give me something. I've got one shot tomorrow to get something in this week's edition. I can't wait for Steem to dance around things."

Noah released a sigh of exhaustion or capitulation, it was hard to tell which. "We have a witness who said Eldon went to see Leo before the market closed for the night."

"A witness?"

"I can't, or shouldn't, divulge who."

Brian thought for a moment. "The clerk? Nyle Potash?"

Noah nodded. "He and Leo were about to lock up when Eldon arrived. Nyle said there was an argument in Leo's office. He didn't hear any particulars, but Leo came out for a moment and sent Nyle home, said he'd take care of locking up."

"So, he didn't really see anything?" Didn't sound like too much of an eyewitness.

"No, but that left Eldon as the last known person to be seen with Leo. So the State Police ran some prints found on the crowbar. Eldon's prints were on it. An exact match."

"Why are Eldon's prints on file? Does he have a record."

"No," Noah said. "All town employees are fingerprinted. Standard policy."

That made sense. Darcie had been fingerprinted when she worked as a school teacher. "Did the State Police talk to Eldon about being at the market?"

"Steem and Wickwire interviewed him. They didn't disclose to me what he said, but something must have sounded off, or maybe he just acted suspiciously. But once the prints matched, they requested a warrant."

"What was their rush?" It wasn't like Winch was going anywhere. He was one of the most prominent men in town. It would have been easy to keep an eye on him. He certainly wasn't inconspicuous.

"This was the first big break in the case," Noah said, shrugging. "I don't think they wanted to waste time. People have been scared these past couple of weeks. They wanted results."

Brian leaned forward in his chair. "They're only charging Winch with Wibbels' murder, right?"

"That's all for now," Noah said. "That will give them time to look at the others from a different perspective."

"Do they think Winch is The Pillowcase?"

Noah sat upright in his chair. "You're the only one I know who thinks The Pillowcase committed these murders. I don't think Steem is even considering that possibility."

"What do you think?"

"I think it's highly unlikely a serial killer would start up again after forty-something years."

"Unless he's been living a respectable life as a town selectman for all that time. Or unless he's been locked up in the Mustard House all those years until he escaped the night of the fire."

"So what are you saying?"

Brian thought for a moment. What the hell was he saying? "I don't know. Maybe Winch killed Wibbels, but what if he had nothing to do with the other murders? After all, there was no pillowcase on Leo's head. It wasn't like the other murders."

Noah rubbed his eyes with the palms of his hands. "Well, that's what the State Police will have to find out."

By the time Brian got home that night, it was so late he decided to crash on the couch. He was only going to sleep for a few hours anyway. No sense disturbing Darcie. He wanted to get up early and into the office as soon as possible. It was going to be a busy day, readying the new developments before this week's edition went to press later in the day. And to think that a few days ago he was wondering what his lead story would be. It was funny how things turned out. And he didn't have to worry about where he covered the Dump Festival in the paper. Neither Eldon Winch nor Leo Wibbels could complain.

Darcie was put off that he hadn't come to bed.

"I don't care what's going on in your world," she said before he left. "I always want you there beside me."

She simmered down once he told her what that had happened.

"Oh my god," she said, her face pale. Then a look of relief came over her face. "Does this mean it's over?"

Brian shook his head. "I really don't think so." And he didn't. There were too many unknowns.

"What do you mean?"

"I can't explain. And I really have to run to the office and redo my front page."

As he was heading out the door, he turned to her. "Oh, I have a chimney sweep coming over later this afternoon."

She put her hands on her hips. "And when were you going to tell me?"

"Right now," he said with a smile. "I just made the appointment yesterday. But I want to be here before he leaves, so call me when he gets here."

"Okay."

At the office, Brian tried to piece the front page together, chugging cups of coffee as he sorted everything out. As expected, he hadn't gotten much new from Capt. Steem, only that Winch was charged in Wibbels' murder. The captain wouldn't even go out on a limb as to whether Winch was under consideration as a person of interest in the other murders.

Brian kept the duck killings and the theft of the pot of bones separate from his murder package. He still wasn't sure there was any connection. Once he had those pieces laid out on his front page, he was able to still make a pretty good layout from the Dump Festival article and photos. He couldn't imagine who would be remotely interested in reading about that with all the other goings-on on the front page, but maybe Winch would get a chance to read a copy in his cell.

Once everything was done and sent to the printer, Brian felt an immense sense of satisfaction. The last two days had been exhilarating. He stepped out the rear door to have a cigarette and relax. It wasn't long before Beverly Crump came out to tell him Darcie was on the phone.

"Hello, honey," he said, once he was back in his office.

"That chimney sweep guy is here," his wife said. "He's all dressed up in a vintage black coat and tails, and he's wearing a top hat."

He could sense her delight and was glad. He didn't think he had left her feeling too reassured this morning, and he worried about that. But he couldn't help it. He wanted to be honest with her.

"I know," he told her. "That's his regular get-up for the job. He's supposed to look like those old-fashioned chimney sweeps, you know, like in that kids movie, what's it called?" He could never remember the names of things like that, but she knew what he was talking about.

"I think it's cute," she said. "Are you going to be home soon?"

"Yes. I'm all wrapped up here. I need to make one last call to the printer, double check that they got the last couple pages okay, and then I'll be home."

When he did arrive home, the chimney sweep's van was parked by the curb. Up on the roof, the man straddled the peak near the chimney, the long handle of his brush thrust down its throat. Brian waved, but the man was preoccupied.

As he entered the house, Darcie was heading out.

"Where are you going?" he asked.

"I'm running over to Gwen Husk's place. I shouldn't be long."

"But what about dinner?" He was famished.

"You can find yourself something or wait till I get back. Promise I'll be quick."

And just like that she was off.

He wasn't too disappointed. He was glad to be alone. As he crossed through the living room toward the kitchen, he could hear brushing sounds from the fireplace and shifting footsteps on the roof above. In the kitchen, Brian went out through the back door. An aluminum extension ladder leaned against the side of the house.

Brian looked at the dying maple in the middle of the yard. He had time for at least one cigarette before Darcie returned. He approached the tree, reaching into the hole and feeling for his stash.

His fingers touched something else—something flat and stiff.

He grasped and pulled his hand out of the opening. His first thought was that Darcie had discovered his secret hiding spot; this was going to be an angry note telling him she knew what he had been up to. His heart sank.

Once he saw the white envelope, however, he knew what it was.

He looked around, even to the house behind his. Its backyard was empty, as were all the others around his house. He studied the envelope and the black ink lettering on it, wondering how long the note had been hidden in the tree and trying to remember the last time he had reached into the hole for his cigarettes. Just the other day, he thought.

He forgot about the cigarettes and took the note to the back steps, sitting down and opening it. The note reminded him of the first one he had received, only it went further:

Have you figured out the secret of Smokey Hollow?
The Silhouette

This time, though, the paper was folded in half, and as he unfolded it, The Silhouette answered his own question:

They're all Loonies

He stared at the message, at first feeling insulted because the Silhouette obviously didn't expect Brian to figure out the answer for himself. But when he saw a black smudge at the bottom, like the ones he had mistaken for ink smears on previous notes and one other place, he was pleased that he had at least figured out one thing without any assistance.

Brian put the piece of paper in his pocket and stood, speaking before he even turned around.

"Can we drop the charade and talk face to face now?" He turned around to see the chimney sweep on the edge of the roof, looking down at him.

Chapter 19

THE ART OF EAVESDROPPING

Corwin Dudle lived on Horseshoe Lane, a U-shaped road connecting with Cricket Lane, in a small, red-brick Colonial with black shutters. Unlocking the front door and leading Brian inside, he flicked a few light switches, illuminating a tidy room. There wasn't a lot of clutter on the walls, and the furniture was sparse.

"How does one become a chimney sweep?" Brian asked.

"In my case," Dudle said, "I inherited it from my pop. I don't think I ever had any other career opportunities." He removed his top hat and black coat, hanging them on a coat rack. "I started young, assisting him while I was in high school, and just continued from there. I think my pop just assumed I'd take over the family business. And I was his only son."

"Did you want to do anything else?"

Dudle paused, showing a slight smile and even a bit of a twinkle in his eye. "Of course. We all have dreams, don't we?" He winked at Brian. "But sometimes our paths are laid out before us and there's no opportunity to veer."

He went into the kitchen and Brian followed.

"You said you had something to show me?" Brian said.

Dudle turned to face him. "I think you will find it interesting. But first, I need to wash up." He held up his sooty palms before going over to the kitchen sink and scrubbing up.

"That's how I figured it was you," Brian said. "The soot. There were smudge marks on your notes. At first I thought they were ink smears. But then I saw the same marks on the flier you handed me at the festival. That's when I knew."

Dudle dried his hands on a dish towel hanging. "It's hard in this profession to keep clean." He approached Brian and held up his hands, backs toward him. "See my nails?"

Brian examined them. Black lines showed beneath each fingernail.

"I haven't been able to keep my hands completely clean in years. I just accept it. Maybe it's why I never got married. Who'd want to hold hands with these?" He winked again and smiled.

Brian laughed. He liked this guy. His cheery attitude reminded him of Noah Treece's, but was more jovial.

"So what do you want to show me?"

"Right this way," Dudle said, leading him to a door. He opened it, revealing stairs descending into the basement. Dudle flicked a light switch at the top and extended his hand. "After you."

Brian looked at the smiling sweep, and a horrible thought came to him. He was alone with a man he didn't know, a man who had sent anonymous notes with information few other people had. Brian had a sudden thought that maybe he had willingly walked into a trap. Did this smiling, kind man hold the darkest secret yet?

No one knew he was here. Sure, he had left Darcie a note, but who knew when she'd be home to see it. Now this man was directing him down into his basement. Brian had often wondered if the killer himself had been sending those notes. It wouldn't be the first time a madman had toyed with a local newspaper. Jack the Ripper wrote to the press, taunting them. Countless other killers had done the same.

What were you thinking? Go down those stairs, and they may be the last steps you take. And who would suspect the smiling chimney sweep who lived alone and minded his own business, who had no girlfriends and sat alone at the bar? Damn you, Brian. You have a baby on the way.

"Don't be afraid," Dudle said, the smile diminishing, as if he understood what was going on in Brian's brain. "I promise you it will be worth your while."

What was in that basement? Maybe there was some clue that would piece this whole puzzle together. That was something the reporter in him couldn't resist. "Sure," he said. Just be on your guard. "After you."

Dudle's smile widened. "Of course. But I want to make it clear, that whatever I tell you and show you is—what is it you say in the business—'off the record.'"

Brian hated that. What was the point of telling him anything if he couldn't use it? But he was tempted by what this man wanted to show him, so he reluctantly agreed.

Dudle started down and Brian followed.

At the bottom, the sweep led him through a door on the right and flicked another light switch. Florescent bulbs illuminated the front half of the room. It helped ease whatever creepy vibes Brian felt. The other half of the room was still shadowed.

A large bookcase stood on his right. The top shelves were jammed with paperback novels, the bindings cracked and yellowed. From the titles, they were mostly murder and detective stories. The lower shelves were filled with piles of pulp fiction and detective magazines. They too were old. The covers depicted scantily clad women in immediate danger.

That was not a good sign.

"I'm a big fan of pulp stories."

"The Silhouette?"

Now Dudle dipped his head and his face grew flushed. "Too corny?" He laughed. "Most of those I also inherited from my father," he said, pointing at the bookcase. "I would devour all those detective novels and pulp-hero mags. I loved them. Maybe it was an escape."

"From what?"

Dudle shrugged. "You asked me if I ever thought of another career. Well, there it is." He pointed at the magazines. "I wanted to be a pulp hero. The Spider, The Phantom, Secret Agent X, The Black Bat. I loved them all. I wanted to be like one of them."

Brian nodded. "So you became The Silhouette."

Dudle nodded. "It seemed appropriate, considering the logo on my van. Not to mention that I'm usually covered in soot." He paused. "Besides, people in town don't generally see me anyway."

Brian watched the smile disappear and sensed the man's loneliness.

"So you're trying to be a crime-solver."

The smile was back. "Let me tell you one of the nuances of my curious occupation. Chimneys have a unique way of funneling sound, specifically voices. When I'm on someone's roof, leaning over the chimney, it's like being on the other end of a telephone. And not just chimneys…duct vents too. I can hear people's conversations. Not always every word, but enough to understand what they are talking about."

Brian was fascinated. "What did you hear?"

"Thirty years ago, I was cleaning the chimney on the church rectory, the one for Father Scrimsher's front parlor. He had a visitor that day. The priest had asked the man to stop by to discuss something important."

"Who was it?"

Dudle smiled. "Dr. Wymbs." The chimney sweep paused for a reaction, his eyes and smile showing he was pleased by the results. "Father Scrimsher told the doctor that he had had a recent visitor in the confessional, someone who had been a patient at the Wymbs Institute. Apparently the man told him that he had been treated as a patient for some time, and that the doctor had eventually released him."

Brian was hanging on every word. It didn't even occur to him to take notes. He doubted he would have trouble remembering what the chimney sweep was telling him.

"Upon his release, this man felt the need to confess the acts he had committed before he had sought treatment at the Mustard House." Dudle ran his tongue along his upper lip. "Father Scrimsher told Dr. Wymbs that the man confessed to being The Pillowcase."

The revelation came like a blow. "The Pillowcase?"

Dudle nodded.

"Who was it?"

"They never mentioned the name."

Brian's excitement dimmed. "And Dr. Wymbs released him?"

"Over thirty years ago."

"Why would Wymbs do that?"

"Why indeed?" Dudle said. "Maybe he figured he'd cured the man."

Brian tried to assimilate this in his mind, but it was confusing. "How did Wymbs react to this?"

"He got very agitated," Dudle said. "I could hear him pacing in the room, stuttering as he tried to explain his methods."

"And?"

"I don't think Father Scrimsher was concerned about that. The Pillowcase had confessed his sins, and the priest absolved him of his wicked deeds."

"Then what did Scrimsher want, if not to turn the man in?"

"What's said in the confessional is sacred. He couldn't do anything about it."

"Then what did he want from Dr. Wymbs."

Dudle took a deep breath. "He assured Wymbs that he would keep the secret safe. But he wanted a favor in return."

"A favor? What kind of favor?" Brian's palms were sweaty and he had a sudden urge for a cigarette, but he figured a man who spent every day around soot and ashes would not appreciate him lighting one up.

Dudle frowned. "At that point, unfortunately, their voices got very low, and I wasn't able to hear much more. But whatever it was, the doctor agreed."

"What choice did he have?" Brian said. "Let it be known he let a serial killer free in the town?"

"Whatever Scrimsher wanted," Dudle said, "it was mutually beneficial."

"And what did you do?"

Corwin Dudle threw his head back and laughed. It was a giddy sound. "That was when I decided my amateur sleuthing career would begin."

"So you became The Silhouette."

"My first case was to try to discover the identity of The Pillowcase."

"And what have you found out?" Brian asked.

"That's what I brought you here to show you." Dudle moved to the side wall near the darkened back half of the room and flicked another light switch. A row of ceiling lights came on, lighting up the back wall.

Brian stood in stunned silence, staring.

Chapter 20

WALL OF MADNESS

"Welcome to Loonyville."

Brian opened his mouth but couldn't find anything to say. His eyes were too busy taking in the wall. A crude map of Smokey Hollow had been drawn on the wall in black marker. Photographs and newspaper clippings were taped all over the map, and notes and comments, names and dates were scribbled on it.

"What the hell am I looking at, Corwin?" There was a small desk and chair before the wall, facing it. On the desk were stacks of notebooks.

"This is thirty years of investigating," Dudle said. He pointed to the chair, and Brian took a seat. "Everything I've been able to uncover, decipher, overhear, and research."

Brian scanned the wall, his eyes jumping from spot to spot. It almost made him dizzy. He wasn't sure what to focus on. It was a big, jumbled jigsaw puzzle, and he couldn't make out the picture.

Dudle stepped to the wall. "I started with this," he said, pointing to a photo of the Mustard House. A picture of Dr. Wymbs was next to it, along with some newspaper clippings. One article was about the opening of the institute, the other was Brian's article about its destruction by fire.

"Do you know why there were no patients at the Mustard House?" Dudle asked. He didn't wait for an answer. "Because they had all been released. Not at once, but over time Wymbs released the patients into society. I guess it would be more accurate to say he re-introduced them into society. Just like with The Pillowcase, he felt that he had treated their disorders sufficiently that they no longer needed to be institutionalized." He stepped back and spread his hands, encompassing the map. "So they all became productive citizens of Smokey Hollow."

"That's what you meant by your note, about the secret of Smokey Hollow."

"Yes," Dudle said, nodding. "Sorry to be so melodramatic. Once I slipped into my role of The Silhouette, it was hard not to be. Too many years of reading bad purple-pulp prose."

"How many?" Brian asked. "How many patients are there in town?"

Dudle scratched his chin. "Hard to say. That's been one of my tasks all these years, documenting and tracking as many as possible. But figure this. The institute had a capacity of twenty-four patients. It was open for forty years. Of course, some patients spent many years there, but even if the average stay was around five years, that would amount to about two-hundred patients."

"And if their stay was less than five years?"

"That number would be a lot higher."

"Oh my god."

"That doesn't mean that all the patients stayed in Smokey Hollow, but many did."

Brian remembered something. "When I met with Dr. Wymbs, he told me the patients were harmless."

Dudle thought about this. "That's what I meant when I said Dr. Wymbs lied. Obviously. He treated The Pillowcase, a mass murderer. He kept that secret. Who knows if his staff even knew about it. And he saw fit to release the man. How many other dangerous patients sought treatment there?"

"Have you found any others?"

"Dangerous? Some. But certainly there are others who weren't ready to be reinserted into society, though the good doctor thought otherwise. Assistant Fire Chief Simon Runck, for example."

"He's an arsonist. That's pretty dangerous." A picture of Runck was tacked on the wall next to the spot on the map that marked the firehouse. Near it was the article Brian wrote about the firefighter's visit to the elementary school with his ventriloquist dummy.

"And more than being a firebug, he was schizophrenic."

Brian remembered the day he had interviewed Runck at the county jail. "He believed Marshall was alive."

"Yes. And blames him for setting the fire at the Mustard House."

"Who are the others?" Brian asked, looking back at the map and the photos of people he recognized.

"Jonas Fitchen," Dudle said, pointing to the picture of the man next to the location of the taxidermy shop. "You saw what's wrong with him at the Dump Festival."

Brian nodded.

"He has a condition known as objective sexuality, where people become obsessed with an inanimate object. I once researched a story of a woman who married a Ferris wheel." Dudle pointed to the Wigland shop downtown. "Ivy Mockler." There was a photo of the woman with blond, curly hair. "You've probably noticed she wears the wigs from her shop."

"I've seen that."

"That's because she's bald. Trichotillomania, it's called, an irresistible urge to pull the hair out of your scalp. She suffered from it so long that her hair never grew back." Dudle stepped over to another spot on the wall. "You've been here."

There was a picture of the rooming house on Cheshire Road, with small photos of several men beside it. "Yes."

"I call this place the 'Loony Bin,'" Dudle said, and in fact those words were scrawled above the photo of the building. "There are quite a few former Mustard House patients who live there. Sherman Thurk, who's a sleepwalker."

"The Somnambulist."

"Correct. And Nyle Potash." He pointed to the man in glasses who worked at Wibbels' Fruit Market and Real Estate.

"Fear of heights."

"Very good."

Sitting at the desk, Brian felt like a student in class, demonstrating to his teacher that he knew the answers. At least some of them. There were still many more questions.

"Linley Droth, you've seen him buzzing around town in his wheelchair. Can you figure out what his condition is?" Dudle waited to see if he knew the answer.

"I don't know. But it seems like he must have been in some kind of accident or something."

Dudle shook his head, grinning. "Not quite. He has what's known as 'body-integrity identity disorder.'"

"What's that?"

"It's a relentless desire to amputate healthy limbs. He cut off his own legs, arm, and fingers. And he removed one eye with an x-acto knife and a spoon."

Brian grimaced at the thought and his stomach squirmed. He wished he had his antacid tablets.

"People with this disorder," Dudle continued, "have something wrong with the right parietal lobe in their brain, which maps the layout of their bodies. The dysfunction causes these people to believe that parts of their bodies don't belong. So they try to remove them. Obviously, Droth succeeded."

"I've heard people refer to him as Doc. Does he have medical training?"

Dudle laughed. "No. He was an arborist. They call him Doc because he was a tree surgeon. When he was let out, he still had both hands and two eyes. It doesn't look like his treatment went well. In fact, I was cleaning the ventilation ductwork at the Loony Bin when Dr. Wymbs paid Linley a visit shortly after one of his latest amputations. He threatened to bring Doc back to the Mustard House for further treatment if he continued to damage his body."

A thought excited Brian. "Was Mrs. Picklesmeir a former patient?" He wanted that to be the case. If anyone was a loony, he wanted her to be one.

"No," Dudle said, much to Brian's dismay.

The whole thing amazed Brian. "Why would Dr. Wymbs release these people if they weren't quite right?"

"I'm not positive, but I've developed a theory."

"What is it?" Brian was fascinated by all the information the chimney sweep had gathered.

"Do you know who owns the Loony Bin?" Dudle asked, pointing to the rooming house on Cheshire Street.

"Eldon Winch," he answered, almost calling the former town official by his title.

"Yes. He's a commercial real-estate developer. He got into that business after the shoe factory closed." He stepped toward the middle of the town map, pointing to downtown. "Winch helped develop many of the vacant downtown businesses. Wigland, the taxidermist shop, Cully's Pub."

"Hale Cullumber, was he at the Mustard House?"

"Yes," Dudle said. "Severe alcoholic. Which is ironic since he owns the only drinking establishment in town. With the help of Eldon Winch, of course."

Brian sat upright. "And Winch was behind the ordinance to allow businesses to serve alcohol."

Dudle smiled. "You're catching on. That's right. This was a dry town for many years till Eldon led the push for the selectmen to repeal the ban."

"So are you saying what I think you're saying?"

Dudle folded his arms on his chest. "The economy has been hurting this town for decades. The storefronts were mostly empty. There are still quite a few vacant spots, like the former cinema, which by the way, Winch bought. Things were bad, especially when the shoe factory shut down." He moved toward the spot near the Mustard House. "The Wymbs Institute was private. It wasn't cheap for patients to be institutionalized there. The patients had money, or as was more often the case, came from families with money, trust funds, inheritances."

"And you think Eldon Winch found a way to tap into that money?"

Dudle shrugged. "It's just a theory. But Wymbs releases these people, and they establish themselves in town, some of them opening businesses in Smokey Hollow. With the help of Eldon Winch, a developer and Board of Selectmen chairman, and real-estate agent Leo Wibbels, who sells homes to most of these people."

"So their money stays in town."

"Adds tax revenues to the town coffers. And speaking of tax revenues. The Wymbs Institute was behind on its business tax payments. About thirty years behind."

Brian's eyes widened. He could use someone like Corwin Dudle working as a reporter on his newspaper.

"Check the records at Town Hall," Dudle said. "It's public information."

"This is amazing."

Dudle shrugged. "A lot of it is speculation, but it seems to fit. I call it the Triple W pact. Wymbs, Winch, and Wibbels."

"And Winch hired Simon Runck for the Fire Department."

"And Sherman Thurk for the Sanitation Department."

"And Nyle Potash works for Wibbels." Brian thought about the people at the rooming house. "Is everyone at the Loony Bin a former Mustard House patient?" He was thinking of the old man, Rolfe Krimmer. He didn't want that to be true.

"No, I don't believe so. There are still people in town I'm trying to figure out. See those notebooks?"

Brian looked at stacks of spiral-bound books.

"I've been documenting as many residents as I can, writing down whatever information I can uncover. It's been a life-long mission."

There was something Brian didn't understand. "Why haven't you come forward to the authorities with all this?"

Dudle's face soured. "I told you, I wanted to be a pulp detective. It was a fantasy of mine, and I got to act it out." He looked over his shoulder at the map. "Besides, we don't exactly have the best law enforcement officials in this town. Chief Pfefferkorn was kind of a joke. About thirty years ago, there was a rumor about a prostitution ring. You can imagine what effect something like that had in a small town like this. It supposedly was run out of a cosmetology school in town." He looked back at Brian. "Developed by Eldon Winch, of course. But one day, the school shut down, and the rumor died. Nothing ever came of it. So Pfefferkorn wasn't much of an option, and this new young chief, heck, he's just a kid."

Brian understood. He liked Noah, but the man wasn't a motivated investigator. "So you've been trying to solve this by yourself. Trying to figure out who The Pillowcase is?"

"Yes, among other things." He pointed to another spot on the map, Walnut Street, which ran behind Brian's house. There was a picture of a blond-haired boy next to where a house was marked in black. "Seven years after I heard that conversation between Father Scrimsher and Dr. Wymbs, another mystery emerged. Little Timmy Birtch went missing. That became another case I wanted to solve." His mouth turned down and his voice grew weak. "That one became more important." He looked at Brian with moist eyes. "And much more frustrating. No clues. Nothing. The kid just vanished."

"Do you think it's connected to The Pillowcase?"

Dudle bowed his head, slowly shaking it. The man seemed exhausted. Maybe the frustrations of all these fruitless years spent on his private project had sapped his vitality. "I haven't been able to make any connections. When those bones were found in Thrasher Pond, I hoped it would lead to some resolution."

"But Pfefferkorn said they belonged to a pig."

Dudle nodded. "Yes. And I should have known better and looked into it myself. But until your article about the Knackerman came out, I didn't know they were human."

"Hester Pigott said they belonged to an adult woman."

"Yes," Dudle said. "Another mystery for The Silhouette."

Brian stood. "You can't expect to solve this yourself."

"All the great pulp heroes did."

"That's fiction. This isn't." Brian wondered if Corwin Dudle had spent time in the Mustard House as well. His behavior couldn't exactly be considered normal. He seemed to know a lot about the patients at the institute.

"I've spent my adult life working on this," Dudle said, stepping back and looking at the wall. "No time for friends or companionship." He extended his palm toward the wall. "Just this." He paused and Brian didn't know what to say. "I often wondered if The Pillowcase was even alive and in Smokey Hollow."

"And then the murders began," Brian said, finishing his thought.

"Yes," Dudle said. "Right after you opened that trunk full of baby skeletons. One more mystery."

Brian scanned the wall, looking at the faces pinned to it. Was he looking at the face of The Pillowcase among this collection of loonies? "Do you think the trunk's connected to The Pillowcase?"

"Seems to be," Dudle said. "The murders started right after the trunk was discovered. It's no coincidence that the trunk was in the home that used to belong to a former nurse at the Mustard House."

"Who was silenced." Brian stepped toward the wall. Something was bugging him. He saw the article on Ruth Snethen near the spot where his house was marked. He looked at the article on Hettie Gritton's murder at the Town Pound. "You've explained the missing patients at the Mustard House," he said. "But what about the staff? What happened to them?"

Dudle shrugged. "Funny thing is, they've been harder to track than the patients. I imagine as the patient population dwindled at the institute, staff members were let go and moved away to find other employment. I just can't find any records of them. Snethen and Gritton were the only ones I knew of."

"And we can't talk to them."

"No. The Pillowcase made sure of that."

Now Brian stepped back to get a full look at the wall. It was amazing what Dudle had done. "This is quite some work. I'm glad you shared it with me."

"It's taken a lot of my time. It feels good to share it." Dudle stepped back and stood beside Brian, the two of them looking at the wall. "It's been frustrating, especially when the murders started. I felt some sense of urgency. I think that's why I left you those notes. From your articles, you seemed like the kind of person I could trust. I saw a little of myself in you, I think."

Brian wasn't sure if he should be flattered or not. Most reporters Brian knew were loners like Dudle. If he hadn't been lucky enough to find Darcie, he might very well be in those same shoes. His work consumed him twenty-four/seven, and he was surprised he had found the time to carve out a life with Darcie.

"You'd make a hell of a reporter," Brian said.

Dudle laughed. "It's a detective I want to be."

Brian stared at the map. A lot of detection that had taken place to construct this. The whole wall was like a gigantic jigsaw puzzle. It was just a matter of finding the missing pieces to finish it.

Chapter 21

A TRIP TO THE LOONY BIN

Brian strolled up the long walkway to the rooming house on Cheshire Street. The afternoon was steamy, and there was not a cloud in the sky to provide any relief from the heat. The week's edition of *The Hollow News* was out and Eldon Winch's arrest for the murder of Leo Wibbels ran across the top of the paper, not that anyone in town didn't already know about it. Word of mouth traveled fast in Smokey Hollow. Of course, Corwin Dudle had shed new light on the story. The only problem was that Brian couldn't print anything about it. A lot of the Wymbs-Winch-Wibbels connection was speculation. But the one thing that wasn't speculation, at least according to Dudle—or rather, The Silhouette—was that the patients of the Mustard House had been re-introduced into society over the years, for better or worse.

At least in the case of The Pillowcase, there was no doubt it was for the worse.

Brian wished he could have gone to Noah Treece with some of this stuff, but he was obligated to protect his source. But Dudle had given him a direction to go in, and now he could try to corroborate the stuff laid out on the chimney sweep's wall. And the Loony Bin was as good a place to start as any.

He figured most of the residents would be at work, but he was hoping there was a good chance Linley Droth would be there. The man couldn't get too far.

As he approached the rooming house, he wasn't disappointed. Linley was there on the first-floor porch in his wheelchair. In a wicker chair next to him sat Rolfe Krimmer, his Boston Post Cane resting across his lap. The two men were playing dominoes again.

"Hello, gentlemen," Brian said as he ascended the steps. "Another hot day."

"Indeed," Krimmer said.

Linley took his Panama hat off, fanning his face for a moment with it, gripping the brim of the hat with his three fingers. His hair was greasy with sweat.

Brian hopped up onto the porch railing. He looked out upon the wide lawn, swathes of brown grass streaking the yard. "Lawn's not looking too good."

"Lack of rain will do that," Krimmer said.

"I'm surprised your landlord doesn't make sure it gets watered." Brian turned his attention back to the duo.

"Kind of hard since he's in jail," Krimmer said.

"Oh yeah," Brian pretended to remember. "Winch owns this place, doesn't he?"

"That's right," Krimmer said.

Droth was silent, still fanning his face, flushed from the heat.

"Kind of crazy, isn't it?" Brian said, watching the two men's faces.

"Lot of crazy things in town," Krimmer said. "Sad to see something like this happen to two upstanding men in the community."

"They seemed very close," Brian said. "I just wonder what drove Winch to the point of lunacy."

Droth looked at Brian with his one good eye. The other looked off to the right, almost as if it were keeping an eye on Rolfe Krimmer. The old man licked his dry, chapped lips.

"Who's to say what's crazy," Krimmer said.

"Not me," Brian confessed. "I've seen so much in the short time I've been in this town. It's all been very mysterious."

Droth placed his hat back on his head. "So what mystery brings you here, Mr. Keays?" the wheelchair bound man finally said, his lisp so prominent it prompted Brian to wonder if maybe the man had snipped the tip of his tongue off as well.

What was he doing here? Brian asked himself. What did he hope to ascertain from Linley Droth?

"I'm just trying to find answers," he finally said. "Like everyone else in town."

"Isn't that a job for the police?" Krimmer said. "They just made an arrest, so they seem to be making progress."

"What answers are you looking for?" Droth asked.

"I don't think the police believe Winch was behind the other stranglings," Brian said. "But maybe he knew something about how they might be connected to the Wymbs Institute."

"And the trunk found in your attic?" Droth asked, his one eye locked onto Brian's.

"They all seem to go hand in hand," Brian said. He tried not to stare at Droth's missing left hand.

"And how can we help you?" Droth asked.

"I thought you might have some insight into the Mustard House."

"Because I was there?" Droth's mouth was rigid, his eye still.

Brian cracked a nervous smile. He wished he could light up a cigarette now. It was hard not to look at the man's missing limbs without thinking of what Dudle told him. A mental image arose of the man binding his upper leg and then taking a tree saw to it. "There's been talk."

"Who's been talking?" Droth asked.

Brian shrugged. "Is that important? I was just wondering if there was someone at the institute who might be a bit over the edge."

"More so than any of us who were there?" Droth's tone thickened.

"Oh, I don't mean to cast any aspersions," Brian said. He wished Droth's other eye would look his way. "I mean no offense. I understand Dr. Wymbs did a wonderful job with most of the patients he treated. But maybe some slipped through the cracks, so to speak."

"Like Simon Runck?" Droth said.

"That's a very good example. His treatments obviously didn't work. And he proved to be a danger to the community."

Rolfe Krimmer had grown curiously silent. Brian wondered if he too had been at the Mustard House as a patient. He hoped not. He liked the old coot. He seemed to remember the man retiring to Smokey Hollow after his career as a train conductor, so it seemed doubtful.

"And are you wondering if my treatments were successful?" Droth asked.

"No. Nothing like that. I'm just trying to find people to talk to who spent some time up there to see if they knew of anyone who might be capable of committing these acts." Brian wanted to go ahead and mention The Pillowcase, but he agreed with Capt. Steem to keep that aspect of the killings under wraps, and he didn't want to impede the State Police investigation.

"There wasn't a lot of integration of the patients at the institute," Droth said. "And people came and went." He paused, staring at Brian with his good eye. "We didn't get too chummy."

"I see," Brian said, staring at Droth's eye.

"Do you?"

"I'm sorry if I've disturbed you."

"No harm done," Krimmer piped in. "Right, Doc?" He looked at Droth. Krimmer stood, tapping his cane on the floorboards. "Now if you don't mind, we have plans to go to the cinema this afternoon." He picked up the dominoes and deposited them into a small bag, leaving it on the table.

Brian watched as Droth motored his way down the wheelchair ramp. Krimmer descended the front steps, not really needing the assistance of his cane. Brian thought the old man just liked it because it was such an honor. He rarely saw the man without it since it had been awarded. Krimmer met Droth in the walkway.

"Where are you going to the movies?" Brian asked.

"Why, downtown, of course," Krimmer said, looking back. "At the theater."

This confused Brian. "But it's closed."

"Yes," Krimmer said. "But I still have a key and know how to run the projector. I often watch a flick there, sometimes with a friend. Of course, there's only the last movie that played there which we never returned, so there isn't much of a variety. But luckily it's a good one." The two men turned to go.

"Do you want a lift?" Brian asked. Even though Main Street wasn't far, he thought he should ask since one man was ninety-six and one was in a wheelchair. Besides, it was so damn hot.

"No thank you," Droth yelled back. "We can do fine on our own."

That was obvious, Brian thought, watching the two men head down the walkway to the sidewalk. After they were gone, he realized he should have asked Krimmer what the movie was. He had seen the "YC" on the marquee for the past few months and still wondered about the title of the last movie that had played at the cinema.

A chime sounded as Brian entered Wigland. Ivy Mockler looked up from behind the counter. She smiled, adding to the creases on her face. She wore a jet-black wig, the hair straight and chin-length. Brian tried to picture the woman bald, and it wasn't a pretty image.

"Good afternoon," she said. Her lips were heavy with red lipstick. She wore long, black, curled, false eyelashes.

"Hello," Brian said, approaching the counter with caution. He felt ill at ease, knowing what he knew.

"Can I help you with something?" Mockler asked.

The grin with the red lips and the fake hair made him feel like he was being addressed by a clown. He looked around at the wigs perched on white Styrofoam heads with no faces. He felt surrounded by an army of decapitated faceless women. He cleared his throat.

"My name is Brian Keays," he said. "From *The Hollow News*."

"Oh yes," she said. "I used to like reading the paper." Her eyes fluttered. "But now it's just filled with the most dreadful news. I can't read that kind of stuff. It makes me ill." Her smile never faded.

"I was hoping I could talk to you about something." As with Droth, he wasn't sure how to approach the subject.

"And what is that, young man?" She was brushing the blonde hair of a wig on a mannequin head on the countertop.

"Forgive me if I sound a bit intrusive, but I understand you spent some time being treated at the Mus—" He caught himself and corrected his query. "The Wymbs Institute."

Her smile dropped but she didn't break stride with the hairbrush. Her eyelashes fluttered. He wasn't sure she was going to answer him.

"I know this sounds like it's none of my business, but –"

"That's right," she finally said. "It is none of your business." She continued stroking the hair. Her knuckles were white.

"I don't mean to be a pest. It's just that I'm writing about the doctor and all the wonderful work he did up at the institute." He thought that was the best approach. "That is, until his unfortunate demise."

"He was a wonderful man," Mockler said, her smile inching back.

"I'm sure he was," Brian said. "So you were there?"

"Yes," she conceded. "That was a very long time ago." Her eyes steeled and bore into his. "I wasn't crazy, if that's what you're thinking."

"Oh no, of course not. That's the furthest thing from my thoughts. I was just wondering if you knew some of the other patients."

The smile disappeared again. "I thought you wanted to talk about the doctor?"

"But how can you talk about a doctor, without talking about his patients?"

She looked him up and down, as if assessing whether to trust him. "We're not supposed to talk about other patients. It was a very private institution."

"Of course," he said. "And I want to assure you I would never divulge anyone's names in the paper. That's not what this is about."

"I knew some of the people there. There was some interaction with other…guests of the facility."

"Were any of them dangerous?"

"Dangerous? How so?"

"Anyone at the institute with violent tendencies or behavior?"

She thought for a minute. "Not that I recall."

"Well, I suppose anyone like that would be kept away from the general population."

"Probably," she said.

"But maybe there was talk, among the other patients or staff, about someone like that. Maybe someone who shouldn't really be there."

She stopped brushing and put the hairbrush on the counter. "I remember there was this one young man who was kind of odd. He was barely out of his teens. Not a very attractive young man. He seemed pleasant enough at first, but then it kind of spooked me when I found out why he was there."

"And why was that?"

"He liked to kill little animals. Puppies, kittens. Dreadful to think of. So I tried to keep my distance from him."

Brian remembered Hester Pigott telling him about murdered animals found around town. "Do you remember his name?"

She looked down, grasping the hairbrush again. "No. I don't recall. He wasn't there long."

"And you never heard of him again?"

"There was talk about him coming back. One of the orderlies mentioned that he was returning to the institute. He must not have fared too well on the outside."

"What did the orderly say about him?"

"Just that he was a bad man. He said a bad man was coming back on the train. That he really didn't belong. The orderly said he wasn't looking forward to the man returning."

"But he did return?"

"Oh no," she said, shaking her head, her black hair swooshing from side to side. "The orderly told me the bad man never showed up on the train."

"He didn't?"

"No. No one seemed to know why. But none of us cared."

Brian wasn't sure that was any help at all. "Were there any other, um, bad men there?"

She took her time to think this over and then shook her head.

"Maybe someone else who scared you a little bit," he said, prodding. "Made you nervous to be around."

"No," she said. "The only thing that was kind of creepy was the crying."

"Crying?"

"Oh yes," she said. "On several occasions, I could hear babies crying."

Chapter 22

A SPECTER IN BLACK

Corwin Dudle stood on the edge of a roof looking down at Brian, who, after leaving Wigland, had tracked the chimney sweep to a house on Willow Street. He squatted on his haunches, broom over his shoulder, his face a mask of soot as he listened while Brian told him of his conversation with Ivy Mockler.

"Babies crying?" Dudle said, rubbing his chin with his free hand. The man had great balance, like a pigeon, while perched on the precipice of the roof assimilating this new information.

"Could it be that the babies in the trunk originated at the Mustard House?" Brian asked, standing in the home's front lawn. The sun was setting behind the peak of the house, leaving the side of the roof Dudle stood on in shadows. "Maybe some of the patients got pregnant? Maybe even impregnated by the staff members themselves?"

Dudle shook his head. "I would think I might have heard about something like that. You sure she wasn't just imagining it?"

"No," Brian said. "She seemed pretty creeped out by it." He thought for a minute. "Maybe I need to talk to Father Scrimsher tomorrow, see if I can get him to tell me about his conversation with Dr. Wymbs."

"I don't think he'll be very forthcoming," Dudle said. "Priests are pretty adamant about their vows of confidentiality."

"He wasn't afraid to break it with Dr. Wymbs," Brian said. "It's worth a try. Something went on up at that place. There's some reason Scrimsher talked to Wymbs. He wanted something in return for keeping quiet about The Pillowcase."

Over dinner at home, Brian was silent. He pushed his food around on the plate with his fork, only occasionally spearing a piece of potato or pea and lifting it to his mouth. It wasn't that he didn't have an appetite. True, his hunger was diminished by acids churning in his stomach that no amount of antacids could help. He felt on edge. It had been a long time since these kinds of feelings had permeated his very being. It was as if his body had been in detox by the mundane news he had been covering the first few months in Smokey Hollow, until the day that trunk was opened. Now all his news nerves were stimulated, and the rest of his body had forgotten how to react. His news sensory system had been overloaded. It was like a recovering alcoholic who suddenly goes on a drinking binge.

The tutorial he had received from The Silhouette had been the catalyst; until then there didn't seem to be any direction for all the ominous happenings in town. The wall in Dudle's basement had refocused everything. Sure there were still many pieces missing, but a picture was beginning to emerge. All Brian had to do was step back a bit and see if he could get a better view. Or maybe he needed to get closer. Maybe he had been standing too far away.

What bothered him was keeping silent about the information Dudle had unveiled. Brian wanted more than anything to share it with Noah Treece. He could use the police chief's perspective. Noah understood the underpinnings of the town better than he. But he wasn't able to let the chief in on what he had discovered. It was his damn obligation to protect the source. But if he could find out a few things on his own, his conscience would be clear about contacting Noah. Not that the chief had shown much enthusiasm for probing this mystery.

But what bothered Brian even more was that he wanted to share the past couple days' events with Darcie. She sat across from him, just as silent. He glanced up from his plate, after inserting a piece of pork into his mouth. She looked up at him and cracked a half-hearted smile. Was something bothering her as well? He knew he hadn't been around much. He just hoped she wasn't reaching out to her former teacher friend. Would she keep that a secret from him? There seemed to be a lot of secrets in Smokey Hollow; why should she be any different? How well did they really know each other? What the hell is wrong with you? She's your wife. Tell her about the chimney sweep's basement. Who would she tell?

Him? Is that what you're afraid of, that she confides in him? You're gone all day and often at night. Who else would she talk to? They're still friends.

He was being stupid. Besides, she's having your baby. What more connection could two people have? It will be a new phase of your lives.

You will welcome that baby into this world. Not like those babies in the attic. Someone didn't want them. Someone shoved them into that trunk. He started to wonder whether they were put there dead or alive. God, he hoped they were already dead when they were wrapped in those newspapers and locked away in that trunk and left to decay in the hot stuffiness of the dusty attic.

Decay. Like the bones in the Knackerman's pot. Bones that had been dragged up from the bottom of Thrasher Pond. Who did those bones belong to? Were Timmy Birtch's bones decaying somewhere, hidden away for more than two decades? Where had you gone, poor Timmy? Who took you and what did they do to you?

"Are you okay?" Darcie asked.

He looked up at her, a couple of loose peas dropping from the prongs of his fork held mi-air before his open mouth. They landed on his plate. He stared at her. Her eyes showed genuine concern. They comforted him. They locked onto his. Not like Linley Droth's wandering glass eye that had avoided his gaze. No, hers sought out his and held onto him.

"I don't know," he said.

At that moment he wanted to drop his fork and rush to her side of the table and grab onto her and hold her. In this instance, she needed to be stronger than he, because he demanded her comfort and support. Things were crazy in this town, and if anything was going to hold him together, it was her.

So he told her.

Not everything. He left out Corwin Dudle and his basement, but he talked about his discussions with people who had been patients, guests, inhabitants, whatever you wanted to call it, of the Mustard House. He let her know he couldn't divulge how he found out some of the things he discovered, and that it didn't really matter. He just needed to let loose some of the bats in his own belfry.

It would be over soon, he told her. He could feel it. And he actually looked forward to it, and things getting back to the dull rhythm that was expected for the town of Smokey Hollow. Then he could concentrate more on her and the family they were starting.

In bed that night, she lay with her back to him, and he snuggled up against her. He reached his hand around and under her nightshirt, but not to touch her breasts, no, but her swollen belly. He caressed the smoothness of her baby bump and the protuberance of her belly button and it aroused him. He felt himself getting aroused and so did she. He moved his hand down, pulling her panties off. She let out a soft gasp. He felt how warm she was when he entered her, spooning from behind as they lay on their sides. It was slow and gentle and ended quickly and that was okay for tonight. He felt connected to her, and that was the most important thing.

In the dark they lay side by side.

He couldn't sleep.

"What are you thinking?" she whispered.

He almost laughed, but caught himself. "You don't want to know."

"I do," she said, planting a soft kiss on his ear. "Tell me everything."

No, he thought. I can't tell you everything. I need to spare you from the worst.

"I was thinking how close I was to that murder in the train station."

She hugged him tight.

"I forget how awful that was for you," she said, her voice soft and comforting.

"I wished I could have seen something. Maybe it would have been some help."

"But you didn't see anything."

"No," he said. "I didn't. I couldn't be of any help. There were no witnesses to any of the killings. If only someone had seen something."

"That guy sleepwalking found the glass eye," Darcie said, her voice sleepy. She was drifting off but was still listening. "That was something."

"Yeah," he said. "But a witness who's asleep isn't much of a witness. He was up there by the Mustard House the night of the fire and didn't see anything. He was by the Town Pound the night Hettie Gritton's body was found, but didn't see anything."

"How do you know he didn't see anything," Darcie said through a yawn.

"Treece, Steem, and Wickwire all interviewed him. But he didn't remember seeing anything because he was asleep."

"Well, just because he was asleep, doesn't mean he didn't see anything."

Brian bolted up in bed.

"Oh my god," he said.

"What?" Darcie asked, sounding more awake.

He turned to her in the dark, barely able to see the confused look on her face. "You're right."

"About what?"

"What if the Somnambulist did see something?"

Brian drove along the quiet dark streets of Smokey Hollow. He had turned left from his road onto Main Street, cruising past the closed downtown shops and empty storefronts. There were lights on at the Odd Fellows Hall, but the rest of the businesses were closed. The cinema marquee still had the "Y" and "C," and Brian wondered if Rolfe Krimmer was watching the leftover film for the umpteenth time.

Brian's was the solitary vehicle on Main Street as he passed the fire station, its service bay doors open and a couple firefighters milling about inside. Town Hall was dark. As he drove past St. John's Church on his left, he saw lights in the rectory where Father Scrimsher and Sister Bernice lived. As he slowed almost to a stop, he also noticed a light in a second-floor window of the vacant brick building that had been the church's old-folks' home.

He took a left onto Whispering Lane, driving by the house Ruth Snethen had been hiding out in, Leo Wibbels' real estate sign still perched on its front lawn. Won't get many showings that way, he thought.

Brian took the loop around Cheshire Road, past the Loony Bin, stopping briefly and wondering if he should just go up to the door and ring Sherman Thurk's bell. No. He knew he'd not find the Somnambulist there. He'd be out here on the streets somewhere, wandering.

He drove off Cheshire and onto Willow, ending up on Hemlock just down the road from his office. He sat in his car at the stop sign, thinking. Down one end of Hemlock he could see the lights on at Cully's Pub, the only sign of life on this Thursday night. He looked to the right toward the other end where Hemlock rose toward its juncture with Ridge Road. He went in that direction, turning left onto the road ascending the ridge.

The dark shape of a tall, thin man with high, tousled hair loomed ahead, walking up Ridge Road, pinned in the beams of his headlights.

Brian parked his car, getting out and catching up to the sleepwalking man. Once alongside Sherman Thurk, Brian examined the man's face. It was dark, and most of Thurk's features were in shadows, but Brian could tell the man's eyes were open. The question was, did they actually function? Were those open eyes capable of seeing things? And if so, did the mind comprehend the images they saw?

"Sherman," Brian said, keeping his voice soft so as not to disturb the man. "Are you awake?" He knew the answer but had to ask anyway.

Thurk kept walking and did not respond.

"Can you hear me?" Brian asked, keeping stride with the man.

Still no response.

The man's pace was steady but slow, and Brian was glad because, as the road inclined, he could feel his lungs strain as they worked extra to suck in air. The effects of his recent relapse into smoking could be felt during this brief bit of nocturnal exercise.

"Where are you going, Sherman?"

The tall man shrugged.

Brian felt good. At least that was some kind of response. That meant the man heard him.

Thurk stopped suddenly and bent down. His fingers grasped a broken pair of sunglasses, picking them up and putting them into his pants pocket. He continued walking.

"I need to ask you some things," Brian said. "I need your help. Did you see anyone at the Town Pound the night you found Hettie Gritton's body?"

Thurk shook his head.

Brian wondered if he would only be able to ask yes or no questions, if the man was only capable of responding by moving his head. But didn't people often talk in their sleep? So why not him?

"Do you remember seeing anyone on this road the night of the asylum fire?"

"No," Thurk said, his voice distant, detached.

He could speak while asleep, Brian thought. That's good.

"Where did you used to live, before moving into the rooming house on Cheshire Street?"

"Here," Thurk said, and stopped.

Brian looked up and realized they were standing in front of what remained of the Mustard House. A metal chain-link fence had been erected around the ruins, with signs posted along it reading: "No trespassing per order police." Beyond the fence were piles of burnt timber from the collapsed mansion. One wall on the right still partially stood, black jagged beams poking into the night. The place smelled smoky, like an old campfire.

"Yes," Brian said. "You were here before, at the institute. You were treated by Dr. Wymbs."

"Yes," Thurk said. He stood before the ruins, almost as if examining them. Brian wondered if he could really see them.

"But he didn't cure you, did he? You still sleepwalk."

"No, he didn't fix me."

"So why did he let you go? Why didn't he keep you here?"

There was hesitation. "He said there was nothing wrong with me. He said I was normal."

"Of course, you're normal," Brian said. "But why didn't he want to keep you at the institute, to continue helping you?"

"He said I should live in town with regular people. He said who's to say what's normal and what isn't. He said there were plenty of everyday people who weren't normal."

True, Brian thought. "But didn't he want to help you with your sleepwalking?"

"He did what he could. He strapped me down in my bed."

"And did that help?"

"It kept me from moving," Thurk said, his voice sleepy. "But when he left me alone at night without restraints, I still went walking."

"Where did you walk?"

"In the hallways."

"Weren't you locked in your room?"

"No," Thurk said. "Dr. Wymbs didn't believe in locking the doors."

"Why not?"

"He said we weren't prisoners. We were patients."

"But weren't some of the patients dangerous?"

Thurk shook his head. "None that I met."

"Did you ever encounter babies at the institute?"

Thurk didn't respond, but his body shook, as if something cold ran up his spine.

"Did you ever hear them cry?"

Thurk started to open his mouth, as if to say something, but nothing came out. His lips closed and his face grew rigid. The man looked afraid.

"Did you see something?" Brian asked. "Did you see anything while wandering the halls?"

Thurk's eyes grew round. "Evil," he uttered.

"What was it?"

"A dark evil. A black specter."

"Where? What was it?" Brian was excited and his tone rose. He tried to control himself. He didn't want to wake the man now that he was getting somewhere.

"In the hallways. I saw a black specter."

"What did it look like?"

"Blackness flowed from its body. Its head was large and misshapen, like a demon's. It looked at me."

Brian stepped close to the man. "Did you see its face?"

"Yes," Thurk said, a grimace forming.

"Did you recognize it? What did it look like?"

"It was hideous."

"What was it doing?"

Now Thurk's eyes drooped, as if he were about to cry. "It was carrying—" His voice choked.

"Carrying what?" Brian was on the edge with anticipation, his pulse quickening.

"The specter had a baby in its arms." In the darkness, Thurk's face grew pale.

"What did it do with the baby?"

"I don't know," Thurk said, sobbing now. "An orderly came by and took me back to my room."

Brian didn't understand. "What happened to the specter? Did the orderly see it too?"

Thurk nodded. "He told me to forget what I saw."

"But what about the baby?" Brian asked, frustrated. His temple sweated. "Did the orderly say what was happening to the baby?"

"He said it was being taken away," Thurk said, and then his body shuddered so hard that Brian thought he was going to go into convulsions. "He said the baby was the devil's spawn and had to be gotten rid of."

Chapter 23

"WE ALL SIN"

Reporters from all around came for Eldon Winch's arraignment at the county courthouse. Even though he was being charged only with the murder of Leo Wibbels, most of the media outside of Smokey Hollow linked the former selectmen chairman to the string of strangulations plaguing the town.

But Brian knew things none of the other reporters knew. Wibbels wasn't strangled, and there wasn't a pillowcase over his head. Brian knew the killer was still out there, and so did the State Police. But Brian also knew a few things that even Capt. Steem and Sgt. Wickwire didn't know. There had been babies at the Mustard House, and someone had taken them away, most likely the person who put them in the steamer trunk.

Brian wondered if Dr. Wymbs had run an abortion clinic at the institute. A little extra cash on the side. But Ivy Mockler said she heard babies crying, which means they were born alive. The questions remained as to where the babies had come from and who took them away. And, of course, why.

Sherman Thurk hadn't been any more help last night at the site of the asylum. He had seen something in the hallways at night, of that Brian had no doubt. But what the Somnambulist had described sounded like a nightmare. Did Thurk's waking state and dream state collide to form a distorted perception of reality? Whatever he saw, the only thing Brian gathered from the sleepwalker's ramblings was that it was large, dark, and hideous. Not much help.

Brian had offered Thurk a ride home last night, but the sleepwalker had declined. Even though he felt a little guilty about that, Brian didn't mind. There was something creepy about holding a conversation with someone who was asleep.

Winch's arraignment was uneventful, a formality during which the accused didn't utter a word. His lawyer notified the court of the man's intent to plead not guilty, and the whole procedure was over in a few minutes. Winch never looked up, keeping his head bowed and not making eye contact with anyone in the courthouse except for his lawyer and the judge.

Outside, on the courthouse steps, Brian spotted Treece with Steem and Wickwire. The three men eyed him when he approached.

"You've been kind of quiet lately, Mr. Keays," Steem said, his tone inquisitive.

Brian shrugged. "There hasn't been a lot breaking in the case," he said. "Certainly nothing you've provided me."

"Maybe the arrest of Winch has quieted things down," Steem said.

"Look, we all know he's not behind the other murders. That's why you haven't charged him."

"It's up to the county attorney to file charges, not us."

"The M.O. wasn't the same as the other murders," Brian said, pointing out what the men already knew. "But I hope you don't think this is totally separate from them."

"Why?" Steem asked. "Something you know?"

"You tell me," he answered. He didn't want to share what Corwin Dudle had unveiled over the years of his investigations, or couldn't actually, at least not with the two men from the State Police. He wished he could tell Noah, but maybe he could work on Dudle a bit and get the man to come forward. But he understood the amateur sleuth's hesitation. The man had spent his lifetime investigating the mysterious case of The Pillowcase and the disappearance of Timmy Birtch, and it seemed like it was so close to the end. He couldn't ruin it for the man. Not after all the hard work he'd put into it.

"If we have any information on the case worth revealing to the media," Steem said, "we will do so at the proper time."

"I'm sure you will," Brian said.

"Any more mystery notes from your anonymous source?"

Brian shook his head. "Not a word." As he turned to leave the trio, he looked back. "In fact, it's kind of funny."

"What?" Steem asked, irritated.

"I haven't gotten any messages since Wibbels was murdered and Winch arrested." He shrugged. "Makes you think."

Of course it was a lie, but why not keep the two detectives wondering. Besides, it brought him a little pleasure to see the confused looks on their faces.

On the way back to the newspaper office from the courthouse, Brian stopped at St. John's Church, hoping to catch Father Scrimsher at the rectory. As he walked up to the front door, a cooing sound drew his glance toward the vacant brick building that had been the diocese's old-folks' home. Several pigeons perched on the edge of the roof.

Brian rang the doorbell and waited patiently. When the door opened, he faced a smiling Father Scrimsher.

"Mr. Keays," the priest said. "What an unexpected pleasure. What brings you here? Did you forget it wasn't Sunday?" The thick flesh around his neck jiggled as he laughed.

Brian returned the man's grin with one of his own. "No, I was just wondering if I could take a minute of your time."

The priest gestured for him to enter and led him to the parlor. There were overstuffed chairs with wooden arms by a small coffee table. Brian sat in one, and Father Scrimsher settled his heavy buttocks in the other. Brian noticed the fireplace at the back wall of the room and thought of Corwin Dudle, on the roof, listening to that dialogue those many years ago and how that conversation commenced the obsession that absorbed the rest of the man's life.

There was movement in the hallway.

"Sister Bernice," Scrimsher called out. "Would you be so kind as to bring us some tea?"

Brian caught a glimpse of the nun in her habit.

"Yes, Father," she said in a low voice and disappeared down the hall.

Scrimsher turned to Brian. "Is this newspaper business? Or maybe a spiritual call?"

"I guess you would have to say the former," Brian said, taking out his notepad and a pen.

Scrimsher gave the objects a suspicious glance. "Usually what's said in these confines is of a private nature."

"I just thought we could have a chat about a few things I've been checking into."

"And what would this be in regard to?" The priest seemed edgy.

Brian thought about how to phrase his questions delicately. "I understand you had some consultations with Dr. Wymbs," he started. "Maybe regarding patients at the institute?"

He watched the priest for reaction. What he saw looked more like confusion than anything.

The priest's eyebrows arched. "I'm not quite sure what you are referring to."

Brian sucked on the end of his pen, wishing it were a cigarette. "Dr. Wymbs used to come here to see you, correct?"

Scrimsher's eyes studied him, giving Brian the feeling that the priest was trying to figure out where this questioning was going. "The doctor was not a regular churchgoer," he said, "if that's what you're wondering."

"No," Brian said. "I was thinking of a visit more on a professional level."

Scrimsher's eyebrows almost collided. "I don't quite follow."

He hoped the priest wouldn't lie—maybe avoid, but not lie. So he put the question more directly. "Dr. Wymbs did come see you, didn't he?" At least once that Brian knew of, but maybe more often than that.

Scrimsher cleared his throat. Before he had a chance to speak, Sister Bernice ambled in, carrying a wooden tray with a small tea kettle, two tea cups, and a pair of matching containers for sugar and cream. She set the tray on the coffee table.

"Thank you, Sister Bernice," Scrimsher said.

"You're welcome, Father." She bowed slightly before leaving.

"Tea?" Scrimsher said, arching his eyebrows as he looked at Brian.

"No, thank you." Coffee maybe, he thought, but not tea. He wished the priest had offered him coffee.

"You were saying?" Scrimsher said, pouring hot water into one of the teacups, steam rising from its surface.

Brian waited as the man scooped a couple teaspoons of sugar into his cup and topped it off with a dollop of cream. He wanted the man's full attention, and he had it after the priest took a slurping sip and leaned back in his chair.

"I was saying," Brian proceeded, "that I know the doctor visited you, and I was just wondering if you provided some service, maybe to assist treating patients at the institute?" It was Brian's turn to arch an eyebrow.

Scrimsher held his gaze, his eyes searching for some hidden motive behind the question.

"I do recall," Scrimsher said, "a day when Dr. Wymbs dropped by for a brief visit."

"I see," Brian said, pretending to jot it down in his notepad, noticing the priest's intense look. "And was the visit initiated by you or by the doctor?"

"Heavens," the priest said. "That was so many years ago. I would only be able to hazard a guess."

"Would you be able to guess what the reason was for the visit?"

Scrimsher's lips tightened. His eyes moved back and forth as if searching for an answer. "I'm sure it was a private matter."

"Were there any follow-up visits?"

Scrimsher set his tea cup down with disinterest and interlocked his fingers, resting his hands on his lap. "If there were, they were most likely infrequent. Dr. Wymbs was a very private man who rarely made appearances in the community."

Brian put the top of his pen in his mouth, thinking. "I was under the impression that the doctor made trips into town to look after certain patients." He watched Scrimsher's eyes.

"Patients?"

"Yes."

"His patients were at the institute."

"But I'm talking about the ones who were well enough to leave the institute."

Scrimsher shifted in his seat. "That's not something I'd have any knowledge of."

"I guess I thought maybe you were assisting the doctor in some way."

The priest laughed. "Assisting? Mr. Keays, I don't quite know why you'd think anything like that. How on earth do you think I was assisting Dr. Wymbs?"

Brian shrugged. "I thought it could be possible you were counseling patients in a spiritual way. Maybe even hearing confessions."

Scrimsher chewed this over before answering. "I hear lots of confessions from my parishioners."

"Of course," Brian said. "And maybe even people who might not be from your parish. Maybe people from the institute who needed to cleanse themselves of their sins." He worried he was laying it on too thick.

"We all sin, Mr. Keays. It's part of human nature."

"I guess I never thought of it that way."

"I'm not quite sure what you are looking for," Scrimsher said. "But I have a feeling I haven't been able to provide any answers." His lips spread in a cheerful smile.

"Maybe I'm just looking in all the wrong places." Brian got up, thanking the priest for his time.

Scrimsher struggled to pull his weight out of the chair, reaching a hand to his back. "Aging is never graceful," he said with a smile. "When I first came to this parish, I was a young man, and quite fit and handsome, mind you."

"No one gets younger."

"And forgive me if I can't quite remember things from a long time ago. The past gets further away every day."

He led Brian to the front door. As Brian stepped outside, he turned back to the priest.

"The vacant building out back used to be an old-folks' home right?"

"Yes," Scrimsher said. "The church ran it for many years, but then funds got tight and the place was shut down. That too was a very long time ago. It was already closed by the time I joined this parish."

"And it hasn't been used since?"

"About thirty years ago, it was used as a haven for troubled teen girls, mostly runaways. Sister Bernice helped run the place." Scrimsher pulled a handkerchief from his back pocket and wiped sweat off his brow. "It only lasted a few years, and then it too shut down. The economy even affects the church, believe it or not."

"I see," Brian said.

"Why the interest?"

He shook his head. "Just too bad to see a fine piece of architecture going to waste." He smiled. "That's all."

He bid the priest goodbye and returned to the newspaper office.

Later in the afternoon, Brian pondered what to do with all the information he had learned the past couple of days. What he needed to do was convince Corwin Dudle to let him share some of the knowledge with Noah Treece. Even though the police chief wasn't half the detective that The Silhouette was, he'd rather Noah get credit for breaking the case than Steem and his henchman, Wickwire.

His head and stomach hurt thinking about it, and he stepped out the back door to smoke a cigarette by the dumpster. The smoke going into his lungs was soothing. It helped him think more clearly. And what he was thinking of was the wall in Dudle's basement. Even though the chimney sweep had provided valuable information, it doesn't mean Brian wouldn't have found any of it out for himself eventually. If anything, The Silhouette had just accelerated the process. And the interviews Brian had conducted with the former inhabitants of the

Mustard House, all his doing, had contributed some valuable pieces to the puzzle. He could certainly go to Noah with that. That wouldn't be breaking his word to Dudle.

After all, the man had been providing him clues since the beginning. What was the point of that if he couldn't do anything with it? He understood Dudle had concerns about who to trust in this town. Who wouldn't, considering how many residents of Smokey Hollow might not be quite right. Certainly one wasn't, no matter what the late Dr. Wymbs had thought. But the chimney sweep had entrusted Brian with his discoveries, so it was really up to him to act before something else happened.

The back door to the newspaper office opened, and Isaac Monck poked his head out.

"Bev says there something on the scanner you'd want to hear," he said.

Too late, Brian thought, something must have already happened.

He stubbed his cigarette onto the side of the dumpster and tossed the butt into the container before rushing back into the office, nearly shoving Monck out of the way. Beverly Crump was standing beside the police scanner in his office. She adjusted her glasses as if to hear better. She looked at him as he entered. He didn't say a word for fear of talking over a vital dispatch. At the moment, the scanner was quiet. He looked at her with querying eyes.

"They've called the medical examiner to Cricket Lane," she said.

"Did you hear an address?"

She shook her head.

It didn't matter. He'd drive down the street and look for police vehicles. He grabbed his camera and portable scanner off his desk and bolted out the front door. He drove down Main Street faster than he should have and barely halted at the stop sign at the end before turning onto Fogg Road. When he approached Cricket Lane, his tires squealed as the car cornered onto the street, slowing down once he was on the residential road. He passed the house he had gone to on the Women's Garden Club tour, thinking how long ago that day seemed.

Up ahead he saw the usual assortment of vehicles, police, fire, ambulance, and, of course, State Police. The medical examiner's car wasn't there, so that meant it hadn't been too long since whatever happened had been discovered. He pulled to the curb, parking far enough back so as not to be in the way. He could feel the excitement in his body as he got out of the car. Even though he was coming into something that was most likely awful, it fueled his adrenaline and he could feel the beat in his heart.

He walked down the sidewalk toward a white gambrel house with cranberry shutters and a large brick center chimney. He spotted Day Shift Alvin posted outside the front door of the home. There were two vehicles in the home's driveway, and as Brian realized who one of them belonged to, his pace slowed, as did his heart. He stopped at the end of the driveway, looking up at the house.

"Oh god, no."

Stuck in the gutter along the front edge of the house's roof was a black top hat.

Chapter 24

WITNESS FROM ABOVE

Brian got his camera out. Even though something crawled in his stomach, sickening him, he looked through the viewfinder at the hat on the roof and snapped a couple pictures. He knew it would be a dramatic shot. It didn't matter at that moment what the hat represented, what he knew it meant. He was a journalist, and he had to set aside the prickling feeling inside and take the damn picture.

He despised that feeling.

But he took the damn picture anyway.

After that, he didn't think his feet would move. They adhered to the driveway, as if the tar had liquefied in this stifling summer heat and swallowed his shoes. But he had to know for sure what was going on in that house, so he got his legs going and approached Alvin at the door.

"Hi, Alvin," he said.

"Mr. Keays."

"I've got some important info they're going to want in there."

"You know the drill," Alvin replied.

"You don't understand," he pleaded. "This is stuff related to what I think happened in there. They need to know this."

Maybe it was the distressed tone of his voice or something Alvin saw in his face, but the cop went inside, leaving Brian by the front steps. He looked around the neighborhood. No one was about, and it felt lonely. I don't want to be alone out here, Brian thought. Don't leave me alone. It seemed to take forever. But then Brian realized he wasn't quite alone. Up on the hill, he spotted a man on the water tower, the same man he had been seeing up there all summer...and now he knew who it was.

The front door opened and Alvin came out with Noah.

"Hey, Brian," the chief said. "You got something?"

"It's Corwin Dudle dead in there, right?"

"Yeah," Noah said, putting his hands on his hips. "Stuck in the chimney."

Brian grimaced. Maybe this wasn't what he thought. Maybe this was just a mishap, the sweep slipping and falling into the chimney and breaking his neck. "An accident?" he asked, hoping but doubtful.

Noah shook his head. "He's at the bottom of the chimney. Owner came home and found him. We can see his body through the open flue." He paused. "There's a pillowcase over his head." The chief looked down.

"Damn," Brian said, and he felt tears well up in the corners of his eyes. "I know why he was killed."

The chief looked up. "What?"

"Dudle was The Silhouette."

The chief's eyes grew wide. "When did you find that out?"

"The other day," Brian said, not trying to be too specific. He spotted disappointment in the chief's eyes.

"Why didn't you say something?"

"I promised him I'd keep it to myself. He didn't want to come forward." Sure, keep telling yourself that, he thought. "But there's more. Lot's more. And Steem's going to want to hear it."

Noah led him into the house, to the living room where a crowd of officers were gathered. Steem looked at him, and he flushed.

"What the hell is he doing in here?" the captain yelled.

"He's got some valuable information," Noah said.

All eyes were upon him, but he couldn't speak at first. His eyes were drawn to the fireplace. Dangling out of the flue, above the grate, was Corwin Dudle's arm. Its hand was open, blackened by soot, fingernails forever dirty. Maybe the mortician would finally be able to get them clean for the man's wake. But considering Dudle's profession, he'd probably wanted to be cremated.

"Well," Steem said. "What is it?"

Brian snapped out of his trance and told Steem everything he knew. He talked about the work Dudle had been doing all these years as The Silhouette, starting with the discovery that The

Pillowcase was a former patient at the Mustard House and that Dr. Wymbs had released him. He described the basement at Dudle's house, just around the corner from here. He gave them all the details the chimney sweep had gathered, about other former patients who were now citizens of Smokey Hollow. Brian described his interviews with some of those patients, telling them about Ivy Mockler hearing babies crying at night, and Sherman Thurk spotting someone taking away a live baby.

When Brian was finished, the looks on Steem's face ranged from amazement to anger. Even Wickwire's usual stolid face became animated as Brian had spun his tale. Noah just looked frustrated.

Steem turned to Wickwire. "Get on the horn," he said to his subordinate. "I want a warrant to enter the victim's house." Wickwire left the room.

Steem turned back to Brian, looking like he was about spew some vitriol at him, but then changed his mind and clamped his mouth shut. He probably figured it would be a waste of time.

"Step outside for now," Steem said to him. "But don't go anywhere."

Brian waited out by the driveway with Alvin.

"What time do they think this happened?" he asked the officer.

"The homeowner said he had made an appointment for the chimney sweep to come over between noon and five. The owner came home around four o'clock."

"Broad daylight," Brian said. The Pillowcase was getting brazen. The other murders had been committed under the cover of darkness. He looked up at the roof. God, the killer must have climbed the ladder and strangled Dudle right up there before stuffing him down the chimney like Santa's sack of toys.

"Hard to believe no one saw anything in the middle of the day," Alvin said, as if reading his mind.

Brian looked up and down the street. He spotted at least half a dozen "For Sale" signs in front yards on both sides of Cricket Lane. All the signs had a picture of a beaming Leo Wibbels.

"Yeah, hard to believe," he said, looking up at the man on the water tower.

They entered Corwin Dudle's house on Horseshoe Lane. Brian felt eerie being in the dead man's house, even more so than on his last visit. In the basement he flicked on the light to illuminate the room, especially The Silhouette's masterpiece on the back wall.

"Wow," Noah exclaimed in wonder like a young boy.

Steem and Wickwire were silent. The captain approached the back wall and stopped, his eyes taking it all in. He put his hand on his chin, tapping his index finger against the side of his head. Furrows ridged along his bald scalp.

Brian didn't say anything, just let The Silhouette's wall speak for itself, since the dead man couldn't. He was forever in the shadows now.

"This is incredible," Noah said, breaking the silence.

It was, Brian thought, thinking about all the work that had been put into it. He looked at the wall, at the pictures of the people he had spoken to, the newspaper clippings, the locations where certain events had occurred—St. John's church, where Father Scrimsher spoke to Dr. Wymbs about his secret, Thrasher Pond, where the rib cage was pulled up by the fisherman; Timmy Birtch's house, where the poor young boy was taken in the middle of the night; the sites of the recent strangulations; and Brian and Darcie's house, where the trunk of baby skeletons was opened. Babies that he now knew had been at the Mustard House.

Steem turned to Wickwire. "I want photos taken of this wall, and we need to catalogue all this information." He looked back at the wall. "And then we are going to talk to some of these people."

Noah left the house with Brian, while the two State Police detectives remained behind. Brian was grateful to be out of that basement. The place seemed lonely without Dudle. He deserved better than his fate for all the work he had put into his pet project.

"I wished you had come to me," Noah said. "You could have trusted me."

Brian felt bad. "I know. I was trying to protect my source." He thought about Dudle's body in the chimney. "I guess I screwed that up pretty bad."

"You can't fault yourself for that," Noah said. "Don't worry. We're getting closer on this thing."

We? Brian thought. Maybe this would help the case for Steem and Wickwire, but he doubted it would make much difference for the police chief.

"I'm going to go," Brian said.

"Keep in touch," Noah said. "Don't leave me in the dark."

"I won't." But he didn't tell the chief what his next stop would be.

He drove down Cemetery Road and took a right onto Breakneck Hill Road. His car lugged a bit on the steep upgrade but settled once the road leveled off at the top. When he got to the water tower, he parked and got out. He looked up, putting his right hand on his forehead, trying to shield his eyes from the sun.

"Hello," he called out, squinting up at the man on the water tower, Nyle Potash.

"Hi," the little man said, looking down at him. "What brings you up here?"

"I was about to ask you the same thing," Brian said.

Potash laughed. "This is kind of therapy for me."

"I see." Brian looked at the town below. It was a reverse image of the view he had had a few weeks back from the Mustard House on the other side of the hollow, same downtown storefronts, just from the opposite side. He looked back up at Potash. "I was wondering if I could chat for a minute."

The man shrugged. "Sure. Come on up."

That wasn't quite what Brian had in mind. He looked at the metal ladder reluctantly. It had rust spots and loose flakes of paint. He stepped over to it, grabbing onto a rung, and began climbing. Brian never had a fear of heights like Potash, but still the thought of falling wasn't reassuring. He kept his eyes ahead, focusing on each rung as he grasped it, not releasing one hand until made sure the other one had a firm grip on the next rung. Before he knew it, he was at the railed catwalk ringing the tower.

"Quite a view," he said as he sidled up to Potash at the railing.

"Yes, it is," Potash said. "I come here quite often."

"I know. I've seen you up here, though I didn't realize it was you at first."

"Dr. Wymbs suggested it as a way to face my fear." He smiled. "I feel a bit safer on this than in the hot air balloon at the Dump Fest."

"This thing is a bit steadier," Brian said, though he had some doubt about its sturdiness, considering the rust. "Have you been up here quite a while today?"

The man nodded. "Most of the day. I have a lot more free time now that the fruit market is closed." He frowned. "I suppose I could make better use of my time by looking for a new job."

"Yeah, that's too bad. I'm sure something will turn up."

"Times are tough." He looked at Brian and his smile was back. "Of course, I guess I can save some money by not paying my landlord, since he's in jail."

Brian laughed. Then the two men were silent for a bit.

"So what is it you wanted?" Potash asked.

"I was wondering if you saw anything while you were up here?"

Potash's eyes from behind his glasses glared back. "Anything?"

Brian scanned the roads below, trying to get his bearings, looking at the rooftops. When he spied Cricket Lane and the house with a ladder leaning against the back, he pointed. "There."

Potash followed his finger but said nothing.

"A man was murdered on that roof a few hours ago. A pillowcase was put over his head and his dead body was shoved down the chimney."

Potash's face whitened, and he grimaced.

"Did you see it?"

Potash didn't look at him, gazing toward the house on Cricket Lane. Finally, the man nodded. "Yes," he said, almost a whisper.

"What did you see?"

He removed his glasses and wiped his eyes with his fingers before putting them back on. "Just like you said. I saw the chimney sweep on the roof, standing over the chimney, running his brush down inside it. I could even hear him whistling, the sound carried all the way up here." He paused. "And then I saw another man climb up the ladder. I thought at first he was a helper...he had something in his hand." Potash's voice started to shake. "And then—he crept up behind the chimney sweep. The poor bastard didn't even know anyone was behind him. Maybe the whistling covered the sound. The chimney sweep turned around at the last second, but as he did the man put a pillowcase over his head and began choking him." Potash took a deep, strained breath and looked at Brian. "I yelled out. I screamed for him to stop." Potash's hands gripped the railing, knuckles turning white. "I don't know if he heard me or if he just didn't care. Then the sweep's body went limp, and the man picked him up and put him head first down the chimney." He released his grip on the railing and bowed his head. "If he wasn't already dead, I'm sure the fall down the chimney killed him." He shook his head. "It was horrible. But that wasn't the worst part."

Brian felt breathless listening to the man's story. He felt horrible for Corwin Dudle. What a miserable way to die. He hated hearing about it, but he needed to hear more. "What was the worst part?"

He turned to Brian. "I think maybe the man did hear me yelling, because he looked up at me. I never felt so scared in my life. I thought he was going to come up the hill after me."

"Did you recognize him? Was he someone you might have seen at the institute?"

"No," he said, shaking his head. "He didn't look familiar."

Brian was disappointed. "What did he look like?"

"It was hard to see from the distance. He was a large, bald man." He shrugged. "I don't know, I really couldn't tell much else about him."

"Did you see where he went after?"

"No. He climbed down the ladder, and I lost sight of him. Too many trees. That's why I'm still up here. I've been too afraid to climb down. Kept worrying he recognized me and might be waiting for me."

"You can't stay up here all night," Brian said. "And you need to tell the police. You're the first one to witness anything."

"I know," Potash said. "I've been thinking about that. But I've been afraid, remembering what happened to those other people, Dr. Wymbs, Nurse Snethen, and Hettie Gritton. Thinking about their horrible deaths and knowing that I saw the monster that committed them. And knowing he saw me." He shook. "It gives me chills thinking about it."

"But you know what you have to do," Brian said.

He nodded.

"Let's go then," Brian said. "Because even I don't like being up here."

The climb down was more harrowing than the climb up, mostly because in order to secure his footing on each rung, he had no choice but to look down. He was grateful when his feet touched ground. He stepped away from the ladder and looked up. Potash still stood by the railing.

"Coming?" Brian yelled.

"I'll be right down."

Brian had turned and begun walking toward his car when he heard a loud thump.

He looked back and saw Nyle Potash's body on the ground, split open like a watermelon.

Chapter 25

A PLACE FOR BAD GIRLS

"I think the fear of what would happen to him at the hands of The Pillowcase was greater than his fear of heights. And he just jumped."

Brian was in Treece's office, explaining to Noah, Steem, and Wickwire what had happened at the water tower. Two bodies were now on their way to the morgue, and Brian's nerves were unhinged. He wished he had a cigarette; instead, he was downing cups of black coffee that sank in his belly like mud. He gave what little description Nyle Potash had given him about the killer, but it wasn't much.

"Maybe this Potash recognized the man from his time at the institute," Steem said. "He might have been too shaken to say so."

Brian looked up at the captain. "So scared that jumping was the better option?" He shook his head. It was crazy.

"We need to talk to some of these other people," Steem said to Wickwire, who nodded. "Maybe this guy wants to get rid of anyone who would recognize him."

"He's trying to erase all traces of himself," Noah said.

"I wonder how he knew about Corwin Dudle," Brian said. "I only found out about him a couple of days ago." He looked from face to face, seeking an answer that would make sense.

Steem rubbed his chin. "This guy's well imbedded in this community. He knows what's going on. That's why he's always a step or two ahead of us." He looked at Brian. "You better stay home and watch out for yourself." He turned to Wickwire. "Let's go."

After they left, Noah and Brian were alone. "You okay?" the chief asked.

"Just a little shaken up. It's been one hell of a day."

"Take Steem's advice. Go home and try to relax."

"Easier said than done." He stood.

"But stay alert. This guy must have known Dudle was talking to you. He knows where you live."

Brian thought of Darcie, and that made him anxious. It would be dark soon. Not that the daylight was any more comfort after a day like today.

When he got home, she was on the phone in the kitchen but hung up as soon as he entered. She looked like she had been crying. His immediate concern was that something had happened to the baby.

He went to her. "What is it?"

"I just—" A sob choked any further words.

"Take it easy." He rubbed her arms. She felt cold.

She gathered herself and tried again. "I'm sorry. I need to tell you something, but I'm having trouble starting."

"Start with the phone call. Who was that?"

She looked at him, her eyes wet, but did not answer.

His stomach dropped. "Was that him?"

"Yes," she said. "I needed some advice."

Brian backed away. "Isn't that what your husband is here for? Can't you get advice from me?"

"You've been too absorbed in everything. You're not even around half the time."

"It's my job!" He didn't want to yell, didn't want to sound angry.

"I know. And I'm okay with that." She took a couple of quick breaths. "And what I've been struggling with has to do with your damn job."

This threw him off track. "What?"

"Just listen," she said. "Don't interrupt and let me get this out." She looked at him, and he nodded. "Can we sit down?" she asked.

They sat across from each other at the kitchen table.

"First, you need to stop worrying about the past."

Easy to say, he thought. The past in Smokey Hollow was causing a lot of worries.

"I love you," she continued. "Nothing has changed. I'm excited to start a family with you." She paused, looking at him for reassurance. He nodded. "I needed some advice because there's something I've been keeping from you, and it's been eating me up."

He was anxious but confused by what she was talking about.

"You know how you have your sources at the newspaper, and you keep them secret?"

He nodded again, not knowing what that had to do with anything.

"You can speak," she said with a smile.

"Thank you," he said, smiling back. "So what are you getting at?"

"I've been keeping information from you that might be helpful, but I swore to the person who told me that I wouldn't say anything."

"But you changed your mind?" He squirmed, dying to know what information she had.

"The flowers that were left on our front steps that day, I know who they were from."

He leaned forward, mouth dropping open but so surprised he didn't know what to say.

"They were from my new friend, Gwen Husk, the waitress from the pub. She believes she's the mother of one of those babies found in the trunk."

Brian walked into Cully's Pub, scanning the tavern for the waitress with gray streaks in her hair. He was shocked that Darcie had kept the information from him, but he had tried to understand. She had given her word to the woman, just like he had given his word to Corwin Dudle. But lives were at stake, and there were already too many secrets in Smokey Hollow.

He walked to the bar and ordered a beer. When Hale Cullumber placed the mug in front of him, he asked if Gwen was around.

"Somewhere," the gruff bartender said. He was drinking from his own mug.

For Friday night, it was quiet in the pub. That was usually the busiest evening of the week. Maybe the murders were keeping people at home. Definitely not good for the economy. He spotted Gwen carrying a tray of drinks and motioned to her.

She gave him a worried look and took the tray to a table of customers. He thought maybe she was going to ignore him, but after serving the drinks, she came over to the bar.

"I know about the baby," he said quietly.

Her frown deepened.

"Don't be mad at Darcie," he said before she got a chance to say anything. "There have been a couple of deaths today, and it's no good keeping things quiet anymore."

She nodded. "I know, I heard."

"Do you have a few minutes?" He looked around again at the scattered customers.

Gwen looked at Cullumber. "Hale, I'm gonna take five."

"Counts as your break," the bartender fired back.

She ushered Brian to a table in the corner.

"She didn't tell me too many details," he said as he sat across from her.

"What I'm going to say is not to you as a reporter, is that understood?"

He nodded and kept his notepad in his pocket. "Fair enough. So what's the story?"

She took a deep breath. He could tell she was hesitant to talk. But she did.

"I lived in a girl's group home as a teenager. It was a place for troubled kids, mostly runaways, girls with drug problems." She shrugged. "I was in a lot of foster homes before that, shuffling from one to another. My parents died when I was young. I ran away from a lot of those foster homes. A lot of the people put in charge of me were, well, let's just say not too nice. So I was finally sent to the group home."

"Where was that?"

"St. John's," she said. "In the old-folks' home behind the church. Father Scrimsher and Sister Bernice ran the place. It felt more like a jail at times. They had pretty strict rules."

Brian kept silent, nodding when appropriate. He watched her expression as she told the story.

"Girls came and went, but there were usually at least a dozen or so at a time. Sister Bernice ran the place mostly, teaching classroom lessons, cooking for us. We all kind of pitched in with chores, cleaning, cooking, and laundry. That was pretty much expected. And then there was our job training." Her lower lip trembled.

"Job training?"

She nodded. "It was a program started by Selectman Winch. He helped open a cosmetology school downtown." She paused.

"Helped how?"

"There was a vacant building, and he found an investor to purchase it and open the school."

"Was Leo Wibbels involved?"

She thought for a minute and shrugged. "I think so, maybe."

"Who ran the school?"

"His name was Preston Creech."

"Where was he from?"

She looked confused. "What do you mean?"

"Was he from town, or—maybe from away?"

"I don't recall," she said. "I didn't get the impression he was from around here."

Brian could guess where the man came from.

"So we were sent to the school to learn a trade…hair styling and coloring, manicures, pedicures, makeup. It was a chance for us to get some career training so we could function in society." She laughed, but it was not cheerful.

"What happened?"

"Let me preface this by saying I was not like some of the other girls. Some of them were a little rough."

"How so?"

She huffed. "I guess 'trashy' would be a better way to put it. Some of the runaways had been living on the street and getting by however they could."

"I see."

"We didn't get paid very much at the school. I guess they figured we were getting an education. We got to keep tips when we practiced on customers, but that was it." Here she drew in a very deep breath. "But there were other ways to make extra cash."

He waited for her to go on.

"Mr. Creech used us to help entertain." Her face reddened and her head dipped.

"Are you saying—?"

She looked up. Tears shimmered in the corners of her eyes. "This is a part of my life that I'm not very proud of."

"It's okay," he said, trying to sound soothing. "Go on."

"We would meet with men, usually men from out of town. Most of them were visitors, older men connected with the shoe factory, investors, suppliers, that sort. We'd be like their escorts."

"But you were teenagers?"

"Hey, with the right makeup and hairstyle, you can make yourself look years older." She bowed her head again. "Anyway, you can probably guess what was really going on. It was a chance for some of the girls to make some good cash." She looked up with a sheepish grin. "Me included."

"And you got pregnant."

She nodded. "It happened to a few of us over time. You get careless when booze and drugs are involved."

"Did Father Scrimsher and Sister Bernice have any idea this was going on?"

She laughed. "I don't know about Sister Bernice, but let's just say Father Scrimsher had his own dealings with the girls at the group home."

"What are you saying?"

"You have to understand, Father Scrimsher was very young back then, and new to the priesthood." She leaned back and her lips spread. "And he was very good looking. A lot of the girls had huge crushes on him."

"And you think he slept with some of the girls?" That was too incredible to believe.

"I don't know for sure, but some of the girls would brag about it. But you have to realize girls are catty at that age and make things up."

He wanted to think, but knew he didn't have much time. "So what happened after you got pregnant?"

"Anytime one of the girls got knocked up, they'd be sent away. At first, no one knew where. And they usually didn't return. Maybe that was punishment for getting preggers. But when it happened to me, I found out."

"The Mustard House?"

She nodded. "Apparently Father Scrimsher had an arrangement with Dr. Wymbs."

Brian knew all about that arrangement.

"Before the girl started showing, they were shuffled off to the institute to hide out in that house of freaks." She shook her head and exhaled deeply. "It was a nightmare."

"So you lived there until you gave birth?"

"Yes. It was surreal. Months of mostly being confined to your room, trying to keep your sanity until it was time to give birth."

"Who assisted in the births?"

"Nurse Snethen. She used to be a midwife before working at the institute. And Hettie Gritton helped, along with this creepy male orderly."

"Creepy how?"

"He was obsessed with the fact I was having a baby. He knew I wasn't keeping it, and he wanted to have it. He said he had asked Dr. Wymbs if he could have the babies after birth, but he wouldn't let him. The orderly said he just wanted a baby of his own, but he was told our babies were evil."

The devil's spawn, Brian thought. That's what the orderly told Sherman Thurk when he saw a baby being taken away in the middle of the night. It must have been the same orderly.

"Do you know the orderly's name?"

"If he wasn't so creepy I wouldn't have remembered him at all. But it was easy to remember because he had the same last name as the new police chief."

Brian's mouth dropped open and his head grew light. "Treece? Are you sure?"

"Yes. I wouldn't forget that guy."

Brian rifled through his memory bank. Could it be a relative? Noah said he was from Ohio and had no connections to Smokey Hollow. Was it a coincidence? That didn't seem possible.

"So what happened to your baby?" That was the big question, though he knew where it ended up.

"As soon as the baby was born...." She stopped, and he could see from her eyes how hard it was to relive this part of her story. "As soon as the baby came, they took it away. Didn't even let me hold it, not even for one second." Tears dropped from her eyes and rolled down her cheeks.

"What did they tell you they were going to do with your baby?"

"They said the baby would be placed in an orphanage run by the church. Nurse Snethen wrapped the baby up and handed it off to Sister Bernice." She wiped the tears from her face.

He wanted to reach out and pat her hand but thought that would be improper.

"Dawn!" Cullumber yelled from behind the bar. "Break time's over!"

"I have to get back to work," she said, rising.

"One more thing," Brian said. "Are there any of the other girls around who got pregnant at the group home?"

She shook her head. "Most of the girls left Smokey Hollow after leaving the home. They didn't want to stick around. But there was one girl I befriended who left the group home without telling anyone she got pregnant. She said she didn't want them taking her baby. Plus she had turned eighteen right after finding out, so she was free to leave. She got to have her baby."

"Do you know where she is now?"

"Yeah. In the cemetery."

"Damn," Brian said. Could this story get any worse? "And where's her baby these days?"

"That's the really sad part. Her baby was Timmy Birtch."

Chapter 26

SECRETS UNVEILED

Police Chief Treece was still in his office when Brian arrived at the station. Everything he had just learned was swirling around inside his head, and it must have shown because the chief gave him a queer look. But Brian couldn't think of what to let out first—his jaws kept opening and closing like Simon Runck's marionette.

"What is it, Brian?" Noah finally asked, standing up.

Brian paced before the chief's desk. Finally he stopped and glared at the chief.

"Do you have family here?"

Noah looked at him, confused. Either Brian was way off or the chief was trying to cover up something. "What are you talking about?"

"An orderly who worked at the Mustard House had the same last name as you." He waited for the chief's reaction.

The chief sat down.

"Where did you hear that?"

"I learned a lot tonight. Missing pieces to this whole damn puzzle, but some of it is still confusing."

"Settle down," Noah said, motioning to the chair opposite his desk. "Take a seat and start from the beginning."

So that's what Brian did, sitting and relating the conversation with Gwen Husk about the girls' group home behind the church, the prostitution ring, and the babies delivered at the institute. That's when he got to the part about the orderly with the same name as the chief. When he finished, he took a deep breath and leaned back, but only for a second before bounding upright.

"Do you know this orderly?"

Noah shook his head. "This is news to me. I told you, I grew up in Ohio."

Brian looked at the chief. "It's one hell of a coincidence."

"Let's set that aside for now," Noah said. "You've uncovered some more important stuff. We know where the babies came from."

"Yes," Brian said, still excited. "But what we don't know is how they ended up in that trunk."

"Then I think we need to pay Father Scrimsher a visit." The chief rose, a smile on his face.

"Should you call Steem?"

"No, no," Noah said, waving his hand. "Let's check this out on our own, find out a little more."

He was surprised. This wasn't like Noah. And for the first time Brian thought they *should* call the State Police. This was information that could break the case open, and he would feel more reassured if the captain was involved. He didn't have all the confidence that Noah could handle this, but he did appreciate his enthusiasm.

"Okay," Brian said.

"Let's go."

The two of them stood on the dark steps of the rectory and rang the doorbell. The light over the front stoop came on, and shortly thereafter Father Scrimsher opened the door. He looked surprised.

"Gentlemen," he said, his voice wary. "What brings you out tonight?"

"Hello, Father," Noah said. "I was wondering if you could help me out with a few questions I have."

Scrimsher shot Brian a wary glance. "Of course." The priest opened the door and motioned them in. He led them to the parlor where they all took seats.

"Is Sister Bernice around?" Noah asked.

Scrimsher's eyes bounced back and forth between the two men. "Yes," he said. "I believe she's out back cleaning up in the kitchen."

"We will want a few words with her later," Noah said.

Brian sat in silence. This was the chief's show and he was willing to let him have the stage.

"What is this about?" Scrimsher grabbed a rosary off the coffee table and began fidgeting with it.

"We've uncovered some information," Noah began. "We know about the girls from the group home who got pregnant."

Scrimsher's face grew pale. Brian could see the man's Adam's apple bobbing up and down in his thick neck.

"There were some unfortunate incidents," Scrimsher said.

"Incidents!" Noah said, his voice rising. He stood up from his seat and took a step toward the priest. "Those girls were used as prostitutes."

"I had no idea any of that was going on," Scrimsher said. "They were led astray by that horrible man at the cosmetology school. I was not involved with that. That was out of my control."

"You were in charge of them!"

Brian was taken aback by the chief's tone. He had never witnessed Noah show this much emotion.

"They sinned," Scrimsher said. "They were tempted by the devil and were out of control. I tried to save them."

"You tried to save them?" Noah said, his tone lowering. "How did you try to save them? By fucking them yourself?" He spat this last question out, shocking Brian. This was not the police chief he had been accustomed to. He went from good cop to bad cop in the blink of an eye.

"That's not true!" Scrimsher yelled back.

Brian wondered if Sister Bernice would come out and shush the boisterous men.

Noah stepped closer to Scrimsher. "You had sex with some of those girls, admit it."

The priest tugged at his collar. His face was sweating. "Things were different then," he said. "I was a young man, fresh out of seminary school. I was struggling with celibacy and they tempted me. It wasn't my fault. They flaunted their bodies in front of me. They teased and taunted me. They seduced me. It was the devil's work and I fought hard to suppress those urges, but, but...." He stopped and began panting.

"But what?" Noah said, leaning even closer to the priest's face.

The priest dropped to his knees in front of the police chief. "I was only human," Scrimsher said. "We all sin. But I prayed and begged my Lord for forgiveness. And I sought salvation from him. I repented."

"And that made it all right?" Noah said.

"It's okay as long as we repent," Scrimsher said, and he sounded like he believed it.

"And you sent those girls up to have those babies at the institute," Noah said.

The priest nodded. "That's right. Dr. Wymbs agreed to help the girls out."

"Because you knew he had The Pillowcase at his asylum and that he let the killer out."

The priest nodded again and his eyes welled up in tears. "The man came to confessional and told me his story. He had been at the institute for several years. Dr. Wymbs released him because he realized the man wasn't really crazy. He was as normal as any of us. The doctor said he could still function in society. He had repented as well and wanted me to absolve him of his sins."

"And when this man began killing again, you didn't feel the need to come forward?" Noah asked.

"The confessional is sacred," Scrimsher said. "I couldn't break the sanctity of that."

"Get up," Noah said, his tone displaying how sickened he was by the priest.

Scrimsher rose and stood before the chief, cowering.

"What happened to the babies the girls delivered?"

"Sister Bernice picked them up at the institute to deliver them to the Catholic orphanage."

"But they never made it there did they?"

"I left her to handle that. As far as I knew, she...." He stopped and a shocked look came over his face. His eyes widened and his mouth dropped open. He leaned forward, looking deep into Noah's eyes. Then he stumbled backwards. "You," he said. "It can't be."

Brian was confused and rose from his own chair. Something had just clicked inside the priest's brain.

Noah began to turn away, but Scrimsher caught his arm and pulled him back.

"Your eye!" Scrimsher said, pointing a shaky index finger at the chief's right eye. "You have a fleck in your eye."

Noah shook the man's grip off.

"What are you talking about?" Brian finally said, wondering what the hell was going on.

Scrimsher turned to him. "He has a fleck in his eye."

"Yeah?"

"I saw that fleck before," Scrimsher said. "On a little boy, nearly twenty-five years ago. His mother had lived in the group home out back." He stared at Noah. "You're Timmy Birtch!"

Brian's mouth dropped open as he looked from the shocked expression on the priest's face to the steady stare of the police chief.

Scrimsher stepped closer to Noah. "I have that same fleck," he said. "I inherited it from my father."

"Are you saying," Brian began, but didn't finish.

"I'm your father," Scrimsher said to Noah.

Brian looked at the chief who just glared back.

"And you killed my mother," Noah said.

Brian was stunned.

"No, no," Scrimsher said. "She died naturally, she was sick."

"Because of what you did to her."

"No," Scrimsher said. "Your mother was in love with me. But I told her God was my true love. She left the school when she turned eighteen. I never knew she was pregnant. She came to Mass one day with you." He bowed his head. "I saw the fleck in your eye and I knew." He began sobbing.

"She was a teenager," Noah said. "What you did to her messed her up. And when I went missing, it broke her."

"Who else knew?" Brian asked Scrimsher.

He lifted his head. "I told no one. I was ashamed."

"Not half as ashamed as I am right now," Noah said.

"Someone else must have known," Brian said. "Someone who kidnapped him."

"I was shocked the day I realized," Scrimsher said. "The only person I breathed a word of it to was Sister Bernice."

"We're going to need to talk to Sister Bernice," Noah said.

In the back of the rectory, a door slammed.

Chapter 27

A MURDER OF PIGEONS

"Don't go anywhere," Treece said to Scrimsher before he and Brian went out the back door of the rectory.

It was dark in the back yard. Brian heard running footsteps and caught a glimpse of a shadow moving. He saw the flowing robe of the nun's habit as she ran toward the abandoned old-folks' home. *(The black specter.)*

"There," Brian said, pointing to the vacant building.

Noah pulled out his gun in his right hand and his flashlight in the other.

Brian glanced at the gun. "Is that necessary?"

Noah looked at him and smiled. "How dangerous can a nun be?" He holstered his weapon and turned the flashlight beam onto the darkened brick structure behind the church parking lot. The bottom windows were boarded up with plywood. The second-story windows were not, but most of the glass was broken.

"You've got a lot of explaining to do," Brian said to the chief. His head was still spinning with what he had just learned.

"Later," Noah said. "There will be time for that."

Brian hoped there would be.

With the chief leading the way they walked through the dark parking lot, footsteps echoing in the quiet night. The front door was ajar and still swaying. Noah pushed it open, shining his light inside. There was an empty, darkened foyer and a staircase to the left. He entered and Brian followed.

Noah shined his light around the foyer. There was a wooden telephone stand against the right wall with an old rotary phone on it, smothered in cobwebs. Brian saw a light switch on the wall beside the door and remembered seeing a light in one of the windows last night. He flicked the switch a couple times. No power. The light he had seen must have come from some other source.

"Hello," Noah called out. "Sister Bernice?"

"Is it wise to let her know we're here?" Brian asked.

Noah looked at him, his face aglow at the edge of the flashlight beam. "She knows we're here."

A floorboard creaked from above.

Noah played the flashlight beam up the stairs. He turned to Brian and motioned that he was going up. He signaled Brian to stay. Brian shook his head. There was no way he was going to stay down here by himself. Noah nodded and indicated that he stay behind him.

The chief ascended the steps, taking each one slow, keeping his light pinned to the landing at the top of the stairs. Brian kept pace with the chief, wincing each time a wooden step groaned under their weight. His hands trembled, and he wasn't sure if it was from excitement or fear.

At the top of the dark stairs, the chief stopped, and Brian almost bumped into him. A long, narrow hallway stretched in both directions. Noah shined his light along the floor. Disturbances in the dust showed tracks coming and going both ways.

Brian looked at the chief and shrugged. He was about to ask which way, when the chief put his finger to his lips. They stood motionless, listening. A soft patting noise came from the left. Noah motioned for him to follow. With the chief's light in front of him, all Brian could really see was the chief's back, and he stayed close behind it. Noah stopped at the second door on the left. He looked back at Brian and nodded.

Something shifted beyond the door. Noah grasped the doorknob, turning it slowly and easing the door open.

Something flew out the door, Noah ducking. It nearly hit Brian in the face. His heart jumped. It was a pigeon, and it flew off down the dark hallway. Noah looked back at him, grinning. Brian let a withdrawn breath escape.

Noah stepped into room. Twin beds were lined up against the back wall, beneath a window overlooking the parking lot. A small bedside table stood between the beds. There were several more pigeons in the room. A pair sat on the window sill, cooing. One was on the nightstand, and a few more perched on the headboards of the beds. Pigeon shit covered the floor, emitting a noxious odor.

"Come on," Noah said, closing the door behind them as they left the room. They tried the next room on the left, and it too was full of pigeons.

Brian scanned the room, which looked identical to the first. An oil lamp sat on the nightstand between the beds, a cross hung on one wall. He spotted something on the floor. "What's that?" he whispered, though even as quiet as he tried to be, it sounded loud in the silence.

Noah shifted his light in the direction Brian pointed. About a dozen dead pigeons lay in the corner. The chief knelt and picked one up. Its head flopped over. He looked back at Brian.

"Neck's broken," Noah said.

Brian shrugged. "Maybe it flew into a wall."

Noah pointed to the rest of them. "Mass suicide?" He stood up. "I don't think so."

They left the room. The chief approached a door on the other side of the hallway and opened it. It had a similar layout, though the windows were intact and there were no pigeons. They stepped into the next room, and it was the same.

Noah shined the light onto the beds. He leaned closer to Brian. "Notice something about these last two rooms?"

Brian followed the chief's flashlight beam from bed to bed. He looked back at the chief and shook his head.

"The pillows have no pillowcases on them."

Brian looked again, and saw that the chief was right. An icy chill crawled up his spine. He thought it might throttle him. He had the urge to leave. This place was creepy. He was grateful the chief was here. He wished Noah hadn't put his gun back in his holster.

He backed out of the room, and the chief closed the door behind him. They went to the next door. Noah stopped, brought his ear closer to the door. Had he heard something? The only sound Brian could hear was his heart pounding. Other than that it was very quiet.

As if on cue, the church bell began ringing. It startled Brian, nearly making him jump, and he turned away, looking toward the stairway landing. Why were the church bells ringing? It distracted him enough that he didn't see the chief open the door and enter the room. He heard the doorknob turn and by the time he looked back the chief was already halfway through the doorway.

That's when Brian saw something grayish-white crash down on the chief's head and Noah dropped to the floor, his flashlight flicking out.

Everything was bathed in darkness.

Something moved in the doorway. He could see only shadows, but the shadows shifted and swarmed around him. A large, black shape pushed him backwards. Brian grabbed onto the shape, feeling cloth. He saw white, and a hideous face leered before him.

Then he was thrust into darkness.

It was as if someone had turned out a light. He was enveloped in sudden blackness. It was suffocating.

A pillowcase had been pulled over his head!

He thrashed, his arms flailing as panic set in. Oh god, he thought. Not me. No. This can't be happening. Where was Noah? What had happened to the police chief?

Fingers gripped his throat, encircling it.

So this was how it happened to the others, death in darkness, not even able to see who was behind it.

Brian fought. He pounded his arms at the hands gripping him. His back was against the hallway wall, and he kicked with his legs, trying to get some leverage. The air was being squeezed out of him and he struggled.

Not like this, he thought. Please.

Brian thought of Darcie, and how disappointed she was going to be in him. And he thought about their unborn baby.

He dug his nails into the arms holding him against the wall. He sucked air in, feeling the cloth of the pillowcase press against his lips. He pushed it away with his breath. The fingers clamped tighter around his neck, choking the life out of him.

I won't let this happen, he thought.

He gripped the wrists of the arms holding him, trying to pry them away. They were strong, but he was determined.

He felt the fingers loosen.

Yes, he thought. *Let go of me.*

Air seeped into his throat. *I can breathe!*

The arms on him weakened.

He brought his knee up, connecting with something solid, and the grip released. His first instinct was to pull the pillowcase off his head. He had to see who was doing this to him. A pale face was before him, crooked nose and drooping skin.

Sister Bernice.

Her powerful arms pushed him back against the hallway wall. He reached up to the headpiece of her habit, grabbing hold of it. She pushed off of him and pulled away. The headpiece came off, and Brian found himself looking at a bald man.

Brian was frozen in fear, gasping for breath. The bald man fled down the hallway toward the stairs. Brian couldn't move. He had the headpiece in his hand and looked at it.

Sister Bernice is a man. It was a nightmare.

Outside the church bells kept ringing.

The footsteps pounding down the staircase echoed in the hallway.

He heard a groan from the room in front of him. Treece lay on the floor. Brian went to his side, helping the chief to his knees. Noah was rubbing the back of his head.

"What the hell hit me?"

Brian groped around the floor, trying to find the flashlight. His hand touched a long, hard object, and he grasped it. It wasn't the flashlight. He held it in front of him. There was enough moonlight in the room for him to see what he was holding.

A human rib.

A light flicked on. Noah had found the flashlight.

When the beam illuminated the bone in his hand, Brian let go, and it clattered to the floor.

"What the hell?" the chief said, still rubbing his head.

"Look," Brian said, pointing to a corner of the room now illuminated by the flashlight beam.

Noah turned and trained his light on the corner. It shone on the ceramic pot of bones that had once belonged to Hester Pigott.

"Who hit me?" Noah said, looking back at Brian.

"It was Sister Bernice. But she's not a she."

"What?"

"She's a he." He helped the chief to his feet. "And he's getting away. We've got to catch her. Him."

The two raced down the hallway and down the staircase. Outside they found the tunic of the nun's habit. Noah picked it up and threw it back on the ground in disgust. The church bells were still ringing.

The two of them looked beyond the parking lot for movement. Brian thought he heard footsteps on pavement, but the sound was overtaken by the ringing.

"Why are those damn bells ringing?" Brian yelled.

"Oh, thank goodness," Noah said. "I thought that was just ringing in my head. Come on."

They ran toward the church. When they opened the door and entered, they saw why the bells were ringing.

Father Scrimsher hung by the neck from the bell tower rope, a chair tipped on its side near his dangling feet and a rosary on the floor.

Chapter 28

IN A DARKENED PLACE

Someone ran through the shadows.

Brian had turned from the twisting body of Father Scrimsher, hanging from the bell-tower rope, and seen a dark figure running down Main Street.

"There he is," he said, turning to see Treece staring at the body of the man who was his father. "He's getting away!" Brian grabbed Noah's arm. The chief spun around and looked at him.

"I've got to call this in," Noah said, dazed.

"We've got to get him," Brian said. "We don't even know who he is."

Noah turned and looked at the body. He looked at the priest's face, the eyes bulging, the tongue extended out of his mouth. "I can't leave this," he said. "I'll call Steem."

"It might be too late," Brian said, his heart pulsing with urgency. They were so close, they couldn't stop now. Who knew where Steem and Wickwire were and how long it would take them to get here. Already the murderer's footsteps were fading into the quiet night.

"Wait," Noah said, dialing his phone while still staring at the corpse.

But Brian was already gone.

He ran down Main Street, past empty storefronts, till he got to the intersection with Hemlock Avenue, where the newspaper office was. His eyes scanned the area, looking for movement. No one was about, except a solitary figure on the opposite side of the street, staggering along on the sidewalk. He was tall and thin, not at all like the man Brian was chasing.

It was the Somnambulist.

Had the murderer taken a side street? Where had he disappeared to? Damn! What had happened to him?

Brian crossed the street, looking through the windows of the storefronts, either vacant buildings or businesses long closed at this hour. The glass eyes in the taxidermist's shop window watched him. Too bad he couldn't ask them what they had seen. The faceless mannequin heads in Wigland seemed to turn and follow him down the sidewalk. They wouldn't be much help either. He tried the doors to a couple of businesses, but they were all locked.

Sherman Thurk shuffled down the sidewalk toward him. The Somnambulist didn't keep his usual steady course. He weaved, like a drunk coming out of the pub. Brian thought he might trip on his own feet and fall face first on the pavement. When he got closer, Brian grabbed the tall man by his shoulders.

"Are you okay?" Brian asked.

There was no recognition behind his eyes.

"Do you hear me?" Brian said. "Are you awake?"

The Somnambulist looked down at Brian. At least he saw him.

"Are you asleep?" Brian asked. He couldn't tell. "Did you see anyone come this way?"

The Somnambulist seemed dazed. "Someone ran into me."

"Did you see who?"

The Somnambulist shook his head. "A big man. He knocked me down. He didn't even say 'excuse me.' No one has any manners these days."

"Which way did he go?" Brian shook the man's shoulders. He still wasn't sure if Thurk was awake or asleep, but he wanted the man to focus. "Did you see which way he went?"

"I don't know," he said. "I was knocked to the sidewalk. He didn't even help me up."

"But where did he go?" Brian was frustrated. He was so close.

"I'm not sure. I saw him go through a door."

"A door?" Brian questioned. "Which door? Did you see which door he went into?" Brian glanced down Main Street. There were too many damn doors. He couldn't try them all.

The Somnambulist shrugged his thin shoulders. "I don't recall."

Brian let go of the man, and the Somnambulist continued down the sidewalk. Brian watched his slow shuffle. Then an idea popped into his head.

"Wait!" he yelled.

The Somnambulist didn't stop. He continued slowly down the sidewalk. Brian sprinted toward him and got in front of him, putting his hands to the man's chest to interrupt his movement.

"Let me check your pockets," Brian said, not waiting for permission. He shoved his hand into the Thurk's right front pocket. Nothing. Then he tried the left front pocket and felt something solid. He pulled it out.

A black plastic letter "Y."

It was one of the letters from the movie theater marquee. It must have finally fallen.

Brian looked up at the vacant eyes of the Somnambulist.

"Thank you," he said, letting the man go. Thurk shuffled down the sidewalk.

Brian tossed the letter aside and ran to the theater, stopping before its entrance. The door was ajar a crack. This was the second open door he had encountered tonight. He could hear muffled voices inside, and something else. Music?

He opened the door and entered.

His eyes took a moment to adjust to the darkness of the theater lobby before him. He wished he had Noah's flashlight. As he waited, the shapes of empty candy counters and a deserted popcorn machine formed before his eyes. He saw the doorway to the theater and went through it. A beam of light projected above him toward the screen. The noise of the movie playing bombarded his ears.

Why was a movie playing? The theater was closed.

He thought about Rolfe Krimmer. He must have come tonight to watch the leftover movie. He surely had no idea a killer was on the loose.

Brian went to the right aisle, looking down the rows of empty seats. He saw no movement. The image on the screen was dark but lighted enough of the seats for him to survey the area. He walked down the aisle, turning his head right to left, scanning the padded seats on either side of him.

On the screen, a man walked up a staircase.

Brian stopped, listening, but the soundtrack prevented him from hearing much else. He continued down the aisle. A loud crash of violins made him to jump. He looked up at a bloody scene on the screen.

Something moved behind him, and Brian started to turn.

A large dark shape rose from behind a row of seats.

Arms wrapped around him, and he had no time to scream, not that there was anyone to hear him over the cacophony on the movie screen. An arm tightened around his neck, and for the second time tonight he found his breath cut off.

No! he thought. Not again.

The arms were powerful, and he pulled at the one wrapped around his neck. It was like a vise. Hot breath breathed onto the back of his neck. He dug his nails into the arm, trying to pry it loose. It was no good.

He began to feel lightheaded and gasped for breath. The arm dug into his neck, crushing against his esophagus. Fluid filled his throat as he struggled to breathe. The muscles in his neck strained, and he felt as if they were about to collapse. He could no longer see what was on the screen. Its flickering light seemed to come through a long black tunnel.

Is this what dying felt like?

He had come so close, he thought. Now he was going to die without solving the mystery.

Blackness started to descend over his vision, like someone drawing a shade on a window. He felt like giving in.

He heard a loud crack, like someone snapping a branch over their knee.

Air flowed into his lungs, and the dots of light he had been seeing winked out. He dropped to his knees, dizzy but able to breath, taking huge gulps of air as his head cleared. An arm grabbed him, helping him to his feet.

A bright light flared from behind.

"Don't anybody move!" came a loud voice.

Brian looked up and saw Sgt. Wickwire standing in the aisle, both hands on the gun pointed toward him. Capt. Steem's bald head could be seen behind him.

Brian stared at the floor and the unconscious body of the man who had been Sister Bernice.

Then he looked at the man who held his arm—Rolfe Krimmer, holding his Boston Post Cane in his other hand, the crack in its middle visible in the light.

Chapter 29

INTERVIEW WITH A MADMAN

The following day, Brian found himself in Treece's office at the police station along with Steem and Wickwire. The detectives had been filled in on everything Brian and Noah had discovered about the connection between the church group-home and the Wymbs Institute. Noah had said nothing about his true identity, and Brian kept quiet, figuring he'd get a chance to talk to his friend about it. There would be time later for that.

"He's confessed to everything," Steem said.

"All the murders?" Brian asked.

"No, not Leo Wibbels' murder. We're still sure that was Eldon Winch. He must have been worried about Wibbels coming forward about their arrangement with Dr. Wymbs and the patients from the institute. Winch probably figured the death would be blamed on whoever was responsible for the string of slayings."

Brian looked at the captain. "Except he didn't know about the pillowcases."

"Exactly," Steem said, pointing at him. "And that's why it was important to keep certain crime-scene details out of the press."

"You're welcome," Brian said. "So who is he?"

Wickwire opened a file folder he had in his hand. "His name is Matthias Letch. Originally from Pennsylvania. Former patient at the Wymbs Institute when he was a teenager. Spent a few years there before being released and going home to his parents."

"What was he there for?" Brian asked.

"He was a brilliant student but apparently had a thing for killing small animals. Dr. Wymbs treated him and then he went home. But it appears the treatment wasn't very successful."

Not surprising, Brian thought, considering some of the other patients released from the Mustard House.

"His parents decided to send him back to the institute," Wickwire continued. He closed the file. "They put him on a train for Smokey Hollow and he never showed up. Disappeared. The family hasn't heard from him since."

"So how did he end up as Sister Bernice? And what happened to the babies?"

Steem looked at Treece and nodded. The chief turned to Brian. "We've got a treat for you."

Brian glanced up, curious. "What are you talking about?"

"We're going to show you something," Steem said. "You actually provided a lot of valuable information on this case, despite my misgivings about you."

"Thanks," Brian said. "I think."

"So we're going against protocol to show you something," Steem said. "Chief Treece suggested you deserved it."

The four of them went to the interrogation room. Noah turned on the video monitor and punched a couple of buttons. A picture appeared on the screen, showing the large, ugly, bald man seated in the interrogation room, hands and feet shackled. Steem sat opposite him with Wickwire standing nearby. Brian sat and watched the tape.

"What happened to the real Sister Bernice?" Steem asked on the video.

Letch hunched his shoulders. "I met her on the train on my way to Smokey Hollow," he said in his gravelly voice that Brian should have realized all along belonged to a man, not an old woman. "We chatted the whole ride. It was a long trip. She told me all about herself and her new assignment with Father Scrimsher at St. John's Church." Letch kept his head lowered so Brian couldn't see his eyes. "I got the idea of disappearing. When we left the train, I offered to carry her bags to the church. Then I took her into the woods and killed her. I chopped her body up with a fire axe I had stolen from the train and threw the remains into the pond. Then I put on her clothes and became Sister Bernice."

"And Father Scrimsher never suspected? He didn't realize you were a man?"

The big man shook his head. "Aren't most nuns ugly anyway?" He laughed, a disturbed cackle. "It's not like there's anything feminine about them."

Steem and Wickwire exchanged glances on the tape. The captain looked back at Letch.

"Tell us about the babies," Steem said. "The babies that the girls up at the group home gave birth to at the institute."

"Those girls were filthy," Letch sneered. "They were wicked girls. The babies in them were evil."

The devil's spawn, Brian thought. Isn't that what the orderly told Sherman Thurk? The orderly named Treece? He looked at Noah.

"What did you do with the babies?" Steem continued his questioning.

Letch chuckled. "I was responsible for making the arrangements for bringing the babies to the Catholic orphanage."

"But they didn't make it there, did they?" Steem asked.

Letch shook his head. "After delivery, I took them from the institute." He lifted his head enough so now his eyes were visible. They were vacant, like shark eyes. "I smothered the babies and brought them back to the church and put them in the trunk."

There was silence. On the tape, neither of the State Police detectives spoke. The four of them watching the tape were just as quiet, soaking in what they were hearing.

After a while, Steem cleared his throat and continued with the interrogation.

"Why did you have to kill the babies?"

"I wanted to protect Father Scrimsher. Those girls were rotten. And the babies evil, they needed to be disposed of."

"How did the trunk end up at Ruth Snethen's house on Ash Street?"

"Once the group home closed, I didn't want to hold on to the trunk anymore." He paused. "It frightened me."

"How did it frighten you?"

"I could hear the babies crying at night." Letch bit his lower lip. "I was afraid of them, afraid they might get out of the trunk. I worried Father Scrimsher would hear the cries. So I asked Nurse Snethen if I could store the trunk at her house."

"Was that because you planned to have her house burned down and destroy the evidence?"

"Yes," Letch said. "I threatened to expose Marshall if he didn't torch the house. You had to talk to Marshall, you couldn't talk to Simon. Marshall was the one who liked to start fires."

"And you got him to burn down the institute to cover up your murder of Dr. Wymbs?"

"Yes. I was afraid the doctor would learn about what really happened to the babies. I did it to protect Father Scrimsher. And it was easy to convince Marshall. I assured him it would wipe out all the records at the institute and the personal files of its patients."

Brian listened as the man spoke with such calculated reasoning, yet it all sounded mad.

"And you murdered Nurse Snethen and Hettie Gritton as well, because they knew you had taken the babies away?" Steem asked.

"That's right. I had to eliminate all traces of what happened."

"And you killed Corwin Dudle, the chimney sweep?"

"He was getting too close," Letch said.

Brian's heart sank as he heard this. Poor Corwin.

"And I wanted to kill that damn reporter, too."

Even though Brian was watching it on the screen, it gave him a chill to hear those words. The monster could have come after Darcie.

"Did you kill Timmy Birtch?" Steem asked.

Brian glanced at Noah, who stared intently at the screen. Even though the chief had already seen this, his eyes seemed fascinated by what was unfolding before him.

"No," Letch said. "Father Scrimsher told me that he thought Timmy was his child. That Timmy's mother had seduced him even though it was against God's will. So I spoke to an orderly at the institute who had helped with the deliveries of the babies. He always wanted to have one of the babies. He kept asking if he could keep one, but I told him they were evil. So I went to him and said he could save Timmy if he took him away from his damned mother. The child could escape the evil with his help."

Brian saw Noah bow his head.

"I didn't want to hurt the boy," Letch said. "He wasn't like the others. He was Father Scrimsher's offspring, so he had to be good."

Steem got up and shut the tape off. Wickwire turned the lights on.

"That's the meat of the matter," Steem said. "The interrogation goes on for quite a while, but nothing important came up during the rest. The man is quite insane."

Brian exhaled, his insides unsettled after watching the tape. But something bothered him. Something was missing.

He looked up at Steem. "Did he confess to The Pillowcase murders from long ago?"

Steem looked from Wickwire to Treece, and then back at Brian. "Letch used a pillowcase in these murders because he knew The Pillowcase had been released from the Wymbs Institute, and it was a convenient way to place blame."

"What are you saying?"

Wickwire opened the folder in his hand again. "We got a hold of Letch's birth certificate from Pennsylvania," Wickwire said. "When The Pillowcase murders occurred in New England, Mathias Letch was only around five years old."

Brian's mouth dropped open. "So that means The Pillowcase is still out there."

Chapter 30

FROM THE DEATHBED

The following Wednesday, Brian kissed Darcie before leaving for work to put the finishing touches on what would be his best issue yet as editor of *The Hollow News*. As he looked at his wife, he could see all the tension gone from her face. She looked relaxed. And once this issue was put to bed, he would feel the same. Sure, there were still the court proceedings and trials to come, but after that he was actually looking forward to the mundane pace the weekly paper usually offered before that day they opened the trunk.

"I promise," he said to Darcie as he held her in his arms at the front door. "Things will be back to normal, and I will be around whenever you need me."

"Once I have this baby," she said smiling. "Things will never be normal again."

He laughed, kissing her again before heading down the front steps. At the bottom, he turned to face her. He was still grinning.

"What's so funny?" she asked.

"I've been thinking. After all the work the State Police, Noah, The Silhouette, and myself did during this whole case, you were the one who held the key that put the final piece of the puzzle in place."

She laughed at that. "Not bad for a pregnant, out-of-work teacher."

As he headed for his car, she called out to him and he stopped.

"And now that this is over," she said. "You need to quit smoking."

Once he got over the surprise, he laughed again. "I promise."

After deadline at the office that afternoon, Brian leaned back in his chair, grateful the work of the past few days was on its way to the printers. It was a gratifying feeling.

What still bothered him was the knowledge that the real Pillowcase was still out there somewhere, not accountable for the grisly crimes he committed. Sure, Steem had said the man might be long dead after all these years. But Brian thought it was just as possible he was still walking around, maybe still here in Smokey Hollow, living a normal life. Could such a killer lead a normal life? Apparently Dr. Wymbs believed so. He thought the man was normal enough to release him into society, and for all anyone knew, the man hadn't killed again. Maybe there was some method to Wymbs' madness.

Brian gazed out the window onto Main Street, at the people milling about downtown. *How many?* he wondered. How many people out there walking around were former patients at the Mustard House? And were any others dangerous, like Mathias Letch and The Pillowcase? It gave him a chill just thinking about it.

Treece came to visit Brian in the afternoon. He had a feeling he knew what the chief wanted. He had agreed to keep quiet about Noah's true identity until after this week's edition was out and they had a chance to talk.

"Thank you," Noah said when he entered Brian's office.

"How did you find out who you were?"

Noah sat down. "My father," he began, and then halted. "I mean, the man I grew up thinking was my father, was a heavy drinker and abused prescription meds. When I was a teenager, he blurted something one night in a drunken stupor. He had always told me my mother was dead, but I had my doubts. He would never talk about her, or her family, if she even had any. So one night when he was drunk, I took a blood sample from him and had his DNA tested, along with a sample of my own blood." He took off his chief's hat and held it in his hands, looking at Brian with sad eyes. "That's how I found out he wasn't my real father. It was then I decided to become a policeman. I wanted to find out who I was and where I came from and how I got to be where I was. When I was a cop I did a lot of research in my spare time." He laughed. "If you thought Corwin Dudle was obsessed, you should have seen me. I eventually traced my supposed father to his days as an orderly at the Wymbs Institute, and I was determined to get a job on the Police Department here." He laughed again. "I didn't think it would be as police chief, but hell, it worked out."

Brian thought about how many times he had doubted Noah's ability as a detective. He couldn't have been more wrong about the man. He had proven to be more of an investigator than Brian had ever imagined.

"What happened to Treece, the orderly?"

Noah dipped his head. "He died, drowned in a bathtub, all messed up on booze and drugs." He looked at Brian. "I didn't feel sorry for him. My mother literally died from the heartbreak caused by my disappearance. My one regret is I didn't find my way back here in time to save her."

"And that's why you bring flowers to her grave," Brian said, his heart touched.

"And always will."

"Now comes the big question," Brian said. "When do you let the world know that Timmy Birtch is alive and well?"

Noah was silent for a moment, fidgeting with the hat in his hands. "Before I do anything, I need to take a trip."

"A trip?"

"To Florida to see Chief Pfefferkorn. I told you how my unsolved disappearance haunted his whole career. When he trained me as his replacement, I couldn't tell you how many times I wanted to reveal the truth to him, to ease his anguish. It tore me apart to keep it secret, but it was necessary for me to accomplish what I needed to do." He smiled. "So I'm going to fly down there and visit him, and tell him everything. He deserves it. God knows I could use some time off. And when I come back, I promise to let you have the exclusive on the story."

That pleased Brian. "And will you become Timmy Birtch again, and change your name back?"

Noah stood up. "Yes, I will. To honor my mother." He placed the hat back on his head. "Chief Birtch. Has a good ring to it."

"Yes it does," Brian said.

"I think you're going to miss the excitement this case brought."

Brian laughed. "In time, maybe. Right now, I look forward to things quieting down. And who knows, I've been thinking I could write a book about it. There's a huge market for true-crime books these days."

"Do you think anyone would believe a story like this is true?" The chief smiled.

"It's certainly not your everyday case."

"Well, I wouldn't mind seeing myself as the hero."

Now it was Brian's turn to smile. "You know who I think is the real hero here?"

"Don't say Capt. Steem."

"Oh no," Brian said. "I think Corwin Dudle would be the hero in my book. He really pieced the puzzle together. He dedicated his whole life to it. That wall in his basement had almost the whole picture. It's what eventually helped solve the case. He was just missing a piece or two."

"Well, there's something that Capt. Steem found out that might change your mind."

"What's that?"

"It turns out Corwin Dudle spent some time as a patient at the Wymbs Institute."

Brian's mouth fell open. He couldn't believe it. He mulled this over and a thought popped into his head.

"What if Corwin had himself committed there in order to further his research?"

Noah shrugged. "I suppose that's possible."

"The lengths that man went to as The Silhouette, it wouldn't surprise me at all. That's the angle I'd like to approach if I write my book. I like him as my hero."

"Speaking of heroes, there's another reason I stopped by today," Noah said. "I came to deliver a bit of sad news."

This town has had enough of that, Brian thought. It didn't need any more.

"Rolfe Krimmer passed away during the night."

Oh no, Brian thought. He really liked the old man, and he had saved Brian's life at the theater.

"What happened?"

"Appears to be natural causes. Died in his sleep."

Brian shook his head. Just when things were getting back to normal, now the town had to deal with another death. "I guess they'll be looking for someone to pass the Boston Post Cane on to."

"Except he broke it over Mathias Letch's head."

Both men burst into laughter, and it felt good, considering the disheartening news.

Noah pulled an envelope out of his pocket.

"I found this in his bedroom at the rooming house." He fanned the letter in his hand. "It's from Rolfe and was addressed to me. I read it. I thought about it all day, wondering what to do with it."

Brian looked at him curiously.

The chief offered the letter to Brian.

"I've decided to do nothing about it," Noah said. "But I want to give it to you to read and give you an opportunity to decide if it's worth doing something about."

"What does it say?" Brian asked, taking the letter.

"Just read it," Noah said. "And then decide for yourself." The chief left his office.

Brian read the letter and then went out to the back parking lot. He needed to have one last cigarette before he quit for good, for Darcie's sake and for the baby. He tapped one cigarette out of the box and threw the rest into the dumpster. He lit the cigarette, sucked the smoke into his lungs, feeling how it soothed him. He would miss it, but it was for the best.

He looked at the letter in his hand from Rolfe Krimmer and then flicked on the lighter and lit one corner. He held the burning paper in his hand as long as he could, feeling the heat from the flames inch its way toward his fingers. When the flames got too close, he dropped it, waiting till the fire consumed the last corner of the letter before stamping out the ashes.

Brian was stunned by what the old man had written. But like Police Chief Noah Treece, soon to be Police Chief Tim Birtch, he decided not to do anything about the fact that in the letter, Rolfe Krimmer had confessed to being The Pillowcase.

THE END

Gregory Bastianelli is a New Hampshire native and graduate of the University of New Hampshire. He worked for nearly two decades at a daily newspaper where the highlights of his career were interviewing shock rocker Alice Cooper and B-movie icon Bruce Campbell. He is the author of the novel *Jokers Club*. His stories have appeared in several genre magazines and anthologies. His novella, *Lair of the Mole People* appeared in the pulp anthology *Men of Mystery Vol. II*. He lives in Dover, NH. Author photo credit: Christine Brickett

ACKNOWLEDGEMENTS

This book wouldn't have been possible if not for the nearly twenty years I spent working at *Foster's Daily Democrat*, a small newspaper in the New Hampshire town where I grew up. I owe a special gratitude to all the wonderful people I worked with in that time span, and all they taught me. Any deficiencies in the skills of the reporter in this story are my own doing. I would like to thank Christopher C. Payne and his staff at JournalStone for the great work on this book, especially Dr. Michael R. Collings, who edited it; and Wayne Miller who did the cover art. I also want to acknowledge the special assistance of Karen Hendrickx with this story. Thanks to my Aunt Robbie for the unending support she's had for my writing over the years. Special love and appreciation of course to Jenna, Brett, Bailey, Jacoby, Casey, Erica and Jace for the enjoyment they bring me. And to Cherrie, whose story I'm still trying to write. Finally, thanks to all the loonies in my life.

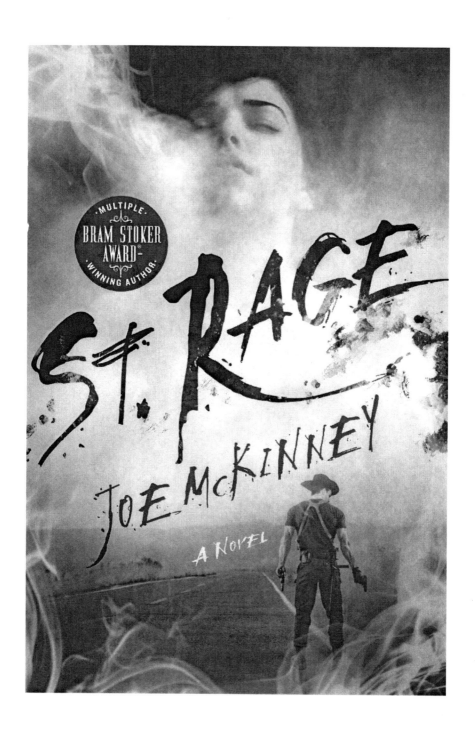

BLACK TIDE

PATRICK FREIVALD

• A MATT ROWLEY NOVEL •

CPSIA information can be obtained at www.ICGtesting.com
Printed in the USA
LVOW10s2330020615

440749LV00001B/41/P

9 781942 712176